WHIDBEY

ALSO BY T KIRA MADDEN

Long Live the Tribe of Fatherless Girls: A Memoir

WHIDBEY

T Kira Madden

TINDER PRESS

Copyright © T Kira Madden 2026

The right of T Kira Madden to be identified as the Author of the Work has been asserted by her in accordance with the Copyright, Designs and Patents Act 1988.

First published in 2026 by Tinder Press
An imprint of Headline Publishing Group Limited

1

Apart from any use permitted under UK copyright law, this publication may only be reproduced, stored, or transmitted, in any form, or by any means, with prior permission in writing of the publishers or, in the case of reprographic production, in accordance with the terms of licences issued by the Copyright Licensing Agency.

All characters in this publication are fictitious and any resemblance to real persons, living or dead, is purely coincidental.

Cataloguing in Publication Data is available from the British Library

Hardback ISBN 978 1 0354 0384 4
Trade Paperback ISBN 978 1 0354 0385 1

Printed and bound in Great Britain by Clays Ltd, Elcograf S.p.A.

Headline's policy is to use papers that are natural, renewable and recyclable products and made from wood grown in sustainable forests. The logging and manufacturing processes are expected to conform to the environmental regulations of the country of origin.

Headline Publishing Group Limited
An Hachette UK Company
Carmelite House
50 Victoria Embankment
London EC4Y 0DZ

The authorised representative in the EEA is Hachette Ireland,
8 Castlecourt Centre, Dublin 15, D15 XTP3, Ireland
(email: info@hbgi.ie)

www.headline.co.uk
www.hachette.co.uk

For Suzanne Hoover.
You told me I could.

But there were too many points at which the other self could invade the self he wanted to preserve, and there were too many forms of invasion.

—PATRICIA HIGHSMITH, *STRANGERS ON A TRAIN*

I once decided to pretend to be angry.
Then I was.

—JANE HIRSHFIELD, *LEDGER*

Dear Reader,

If you would like the opportunity to review a content warning before reading, please see page 367.

I

BIRDIE

I DIDN'T KNOW ANYTHING about Whidbey Island when I chose it, only that it was far. Only that it would take a great deal of work to get there, and more work to be found. When I say I closed my eyes and pointed to a map, I really mean that. I did. Red votive candle dripping over foil in the center of our dining room table, my girlfriend, Trace, sitting across from me, a full moon over north Brooklyn. *Safety*, we repeated, a Trace manifestation, and I hovered my hand as if feeling for heat—but when we opened our eyes to Elko, Nevada, it wasn't exactly far enough, so I moved my finger further west to Whidbey.

One month later Trace flew me to Seattle. We bought the one-way ferry ticket online, drove to the Mukilteo terminal. Then, there was my boat pulling in. Huge and white with a green lid over the top deck windows, a monstrous face to it, the gaping garage. Cars thumped from the ramp onto the ferry as I stepped on board, and it was dark in there, between all that machinery. I rolled my suitcase between cars and cinched my shoulders for better posture, wondering if any of the passengers were wondering about me. *Who's that girl with the practical green suitcase?* the faces would ask. *What about her?*

When I had thoughts this self-dramatizing, which was often, I imagined being hurled down a flight of stairs right after thinking them. Sometimes, knocked out by a mail truck, envelopes bursting onto a wet street. On the boat I followed passengers, and one of them—a gaunt freckled woman smeared white with sunscreen—held a door for me at the side of the garage. Thanks, I said, and trailed her and the others up the damp stairwell, like I knew where we were all going. Rather than carrying my suitcase by the handle, I let it clack-clack on each step, the sound echoing awfully. A few of the people looked back at me, just to see who, I guess. I had to commit to the choice now. I clacked all the way up.

The second door brought us to a passenger seating area, and for a moment I was back in Penn Station. For a moment, I'd never left. A white sign read Upper Deck, and windows dotted the whole perimeter, casting a greenish pale light; tables, bolted between pleather booths, collected glossy half-finished puzzles. The room wafted fried fish and cleaning products, and doors led out to a deck. Out there, the day drizzled sloppily over the parking lot and water. Late May, first breezes of summer, but still a cold that crept up shrewd. People walked past me out onto the deck, no umbrellas or anything; they just stood beneath the rain, jackets darkening. They smiled, white caps melting on the mountains behind them, phones clamped onto sticks.

I found a seat inside at the rear of the boat, and with an uneasy quiet, the glass window vibrated, woke to movement. The shoreline of Washington, the trees, Trace waving from our rented Honda Civic, they all grew smaller.

Children chased each other down the aisle between the ferry's benches. I flinched at their sounds, their little squawks and shrieks, thump of a tripped sneaker. One child aimed a toy slingshot, and powdery glittering balls arced through the air, fell slowly. Laughter, their mouths all laughing, before a man tiptoed beside them, arms up in a playful shield.

Then he sat across from me.

I'm Rich, he said, extending his hand. He gripped mine in that firm too firm single thrust *this is a professional handshake* way.

He was handsome, for a man, with black seal-like eyes and a tight stern forehead, hair blown back as if in motion. He carried a plastic drugstore bag lumpy with clothes, which he twisted, then let spin around his wrist. He looked around my age, mid-twenties, Middle Eastern—from where I couldn't tell—and a bright rope of scar ran up his forearm and into his sleeve. I wondered if he was asked about that scar a lot, maybe the reveal was a benchmark in his romantic endeavors.

Finally, I said, I'm Birdie.

I'd introduced myself with pseudonyms off and on for most of my life, names I'd lifted from films, sometimes historical figures. When forced to sign Greenpeace clipboard petitions, I was Judy Barton. My coffee orders and library books belonged to Mary Ann Zielonko. Online, hotel bookings, mail: Wilma Dean Loomis or Jacy Farrow. *It's good, sometimes, to be another person*, one therapist had said, long ago. The sound of my own, true name prickled, an ash in my mouth, and already I knew I was getting away with something. Birdie Chang, I told this man.

Rich was holding a paperback copy of Animorphs, a series I'd loved as a kid. On the cover, the boy in a brown jacket transformed into an eagle in vivid, holographic layers.

Haven't seen one of those in years, I said, pointing.

He bent the book back and forth in his hands, testing its flexibility. It made no sound. One-dollar cart at Elliott Bay, Rich said. Collected these as a kid. Guess I wanted to take a trip back in time. And you know, the story really holds up. He slapped the book with the back of his hand. There's some serious literary merit here, he said.

I hated men. More precisely, I hated how a man like Rich could carry a book like Animorphs on a boat, unashamed, gleeful. He could slap it. *Some serious literary merit*—he could say something like that, and it would be considered refreshing, sweet. *What a confident man*, my mother, Wendy, would say, *not trying to prove a thing*. Another woman might note his *vulnerable masculinity*, of course she would, he'd asked for it. But we were all trying, all the time, I reminded myself. That's how we become the people we are, impressionistically, chiseling lumps of selfhood off the truer, moldering form. There was always the effort to prove, though only certain people got to do so with pleasure. I tried to reel empathy from any part of myself.

I used to like that story, too, I said. Same generation, I guess.

It ends sad, he said.

It had to.

Rich spun the bag of clothes again. The plastic left pale ridges across his wrist. He said, what are you, twenty? Twenty-three?

Twenty-eight, I said.

No shit?

Asian genes.

Same, he said, tilting ear to shoulder.

I must have looked confused. I said nothing. There was nothing I could think of to say. Rich waited for me to go on, then smiled. He said: You Stanford sun-hat Asians always gonna forget brown Asians.

I rolled my suitcase directly in front of me, snapped the handle down. Then I wrapped my legs around the sides of it and squeezed, remembering the book that was inside.

You don't know anything about me, I said.

I think you're tired, this man said. Real tired.

I am tired.

What do you have going on on the rock?

The rock?

On Whidbey? he said.

Trace and I had rehearsed several potential responses: I was *visiting family* (boring, no follow-up questions). I was *meeting with researchers to study moss and hydrology* (for this I'd googled the absolute basics). Always I could default to *I don't speak English*, the quickest way to be left alone, forgotten. But Rich was frank and direct and didn't regard me with pity; no, he didn't have that pitying scrunch between the eyebrows, the soft tone—it wasn't there. He knew my real name, and speaking to him felt like a challenge, one I shamefully, senselessly, wanted to pass. So I told him the truth: I'm hiding from someone. From a lot of people.

Rich fanned the corner of the book with the tip of his thumb. Back and forth, tightly, like a deck of cards. He looked right at me, unmoved, elbows on his knees.

Someone, Rich said. He hurt you, or he wants to?

He already did, I said. He's a pedophile.

Rich didn't budge. His big seal eyes blinked sleepily. Trace would toss me off the boat if she knew I'd shared this much. My mother would say, *You have got to be joking*, maybe even get uncharacteristically violent. I knew better than to spill; I knew anyone could be a friend of Calvin's, maybe someone he'd met inside, someone with my photo and information printed and folded in their wallet. But there were so many lessons I'd never learned in my life, so many mistakes I'd continued to make, and some thrill giving up and into that person.

So you're hiding? he asked. Why now?

Now people know about it, I said. So he's back.

I don't know about it.

Other people know, I said, trust me. I thought of the book. The photo on the cover. The New York Times Bestseller stickers glinting from her cheeks on the wall display at the airport. Trace had pulled my hand to keep walking. I was supposed to spend the summer on Whidbey to *reset* and *recalibrate* unplugged, to find that *safety bubble*, at last. These were other peoples' words, but I knew how to use them.

What does this guy say he wants? Rich said.

He says all kinds of stuff. Says he wants to apologize.

Does he, apologize?

Depends.

On what?

On how you see it. How you think of apologies.

So what's your issue? he asked.

A woman pushed inside from the deck, and the wind fluttered Rich's hair before the door snapped closed. She was yelling into her phone to someone named Joey, and she said his name a lot: Joey, I said what I said. Listen, Joey, I'm not coming to Ballard, Joey, don't be so stupid.

The issue, I said, is he finds me. He doesn't go away. He's out now, and he writes me—

Words aren't violence, Rich said. He shook his head.

This is a violent person.

Well, Rich said. You say he's a pedophile. Why would he care about you now?

I didn't like somebody else talking about Calvin like he knew him, coolly calling him a pedophile. It was unnerving to hear it so casually with no bulk to it; his tone ground my deliberateness and my fear to dust, the life I'd lived leading to that word of who Calvin was, and the thorned acceptance of what that made me.

You don't know what the fuck you're talking about, I said. I looked him in the eyes.

Oh, there it is, Rich said. He smiled again. There, that's where it lives.

I looked down at my fingers as if something were stuck there, something to be addressed. My fingertips, frayed from picking. Blood dried in horseshoes around the nail beds. I tried to focus it, the swell, the heat rising inside, a crimp in the gullet. Not the crying kind—but the other feeling. *There it is.* I looked back up at Rich.

It's 'cause you're too nice, Rich said. Guys fuck with girls like you because you let them.

I'd kill him, if I could, I said. I'd shoot him in the dick.

That's how you'd do it?

The dick, then the head.

Nah, you wouldn't, he said. Let me guess, you sleep with a gun, right? What kind?

I said nothing. Rich leaned closer. A focused crouch, hands ready, as if dribbling a ball.

Tell me. Smith and Wesson, 38 Special? You sleep with a big boyfriend, too?

I'm a dyke, actually.

Hey, girl, I'm cool with that, he said. Then, a thought behind his face. Slightest twitch at the corner of his mouth before he said it: You'd let him do it again, before shooting him. You don't have that in you. Guarantee.

You have no idea, I said, and we sat there for a moment, the fluorescent ticking overhead. The boat slowed. I didn't go to Stanford, I said.

The woman screamed at Joey some more from a nearby bench. She plugged one ear as she listened to what he had to say. I thought Joey had been a boy, but now it sounded as if he had been a lousy lover and owed her money. She hung up and threw the phone into her big purse, said, *Unbelievable*, to the rest of us.

Where's the bad guy live? Rich said.

Florida.

Florida Man.

Don't shit on Florida, that's a boring thing to do, I said.

You still live there?

No.

Exactly. So where's he in Florida?

Do you know what a pervert park is? I said, trying to prove a lax knowledge of my own life. That's what they call them in Florida. Where he lives. It's called Gateway to Grace.

I work East Coast a lot—cargo ships, cruise lines, Rich said. I'm down there next week, staying through summer. I got friends in Opa-locka.

What do you do, exactly?

Rich nodded his head like he was thinking. He said: Boats. Marina stuff.

He slapped the book down next to him, then buried his face in both hands, breathing in hard. He flicked the tip of his nose with a thumb. Sniffed. Outside the glass doors of the ferry, a little girl on the deck threw pieces of bread, or crackers, at some gulls that curved down to them. Behind her, the clouds parted a Magic 8 Ball blue.

Well, Rich said, looking up at me. He looked calm, almost sedated. You want me to kill him for you?

I glared at him. His stubble, his dry knuckles. I imagined him snapping off gloves, a dirtied spade, wiping prints from a revolver with a soft, meshy cloth. Then I imagined Calvin—bound and blood battered—screaming for his life in a ditch near the Everglades. A gator would finish him. It was all ridiculous.

I can do it for you, Rich said. It'd be my honor. Even the score in this small way. For the sun-hat nice girls.

He leaned back and crossed one foot over a knee. I crossed mine too. The children in the aisle were gathered by their parents. Backpacks and strollers. Arms flung around necks.

No one would ever connect us—who could connect us? I'd have no reason to kill this guy. But I could. Easy, without a hitch, trust me I could.

What are those people eating? I said. Rich looked outside, where I pointed. The birds multiplied and the little girl screamed. Orange life buoys clung to the deck gates, quivered brightly and weakly as the boat moved.

Probably chowder bowls, he said.

They love chowder here.

It'd be fun actually, Rich said. Taking your guy away.

I liked that he wouldn't drop it. That he was asking something of me. A permission. He needed me to play along, to assuage some want. I knew what that looked like.

I told you, I was going to kill him, I said.

You don't have it.

I can be scary, I said. Ask anyone who knows me.

I don't know anyone who knows you. Then, after a pause, he said, You couldn't scare anything.

I scare.

Scare me now, Rich said. Come on. Gimme your best. Scare me good.

I looked out the window to the water, the deep blue mat studded with white. An identical ferry passing by. Mount Rainier glowing like a postcard. I once went on a date with a woman who said she'd never get serious with someone who rolled a suitcase. That it was a lazy, humiliating thing to do—to not hold a suitcase by the handle, a proper handsome Samsonite from long ago, luggage with dignity. I didn't know how to scare this man. I never would.

Are you lying? he said.

I'm not.

You seem like a liar. I just need his name. Gateway to Grace. Give the name. After this we never met. You'll never hear from me again.

Give me your name, I said.

Rich Amani, he said. Do you trust that I'm a good person?

Absolutely not.

I respect that, he said. That's fair.

Do you think I'm a good person? I asked. Out of the ferry's loudspeaker, words clanged, indecipherable. The boat slowed even more. The island: closer.

Good and nice aren't the same, he shrugged. Does he deserve to die?

He doesn't deserve to live.

That's the same thing, Rich said.

I don't think it is, actually.

Say it, Rich said. Just say it out loud. It's good for you.

Passengers opened the doors to exit. Cold air trailed through the room, and I pulled my jacket tighter to my chest. The ride was ending, a ramp ahead lowering to the boat, bridging to the rest of my life.

I said, Every day, when I wake up, it's the first thing I wish for. Him gone.

Well, give the name, then. If you want me to.

I stared at Rich and he stared back. A dare with our eyes, who'd break first. That Disney villain scar, his twisting bag of clothes— I smiled, caught myself, straightened back up, serious now. Scary. Something mirrored between us, but he still didn't think I could.

Calvin Boyer, I said, and Rich stood as soon as I said it.

Well, that was easy, he said. Birdie, good for you.

He slipped the book in his back pocket and walked away toward the deck.

MARY-BETH

WHEN MARY-BETH BOYER agreed to spend her life with Tommy, she'd asked for two children. *At least that*, she'd said, *in case one of them dies*. Tommy suggested she talk to someone about this, someone who might ease her down from that kind of whack-a-doodle thinking, someone with a framed degree, but she didn't, and they'd dropped it, and he'd married her anyways.

Then, Tommy left them—Mary-Beth and Calvin. Wanted little to do with his wife and son, no holidays or questions, only checks in the mail for absolute necessities. That was a long time ago, and Mary-Beth remembers all this when she hears her only son is dead, dead for real this time, not just disappeared again or MIA—she remembers she'd once wanted another child. She'd asked for it, even. Two, in case one dies. At least that.

Identify body, her own handwriting said. There was a phone number written down too. Blue ink. Legal pad, torn. The page on her coffee table ringed with condensation from her drink, the letters and numbers spreading like flame.

Mary-Beth would have to *identify body*. But right now, her living room flooded with afternoon light, she decided not to move. Instead, Mary-Beth Boyer, fifty-six years old, would stay put right here on her pink floral couch, bare feet firmly planted on the tile floor. Her feet were cool there despite the creeping fever of July, a blurred, ghosted outline of steam around them. New urine ringed around her on the cushion like an oil spill. Now she'd have to clean that up, too.

Mary-Beth was out of Mistys and in need of a smoke. She looked at her face on the mirrored wall opposite her, behind the blank-black television, and tried to keep it as still as possible, like a game. Her blonde hair clung to her forehead, and it shone greenish always, a chlorinated color, though Mary-Beth never swam—not anymore. Was anyone else's face in her face? Was her son there? She looked hard but did not know.

Her right ear was still hot. The police had called, or was it Calvin's case manager? Or his parole officer? Or Betty from Gateway to Grace? Mary-Beth had received many calls since that morning, all in the same rushed tone: *I'm sorry to say / found him / need you to identify the body as Calvin's.* Maybe the officers had come to the front door of her Palm Paradise condominium, unit N253 with the Burbank Blue door, her plastic flower wreath leached colorless from the sun. Or maybe it was several officers who'd delivered the news, walking the ring of the complex looking for her, caps to their chests—*Are you the mother?*

Now she wasn't even sure any of it had happened at all.

The note she'd left herself, *identify*, still blurry. Maybe she'd copied it down wrong. Maybe she'd heard all the wrong things—sometimes she did that. Now her landline rang and rang, and her cell vibrated across the glass coffee table until it plinked onto the floor. No calls with Calvin's Cat Stevens ringtone. "Moonshadow"—he'd set it himself, knew all the words.

Mary-Beth's little brother had died when he was six. Mary-Beth was thirteen. Alfie was his name. He was so quick and so beautiful, and he'd died on a swing set, jumping off. Mary-Beth was there and she couldn't believe how fast it could happen, life and then no life in an artless snap. And thank heavens her parents still had Mary-Beth and her younger sister, Syl, once the boy was buried in all that sandy soil, two girls who could keep Alfie's likeness alive by memory, by the act of pure witness—*he was here, he was like this*—and anyway they'd helped around the house in those years, too. This: why Mary-Beth had the hunch, this feeling—*in case one dies*—sometimes she could still see little Alfie in Calvin when he'd made certain faces. Frustrated faces. It was in the eyebrows, the pulsing nostrils—DNA was really real, she thought. Now it was as if she'd lost her brother twice.

Mary-Beth straightened her posture. She wore a Florida Marlins t-shirt, no pants. She drank from her little glass, her special blue glass for special occasions, and refilled it a few times with the Skyy bottle, propped between couch cushions, next to her. It had been a long time since she'd had a drink. Mary-Beth will be still for a while, she told herself, as long as it takes.

A knock on the door now. Hard, insistent knocks. Her whole life it'd been those same hard knocks. She thought she heard her name—*Mary-Beth? Come on.* She refilled her glass again. The sun shone so brightly through the sliding doors her face looked faked out on the mirrored wall, only a streak of light with white eyelashes, not even fluttering. The phone jittered across the tile floor.

She'd talked to Calvin three or four times a day on the phone, even when there wasn't much to speak about. There was never much to speak about. He called to wake her, or to catch her before clacking her blinds closed, the deep morning sleep after working the graveyard at her gas station, North Pole Florida Gas & Save. He said, *Sweet dreams, Mama. Mama*—he'd never get too old to use that. Then he'd go off to work in the sugarcane fields and the community pond doing brutal things with his hands, and then he'd call again before afternoon group sessions, and then sometimes even again before prayer service, then good night. Gateway to Grace didn't supervise his calls the way other halfways had. Calvin's computer was monitored, but not his phone. He was going to become independent at Gateway—a chance at friends, a trustworthy man, maybe even a name tag again one day.

Mary-Beth didn't hear from him that morning, before the other calls started in. None of them his ringtone. That's all it took for her to know.

Knocks again and it was Syl at the door. Mary-Beth didn't remember how long ago she'd arrived, how long she'd been knocking, and as she opened the door, it didn't quite register that it was her little sister standing there dripping wet, her sister with that clammy look on her bloodshot face, mouth gaping wide like a painting of grief, a little fatter than the last time she'd seen her, but Mary-Beth hugged her anyway and held her body as she wailed, and eventually it clicked: Oh, fucking Syl's here.

I thought you were dead in there, Syl said in the doorway. Mary-Beth looked behind her sister into the communal lot. There were no officers, no unfamiliar cars. Syl cried into Mary-Beth's shoulder for several long minutes. She said, *There are no words*, over and over again—there are no words! And Mary-Beth did not understand this either. There are words, she thought. You're using them now. These are the words you are absolutely saying. Then Syl moved inside with her old leather suitcase, tongue of neon pink duct tape flapping from the handle.

Mary-Beth passed the kitchen and walked back to her couch. She lifted her arms as if to say, *Check this place out*, her pale butt cheeks exposed with her arms like that, but Syl had been here, to her sister's condo, many times. Mary-Beth had moved often, but her homes always looked the same—one small bedroom for Mary-Beth and, budget permitting, another for Calvin's eventual return home, still decorated with his childhood posters. Mary-Beth's living room setup: ceramic ashtrays on the armrests. Too many remote controls. Warm liters of Pepsi. Her phones. There was nothing really new to see.

We're going to get through this together, Syl said. She stood near the TV, in the middle of the living room. Nodded her head, which jerked unnaturally and chicken-like, as if she might yack all over. What's that suitcase about? Mary-Beth asked. Why are you wetter than a tramp?

Sweats, said Syl. They come on all the time now. She wiped at her forehead, then her lip.

Hoo-ha dried up? Told you.

Syl waved her off. The suitcase is 'cause I'm staying, Syl said. I will not leave you alone with this. I told Howie and everything, he's fine, knows I'd never leave you alone with this, he seemed relieved, almost, like he'll go all bachelor on me, we'll see. I'm not going anywhere, we're going to get through this the way we always do—you're my sister.

Mary-Beth said nothing. She was used to ignoring Syl, and quite enjoyed doing so. Syl crossed the room, moved toward the sliding glass doors that faced out to the lake at the center of the development. She opened the door and spoke facing the water. No one's heard from you, she said. We were worried you'd—

You auditioning for Lifetime?

Who all's been here yet? Syl said. You been over to Gateway?

I've been right here, Mary-Beth said. She dug her pointer fingers into the cushion, *right here in my spot*. Then she said: That show's on tonight, the one with the New York sluts. I'm all out of Mistys.

Syl's outfit annoyed Mary-Beth. Instead of her usual barn clothes—smeared blue jeans and a baseball cap, t-shirt reeking of tack oil—she wore a black polo shirt tucked into a knee-length denim skirt. Her damp dark hair bobbed at the shoulder. Always strange to see it down and not tied back, or flipped up into her cap, *like a redneck Sally Fucking Field*, MB had called her. Syl wore flat Mary Janes on her feet, her one pair of formal shoes she'd worn for every nice occasion since her prom in Destin, Florida. She looked so sensible standing there with her suitcase, Mary-Beth thought. So eager with her ham-pink skin, her doleful eyes.

MB, do you understand? Syl said. I need you to understand what's gone on. I wish I was here sooner, I know. I drove straight down when Tommy rang, didn't even turn out the animals, barely stopped the whole drive—

Tommy? Mary-Beth said.

He said he called you.

Mary-Beth refilled her little glass. So Tommy was involved. So Tommy knew something. Mary-Beth laughed a little, and Syl said, MB, what could you possibly think's funny here?

Then a tear came from Mary-Beth's eye so suddenly it stunned her. She licked her upper lip and it was wet, her eyes leaking now, the whole mess of her heart curving her cheeks and gathering there at her mouth. She blinked hard and fast, swatted away nothing in front of her face. She smiled.

Have you called North Pole? Syl asked. Would you like me to call them for you?

My day off, Mary-Beth said. Whoopee do! Finally a day off.

The landline rang again. Syl picked up the phone from the coffee table, moved it back to the wall mount, still ringing. Need to keep this charged, she said. How many times do I tell you that?

Mary-Beth sipped her drink. Then cupped her hands over her ears. Why the hell should Tommy know? He'd been in and out of their lives two decades, since Calvin was accused of the first girl. Cal was only sixteen then. Tommy knew nothing about Calvin as a real grown-up, not the weather he liked most or the movies he found funny or the way he tended to sick bonsai trees and hypothermic iguanas. Calvin loved dogs. He could name stars in the sky. He was an excellent driver (despite the violations) and liked to dip his foods into sauces, nothing smothered. Tommy wouldn't know any of that. He'd abandoned them both—refused to offer character statements to the courts, to humanize Calvin. Cal had gotten it worse because of that, Mary-Beth knew, because his own father didn't even love him enough to help. And now, after all the big absence, all the not knowing, *Tommy* had called Syl. Tommy got to have a dead son, a loss others would pity, maybe he'd even receive little gifts, 3D greeting cards, cellophaned baskets of shining fruit, a girlfriend. Because Tommy wouldn't have to share anything about Calvin's hardships to those in his new life, no details or specifics. A dead son is a son is a son.

Syl walked over to Mary-Beth's open kitchen and filled a glass with tap. Mary-Beth watched her through the cutout, the tap water milky with carbonation. Tastes foul, Syl said. Way worse than mine. You still on that well?

Someone said I have to identify the body, Mary-Beth said, pulling a rubber band from the coffee table. She snapped her hair into a pony.

Tommy's come up from Miami, Syl said now, maybe he should do it. You want some coffee, Elvira? Think you could use some. Her eyebrows lifted up and up—an expression of judgment meant only for herself, but Mary-Beth noticed. She always noticed. Mary-Beth wanted to crunch her up into her suitcase and zip it for good.

That was my boy, Mary-Beth said. I'm gonna do it.

Syl opened her sister's fridge and sighed dramatically—there's the breeze, she said. Oh, I'll stay right here. She swung her arm over the fridge door.

That was my Cal.

I know, sissy, Syl said. Then, after a long while: You don't need to keep onions in here, you know.

BIRDIE

THELMA GREETED ME outside the cabin when I arrived. Welcome to Whidbey, she said pertly. Any whales sniff your boat? With her cropped silver hair, purple cord jacket, socks printed with chickens, Thelma looked like a lesbian, there was no mistaking it, and this was a comfort. Her account on the rental website hadn't displayed a photo, but the reviews of Thelma were all favorable, kind. *Great communication!* was the only part that left me uneasy.

No whales, I said to Thelma. I'm Wilma Dean. I raised an *all good* hand to my cab driver at the bottom of the gravel drive, and he pulled out.

The cabin looked plucked from a storybook—an A-frame with scalloped wooden siding and a farmhouse door. It was shaded over with lush forest that dripped fresh-smelling rain onto my hair, and it was somehow more viscous here, syrupy. *The experience was too isolating*, some reviewers had written. I'd liked that.

Thelma messed with some keys on her carabiner and slid a few off. Wilma Dean, I'm Thelma, she said. Thanks for choosing Thelma's cabins! Already put your boxes inside—they arrived yesterday. Always fun to have folks here from the city that never sleeps. You sure will sleep here, frog songs, everything abloom in May.

Are those all your properties? I said to the keys.

Sure are, Thelma said. She nodded sadly, then looked out to the empty woods. We've turned all our structures into these cabins, cater to all different needs. The rental thing isn't really the local yokel way, but we're getting drained by the newbies on the bluffs. That means we natives gotta make do, adapt with the times. I watched the chapped tip of Thelma's nose as she spoke.

What kinds of needs? I asked.

Oh, some people with their kids, don't want them climbing up ladders and such to go beddy-bye, so we have cabins for that. Mostly it's kid needs.

Kids come here?

Parents like the disconnected aspect for the kids. That's a thing now—*screentime*. And that lasts about three days and then it's the parents who want out of here, off to a hotel. Ha! Thelma lifted the proper key, then released the iron door latch. She carried my suitcase inside. In the doorway, silent and inelegantly, we both removed our shoes.

The inside of the cabin smelled charred, like incense, and Thelma told me all about the red cedar used in the frame, the western hemlocks and firs, miscellaneous wood things I couldn't follow—*alder splits like a dream*. Logging, she said, that's our real business here. Just me and the hubs, Hal's his name. Still uses a winch and a tractor, bless him. And we still float the timber.

I said, That's so interesting.

The room had a high cathedral ceiling and windows that looked out into the trees, one with a cushioned window bench below it, quilted blankets with eagles and stars, a carved sign that read WOOD YOU BE SO KIND AS TO REMOVE YOUR SHOES? on the mantel. The bed was lofted in an open space at the top of a ladder, and Thelma told me all about the buckwheat pillows she'd arranged there, just for me. Wait'll you hear the toads, she said. The ones that sound like demented water droplets (she imitated their sound, pointer finger in her cheek)—they're invasive little shits. You can squash those if you see 'em.

I imagined it, pressing one beneath my boot. *I scare.*

Rentals, animals, the farm—that's all just a plus, she went on.

People sure like our eggs, and we get more than we need in summer, lay like crazy. I'd tell you to check out the salmon, take some pictures, but the pinks aren't running yet. Are you used to wildlife, Wilma? Thelma opened and closed cabinets, one after another; she appeared to be counting things. I could tell she was lonely.

It's kind of freezing, I said. Is there heat?

Thelma opened the iron woodstove and showed me how to load logs. Till end of June—you'll need it, she said. She lined up the first two logs parallel, a slight gap between, then said to *fill the middle with whatever till she blows.*

Only rule here's no candles, she said. That's a hazard, you get it.

I can do that, I said.

Anyway, the way we do things is you can come on up to our main house about a half mile away if you'd like snacks, famous eggs, coffee refills, company, that's on us—but you can keep to yourself, too, if you're like that. Probably you are if you're here. On Fridays we make a grocery run—you need any food, essentials, booze, leave cash in your mailbox with your list, and we'll drop the goods at your door. No others renting just yet, she went on—true summer, though. Gosh, wait'll you see this place.

I pulled my phone from my jacket pocket. No bars, as promised. A few texts from Trace. I didn't open them.

What's your business, Wilma Dean?

Film, I said.

I knew you had something Hollywood about you, I felt it. Thelma shook her pointer at me as she walked to the door, then slipped her shoes back on.

I'll take you to the pumphouse now, she said, where you'll pick up firewood. And that's where you'll find the landline guests can use—I assume you gave your contacts my number for emergencies, otherwise feel free to use the pumphouse line. You'd have to go two, three miles west for cell service.

Thelma pulled a yellow helmet from a nail on the wall, next to the door. On the back: two feathery, mean eyes, painted in cracked acrylic. Owls, she said, knocking on the helmet—after dark, they'll getcha by the hair.

Trace couldn't join me on Whidbey—the aloneness was kind of the point. The Walden experience. The great quiet. The anonymity. I'd lost my role as a film projectionist earlier that year when my East Village theater went digital. Now, with automated DCP projection, anyone could do it—push buttons, press Start, replace me. Trace's advertising job paid well and offered domestic partner benefits, and because Trace was Trace, she'd flown me cross-country just to drop me off. As my hands shook those plastic airplane cups full of vodka, she steadied them, repeated her Traceisms: *You're taking care of yourself; self-care is radical; rest is reclamation.*

On Whidbey, I'd breathe new air. No more phone calls or tabloids or news bits. No *Check out your next best read, suggested for you!* On Whidbey, I'd simply be Wilma Dean.

Trace and I spent one night together in Seattle before the ferry. At a restaurant strung with fishing nets, we pretended things were fine, the same, like it was another Thursday back in Greenpoint. We ordered Dungeness crab and a fried rice special and said hollow things like *West Coast oysters really are better,* avoiding the more pressing topics—the phones silenced in our pockets from the relentless media calls, the *bestselling* memoir, Calvin's letters, and the court dates. It was more comforting to observe the immediate, what couldn't be challenged: This menu is pretty. The bathroom line is long. Haven't heard this song in years. We clinked glasses and took pictures of each other on my old Pentax, pretended we were on vacation, a couple who'd patiently waited for this time away, this beautiful meal, a sweet occasion to look back on.

We stayed with a cousin of Trace's, a night nurse with a night off wearing a sorority t-shirt with the collar snipped. Her name was Havi and she regarded me with a solemn, fixated sadness. The sadness was in the way she laid the fresh pink towels on our bed, folding and petting them like they might bite. I knew right away Trace had told her about me.

If there's anything I can do, Havi said from the doorway, *to make you gals more comfortable, you just let me know*. She was emaciated with bulging blue eyes, an elastic headband revealing a crown of extensions. She wore a sagging sheet mask and carried around a gray cat who clawed at her face in quick strikes—*This is Patricia, she's shy, hates the masks*—and I nodded. I looked down at my feet. The whole thing had me wanting to leave an impression, a story she might recall to her friends later or write about in a diary, the time she served as a safe haven, a true refuge, for that traumatized gay girl.

The guest bedroom had no nightstand, so I used a decade-old tabloid magazine to balance a glass of water on her carpet. The glass left a dark, sunken ring across the stomach of someone beautiful.

I returned from the pumphouse alone with a few splits of wood. Hung the helmet at my door. Thelma had left me a basket full of pretzels and a bottle of wine near the hot plate. A little purple card with scalloped edges read *Welcome Wilma Dean!!* in shaky, careful handwriting. The boxes all had Wilma Dean Loomis's name on them, and as I slit each one open with the cabin key, I pretended I was going through someone else's stuff. Folding someone else's sweaters; stacking someone else's DVDs. Wilma Dean lived in the woods, near chickens. Wilma Dean wasn't afraid to be alone, maybe she was even a woman for long baths, Russian novels. Wilma Dean had a radial purity to her aura; she used words like *radial* and *aura*; she was firm and placid and unpetrified.

Birdie Chang was none of those things. Or, I hadn't been.

In the cab from the ferry, I'd been greeted by a welcome sign painted with Orca whales and eagles, the kitschiness reminding me of childhood trips to Key West. I'd passed shivering rows of crops and fields of llamas and places to buy loganberry pies and jars of dahlias. Weedy yellow flowers dotted the road. Whidbey was more rural than I'd expected, the trees much taller, dwarfing everything into a toy. I wondered how I'd one day remember this place, if I'd dramatically, tearfully exit a room if this summer were brought up.

I liked the company back home of cars exiting off the BQE, the traffic outside our window on Apollo Street; already I missed the wrinkled dog scratching above in 3A, and his owner's phone as it vibrated from his floor into our ceiling; I missed our drunk Polish landlord smacking the radiator with his cane and practicing alto sax to Charlie Parker tapes. Most of all, I missed the cold clashing sounds of my projection booth in the theater. The dark, steady sixty-two degrees in that slow pocket of life, AC howling over audio to protect the reels. Every frame of film magnified out the port glass, the subtitles too. For those hours and years, drowned in my wind tunnel, the movie was all I had to think about. That was all gone now.

Here, in my cabin, there was so much nothing my ears felt plumbed straight to water. I opened Thelma's gift bottle of wine, and the sun eventually slipped between the trees, went away.

Two lamps in the cabin, a pleasant orange glow. I unpacked boxes of miso soup packets, instant noodles, just-add-water foods that would get me along without doing much. I arranged picture frames on the corner desk and mantel: one of Natalie Wood, one of my father. I stacked my film books and DVDs against the wall, the notebook where I might one day write my screenplay, then lined up boots and galoshes. I unwrapped my dad from a ball of newspaper—I kept him in an old Chinese tea canister—and he was leaking a little, the tin dusty. Sorry, I said, wiping him off on my jeans.

My cell phone—still no bars. Not even a flicker. Not even on the windowsill or when I waved it slow over my head like a torch.

I turned it off. *You can put your device to bed here,* Thelma had told me, offering up a tiny wooden bed frame she'd carved for this purpose. The miniature bed had miniature crocheted blankets for the cell phone to rest. The pillow was a tiny knot of straw. *You tuck it in, so it's intentional.*

I threw my phone in the desk drawer.

Then, kneeling beside my suitcase as if performing a ritual, I took out the book.

I'd hidden Linzie King's memoir in an additional zippered compartment meant for electronics. I knew Trace wouldn't look there. The book was still in its brown paper bag with a pink receipt from the bookstore. I'd bought it a month ago at the end of April, the day it came out, and since then, it had lived under our mattress in Brooklyn.

Now I held the book in my hands. There was no one left to hide it from. It was cold.

The cover featured Linzie's face, a black-and-white photograph airbrushed glowy and smooth, cartoonishly bulb-lit eyes peeking over her bare shoulder. Her expression: a *who me?* humility. Above her head, in bold 3D letters, the title—*MY TURN: A Memoir of Survival*—printed on red reflective foil, and across the skin of her shoulders, in script: *From victim to victor, one brave woman's journey.* Quotes on the back read *Startling and informative, For the modern day feminist!* and *King is more than your girl next door.* I didn't find her pretty. I flipped the pages just as I'd done in the bookstore, looking for Calvin's name.

Trace and my mom had banned me from reading it. Of course I knew it was coming; Linzie had been reaching out to me for a year leading up to publication. *I promise to respect your time and boundaries,* the emails had read, *but I would really love to ask you some things, even over email. I think this could be healing for the both of us.* Sometimes, as a mental exercise, I pretended to remember

Linzie from school when we were both students at Dole Grove; I made up whole scenes of us together in the locker room, the library, convinced myself of the way she wore her hair (braids), and the way she dressed (*The Secret Garden*, 1993, lace collars) and that she'd changed her name from Lindsay to Linzie to come off more interesting (this was not true, as proven by yearbooks). But really, I had no idea. I didn't remember her at all. If she came to my parents' restaurant, she likely looked like every other white girl in Florida. She was four years younger than me, had only begun high school when I graduated, and in court, they'd kept all of us apart.

Two years before her memoir's release, at twenty-one years old, Linzie appeared on half a season of *The Dating Show*. There, she first revealed her big sad truth, sobbing at the camera over a plate of anemic-looking fish. Her potential husband wiped a tear from his own eye, then swiped at hers. *This is so fucking scripted*, I said to Trace when Linzie sent herself home, unready for real intimacy. She smooshed her face against the car window as it drove her away, red lipstick smudged to her chin. In bed, as the sad music played, I clapped the laptop closed.

King astonishes, another endorsement read on the back cover. *Distantly related to Stephen*, I bet she'd lie—*writing's in my blood!*

I never responded to her emails.

Linzie was allowed to use Calvin's real name because of public court records, and this felt exploitative to me. *Why couldn't she write her story as fiction? Like a novel or something?* Trace had asked, impressively and loyally irritated; this, when the book was first announced, when, as a result, Calvin's name started appearing everywhere (*Convicted Son of School Bus Driver Identified. Years later, there's trouble!*). But that answer was simple. Before the book was even published, Linzie was on *Late Night*. She was interviewed by *Teen Vogue* and then real *Vogue*, her life hacks and daily eating rituals were debated on the internet. Of course she'd written a memoir. She needed everyone to know just how exceptional she was for having endured any bad. She needed the world to see that white, lovely women could suffer monumentally, excruciatingly so, and still hold on, keep it together, emerge *survived*.

But it happened to me when I was nine. Linzie was touched eight years later, and she was thirteen. I'd never needed an audience or judge or jury to name my suffering to know its volume and realness; it happened to me, and I could never, would never, capitalize on it.

Linzie was a teen. I was a child. To me, there was a difference.

By the time I left for Whidbey, Trace and I hadn't had sex in almost a year. This coincided with Calvin's most recent prison release, as it often did. In the beginning, we liked fucking in other peoples' homes, or out in public restrooms; she'd even given me head on the slow Epcot time machine ride—a queer reclamation of space, we'd called it, rerouting the trauma of growing up in Florida. Then things shifted. Our couples counselor, an older Danish butch, told us we should take our time returning to intimacy. *Sex will likely ebb and flow throughout your life*, she said. *None of this's linear, what's the rush?* At this, I cried. I hadn't cried in all those sessions. Not when I described what had happened to me. Not when I described what was still happening to me, how the once wasn't actually once but something viciously ongoing, the movie villain thrown from a window or shot ten times, and yet—the gasp. The eye, opening. Always, a resuscitation. Furiously alive.

Whidbey was supposed to fix all that.

I checked my watch. Almost ten p.m. My tailbone ached from sitting, my left leg asleep. One a.m. in New York; three hours into the future, Trace had landed. Trace would now stand up in her airplane aisle, twisting the little air knob off, hunched and impatient. She'd snap some gum after a long plane nap, wind through the corridors of JFK, then wait, dazed and a little hungover already, for a taxi to drive her back to Greenpoint. She'd direct the cabbie the whole way—*middle lane until the Kosciuszko*—then have him drop her off a block or two from our apartment; she'd never let anyone see where we lived. Upstairs, she'd turn on all the lights, check the rooms, the closets, behind the shower curtain, under the bed, under the sink. Then she'd check again. She'd shout, *I'm here if you're here, motherfucker*, the whole Coming Home Routine she'd perfected, announcing herself, exhausted. *This kind of trauma can be a family illness*, another counselor had said, before strongly suggesting Trace seek independent therapy. I'd hated her for saying that.

I fed the woodstove some used tissues and picked up the fire poker, testing its weight, its grip. I didn't bring a gun or bear spray or Mace to Whidbey—there was, of course, no way to pack any of it—though Trace had shipped me a switchblade and spiked key chain with individual holes for my fingers. The fire poker was so sooty it left dark marks as I played with it, a pen stabbed into a palm. It would do.

I brushed my teeth and slid on a second sweatshirt. Upstairs, in the dark, I sat on the bed, dropped the book on my nightstand, then moved under the stretchy covers. The buckwheat pillow crunched like a beanbag. I tucked the fire poker beneath the sheets with me, still warm from the stove. In the window, cut by the banister, a hook of midnight so flooded by moon it was as if I was right in the pith of the world. Maybe there would be a life for me after all this, a reason for Whidbey, a purpose, a tomorrow.

Safety—would I know it if I ever felt it? I thought of Rich. His face on the boat, the way he walked away from me. *Good for you.*

I pulled the chain of my bedside lamp, folded over Linzie's face, and found the dedication page. *For every girl out there who needs this*, it read. *You are never alone.*

MARY-BETH

SYL DROVE. THE sisters took Mary-Beth's Mercury Sable so Mary-Beth could drink from her glove box mini-bottle stash. The Gateway to Grace Reentry Compound, where Mary-Beth Boyer would *identify body*, was an hour away, near Belle Glade, tucked between blank fields of charred cane and rotted muck soil which was, after all, the objective.

On the way they stopped at Mary-Beth's place of employment, North Pole Florida Gas & Save (*plus casino!*), so she could pick up a pack of Mistys. Rather than using Mary-Beth's reserved parking spot, Syl pulled right up to the front.

Mary-Beth opened the door to the station, setting off the bell. She was not used to entering like this, in her regular clothes—not an elf, but a customer.

The shtick of it was Christmas year-round, every inch of it. Tinsel fringe stapled to the walls wiggled by the AC. Carols played on their scheduled tracks, the women employees dressed as elves, the men as reindeer, and once a year, to celebrate back-to-school—Snow Day—when Joe the Snowman came with his truck and cannons, his grunting hose spewing snow over the parking lot. Mary-Beth wished Calvin could see the snow, could see her single day as *Mrs. Claus*, but he never did—2,500 feet. Eight football fields away, as mandated by lobbyist Ron Douchebagel Book, from anywhere children could congregate. Not where, or would, but *could*. Like if kids felt like going to the corner of

Douglas where Old Nick sells reptiles out of his cooler, if they wanted to see snow dissolve in their little palms—*BAM!* That's a children congregation.

Petra and Stanley were working today, both on step stools hanging a God Bless the USA banner from hooks above the sleigh. Mary-Beth was relieved to see Petra, her friend for years, her purplish dyed hair, lipstick matching. Petra had been struck by lightning not once but twice, and galactic scars webbed out across her neck and chest—*gotta protect her with Bullfrog*, Petra always said, swiping SPF 50 over the scars before the sun came up at the end of their night shifts together. Petra understood Mary-Beth, two boys of her own in Dade for armed burglary, and with every creep that walked in and out of North Pole, with every man saying the slot ate his goddamn money, for every temper and licked lip and sweat-liquored face, Petra would stand ever so slightly in front of Mary-Beth, one hand out as if Mary-Beth were a child about to crack through a windshield, the other hand balling to fist quicker than a spider touched.

When Mary-Beth told Stanley and Petra (*Something happened to Cal*, is how she said it, as she straightened a Monster can on the reindeer sleigh), Stanley stepped behind the counter, grabbed her a whole carton of Mistys instead of the pack. He squeezed her once, hard, at the shoulder. Then Petra came in for a hug. Neither said anything about God's plan, no glum corniness or platitudes, they just held her a moment, asked no questions—they knew. North Polers were the truest friends Mary-Beth had ever had, and she noted this as she and Syl pulled out of the station and back onto I-95, a new bag of mini bottles at her feet, Mary-Beth lighting up.

The day was interminable. It had gone on and on, and it felt like the sun might never set, and Mary-Beth didn't much want it to. A sundown would mean a full day of life on earth without her boy—she was beginning to understand that now, the fact of it pluming through her blood as she stared out the window. July 4, 2013—this would always be the day. It had been a relentlessly stormy summer, but today was clear, perfect for the fireworks. Calvin's favorite. Mary-Beth pushed the window crank around and around, toward her, then away, toward her, then away, and the glass rose and fell. She pretended for a moment she was captaining a very important ship, and these small rotations of her wrist would determine what new world she might find at the end of this hot, courageous journey.

Syl had been blabbering about all sorts of things in the car, everything having to do with *arrangements*. She got fixed on big euphemistic words like that, repeating them until they were acknowledged—*ergonomics, existential,* when she was a little girl: *conciliatory*! Always Smart Syl, Syl the Smartest, now her *arrangements*. Before they'd left the house, Syl had stripped Mary-Beth of her Florida Marlins shirt, underwear too, and dropped the damp clothing into the empty bathtub, a single sound to indicate that she had done it. Then she guided Mary-Beth into the tub to sit with her feet next to the garments, and as the water ran Syl soaped her sister's body with a stern, rough sympathy.

The saw palms wilted on the side of the road, mottled brown where there had once been life, and Mary-Beth said: Would you stop yapping already and let me goddamn think? Syl followed a green exit sign. They passed the horse show grounds of Wellington, they passed Lion Country Safari. They'd hit dirt roads for miles now, drive all the way west to Okeechobee, and on the radio, Mary-Beth's favorite DJ asked if anyone had seen the signs of our Lord today. Mary-Beth asked Syl to pull over for a piss.

Mary-Beth couldn't allow herself to think of Calvin, though he kept pushing on a place deep and sick in her chest. She pulled her pants down on the side of the road—her fancy blues, embroidered on the right thigh with a rhinestoned eagle—and left them scrunched at her knees. She did not like that Syl chose these eagle pants for her, didn't much understand the decision. As she peed and spread her feet to avoid the run, she thought of him, Calvin, their last conversation on the phone the night before, around ten p.m.: *I'm getting good at shooting hoops.* When the words came to her in his voice, she screamed and said, *Out! Stop it!* and her shouts must have been louder than she thought, because then Syl was at her side rubbing Mary-Beth's back in tiny irritating circles, asking what just happened. What just happened? The Mercury wheezed six feet away.

In her mind's eye Mary-Beth saw her boy's face and then his fingers, first young little boy fingers and then grown, the square cut of his nails, the yellowed fingertips that had matched hers from smoking, and as she pushed these images out out out, she grabbed a fistful of gravel from the shoulder and pushed it into her mouth. She coughed it right back onto the road.

Now, what're you trying to accomplish with that, Syl said, wiping Mary-Beth's chin with her hand. Let's get you back in the car. Mary-Beth pulled up her pants and zipped but let her brown belt stay dangling, and as she walked toward the vehicle, the air warped and magnified like she'd stepped inside a blown bubble. Gnats tickled at her face in the heat. She wanted to be sick. She wanted everything inside of her to come out her mouth and ass and eye sockets and every pore of her skin; she wanted to be emptied, her soul a splash of nothing, that might help with the pain. But this didn't happen, and the sun kept beating her skin and she fell back into the passenger's seat, the seat belt metal bright hot on her biceps as she curled up and said: Just go.

Syl spoke into her BlackBerry several times as they drove, mostly answering in short, quiet bursts and plenty of *mmmm*s. It took several calls for Mary-Beth to realize that Syl was talking to people about Mary-Beth and Calvin and the whole bad situation. This struck her as surreal—Syl's life had always been so separate. She had trouble imagining her sister ever talking about her at all, and the fact of her on the phone now, her hushed voice, her squeezed eyes darting over to Mary-Beth to see if she was listening, meant that this all must be a big deal. Mary-Beth knew her son wouldn't be calling, but still she panicked for a moment, smacking at her pockets to look for her own phone in case he'd tried.

I've got it, your phone, Syl said. Mary-Beth lit a new Misty with the tip of the one in her mouth, then replaced it, flicking the old out the window like a nub of French fry. That's something she and Calvin used to do—play with their food. They both liked the greasiest, sweetest, floppiest fries at the bottom of the red cardboard container. Mary-Beth emptied another mini bottle into her mouth, the Skyy glugging out so quickly it sang a scale.

Sure is far out here, Syl said. Can't believe you do this drive.

You get used to it.

I've arranged it so Howie and the girls have all the instructions they need to hold down the barn, that way I can be with you indefinitely, Syl said.

The girls?

They're home for summer. It's summer break, MB, you know that.

Of course she knew that. Syl loved to talk to Mary-Beth as if she were crazy all the time, as if there were an audience always nearby to laugh at her, *That Mary-Beth Boyer sure is crazy!* Syl opening her arms like Oprah on TV, nodding, *Like I told you! Exactly like I said!* It was summer, but no, Mary-Beth hadn't kept track of Syl's children's academic schedules, so sue her. The car whipped past fields of green beans and corn, cane trucks and tented palms, and Mary-Beth said, Shit goddamn, woman, how many instructions they need? What's the fuss?

Horses take a lot of care, Syl said, nodding slowly to herself. All animals do.

Do not, said Mary-Beth. They roam around doped in your yard when they should be wild. You treat 'em like a spa, but that doesn't mean they need it.

We don't have wild horses, MB, and no pasture puffs either. We have domesticated, working horses, and that means big needs.

That means I'm paying out my asshole for an assistant trainer so I can be with you. PT, acu, chiro, magnets, lasers, injections, supplements—every day it's something. These are prancy people who board with me. Ocala people. You know I'm up four a.m.—

I'm still working four a.m. in Santa's workshop, getting half fucked by frat boys, Mary-Beth said. You think this means something to me?

Mary-Beth wasn't used to Syl's face in profile like this, driving. She noticed how her sister had aged since the last time she saw her. Straight on, Syl was just Syl. But from the side, her neck sagged in overlapping tanned folds, and when she spoke, the paler slivers of skin flashed decadently.

Well, they've got it handled at home, Syl said, so I can help down here. And Stanley'll take some of your shifts, I'm sure. I don't want you thinking about work. I've got you for cash.

They need tits at North Pole, Mary-Beth said. That's why they use me nights. Stanley won't do nights. It's me or Petra because Margail dances nights. Can't put that all on Petra.

I'm sure they can scout another elf, Syl said, and Mary-Beth knew it right then—Syl's mean bone was coming out. Always the predictable amount of time, speaking like she had an iota of respect for Mary-Beth and Calvin, as if she found them human and worthy, the sweet-talk up—sure, they had their quirks, but they were hardworking, full of good love, *family*—until the mean bone came out. Next, usually after a few beers or mugfuls of box wine, Syl would fling some shard of truth, then say she was just kidding, swear it. Syl thought of them as low-lifers, Mary-Beth knew, embarrassed of her sister working the gas pumps, her nephew on the *you-know-what* registry—unless she was swooping in to help them. Only then was Mary-Beth of value to her sister. When Syl could play martyr and Mary-Beth could be saved.

That's why she was here.

I bet your girls are slutting it up at college, Mary-Beth said, sucking the Misty. Her cheeks were concave, pinched even when she wasn't smoking these days. Syl had commented on the sharp-boned points of her sister's frame, MB's jeans crimped around the hips like cupcake liner, and she'd had a lot to say about eating right. She didn't like the baby food pouches Mary-Beth sucked (they were easy on her teeth!), and Mary-Beth knew it was her sister's way of defending the weight she herself never seemed to lose, no matter how hard she worked at her barn and wheelbarrow, no matter how many sun-bleached books about cottage cheese and cabbage she'd dog-eared and reread.

I don't stoop to that talk about my girls, said Syl. I don't stoop, Elvira, and you know it. *Elvira*, what Syl had called Mary-Beth since they were kids. No one remembered where that had started or why, but Syl always used it. Certain moods.

Oh, you stoop, Sylvia.

Mary-Beth loved children—she was Mrs. Claus, for God's sake!—but she had never liked Genie and Nicola, Syl's daughters. Sure, they were her only nieces, but Mary-Beth didn't feel connected to them in any real way. They were born twins, and from the start Mary-Beth hated the preciousness with which they were regarded, what with their matching onesies with beaded buttons, double birthdays and therefore double-the-price birthday presents, cutesy haircuts and matching glitter nails. Mary-Beth never felt as if she could get through to either one of them because they spoke only of French classes at school and their future aspirations as exotic animal veterinarians. Even when Nicola went through a punk phase—thick makeup, wrists looped with colorful rubber bracelets practically to her elbows—her whole angsty thing felt rehearsed, drama that could fool others but not Mary-Beth. *A cola passed off as Pepsi*, Mary-Beth had thought (she'd told Calvin this, proud of the comparison), *would never fool me*. And now they were at college in Orlando, less than two hours south of Syl and Howie, and it occurred to Mary-Beth again, in this very moment of resentment, that her son—her only child—was dead. Abominable, that Syl would mention the stupid girls at all.

Syl slowed the Mercury and Mary-Beth listened to rocks springing against the undercarriage. She felt each pang. Out the window the shadow of Mary-Beth's smoking arm stretched across the road, the sky softening pink by a wounded sun, though the heat did not waver. The area smelled of rotted fish—Lake Okeechobee was algae-choked, dying—and the muck from the crop fields was churned velvet, the blackest of black. Cicadas chattered their tongue-rolling sound, all wrong like air squeezed from a balding tire, and Syl said, Oh dear . . . this it? Mary-Beth saying, Not yet, still around the corner—before she noticed gradually and then quick why Syl had slowed the car in the first place.

The graveled intersection right outside Gateway to Grace was squared off by yellow tape flipping back and forth, like a coin tossed into the light. Pink sparklers lay askew on the ground no longer ignited. Surrounding the tape stood Betty and Lief and Charmaine, people who'd become like family to Mary-Beth and Calvin. Lief smoked his cig, his shorts hung low exposing Ren & Stimpy boxers, and he aimed his flip phone at the not right red of the road inside the tape. Mary-Beth opened the car door and tripped to her knees as she came out of it—the car had still been moving.

MB? Betty's face was pruned with sorrow. She walked, then half jogged over on sturdy legs, feet and flip-flops mud-spattered. She helped Mary-Beth off the ground and held her body tight. Oh no, she kept saying to Mary-Beth, oh no, oh no, poor Cal, poor Cal, in a tenor Mary-Beth recognized—a low note distinct to a woman in pain. Betty took Mary-Beth's face between her palms to get a good look at her, to make meaningful eye contact, but Mary-Beth's face didn't do much or feel much in her hands. Instead, Mary-Beth really took Betty in, her tattooed eyeliner which had faded to a dark cobalt ring, her thin, bleached curls tucked high in a tortoise clip.

MB, what're you doing here? Betty said.

Came here for my boy, Mary-Beth said. Mary-Beth breathed in

sharp through her nose, straightening her back. She hiked up her pants, fixed her belt.

Oh, honey, he's off back at the station—or, I mean, the coroner's, oh, honey, what did they tell you? Did they tell you to come over here? How come?

Was Mary-Beth told to come to Gateway, or was the drive to Calvin this automatic? She couldn't remember anything she was told at all. Had someone told her sister where to go? Syl was on her BlackBerry again, pacing the side of the road, the car blinking its cautions on the shoulder. Usually, cane trucks shot down this street. Today, no other traffic.

Fairy-Beth, Lief said, we're gonna get the guy—I swear to fuck I'm gonna nail him.

The boys had all taken to using *Fairy-Beth* soon after Calvin moved to Gateway to Grace last December. She was their fairy godmother, always bringing extra smokes and pork rinds from North Pole or Pahokee, and she'd helped them hang curtain rods and framed pictures, tidied up their rooms with plastic flowers, gift wrapping paper taped around their beds like fresh coats of paint. Mary-Beth had always been interested in interior décor, creative like that. She couldn't remember who'd started the nickname, but she loved being trusted, one of the few guests welcomed on the compound premises. I'll fuck him right up, Lief said.

Syl got off her call and walked toward Mary-Beth. A thin, focused woman in a white polo with a lanyard dangling from her neck crouched inside the tape with a small baggie and tweezers. She tweezed dark glass from the ground. Mary-Beth didn't understand what was happening.

What's happening? she said. Why was Cal off the premises? Was this after curfew?

Syl swooped her arm around Betty and said, Betty, may I talk with you for a minute? They walked ten feet away, the two women speaking with fierce seriousness, Betty's hands pinching nothing in front of her face to emphasize whatever it was she was saying. Then Betty's hands went *SPLAT*, and she cried out with a wild contortion in her face. For a moment, Mary-Beth told herself she was watching a joke being told.

Lief was still talking to Mary-Beth, though she'd turned his voice off. He was a jittery boy in his early twenties, covered with pink skin and scabs, freckles that clustered more on his lips and kneecaps. He'd been clean off nitrous for a while but still had the tweakishness of that life before, dark scarring around his mouth from the time he huffed directly from a tank instead of a balloon, and very blue eyes that sat so wide on his face Mary-Beth thought of him as a hammerhead shark, slick and precious. Mary-Beth loved Lief—he was Calvin's first roommate at Gateway—and she took a great interest in his situation: he'd been arrested, convicted, and sent to Gateway on the registry for sleeping with a girlfriend who was fourteen when Lief was eighteen, but they were official and in love, and the girl had lied about her age, Lief swore it. The Romeo and Juliet motion did not work for Lief's case, and it was one of the stories that kept Mary-Beth up at night. Because of one girl's lie, Lief would be pariahed forever.

Fairy-Beth, I got pictures before they took him, before they got Cal, Lief cried, his voice pitching up. He wiped his nose erratically with the heel of his palm.

Who got him?

The police, the medics and stuff. They scraped him, it was fucked. But I got pics on my phone, I got evidence, Fairy-Beth. Cal didn't have shoes on.

He was here? she asked. Calvin was here?

This is where they got him. Right there. Lief pointed to inside the tape, the woman still crouched with her baggie, a clipboard, too.

Mary-Beth did not know how her son had died until that moment. But in a way, she felt she did know. Of course she knew. In a way, this patch of road, the unlit sparklers—the fact of murder— did not surprise her, not even at all. How was that? Had somebody told her and she'd forgotten? Or had she intuited it, felt it somewhere in her body, maybe while she was sleeping? Goddamn her for sleeping. The tingly thing, she'd felt this for Calvin all her life, since before he was even born. His big, too-big heart the size of an animal's much larger. His fears. His sickness.

Calvin was thirty-one years old when Ron Book's Florida sex offender legislation moved him under the Julia Tuttle Causeway Bridge (later known as Bookville). To *reside* in a place simply meant to sleep there—Cal and Mary-Beth had learned that fast. But Calvin did not sleep. From ten p.m. to sunrise, the bridge was his legal address. Mary-Beth brought dinner, a Styrofoam box of Pollo Tropical warming the passenger's seat as she drove. Then Calvin ate while plugged into the generator—seven ankles, seven men at once—which buzzed, spat sparks, and killed things on the shoreline.

Mary-Beth would swear forever she knew the percentage left of Calvin's monitor's battery by a feeling in her chest, could sense the sheets of rain knifing over Biscayne Bay before he did. She drove back and forth across that 2.5-mile bridge every night, pulled off into the grass so she could run down the slope and through the mangroves to her son, for whom she'd bring a tarp, a Mylar blanket, a toothbrush. Mary-Beth was sick, too, but in different ways. She hadn't known but she knew, of course she knew, that someone would get Calvin eventually, take him from her. It was a fear so common, so everyday, that this event inside this tape felt like only the very top layer of something else. The gray scrim of fat over her chilled, leftover food.

Syl and Betty were still talking, mouths moving fast. Syl looked dressed up next to Betty—those filthy flip-flops—and Mary-Beth knew Syl felt good about the difference. Lief, baby, I got to talk to my sister right now, Mary-Beth said, pointing over to the women. I can't listen right now, baby. Lief crouched so his butt almost touched the pavement and bounced a little, crying into both hands, cigarette leaking smoke from between his fingers.

Mary-Beth approached Syl and Betty, and as they saw her coming, the women turned away from her and lowered their voices. Screw that, Mary-Beth thought, there was nothing her sister could or should know that Mary-Beth shouldn't know herself. That she shouldn't know first. Betty didn't know Syl. Syl had never even been here. Syl was a woman who picked her molars with paper clips and sucked on crackers before a spit cup. Mary-Beth pushed the two women apart. Hey, what are you talking! Mary-Beth shouted. What the hell are you talking about?

MB, I'm just telling your sister about the condition, Betty said softly.

What condition?

MB, Syl said, I'm trying to take care of things for you. You've got enough to think through, these details shouldn't be of your concern.

Take me to the coroner! Mary-Beth said. She spun around. Betty, take me—

I have to stay here, sweetheart, Betty said. We've got session soon, I can't leave.

You're holding sessions?

The boys need their sessions and service more in hard times, MB, I can't go'n cancel on them. And they love their fireworks—that's something nice for them. Something to look forward to later. But we'll all be praying for Cal tonight, under his name . . .

Sissy, get in the car, Syl said to Mary-Beth. Sounds like he's at the coroner's over east.

Mary-Beth ran to the woman inside the tape. What's in that baggie! The woman flinched. Gimme that bag! Mary-Beth would learn in the weeks to come how to be offended for her boy after his death, because only by death could she finally find the traction, the right.

A young officer clinked over, from where, Mary-Beth didn't know. She hadn't seen anyone else around, only Charmaine—big, kind, and braided Charmaine, on the registry for public urination—

who'd stayed quiet, staring at the road like she was under a psychic spell.

Miss Boyer, the officer said, writing something down. He was standing too close. He said, I'm kindly going to have to ask you to back away from the secured area.

My name's Mary-Beth, the mother, she said. And you can go fuck a rabbit.

MB, get in the car! I got the info! Syl screamed. Syl opened the passenger's side door and pointed in, in—now! Don't be incensing that man!

Your son's no longer here, the officer said. Breath that made MB's eyes water. Crack of blue-green gum between his front teeth. They shoulda called you over to identify his body.

He's got a SCRAM monitor with GPS, Mary-Beth said. How hard's it to identify? They know where he's at every second, and now that he's dead, nobody knows where he's at?

He's with the coroner, the officer said, we know where he's at, ma'am. The woman with the baggie jotted some things down on her pad, unbothered. Mary-Beth took in the deep stain of the road and the rocks. The red, the black, the pinkish areas, too. All this dirt was her son. What had he been wearing? She wanted to pack all the colors inside her own baggie now, a million baggies, load the car up with bags and bags of Calvin, take him with her.

The officer looked at her with great concentration, and Mary-Beth thought he must have felt very official, looking at her like that. Bigger than her, and more important too. A cloud rolled over the sun until it outlined with glow. Betty let loose, shook out, then reclamped her hair, and a bottle rocket sent birds to the power line, where they eventually settled.

Mary-Beth walked over to the Mercury and slid into the passenger's seat next to her sister. Let me see him, she said.

BIRDIE

I DID NOTHING but read the book for the rest of May and into June. If I slept, I barely knew it. If I dreamed, I dreamed only of the book. By the third read, I'd begun to memorize page numbers and passages, and by the fifth, I knew the book spatially; left side, two-thirds down, after the break on page fifty-four—that's where Linzie did it. That's where her version of my story began.

I was a minor, a Jane Doe, when my parents pressed charges against Calvin; I couldn't even sign anything myself. My real name brought up nothing on the internet—Trace and I had paid a company, via annual subscription, to wipe any digital footprint. But recently, scans of all case documents appeared on the web for law students and gawkers to peruse, the names of minors redacted under stretched black boxes. Linzie used it all. The witness details, the statements and testimonies, transcriptions of interviews I sat through with so many rotating suits in my childhood living room, at the Broward County station, in the office building with palm trees planted under the lobby's pallid lights. Those details and memories had once been mine, alive in color and temperature only when I let them in, chose them—mine. Now they weren't. I had never even read my files until they were excerpted in the memoir's pages, paraphrased and analyzed in her words, her name on the cover, her picture, her book.

Some mornings I sat on the toilet with the book in my hands, feet and legs stinging a numb vibration. Whole days passed like this, my awareness of time only coming to when I'd urinate every few hours, my ass bleeding drops into the toilet from sitting too long, my mind in 1995. Ever since Calvin, I have struggled with this: moving. Simple movement. It's what made me a decent projectionist, legs spread in stance, eyes fixed at the port glass of the theater, waiting for the changeover cues. Outside of work, long stretches of time might pass before a flash of rope above me—usually my mother's or Trace's—*you've been staring for hours; you haven't left bed for days; you can't drive with this tendency; do you think she's epileptic, narcoleptic?*—and I'd do my best to catch the end of that rope, a ladder let down in the dark, whipping and merciful.

And really everything bled in those early days with the book, all the way into June. My period came off schedule; my nose ached and cracked from the woodstove, plastic sharp inside the nostrils, then: blood. More blood. I bit my fingers, picked and ripped at them, though I was never conscious of doing this. The book's pages went splotchy with comets of red that oxidized a dull brown. Tissue wads littered the floor.

After every full read, I closed the book to stare again at the cover, looking Linzie right in the eyes, expecting to find something new, like she'd move her lips and talk to me. The photo of her inside the back cover showed a different Linzie—a girl beaming with the open-mouthed smile, phony black hair backlit by sun. She wore a silk burgundy blouse in this photo, arms crossed over her chest, a small gold pendant around her neck in the shape of a rabbit.

Jade Suzuki, I will call her, my section began.

Jade—to protect her privacy. Jade, an appropriate mineral, rare and heavenly. Picture Jade here. Bring her to life in full-fledged color. Picture her eyes, two salt-dusted almonds, her childish knock-kneed posture, the smile that eventually got wiped away. An only child born in Miramar, Florida—just like me. Jade's parents stayed together; a Chinese father (deceased, cancer, 1997) and mother made a tight family unit—not like me. Jade's parents owned a popular Asian-fusion restaurant called Hei Baby in the Plantation area. I ate there once. There are so many experiences that separate us, but so much that brings us together.

Jade was nine.

Not even close to my age when it happened. I was a teenager, someone with more maturity, more context and tools for self-care, a will to survive already established. I was somebody destined to one day speak her truth.

But Jade Suzuki was guileless, defenseless, nine.

She deserved more life than what Calvin did to her. She deserved her American Dream. She deserved so much more! I read Jade's records and transcripts and have looked her up, just to see her face. Once, and only once, I saw her on a university's website—I cannot, for privacy reasons, disclose which one. She was graduating in a purple billowing cap and gown, and on her face, a nervous half smirk, like she wasn't sure if she wanted to be in the photo. I reached out and actually touched my laptop screen when I found the picture, running my fingers over the low-resolution image, moved beyond measure. To this day, it is a feeling I can barely describe. Me too, I wanted to say, cliché as that may sound. He hurt me too, Jade. I wanted to hold her, this cracked porcelain doll, for we women were soulfully linked in ways almost incomprehensible. I wanted to mend all the fractures. Where did he put them, Jade? How many were there, and how deep did they run? I wanted to tell her we could—we would—*survive him, together. We would be okay, even more beautiful in the fractured places.*

Show me your scars, reader. Now trace mine, too.

I reached out to Jade a few times but let go, eventually. Maybe she wasn't ready, maybe she still isn't. Or maybe she's reading this today. It is my greatest hope that she is. I've always known that we would travel forth alone on our own unique journeys, because that's the way of these things, the one true current of survivors, this suffocating loneliness. Calvin made sure of that. But still, I ache for a connection. It feels like very little to ask.

Jade was nine. You should know what happened to her. She wasn't the first, or last, of Calvin's victims. She was only in the third grade. Yet, with ample evidence and even video footage, the courts dismissed Jade's case. Calvin was punished for the others, but not for her.

I will do my best to re-create Jade's story, to share this wrongdoing and therefore offer her experience more gravity. It's a privilege I don't take lightly, to speak for those who can't speak, who have been left voiceless. You might know a Jade yourself. Statistics say you probably do. Someone, perhaps, without the privilege I have of sharing.

To the Jades of the world, I want to offer my humanity, my voice, and my strength. It is my purpose on this earth, I believe, to help and to humbly serve, to light up the darker places where there is only silence and pain. I see you, I love you, this story is exactly for you.

Reader, to understand Jade's story is to understand my own.

Then that bitch went on to tell it.

MARY-BETH

MARY-BETH EXPECTED TO be led into a room with blue tiles. She expected a pristine sheet hovering midair, as if a caped magician or the grinning host of *Iron Chef* would pinch and lift it, revealing a body ready to be transformed. She expected that body, Calvin's body, to be stark white and shirtless beneath the halogens, angelic in a final, hard-earned peace. She would hold him, kiss him, and by that touch, absorb some version of the truth.

Instead, she was led into a cinder-blocked county office thirty miles east, fax machines and phones chirping, Syl gripping her by the elbow as if to keep her in line. The station lights shot yellowy and harsh like a rest stop bathroom, and a square-jawed Black woman scooted a chair up to the desk, facing Mary-Beth. The woman wore honey-colored contact lenses, which floated over her irises in small, pixelated dots. Mary-Beth noticed the dots from a desk away. The woman's face was perfect, Mary-Beth observed, like an America's Next Top Model. Who really was she?

Again, Miss Boyer, the woman said, I'd like you to take all the time you need with these photographs.

A folder in front of her. Mary-Beth hadn't remembered a folder there. There were folders and papers all over the place now, though she wasn't sure which were important, how long she'd been sitting in this seat with her sister's firm clutch at her shoulder. The station smelled like Hot Pockets and burritos, too many meats microwaved without ventilation. It was the smell of jail, and prison, all the waiting rooms and visiting rooms she'd sat in for Calvin, holding her breath before easing into it, every time. Unmistakably, stagnantly microwaved, these places—meal atop meal atop meal, years of peeled plastic dappled with condensation from the globs of flash-frozen greens—these were the homes of her son.

I'm not sure I understand, Syl said, why my sister's got to go through this business with the pictures. Calvin wore an ankle monitor.

Lady, what's your name? Mary-Beth asked.

Officer Durham, said the woman. Carmen Durham. You can call me Carmen, if that's comfortable. Here's my card. She pushed a white card across the desk.

Wouldn't the monitor be all you need? Syl continued.

I understand how that would make sense, Carmen said. She wove her fingers together in front of her—long fingers, painted acrylics in a Band-Aid beige color. Wrong nails for an officer, Mary-Beth thought. Who was this Carmen after her shift?

Unfortunately, we still need to move forward with the standard process, Carmen said. Believe it or not, the wrong wallets and IDs and, yes, even monitors, have been found on deceased persons' bodies. In a situation like this, in . . . an exclusive community like this, it's important we move forward fastidiously. The medical examiner's office will—

Mary-Beth did not appreciate Carmen's calm patter. *Exclusive community.* People often used words like this: *exclusive, unique, exceptional,* to describe programs and compounds for registered offenders, programs like Gateway. *Exclusive,* like they lived in fucking Mar-a-Lago. Like they spread picnics over a putting green.

You can't get that monitor off, Mary-Beth said to Officer Durham. My son stays plugged into a wall half the day to keep the shit thing charged. We pay five dollars a day to keep it on, and when he lived under Julia Tuttle bridge, he almost lost his foot to sepsis being hooked up under there. They had him chained to a hospital gurney a full week. You think he'd do all that if it came off like a little locket?

You can take as much time as you need with the photographs, Carmen said.

Where's my son? Where's my son, Carmen?

Carmen said, Now, the body you will see shows severe primary impact injuries as well as secondary impact injuries—that's common for vehicular pedestrian collision. You will also see avulsions of the skin due to what we call a rolling injury. These dark contusions are created when the tires—

Why are you telling her this? said Syl. She shook her head as if disappointed, pulled out her flat pack of gum. Her front teeth slid a chalky stick from the foil.

It's standard for us to describe what you're about to see in these photographs insofar as—

Mary-Beth opened the folder. She didn't expect to see someone else in the photos, but she also hadn't expected to see her Calvin. The splotchy hair on his calf, always darker than the hair on his head. His slender bare foot—his good, uninfected foot. And some part of Calvin looking like a jumbo spat-out gristle of steak.

I'd like to confirm, Carmen said, Mr. Boyer's ID indicated he was not an organ donor—

He had an ID on him, too? Syl asked.

You're goddamn right he's not, Mary-Beth said. Me and Cal, we'll rest in peace, not in pieces. It occurred to Mary-Beth now that this little thing that they had always sworn was no longer true. Calvin was, indeed, in pieces. But nobody would cut him up even more. Nobody would take his parts, his eyeballs or ears, whatever was left and good of him.

Due to the nature of the multiple avulsions and the quantities of fractures, the medical examiners have estimated your son was impacted several—

Impacted.

Rolled several times—five times, to be exact—back and forth.

The spiral fracture / bumper shard / pigment found in / chest sunken / be determined but / over the extremity of the—

She couldn't listen. She thought of hoops. That's what Calvin wanted to talk to Mary-Beth about the night before. He'd said, *I'm getting good at shooting hoops, Ma.* And Mary-Beth had thought, How wonderful.

Under the chassis / because the gravel / blood—see / where the victim / would you like a glass of water, Miss Boyer? / recumbent limbs / with the nature of / what the sample will tell—

Mary-Beth said she wouldn't believe it until she saw it. Said he'd have to show her some slam dunks next visiting day, like Shaq before he betrayed the Heat. Mary-Beth had felt so moved that the other boys were teaching Calvin a sport, that they'd created teams, played games. She thought, My boy will get his boyhood back. At last, close friends, a tribe, inside jokes she'd witness between them, people who'd see him all the way through. She imagined designing and sewing the boys' uniforms for future basketball teams, should they be any good. She'd finally learn to sew for that.

Carmen placed a cup of water on the desk.

My sissy can't drink cold water, Syl said, baring her own teeth, pointing to them.

Carmen said, we're handling the questioning here at the station. Does anyone specific come to mind, anyone who might have had a grudge against your son? Has anyone recently made any threatening—

Everyone hates my son, Mary-Beth said.

Can you be more specific?

You and me . . . we know what goes on at Gateway, what people do to those boys, what they think of so-called *kiddie ticklers*. Mary-Beth waggled her fingers, made an O of her mouth like a Halloween witch. Syl shifted in her seat. She could never sit still.

There was a sharpness to Carmen now. Tongue rolling against her upper teeth, a vole under grass. I understand that a book came out in April, Miss Boyer, she said, detailing a few cases where your son was involved in—

It's *abuse*, Mary-Beth said, what the locals do to those boys. Rats in pillowcases. Graffiti. Sugar napalm, melting their fucking skin off. Tasers off eBay. Those sting ops with your guys, *your* men, acting like prissy little girls on the internet. That's entrapment. Your side's full of sickos, you know that, Carmen? Why do you think your guys spend all that time in the chat rooms? Just playing around, I'm sure. You know someone even killed the Gateway dog, for God's sake, a DOG! Drowned an innocent dog in the pond. Mary-Beth sat back in her chair, crossed her arms. Now, would you believe that, Carmen? Cruelty like that?

Carmen took a Pop-Tart out of her drawer, tore open the chrome wrapper. I understand, Miss Boyer, that this is a lot.

No, honey, you don't understand.

We'll do our best, Carmen said, breaking the Pop-Tart in half. S'more flavor.

What comes next, on your end? Mary-Beth asked.

We'll call you, Carmen said. We have your information written down.

You want to start somewhere, said Mary-Beth, maybe start with his deadbeat daddy. Thomas Pinball-Brain Boyer. You can write that down. Ruined Cal's life already—wouldn't surprise me if he did it again.

He's already in for questioning, Miss Boyer, Carmen went on. She flipped papers like it was nothing. Chewed on her snack. Eventually, she pulled the folder from Mary-Beth's hands.

MY TURN

Pages 2–3

I was born Linzie Gwendolyn King on December 21, 1989, a Sagittarius Capricorn cusp. Winter solstice, and one of the coldest Florida Decembers on record. Miami froze. Governor Bob Martinez declared a disaster. Iguanas plopped paralyzed from trees. They called it the Christmas Coastal Snowstorm, with flurries dipping all the way down to Sarasota. Floridians mummified their outdoor plants in all the clothes and tarps they could gather.

Which is to say, I was destined for an extraordinary experience. A path unexpected, sometimes confusing, and rare. Astrology says the Sagittarius Capricorn cusp makes a person primed for prophecy. In my experience, I have always known I was born for love.

As an only child, my first true loves were my parents. My father, Doug, served nobly in the US Navy and was stationed in Vietnam at eighteen years old, then Hawaii. I grew up with his tales of jungles and rice paddies, hard work, rescue missions. A true blue American, he can still make a gadget of anything and tell you the ins and outs of any machinery (cars, toasters, a plow shaft, you name it!). He's a freight dispatcher now, and we spend a great deal of time together in the modest South Florida house I grew up in. He's been there for me through everything—middle school dances, the death of pets, and, yes, even Calvin; my father is my true rock.

Growing up my mother, Irene, was a traveling entrepreneur. When I was young, she went door to door around the country, selling supplements and beauty products she made herself and really believed in. An avid gardener, she was always making special "potions" in our kitchen and bathroom from her bounty: lavender soaps, rosemary tonics, carrot face masks (the first time we yanked up carrots in our yard, we laughed and laughed at the square shape of them . . . Hot tip: Florida coral will make for some interesting gardening!) Eventually, she and my father parted ways, amicably. My mother moved to Buffalo, New York, where I often visit her on her sustainable organic farm. She is resourceful, an avid canner, and now I am, too. Once your jeans are wiped with soil, it remains there forever—and in your blood. I dearly hope to one day have a farm of my own.

My parents showed me true love. But let's back up here. Or, perhaps, fast forward.

I was born for a rare experience. And despite my parents' love, as an only child of divorce, I still felt a profound lack, like I wasn't wanted or good enough. I stood too long at mirrors, pulling and prodding at my face. Was I beautiful? Could God make me beautiful if I was good? When my parents separated, my dad worked all the time, and I looked after myself a lot. I taught myself female things like how to do makeup and how to use a Tampax. Which is to say, even then, I was already primed to be a girl on The Dating Show. *Conditioned to be a girl to break down, to need validation, to want flattery and care—however shallow.*

Who doesn't want to be special?

Calvin Boyer made me feel special. Before we get to the villain of him, you should know he listened to me. He was kind to me, an online companion, and the son of our school bus driver—there was no reason not to trust him. Calvin asked about my favorite songs and movies, speaking often about what kind of adult I could one day be. That kind of belief is powerful, intoxicating. Later, I would recognize signs of his narcissistic behavior, but narcissists are often charming, and they know exactly what to ask. It's part of their spell, their expert manipulations.

Narcissism. Manipulation. Abuse. I know the telltale signs by now. By the end of this book, reader, you will too.

BIRDIE

IN OCTOBER, EIGHT months before I packed for Whidbey, I printed out Calvin's emails and gave the stack to Trace. We stood in our Greenpoint kitchen. Seven thirty a.m., right before she was headed to work. Stray cats screamed down on the landing outside the window. Leaves twirled, dead as pencil shavings. No frost yet. A squirrel scurried the power line.

I didn't want to bother you with this, I said to Trace, but he's back, just like I said would happen. You said it wouldn't happen, and now, look. It did.

The light in the kitchen was butter yellow. The espresso machine hummed. Two eggs, hard-boiled and peeled, rolled lazily in the bowl Trace handed to me.

Trace wore a denim button-down shirt tucked into jeans; they were two different blues. Her hair was still wet from the shower, black curls slick and sweet smelling, her face still bloated by morning. I felt so bad for her, clean like that, clutching those pages. She stood with one hand on our tiny drop-leaf table, anchoring herself. The table came down from the wall. Every day when she left for work, it went back up like it was never there.

Six years before this moment, I'd met Trace on a film set. A small-budget indie that only made two bootleg festivals, never a real theater. The film was called *The Talent*, a campy and meta film-within-a-film in which a group of small-town high school extras get all screwed up with adult actors playing the high schoolers. It was honestly quite good.

The Talent was my first college job, as a set PA, when I could still work alongside people. I continued those gigs for a while, as much of it suited me. The long, impossible hours. The artifice, the lighting. Blacks on the windows or Tungsten bulbs and like that—you could be anywhere. It was my job to charge and manage the smoke machines; little babbling guns that ran out of fluid often. The PA's job is to remain anonymous, a nodding ghost in black clothes ballasted by walkies and pliers and fanny packs, rings of neon-colored tape looped onto the belt. I marked the ground, pointed the talent to where they needed to be. I delivered milky coffee to the script supervisor, Raksha, whom the white DP called *Rock Star* because he couldn't be bothered to remember. I delighted in the calming duties and tasks, the rigmarole of call sheets.

The best boy gaffer, a Portuguese dyke named Renata, was famously fucking one of the HMU artists, Quinn, who had a long-term cult-affiliated Republican boyfriend. Renata was strong and red-faced and took amphetamines when prompted by a phone alarm. Tattoos of numbers crawled down her calves—geographic coordinates of where people she loved most were born, which I found a little corny. One day, worked up over Quinn, Renata slashed a bounce reflector with an X-Acto blade and blamed it on one of the grips. I was so jealous.

It was a warm Monday morning, 2007. We were shooting at a bar in the East Village. Blacks on the windows to cheat it as night. Between setups, Renata and I stood outside cupping smokes, pigeons coming for our shoes, Renata going off about Quinn needing to buck up and come out already—Renata would email the boyfriend and tell him everything if she didn't. *Don't do that*, I said, *the cult may come after you.* I made up a recent ex-girlfriend I didn't have so Renata would know I was gay. *Maybe there's something better out there for the both of us.* I shrugged. I repeated things therapists had told me about what we could control, what we couldn't. *You're at your pinnacle*, I said, serenely, *and she's still a chrysalis*. I smoked with purpose, held eye contact. I hoped she might mistake me for Buddhist.

Then Trace appeared, from around the corner. A simple white t-shirt. Black pants and black All Stars. She was butch and maybe six feet tall, brown skin and shy brown eyes. Her dark hair curled on top with tinsel-like grays that tendriled over her forehead; the rest was a fade. Her hipbones were like handles I wanted to grab hold of and bow to. I saw her and I thought, There. There it is. The beginning or the end of my life.

It took me a few minutes to notice the crumple-nosed dog Trace had on a leash. The dog jumped on my leg, and I ignored it. I was watching Trace's mouth as she said something about this being Renata's dog, and how she'd walked the dog all the way over the Williamsburg Bridge to say hi. Trace rubbed her magnificent hand down her mouth like she was wiping it—a nervous habit, I'd later learn. Her hands: huge and veiny and spangled with rings. No dick in the world was necessary with hands like that.

I made a fuss over the animal then. I remember we all smoked and talked, and I easily aligned myself with Trace, Renata's mature roommate Trace, Trace who played in a queer basketball league at Chelsea Piers, who had also escaped from Florida, and who also knew Renata should give up on Quinn. Suddenly Renata looked so small and childish, two eggs over eager. Trace was calm and listened intently as Renata explained, *This is my bud Birdie. She just went through some dyke drama herself.*

I nodded along sadly and told my fake story. Told about my fake girlfriend and our fake dramatic split, the lost custody of my own fake dog. A chocolate lab. Pink collar. I missed the dog and was all torn up about it, I said. Late at night and around the holidays, especially.

What I mean to say is, we started with a lie. Trace listened and asked for my number, bashfully, once Renata walked away. Her thumbs shook as she punched the buttons of her phone. I kept up the lies. Very quickly she fell in love with me. Dizzying love that left sweet notes tied to my bike. Bags of my favorite juices delivered, by surprise, to wherever our set location was. Trace didn't yet know about me, or Calvin, or anything that happened in Florida. She wouldn't for some time. I loved her back, a quicksilver love that rendered me ascetic and numb to the rest of the world, a love that kept me so happily nauseous I wouldn't eat for days, I didn't need to, because there was her. There was Trace. And a whole new life I could picture, just the two of us, reborn without history.

We were still in our Brooklyn kitchen. I held the bowl of eggs in my hand. The morning sun feathered across the wall like the bottom of a pool, and if someone had seen us through the window without sound or explanation, they might imagine between us a sedated, comfortable calm. I'd taken a bite of the egg at some point while Trace wiped tears from her chin, blew her nose. The egg yolk was pale, chapped. A ring of deep green.

Bird—Trace said. She read one of the emails, then held the papers to her chest, as if to shield me.

I've read them all, obviously, I said.

These are bad, said Trace, these are worse. She sniffed, then swallowed. From the fridge, our own faces smiled at us in photo strips slipping from their magnets.

I told you this would happen when she went on that fucking show, I said.

You shouldn't be reading these, Trace said. What's it Dr. Lindenmeyer says about—then Trace went into her monologue about *radioactive material*. Radioactive material, Trace repeated, maybe a dozen times. Dramatic hand gestures. *Calvin content is radioactive material*. It is toxic. It is not for your consumption. It lives and remains in the body, hollows you out like the heart rot of trees, an organ-eating decay.

He's going to find me, I said. Any day now.

This violates the order of protection, Trace said. This violates his probation. He can't just say these things. Trace walked over to the metal trash can next to the kitchen sink. She stomped the trash pedal like a wedding glass, then chucked the pages into the bin, as if that could do anything.

I guess we can try again in court, I said. I'll forward them to his parole officer.

Trace nodded blankly. Helplessly. Her eyes—the wide-open dazed look that comes after a long cry—had nothing left to give me.

It was a look I was used to.

MY TURN

Pages 61–64

Calvin never once came to my house. That didn't keep me from fantasizing about the possibility of it. In reality, he was "hot Calvin" at the front of the school bus, sitting quietly next to his dad, and he was FrogPrince3609 when he messaged me on AOL. When the creaking sound effect came through my computer speakers to indicate he'd logged on, it was like a light turned on inside of me. I felt like the whole world was possible in that one, simple sound.

In my imagination, Calvin and I went on dates. I was more grown-up, of course. I pictured him as the kind of guy who would never dare honk his horn outside our house. He would grip flowers in his hands, something thoughtful, like daisies. He'd show up wearing an icy cologne and an ironed shirt, just for me. He would possess great manners. He'd knock. My father would open the door. The front door opening would sound just like FrogPrince logging on. Then the two men would turn to take me in, dazzled, and I would feel pretty.

Our true relationship was not quite like that, of course. It was hidden. That's how predators function—so powered are they by secrecy, by isolating their victims. At twelve years old, I was the most alone I had ever been. My parents were fighting constantly. I knew they would probably divorce soon, and I looked anywhere and everywhere for an outlet for that pain.

It all started when Calvin passed me a note outside the bus. He put it in my hand as I walked up the bus steps. It was the first month of the eighth grade. The note said, hey gorgeous, what's ur screenname? *I didn't wash the hand he touched for a whole day. My hand felt tingly from this older guy, Mr. Boyer's hot son, touching it. I didn't know Calvin was twenty-five—people sometimes ask me that, did I know? But if I did, it wouldn't have mattered. Nobody had ever called me gorgeous before. Plus, he looked young for his age. So when Calvin messaged me later that night, when the sound effect went off, I never even asked.*

♥

There are child molesters, sexual abusers, pedophiles, and then there are Calvins. These terms can overlap, but they don't always. I have tried to seek knowledge and therefore find an inkling of empathy in these categorizations, with hopes that, by learning more about what makes people do evil things, I might find within myself a bright place of forgiveness. Reader, I'm sorry to say I don't think I'm ever going to find it.

Picture the above terms in a Venn diagram. Find that center space, the all-encompassing. Now, shade it in. That's Calvin. Through research, soul searching, and many sessions with my life coach, I have learned that sexual abuse (including abuse against minors) is often about control. To me, it's also something deeper and more sadistic; I can't ignore that feeling. But my feelings don't matter, feelings are not data and cannot be measured scientifically. I suppose this book is asking how one might measure that which remains unfathomable, mysterious. Feelings that cannot be quantified.

Some argue that pedophilia is a paraphilia that develops in utero. That this attraction/affliction can be proven in the brain (see: sexologist Dr. James M. Cantor of Toronto, appendix 2B). While it's not a popular opinion, one barely studied, MRI scans have shown that the prefrontal network of a pedophile's brain functions differently than an average person's when viewing images of children. The pedophile's network is, quite simply, broken. Rather than feeling a desire to protect or a desire to nurture, arousal dings like a relentless bell.

Do I believe in this theory, reader? In this "scientific explanation"? Well, I've never seen the inside of a person's brain, and I have certainly not looked inside of Calvin Boyer's brain. I do know the ways in which Calvin acted on his impulses, though. Ask anyone shaped by monstrosity, and they can tell you just how real "monsters" are. Monsters are shape-shifters. They transform from the imaginary, the thud from inside your closet or beneath your bed, to something lurking in your own psyche. Monsters move. In this way, they can never truly be slain.

When I was a little girl, my mother, Irene, used to read me the story of "The Three Billy Goats Gruff." This was before she moved to Buffalo, New York, before the divorce, so of course I remember it all, every tuck-in in my palatial princess room with a canopy bed, every good-night, my mother's heartbeat as I lay on her torso. In the Norwegian fairy tale, three goats are hungry, and they long for the lush meadow on the other side of a bridge. The catch is, they must survive the troll lurking beneath. One by one, they tell the troll to wait for the next goat, and the next; they promise the troll can eat one of them, the fattest one, the next one will be best, the troll just has to wait. And wait. And wait. He does.

Of course I've thought of this fairy tale often. I think of Jane Doe 1, "Amelia Sanchez," with the beautiful voice on the choir bleachers. I think of Jane Doe 2, "Jade Suzuki," and her slashed American Dream. I think of my own young self, my confident childish shoulders that eventually hunched with shame. After Calvin was convicted for statutory rape, once he was released from Dade Correctional, he was sent to live with the other registered sex offenders under the Julia Tuttle Causeway Bridge over Biscayne Bay (appendix 4C). As mandated by the ordinance of lobbyist Ronald L. Book in 2006, this was the only place sex offenders could live: 2,500 feet away from children, even their legal IDs listing the address of that bridge. I cannot tell you what it felt like to know that my abuser lived there, under a literal bridge, fishing in those murky waters. I cannot describe what it felt like to know that, while tourists and locals and girls like me were crossing that bridge for a carefree day or night in Miami, he was there. All of those predators dodging water rats, waiting for their own Jane Does, their next prey.

Monsters are real. I should know.

The troll waits for the last goat, in the fairy tale. He waits for the fattest one of all, the one he can finally eat, a reward after being so patient. But the troll makes a mistake; he leaves his spot under the bridge. He comes into the light, ready to feast. He dies that way, the goat knocking him off the bridge and back into his own waters. The troll drowns. He's swept away by the currents.

I have never trusted that happy ending. Where there is one troll, others always lurk.

I have already mentioned most people refused to be interviewed for this book. Many never responded to my requests, and I don't blame them for being distrustful. There were exceptions, though, and few as insightful as Calvin's aunt, Sylvia Packman, an equestrian instructor and horse breeder in Ocala, Florida, who once knew her nephew well. While I offered to conduct interviews via email, Sylvia, or "Syl," invited me to her family's ranch, River Run Farm, in December of 2011.

Around eight a.m., on a damp and foggy morning, Syl Packman opened her front door with a baseball cap on her head, ready to talk to me.

"Coffee's going, and I hope you like it strong," she said, before inviting me inside.

BIRDIE

I STARTED WALKING in June. Walks were hours I could commit to being away from the book. Instead of reading, I wanted to explore the grounds and become a woman who knew the woods, this verdant sponge of land; I wanted to identify berries—poison or balm, invasive or endemic—like I was meant for any other kind of knowledge.

I'd moved from Florida to New York at seventeen, right after graduating from Dole Grove. I never went to the Sichuan province of China, where my father was born and raised, never smelled the fermented howl of chilies drifting in his hometown's air. I never saw the humped Appalachian Mountains of my mother's life before me, purple and immediate. I only knew where I was from and the escape routes that followed.

Beyond my cabin, beyond Thelma's farm, beyond the duck lagoon, a winding road with sharp turns led out to Useless Bay. The beach was usually empty, mostly driftwood—hugely white and tangled—a shore of beheaded Medusas. Seaweed fluttered from the sand like weathered grocery bags; you could barely tell the difference.

The air, near that water, never felt warm. It still rained, daily. At twilight the bay receded, curving into perfect mirrored pathways that beamed back only sky. It was as if a whole twisting highway formed on the ground like that. Birds jumped along the sand, and it shone like slick putty. As the birds walked beside me, dark auras pooled around their webbed little feet.

If a person passed me, I'd shoot my head down, clutch my owl helmet to my stomach. Some afternoons, if the figure was just right, I imagined it was Rich walking toward me. Other days, I imagined Calvin. For years, I'd lied to Trace, to my mother, to my therapist; I'd told them all that in my visions of Calvin, I killed him—strangulation, a knife, anything that allowed eye contact as his own life faded, his body collapsing into a kneel before pitching forward into a meaningless after. *It is good, to identify and place your anger*, one therapist said. But my truest, fiercest fantasy was this: Calvin simply apologized, flatly, almost silly, and together we'd decide all of it—all the years and losses, all the court appearances and sentences and evidence and dismissive judges and lukewarm coffees—had been some wild and complicated misunderstanding. Then we'd find things in common, two unlikely friends laughing at a recent news item, bonding over a mutual favorite film, staring out at the horizon, relieved, healed. But the people on the beach were never Calvin or Rich, and my eyes bolted to my boots every time. Sometimes these people would toss out a *hello*, but never wait for an answer.

The bats—Thelma said—it's like they're on steroids. Did they swoop you?

Then she said, Come on, now, Wilma, keep the heat in, inviting me inside.

I'd been walking the beach, then the woods. The sun was out but then it wasn't. I knew my way but then I didn't. The bats, indeed, swooped me as the temperature dropped. Then the owls called. When I couldn't find the path to my cabin or the pumphouse, I saw the cedar-shingled home with a single porch light on—Thelma and Hal's. Now I stood for a moment in their living room. Thelma said, it's easy-peasy to get lost. Glad you knocked, Wilma! Were you wandering long?

Not long at all, I said. Just lost track of time.

Thelma and Hal loved large, ornate accent pieces—candelabras, grandfather clocks, brass figurines and planters, turquoise whales aged by a specific paint that had crackled them—*like an Italian villa*, Thelma explained, though I didn't quite follow the reference. Smooth jazz played from an old black stereo.

Just in time to join us for supper, Hal said, entering the room. Then he ushered me down the hallway to the kitchen. Do you know about solar? Hal asked, as he set the table. Been meaning to install solar lights on the pathways.

Hal was a short man with bright eyes made brighter by deep purple bags beneath them, as if he'd just recovered from a face lift. *Extra pigmentation*, he explained, without my asking. Makes me look tough, don't you think? He walked with a slight limp, muscular and bowlegged, and his hands placing the silverware had a sturdy elegance that made me miss my father.

We have a tenant coming tonight, actually, arriving *late late*—Hal said—we hate that.

The two of them were dressed up in button downs and silver jewelry for their dinner alone, which gave me a pang of embarrassment. I wore my old Levi's, one of Trace's navy sweatshirts, thick wool socks. I'd left my boots at their door. I listened to them describe the wine they poured me, some variety they'd learned to love on a cruise they'd taken for an anniversary trip. They had a wine club subscription to mark the experience. That's how they get you, Thelma said, wait until you're four bottles gassed before handing over the form. I drank and listened. Hal leaned over the dining room candles with a long butane lighter, holding his tie. He was talking, now, about tamping gravel.

Hey, no candles allowed! I said. Thelma and Hal both stopped what they were doing and looked at me. Rules are rules, I tried again. Hal gave a quick nod and carried on lighting. Well, then, I'm sure to be careful, he said.

The worst part of being alive has always been my general loathing of people but my sporadic, frantic need for them. New people I needed even more. With new people I could try out anything—an accent, a faith, opinions about rising sea levels, national allegiances— I could practice a new posture or way of sitting, a different pair of earrings, a joke. Without these rare occasions, I feared I would never exist again, could never be somebody else. Without them I was only Birdie.

Hal sat at the head of the table, and I sat across from Thelma. Toward me, she pushed a cloth napkin that didn't match the others, forest green with oil stains. Then she brought over a clay pot, oval and burnished, and when she opened the lid, steam roiled out. My God, woman! You've outdone yourself! Hal said, clapping his hands. The chicken looked rusted under mottled paprika.

The key's to soak the pot in water first, so it doesn't stress in the heat, Thelma explained to me. This pot's older than you are. It has to be gradual, you see, otherwise she'll crack. And this isn't our chicken—she pointed to the bird. The neighbors have meat chickens, she said, not like the ones outside. Pets aren't livestock. Livestock, never pets.

Hal asked: What have you been up to, Wilma? Disconnected out here on the rock? Feel like I know you a little since I fetch your groceries Fridays. Hope those Oregon Cabs have been buttering the biscuit.

Yes, the wine's been great, I said, a little embarrassed. I've also been reading. Every day. I've become a big reader here.

Ah, have you read *Memoirs of a Geisha*? asked Hal.

They both looked at me.

I haven't, I said. I pulled chicken from the bone, slipped the skin with my knife. I held the silverware like a child, knuckles out, thumbs tucked in, embarrassed of the blood of my fingers, the wounds, the severity of which I only noticed in the presence of others.

And what do you do back in New York? Thelma asked. I can't recall.

I work at a theater, I said. A movie theater. Well, I did.

Selling snacks? Or tickets? Hal worked at the breast of his chicken, cutting many bite-sized pieces and moving them to the side of his plate. There was a whole system, it seemed.

I'm a projectionist. A technician.

Thelma whispered, *Is that right?* without interest.

Actually, I continued, they recently got rid of our Century. That was my projector. Everyone's going digital, even though when you say the word *film*, like, *Hey I'm going to see a film*, you're talking about celluloid, polyester—maybe acetate—not digital images. But no one seems to care about that. So there went my life, and my job, and the one thing that made me happy. Then some personal stuff happened. I got outed, in a way, my identity, and had no choice but to leave New York because of that. I had nothing left to lose really, without my job, so now I'm here.

Outed—as a homosexual? Thelma asked.

And isn't it nice to unplug from all that hubbub? Hal said.

It is, I said.

So do you project digital movies now? Thelma asked. That sounds kind of easier, more streamlined. They just switched over at Mike's place, our local haunt. Mike said digital's the future, like it's happening right in front of you. Easier is always an improvement.

I thought of my Century JJ machine. The rollers and sprockets and cast arms. The finger loops. How I'd arrived early all those mornings to oil and care for it, toothbrush and alcohol in the sprockets, the blitz of canned air, the Century an extension of my own body. It was sacred and mine; that one, tender thing. Then it was dismantled in the lobby, sold for parts.

I respectfully disagree, I said. Then: How'd you decide to do the unplugged thing here? That seems like the opposite of what you're saying. In terms of ease.

Thelma cleared her throat. Coughed into a fist. It's cost is all, she said. All that power's hard to run. Some of the cabins don't even have electric and water like yours, only propane and an outhouse. Would you like to switch over?

I love movies, said Hal. Always wanted to direct them, myself. Then he stopped and placed his fork down on the table. Thelma reached over and grabbed his forearm, though she kept eating, studying her plate. Her thumb smoothed the hair around his watch.

I'm sorry, said Hal, I am not being altogether truthful. I have never wanted to direct a movie, Wilma. He wiped his mouth with a monogrammed napkin. His eyes flashed.

Oh, that's OK, I said. You can still like films. The song on the stereo switched to something up-tempo.

So what's next for you, in this great big digital world? asked Thelma.

Maybe I'll be a phone psychic, I said. Or maybe—I always wanted to write a screenplay.

I used to call phone psychics all the time! said Hal. Then he paused again and shook his head. I'm *so* sorry, Wilma. Again, I have never done that.

Hal's in a special treatment for lying, Thelma said. It's pathological, neurological. It has to do with brain routing, he can't help it. It's just the way he is. We're all born one way or another, aren't we. Once Hal starts, it goes and goes.

White matter—said Hal—in my brain. Then he shrugged.

That's it, white matter, Thelma picked up. He has too much white matter in the hippo. Which makes him too imaginative sometimes, which, to some, might sound like a gift, but, well. She looked at Hal. She loved him, the way she was looking.

What other matter is there? I asked.

Gray matter, they both said at once. The brain is complicated, Hal said, big as this table if you flattened it out. Could be a tablecloth! Pretty unseemly.

We're all proud of Hal, Thelma said. Big family, and everyone's proud of Hal.

So why Whidbey? Hal asked. Usually when people do these retreats, especially monthly, it's a group thing. But you're a young, very beautiful girl alone in these woods.

Meditation? said Thelma. Young people do that. Hal, remember the girl with the tooth?

I thought about which story to tell them, which story to try. The moss and hydrology research felt stupid now that I was a little drunk, and I couldn't try *visiting family*. I hadn't even thought up a family name.

I'm hiding from a criminal, I said, a felon. Recently released. He's after me.

Thelma leaned in. Oh, is that right? She suddenly chewed with her mouth puckered formally.

I'm creating my own witness protection program, I said. That's why I chose this place.

Hal raised his glass as if to give a toast, an immediate reaction that seemed to confuse even him. Then he lowered his glass back down.

I'm kidding, I said, I'm not being altogether truthful.

Then we laughed—me first, as if to give permission. Hal smacking the table with his married hand, for emphasis.

Later, the three of us sat in the living room on a velvet sectional couch, near their woodstove. I drank several glasses of their subscription wine, then a bourbon tasting from Hal. The channels of my ears throbbed and flushed. We were talking about fear.

Well, why on earth would you need a new name? Thelma asked. *Birdie* is beautiful!

Hal stood often to walk to the window and play records, flipping them mid-song, then replacing every choice with a new one from their collection. He said, *No, that's not the mood now is it?* many times, though no one answered him.

I don't dislike Birdie, I repeated. I like my name. But Wilma's kind of a comfort blanket. My therapists have told me it's healthy to be other people when I need to be. To role-play. You could say I'm kind of a paranoid person.

How many therapists? Thelma asked.

Paranoia is allowing fear to rule you, to win, Hal said. Do you want to be ruled by fear?

But Birdie is really so . . . unique, Thelma said. She was drunk and slow, her words gummy. She pulled a cuticle clipper out of her back pocket, then went at her fingers. She piled nail and skin on the leg of her pants until it was a tiny mound of grated cheese, then swooshed the pile into the woodstove, wiggling her fingers. It made me want to pick. I set my glass down on a tree ring coaster and sat on my hands.

Asians, they have a close relationship to the birds, do they? Hal asked. It seems they enjoy birds very much. Shall we call you Lark instead of Bird?

I did think *Wilma Dean* was a bit different—Thelma said—with your descent. But I know they choose American names sometimes. You know, like Jennifer.

Outside, a motion light blinked on. All of us stopped talking, Thelma and Hal mouthing words to each other—*Hal?* Someone knocked at the door.

It had not occurred to me, not until that moment, that the island was small, and Rich might still be somewhere on it. Rich Amani—a stranger, a man unstable enough to offer murder—may have been lying about going to Opa-locka for summer. Of course he would lie. Maybe this man was a Whidbey local. Probably, he was. Maybe he was a known killer, his face xeroxed on flyers circulating all the way to Tacoma. And Rich knew me, the real me, a *beautiful girl* alone in the woods. I had never even looked behind me in the cab drive to Thelma's to search for a window-tinted vehicle in the distance. When I came here, I'd wanted to leave that girl behind.

Hal went to the door. Thelma and I both watched silently. When he opened it, it was Rich's broad shoulder until it wasn't. A woman stood under the weak light. Burnt orange jacket and a colorful scarf. She wore a beanie over chopped red hair, camo pants.

A husky higher than her knees. Moths dived at her head, but she did not swat them.

Oh hell, the Turk and her dog, Thelma said. The late check-in.

The woman outside shook Hal's hand. I heard her say: I'm Nevra. My dog's Amanda.

That young lady over there's our friend, your new neighbor, Hal said, pointing at me.

I'm Jade, I said to the door.

Oh, Christ, you girls and the names, I can't keep up, Thelma said. Then: Hal, go fetch the Turk some keys!

And even later: Hal refilled my glass, clinked his against mine saying, *Nostrovia*. He asked me to find the cinnamon notes, bark too. He sniffed and swirled, and I copied. I didn't taste any of it.

You know, Hal said, sitting down next to me, kids your age with the gadgets. It's making valuable stuff, stuff with character and craftsmanship, obsolete. Just look at film.

I know, I said. That is literally what I do.

That's right. Hal nodded to himself. Our thighs were half a foot apart, a distance I always gauged. He said: It's nice to see you wearing a watch; kids these days don't even know how to read them. They can't even read cursive. You should be proud of yourself, doing a summer like this. Back when people were good, safe people, I used to hitchhike cross-country. While high, very high. Thousands of miles I did like that with no real trouble.

I wanted Hal to stop talking. I wanted him to liquefy into the couch cushion, or maybe choke on shaving cream. Nothing fatal, but inconvenient. The real reason I'm here, I said, leaning back, looking at Thelma, is nobody loves me. Because I'm a crazy person. I heard the slur in my syllables, slow and numb. Like that, my mouth remembered winter.

Oh, come on now, everybody's a little crazy, said Thelma.

It was my first therapist's idea to use BC and AC for Before Calvin and After Calvin, a way to identify the two distinct Birdies in order to marry the whole girl back together. I had to make lists of those separate selves. Things BC and AC Birdie loved, feared, remembered, valued. At some point I wondered if I'd settled entirely into After Calvin Birdie, someone distant and opaque, with no chance of finding who was there before.

A bad man, I said. A man who's made me crazy. I'm being serious now.

The criminal on the loose? Thelma asked, winking.

He wasn't a boy, I said. They called him a boy, but he's a man. A rapist. He took my life away. I picked up my glass again. He's a boy like I'm Jade Suzuki.

I see, said Thelma. Her whole face tightened. She looked tired, eyelids sticky like a doll's. Then she pinched at her tongue as if trying to locate a piece of lint.

Even under the booze I knew my own rules, how unfair it was to tell someone the truth. How, whenever I said the R-word or the P-word, whenever I brought a child in, it was no longer about me. The truth had a way of sprouting new roots into a person's mind, demanding their own reflection, their own space, too dark for them to comprehend unless it had happened to them, too, and even then, even if they knew the feeling—if they, too, were a child touched into a death—they'd wander quick and deep inside themselves into their own entropic past, leaving no more room for me.

Well, this all sounds rather lousy, Thelma said, shaking her head, and I saw in her expression that it hadn't happened to her. I was alone in it. I knew the look of recognition in another person always. That flicker of wreck. To be alone with it was better.

He'll never stop, I said.

Raping?

He'll never go away. I started crying, then. Humiliating, I thought, but also nice, to cry. Proof of something you thought you'd imagined—a specific, throttling smell through the crack in your window, lashed out from nowhere and then you're a kid on A1A again, your parents driving the car, tide rising with the arms of the bridge. Before Calvin Birdie.

Actually, he *is* going away, I said. I emptied the rest of my bourbon in a big gulp and lifted both eyebrows, pointing to Thelma and Hal like, *You'll see*. I said: Hitchcock shit. I met someone on the ferry.

Hal was silent. He leaned forward on the couch, curved spine of a turtle. Then he said, do you need to head on home soon? I can zip you right over on the golf cart. Thelma flapped her hands at him, and he trailed off, scratching behind his head. It's just that I have to rise very early tomorrow to take a load over to Coupeville, and the fella who runs it there—Hal stopped.

Not even gray lies or white lies, said Thelma. Hal, good on you.

I woke early in their living room, a dull drumming at the temples, heart hammering my body into shakes. How many hours had passed this time? I'd dreamed of drought, of drinking from dog bowls, toilets, puddles, desperate and clawing. The house was quiet; blue light jammed in from between wooden blinds, which Thelma or Hal must have snapped closed for me.

Often, I woke with this smog of shame, even if I hadn't been drinking. The many nights I'd drunk too much had conditioned my body to wake with it. A fleece blanket printed with flying pigs covered my legs, and I felt moved at the image of Thelma tossing it over me, protective. I sat up and folded the blanket. At the door, I slipped on my helmet, my boots.

Branches snapped under my feet as I walked back toward my cabin. My skin cooled as snippets of the evening wound back— *I'm not Wilma Dean. Raped*—nausea running all the way down my arms and legs, sour stomach in my knees. Thelma and Hal would worry now, with the understanding that they'd rented to a psychopath, a *crazy person*, a fake. They'd kick me out, maybe wait a few days to pretend it was for unrelated reasons: a burst pipe, termites, rot in the walls. Thelma would do it; she was still allowed to lie.

A rooster crowed somewhere off key and off time. Then I heard a dog barking in the far distance. I thought of the woman in the doorway with her husky the night before. Her red hair, no smile. She'd looked at me like she knew something.

My helmet rolled jaggedly as I fell. A sturdy root, knuckle round, hovered above my foot. I pushed my hands into the soil. Bright gold slugs shiny as pencils slid along beside me. I didn't see them move though I know that they did, even when I stared and stared, I saw no will outside the jelly twitch of their antennae. Beautiful, I thought. Go. Be alive. And I stayed right there, lying with them, like it was the only thing to do. Next thing, maybe a moment later, maybe an hour, maybe more, the ground was wrapped in the cellophane their bodies left, dead leaves and earth under their canopy of translucence, slimed and shrunken without air, like a world perfectly packaged.

Odette Carlisle <Odette.C.Carlisle@gmail.com>
to me

Mon, April 12, 2013, 9:43 PM

Dear Birdy,

    You don't know me, but I know quite a bit about you. My name is Odette Carlisle, and I've taken a real interest in your case. I hope that doesn't sound callous, quite the opposite. It's not the oogling rubbernecking interest you may be used to given your history, plus the added gaze of Linzie's forthcoming book (which you appear in, as I'm sure you already know). I can't imagine how hard it's all been, and I won't pretend to. No one should be market strategizing and profiting off your pain and private experiences, which brings me to the below.

    A little about me. My father was a plaintiff's attorney, and I too once imagined myself in courtrooms, standing up for those wronged, fighting for just causes. My path led me to media instead, which is what I studied at our shared Alma Mater, NYU, from which I recently graduated (class of 2012, you can confirm this here; I spoke at graduation). It is in this way, media, where I personally feel I can make the greatest impact in the world, and hopefully make some positive changes. How? You might be asking? By bringing to light the cases and crimes that are owed a closer look. Your case is a fascinating one, and I'm glad I've done the work of finding you (Did you know that someone can access the court records of a minor simply by looking for their parents/legal guardians? You must know this but if not, you should. It was not difficult to identify you by the pseudonym used in the book, which reeks of racism. I assume from your last name you are of Chinese descent, not Japanese, but I digress . . .)

What happened to you was wrong. I know this and I wholeheartedly believe you. I also have skin in the game here . . . when I was ten years old, my mother's best friend sexually abused my cousin and my mother did nothing about it. This has changed the makeup of my DNA and how I interact with the world. I want to say here that I believe your case has the potential to be reexamined in the public eye. I understand that Calvin Boyer is under Community Control in Palm Beach County's program Gateway to Grace. If you ask me, that's not enough. Pedophiles don't need rehabs, or special treatment centers, or "re-entry" to anywhere. They should be shot or castrated or both (sorry not sorry:/ you will learn I'm blunt).

Your case should not have been dismissed when the other survivors got their due diligence. Francine Gerber pushed the needle (selfishly I must know, do you two keep in touch? I haven't been able to reach her) and Linzie linchpinned it, but what about you? I happen to think it's because you're a Queer Woman of Color, and the world treats QWOC differently than those considered "of the norm." But things are changing. This I know from media trends I've been following, and nothing puts pressure on the legal system quite like public opinion. Also, there's nothing America hates more than a pedophile, which is to say fortune's on our side here in 2013.

So here's the headline, what I've been building toward. I plan on recording a podcast about your case, and about Calvin, exploring how child sexual abuse impacted me, and countless others. The working title right now is *Carlisle Files*, but I'm not sure yet. While I don't need yours or anyone's permission to make my podcast (I should add, significant sponsors are already interested), I'm hoping you would be willing to talk to me for it, on the record. I want to hand you the literal and figurative mic, and promise to respect your story as if it were my own. In a way, it is. By engaging in this contemporary form of storytelling, I think we could reach audience numbers you may have never imagined reaching. And by reaching that audience, you'll be helping victims everywhere, and will likely save more girls Calvin has yet to harm. Please think of those girls, imagine their futures, before you respond to this request.

We can take it slow, though not too slow, I hope. With Linzie's book out later this month, interest is hot now, and will wane fast. I got my hands on an early copy (a "galley") of her heroic tale, which I've determined to be mostly untrue and essentially *fiction*. Together we can prove this. You can take the reins back. I'm a good listener, and there may even be compensation involved if I can secure more advertising (I have substantial reach on social media, which you can see here and here).

I look forward to hearing from you, and I am sorry again to learn about your myriad misfortunes. It has obviously deeply affected me, and I feel like I know you from reading your records. Please consider the podcast my small gesture toward trying to make things right, but please also know this will happen, with or without your consent. I hope we can be on the same team, dismantle the Linzie of it all, and go forth fighting for truth and justice.

Kindly,
Odette Carlisle

MARY-BETH

THERE WAS RELIEF, to Mary-Beth, in planning her only child's funeral. She felt guilty for the feeling. To plan a funeral meant to admit defeat, Calvin's defeat and hers too, both of them squashed out at last not only by Tommy but the girls, and the Pigs, and Ronald Lee Book, Unofficial Mayoral Douchebag of Miami, and the teachers and parole officers and correctional officers and social workers and *Your Honors*, and the system of selective lifeboats (*MONEY! It's always the money!*), and the cuntish polo-shirted neighbors who'd kicked Calvin like a Hacky Sack from place to place, who'd painted *LUCIFER/AURORA* on Mary-Beth's Burbank Blue door, and Syl's *I told you so*s, and Cal's episode of *Cops*, and the snitch therapists, the *whole world* it felt like most usually, and of course, Mary-Beth would not leave out the person who'd run over her son.

Five times, forward and back.

The steps of planning a funeral transformed the taut pain of her chest into something coherent, productive. She remembered Calvin telling her the universe was always expanding, like a strip of dulled elastic, a rubber band at the bottom of her junk drawer. One day, without warning—Calvin had said—it would all snap. That's how this death pain felt, a rubber band stretched beneath the bones of Mary-Beth's feet, then secured at the top of her skull where headaches came on. She was an overblown balloon animal, skin thinning, and though her whole life had been spent waiting, she knew now, without Calvin, that annihilating snap might arrive sooner. There was some relief there, too.

Detective Carmen Durham hadn't called Mary-Beth since she identified the body one week ago. Nobody had called her. There was no police unit left in the town nearest Gateway, the station boarded up for years (only Luckens selling bootleg T-Mobiles outside the station's old door), so they were *outsourcing* the investigation to other units now. That's what Syl said.

Ordering the finger foods, choosing a picture of Calvin for the program, selecting a nice and respectable place for a funeral—these tasks felt easier. Soothing, almost. These tasks were, simply, something Mary-Beth could do. For days Syl brought her the options—Deerfield or Palmetto or Broward, Pastor James or Pastor Finley, how many speeches, what songs—and Mary-Beth would close her eyes and picture it before offering an answer.

Syl had moved into Mary-Beth's bedroom, Mary-Beth in the living room. This was on Mary-Beth's insistence. She was more comfortable on her couch, ashtray one reach down, whorls of the TV glow reflecting in her special glass, upside-down little people in there, lulling her to sleep.

In the week since her arrival, Syl had begun to stink up the house, and Mary-Beth told her so. It always smelled like *something* now, someone else—those Indian meals from the fancy row of the Publix freezer, cloudberry angel wing perfume, lemon bug repellent, the LA Looks hair gel that farted out the bottle and into Syl's palms. That, and all of Syl's shoes and clothes smelled like horse shit, no matter how often Syl said that shit was just grass and grain, molasses concentrated, it was still *shit*. Mary-Beth hated living in grief with those smells.

Syl always hiked the AC way down on account of her hot flashes, which slicked the tile too cold. Mary-Beth had to wear her North Pole elf clothes around the house, those green and red stripes, bundled. When Syl needed formal paperwork signed, Mary-Beth would take the whole operation out the sliding glass doors to the back lawn, remove a few layers of clothing, then scribble her name a million times on the dimpled glass table. She sucked her orange baby food pouches—her toothaches worsening by the day. She wiped Misty ashes from the pages, leaving gray smears and tiny burns on words she could read but not understand. What casket? What wood? What money? The papers crinkle-shrunk in the humid air. July wrapped her body and squeezed.

Mary-Beth's yard dipped down to the communal lake. Encircling it: identical condos like a roll of Smarties, and a few gators spread out on the shoreline sunbathing at all hours, iridescent in stillness, even at night. *The Lakeness Monster* she used to call each gator when Calvin was little. Back then they'd lived in Dade County on a different canal, but still—those goddamn gators. She dreamed constantly of Calvin's legs and little feet dangling from the open jaw, then disappearing under a body of black water. *Never get too close to sitting water*, she'd said to Cal. *Never make eye contact. And if the monster comes at you, throw your arms up, make yourself big, and run a zigzag fast as you can.*

The zigzag thing. Thinking of it now, she wasn't sure where she'd heard it, if it were ever even true.

The theme of the funeral was Calvin's favorite things. *A funeral doesn't need a theme, the theme is funeral*, Syl had said, but Mary-Beth would make sure people knew more about her son than what they'd read or heard. She wanted them to know there was so much at the core of him, so many things he loved, curiosities, even things he collected. She spent hours outside at her little table, chair wobbling on grass, clipping images from magazines and catalogues and the *TV Guide* too. With a glue stick, she collaged using sheets of construction paper, swatting mosquitos right onto the pages.

What she could afford in the end was the Bohner and Sons Funeral Parlor in Boynton. She hadn't expected anyone to come. Mary-Beth had considered holding the funeral at Gateway to

Grace so those monitored could attend—but she'd also wanted something nicer than the Gateway chapel with its papier-mâché crosses and hearts. She wanted tasseled embellishments for her son. A pastor in a heavy robe. Real, breakable plates. A carpet.

Bohner and Sons had one room for the service, and another for food and beverages. Arriving early, Mary-Beth and Syl wedged collages between clip stands they'd found at the Festival Flea, copper coiled hearts that held the images upright in the center of every table. The colorful sheets lit up the parlor, and this small detail will be one of the few things Mary-Beth will remember of this day, a fleeting sliver of beauty, all those glossy cutouts—Will Smith, the solar system, every breed of dog and reptile, Cartman and Chef from *South Park*, hermit crabs, the gecko from that Geico commercial, Kid Rock, Harrison Ford, bald eagles, *Animorphs*, French fries, images of surfers, wakeboarders, mountain skiers, waves from the pipeline of Hawai'i, Sylvester Stallone, the Eye of Providence Illuminati pyramid, and of course, photos of Mary-Beth and Calvin together through the years.

Mary-Beth hadn't expected so many people to walk in, find her sitting alone at a table, greeting her early. Ten people, then fifteen. Twenty! Prolonged eye contact as they clamped her hand between their own and said *very sorry*. She knew from working the gas station that direct eye contact meant two things: aggression or respect. Often, she'd found, it was a little of both.

Thirty people, then forty. Mary-Beth got up and stood near the door of Bohner's in her black blazer and skirt, shoulder pads sewn in from the '80s with rhinestones glinting at the seams, doing her best to remember each face. How did they all know her son? Surely, she thought, she'd know every person who'd ever mattered to him—Rhea, the server at Jack in the Box, who sometimes brought the boys food when they lived under the bridge; a few guys released from Dade Correctional; everyone from Gateway without a monitor—but most of these faces were new. After a while, Mary-Beth sat down at the table again, stopped counting.

A gilded mirror hung across from her in the parlor. She could see those entering behind her, and her own reflection, too. Syl had French braided her hair tight for the occasion, and Mary-Beth had carefully shaved her own face and neck, no chin stubble. More people entered. Walter from the pet store. Howie and the twins (ugh) who slow-hugged and regarded Syl as if *she* were the mother in grief. Then more strangers, whispering. Drinking from water bottles around the doorway. Plucking the collages from their clips, inspecting Mary-Beth's work. Mary-Beth knew the look of junkies—she always knew—they stood out in the crowd like a comfort, their ill-fitting clothes and jitters, borrowed black suits, one lady still in her coochie-cutters, those who called her Fairy-Beth. But these other strangers were prancy, collared shirts and hair a single color. Who were they to Calvin? Were they undercover investigators, finally doing their job? Mary-Beth gave the third degree to anyone who'd ever stepped into Calvin's life, asking after their faith, their motivations and intentions, but this was always and only to protect him. At that, her life's main purpose, she'd now failed. So she didn't ask.

As she looked from person to person, only one question remained: *Did one of them do it?*

The priest led the way down the aisle, holy smoke rising from his thurible. The censer swung from a chain in his fat chapped hand as the room wafted wood and spice, everyone turning in their seats to watch Mary-Beth follow in her performance of mourning. Because that's how it felt to her in that moment, like a performance. Her pinkened eyes darted from face to face, because she thought they should, because she wanted everyone to know something of her pain, of the unjustness of the whole terrible ordeal. Then she thought of that road again, the blood of it. The red and black rock of her baby. She wanted to be back at the scene of the crime, or in Calvin's studio apartment at Gateway, or in the McDonald's drive-thru, anywhere other than this parlor with its artificial rose scent and shampooed rug; she wanted to be anywhere she might feel him again. She accidentally smiled in all this emotion, a misfire of the mind. She remembered her own gums, her two graying front teeth and wide gaps around them. She pinched her mouth closed.

The priest spoke. Mary-Beth did not.

Instead, Mary-Beth had asked Syl to read from pages she wrote. Syl stepped up to a podium in fancy black nylons and those same stupid shoes. Howie must have brought the nylons down from Ocala specifically for this. Syl made a whole production of wiping a single tear from her eye with an old-lady handkerchief, and already Mary-Beth regretted asking her to read.

Sylvia Packman here, hello, Calvin's Auntie Syl. I'm going to read on behalf of my sister, Mary-Beth Boyer, she began. The crowd all turned to face Mary-Beth in her seat. Syl tried for her eyes, trying for a special *moment*, but Mary-Beth stared straight ahead.

Anyway, these here are her words, Syl read.

Life was hard for my boy since the day he was born, and it didn't get much better from there. He had his health issues as a baby, and they put him in a box of light, to keep him alive and breathing (I was there for that—Syl interrupted—that's true, that was a hard time. Bless our doctors, Lord, bless them). *Calvin held my finger every day just wanting his life, and I did my best to give that to him. I would continue to always give that to him.*

Calvin loved to skateboard as a kid and he loved water sports. He loved all animals except mice (I'll add, Syl said, he was an adequate stable hand), *he liked cars and NASCAR, and he talked like he could be a mechanic one day, because he understood engines. There are too many things to list that my son, Calvin, loved, so I encourage you to take time with the collages I made about him. He could have had a lot of different futures if he'd had the chance.*

My son was my best friend, and he overcame so much, more than most people in their whole lives, and he was thirty-five when he got murdered, only just beginning. The government fucked him, excuse my language (Lord, these are my sister's words, remember, she chuckled), *but he dealt with it with the presence of our creator and in keeping good spirits. He had demons like the rest of us* (Syl paused here; she looked up and around at the crowd like her sapped face had something to say), *but he worked hard to overcome these, too.*

He was special, Syl read, toward the end of the speech. *And God knows he will be missed, and in time, with the prayers of others, justice will be served for this horrible, horrible tragedy. I promise not to rest until it is.*

Syl didn't move from the podium when she finished reading. She fussed with the paper, which crinkled at the microphone with awkward noise. Then she closed her eyes like she might add a memory or two. Maybe something was coming to her. *Say something*, Mary-Beth thought. Just one, happy thing.

Syl did not, though she tripped a little as she stepped away from the podium in silence. She'd folded up the speech into a slender, white baton.

Cars trailed the hearse a few blocks to a cemetery, where Mary-Beth stood near the hole a tractor had dug, bouncing her knees. She couldn't stay still. She looked for birds, planes, sky writing, any sign from Calvin, but there were none. Everyone gathered, looking down into that hole. Mary-Beth stayed looking up.

As the priest recited Scripture, the casket lowering in uneven, harsh jerks, Mary-Beth remembered the first time and then the many times after that Calvin had kicked in her stomach. Before he was born, they'd had their own ways of communication. When she'd asked for a signal, he'd kick, a thud so real, knocks coming in elaborate patterns like a Morse code only she understood. Moving like that, her unborn son reminded her of a dog twisting and shaking in his own dream, running after something no one else could ever know. Stouffer—that was their dog's name, their old lab mix, Cal's first dog. He was a good dog. He, too, had been flattened by a car.

Keep us in life and death in Your love, and, by Your grace, lead us to Your kingdom, through Your Son . . . the priest went on.

Dirt hit the casket in pebbled smacks, then the three holy palmfuls were done. The dirt smelled blank, originless. The prayers, suddenly over. People moved and hugged Mary-Beth, though she didn't lift her arms to receive them. Birds cawed, and the sound of a soft rain came on, leaves stinging with drops. Genie or Nicola, she couldn't be bothered to tell which niece was which, said to one of the strangers: He was a friend to some and an enemy to others. Mary-Beth pocketed this as something to ream Syl about later. Disrespectful little bitches—the girls weren't even wearing black, not even chinos, they wore *jeans*, for Christ's sake! She imagined pushing the talking twin into the hole, but didn't want her anywhere near Cal.

No Tommy in all this. She'd looked for him at Bohner's and again here. No flashed badges either, no cuffs suddenly revealed to click behind the proper person, her son's killer. The disappointments would always keep coming.

Mary-Beth looked down at last. It seemed so shallow, for a grave. Lime rock and sand, not as dark and endless as she'd expected. Cal was right there. From her jacket pocket she pulled a green plastic Citra Sipper plug, the hard straw used to jab citrus, to drink right from an orange—Calvin's favorite pastime. She tossed it in the hole, and it let out a tiny, unsatisfying *plink* on the casket before rolling off into the dirt. Mary-Beth said, You keep that, baby.

No more tears. She wouldn't give that to Syl, or the girls, these strangers, whoever else was watching. *You keep that.* She held her eyes on the wood shine. She could see dark clouds rolling, stretched and distorted, in the lacquered reflection. It occurred to her that this, this view here, would be the last time she'd ever see her son. Of all the surfaces that had ever divided them—phone receivers, panels of bulletproof glass, brick walls, the chain-link fence between the underbelly of the bridge and the highway, the windows of her car, of police cars, windows upon windows upon windows—this would be the last.

Mary-Beth could not immediately situate the sound. She thought, Oh, even more people, when the crowd came screaming. Fifty now, maybe sixty, rounding a stand of trees. But these new guests had signs, and those signs had photos of her son. She thought, Oh, where have these signs come from, she hadn't printed any, and what an effort to have made them. It wasn't until the crowd drew closer that she could make out what was what—the crowd in green wigs and stretched burglar masks, and then she could hear them, too—the prancy strangers around her joining in, the priest asking for silence, robe spinning—then one massive chorus: *God Hates Calvin Boyer. All Pedos Fry in Hell. Justice for Survivors. Save Our Children.*

Mug shots of Calvin, her boy looking frightened, teeth crossed like pick-up sticks. The signs bobbed up and down.

And on other signs, enlarged yearbook photos of Linzie King. Elastic choker, chapped lips and blunt bangs, Linzie, a little girl then. Red letters stamped over her cheeks, dripping like movie blood. The signs read *HER TURN.*

Dear Birdie,

I don't think about the other girls but I still think about you and what happened at my house. I hope you don't hate me for that. People from where we're from are not always kind but you were. Not just to me but to everyone. You were different. I remember when you used to let the loud mean girl Missy copy your homework pages on the bus. I memorized where all of you sat. This was not only because I liked you but because where you sat told me a new story every day. It was like a food chain of who got the back of the bus and who got the window or the middle or the messed-up seats with all the duct tape on them and the stuffing that came out. You always sat with Francine but when you got in fights or when Francine wasn't there you sat up front behind my dad and I thought that was because you wanted protection from something or someone. I'm sorry that I only thought I was protecting you. I thought and acted wrong.

If a genie came to life in front of me and said OK Calvin now you get three wishes, I would use all three to fix myself. I know it's wrong to hurt children I really do. But it's easy when you want something to find a way to believe that hurt is gonna happen anyways. Or that something done with love intentions would not hurt at all. Do you ever feel this way? That you want something to be true so bad you'll find the craziest reasons to make it sound right?

I used to wear St. Christopher around my neck, do you remember that? I would rub it and I would pray to it and even kiss it. I begged for strength. I would say the rosary until my knees ached. I believed in a lot of things back then. You seemed so mature. You didn't seem it, you <u>were</u> mature. More than Francine even if she was older. It's not an excuse but only something I wanted to mention here. I think when you've been through a lot the way you and I have you grow up quicker. I don't know what you have been through in your lifetime but it seemed like there was already something very sad in you and that was before me. Birdie I still pray sometimes that I'm not the one who did that. I know I hurt and disrespected you, but I couldn't handle living with putting out some kind of light in you.

There were others, which I'm not proud of. I wish you were the only one. Eventually I did learn children don't say <u>yes</u> and really mean it. I have made mistakes but Birdie I hope you don't hate me for saying this, but it felt like true love with you. I am not some pervert who <u>wants</u> to rape kids or some heartless guy who wants to murder them. I just see good and then I <u>want</u> it. You are obviously a great girl and that doesn't just go away. I regret what I did to you only because you made it clear after that you didn't want that. Otherwise I would have regretted the others but never you.

Hopefully with these letters I can explain. The things Lindsay said about me on TV are <u>not true</u>. I don't want the world to think that way about me and I hope you don't and maybe before the book comes out you can help me share that she's a lying bitch and we can make this right. You knew me Birdie and that means you still know who I am. You have seen me through it all. I never wanted to hurt you and you know that. People hold all kinds of mercy for other sick people so why not me? God says it is human to make mistakes and I have listened to mine. I hope you will write back and one day maybe you would visit me here at Gateway. It is a compound made for healing and you are a big part of that for me.

Sincerely,
Calvin

BIRDIE

ON THE LANDLINE in the pumphouse, Trace said I didn't have a choice. She was coming to Whidbey. That was that.

Trace said the way I'd been sounding on the phone had been worrisome. Taciturn. Something about the jokes I made, too. *You're going dark again*, she said, when I told her about the slugs; my time, lately, on the ground. So she took a few paid days from the ad agency, packed a carry-on, and said she'd arrive by sundown the next day.

That's that.

I said, *Alright, then.*

I showered. I brushed my hair. Moisturized my face and hands with body balm, swiping a hole so deep in the container it shone like a throat. Then I hid the book in several places: back in my suitcase; in the desk drawer with my cell phone, which had remained off since arrival; in the large pot in the kitchen cabinet. I felt guilty bringing Trace into the home I now shared with Linzie.

I imagined Trace on the ferry. Those seats again, the brown cushions, that pale green light. I wanted to smell the stale fry oil, walk the linoleum tiled checkered floors, check the unfinished puzzles, which might now be complete—anything that would bring me back to Rich. If only Trace could have heard the way I'd said Calvin's name. The way I'd said my own, abrupt and dimly hopeful. I'd been someone new on the boat, someone possibly terrifying, which is to say for a single afternoon, for one day of my life, I had perhaps been myself.

The spinning bag of clothes. Rich's scar—if I'd taken a picture on the boat, I'd zoom in to see it all again, just to find him.

I boiled some leaves and cinnamon sticks and orange rinds on the woodstove to make the cabin smell sweet. Thelma had told me to do that. *No candles!* I'd kept my word.

Then, when all was clean, I hid the book again.

I was writing in a journal at my desk when a car door slammed shut, setting off the neighbor's husky. Out the window, Trace pulled a duffel bag from the passenger seat of a Subaru, adjusted the brim of her baseball cap, and walked up the drive toward the cabin.

We stood a long time in the doorway letting the bugs in. Trace said, You got taller, didn't you? fussing my hair. It was a modest, clumsy greeting. We didn't kiss.

Inside, I made us tea. I showed her the woodstove and how I'd learned to use it. Six years together, only this one month apart, and already I felt as if I were presenting her with my great new life. One I had built alone. The way I had to smack the hotplate to turn it on, muddy shoes on the doormat. My owl helmet. Amanda, always barking around dusk. *Holly's invasive here*, I said. *They have to stab it with a poison pen, a lance*—these facts were all mine.

The trees are moody, Trace said. Dr. Seuss trees.

They're more Matisse, I said, handing her a warm mug.

This is *nature* nature.

Trace sat with her knees up in the window seat. She wore thick socks, watched me blow into the crescent mouth of the woodstove. With the generic plaid mug in her hands, an image removed from our home, I felt our early days again. The nerves. A charged, cautious distance. The way she looked at me, tilting her head, watchful. She sipped her tea, and steam pulsed on the rim of the mug, flickering like breath.

Should we go out tonight? she asked.

I nodded, Sure.

There wasn't worry in her voice. It was something different.

Trace drove us to Bruno's in the rental Subaru Crosstrek, which she'd driven onto the ferry. It's a nice view from the boat, she said. Shorter ride than I thought.

Did you meet anyone on the ferry? I asked.

Sorry, was I supposed to?

We pulled into Bruno's bar. Walked the crunchy path to the door. Inside it was a dive lined with '90s track lighting, '70s music posters curling from the walls, pickled eggs packed down into a jar. A man in a fedora tended a resin-glossed bar top. When we ordered, he repeated our words back like an infomercial.

Trace liked that the place had a jukebox and went over to feed it, her fingertips on the glass. I brought my drink to a high-top and studied her. She was so absorbed, easy to entertain in these small, predictable ways, and as I watched her bend down, quietly flipping the records, punching numbers for Connie Francis, boxers showing above her pants, I felt so guilty. If that moment were the first time I'd ever seen Trace Marie Levenson—Carhartt jacket and bowling shoes and dimpled, focused chin—I would still choose her, beg for her. On my knees. Exactly her.

She came back to our table, and the song changed to Elton John. We'd have to wait for Connie. I sipped whiskey, neat, and she drank fast from a bottle of beer, her lips already bubblegum wet in the way that meant she'd be drunk soon.

So what's up, Chang, she said, her tone descending, and with this I knew: we were about to talk about something serious. Calvin oriented. Or maybe my mother. I took a fuller sip. My face throbbed. *Your Asia glow*, Trace used to say in the beginning, but now it was a constant.

You've got to call Wendy from the little pay phone, she said.

Without you calling her, I hear from her before I even eat breakfast.

You don't eat breakfast, I said.

Chang, just once a week. You know your mom. She worries. Trace placed her phone on the table, as if for proof. We both looked at the dead, mirrored face. It reflected the track lights, nothing else.

Aren't we supposed to be *preserving* my peace? I asked. Isn't that what this is all about? To reset the nervous system, find my center?

I knew how to use Trace's own language to get what I wanted.

My mother, Wendy, had lived eight hundred lives. At my parents' restaurant, Hei Baby, she was front of house, a local legend, a jolly and theatrical white woman easing fellow white diners into cashew shrimp, pearly lobes of chicken. Every night, she would pause dinner service for her Speech. The Speech was about meeting her husband, Hei, and crossing racial lines for love, and opening their dream restaurant, uniting people to eat traditional food with an "American twist." The Speech thanked the military and police, it welcomed new diners, then a shout out to the loyalists so they would feel at once humbled and magnificent. She sang a cappella Billy Joel, Bette Midler, Neil Sedaka; her hair—auburn red curls with an Aqua Net sheen—swung immaculately. I used to accompany her, standing on my chair the way everybody adored, harmonizing. We were a multiracial, wholesome family. We were an inspiration.

These days, my mother worked as an orthodontist's assistant in West Boca, and recently, Trace and my mother had *connected* on a *spiritual past-lives level*. They attributed this to their *mutual devotion to feminist causes* and their love for me. They talked on the phone, emailed, texted each other memes and meditations and Internal Family Systems reading lists.

Have you read the book yet? Trace asked, finishing the last of her beer. Be honest. Did you go out and find it?

I haven't gone anywhere, I said. Just my walks to the beach.

See, that *is* progress, Trace said. You're healing here. The ocean, it has all kinds of healing ions. And all this time in nature, do you know it's been said—

How's the book doing? I asked. Do people believe her? I imagined Linzie being invited to speak at universities, healing breathwork retreats, and sweat lodges in Sedona. The kind of retreats Trace would attend.

The podcaster keeps reaching out, Trace said. She looked down at her bottle. Twisted it in her hand, the metallic label spinning. She says the book is all lies; she can prove it. And your mom thinks we have a real shot at the next hearing. With the new emails, she thinks he'll get the violation, it'll be clear cut. So maybe Linzie escalating things was actually a blessing in disguise.

I'd been trying not to think about the next hearing in Florida, end of summer. Every year I flew down to renew the order of protection against Calvin, which would soon be expiring again. Trace would be there, as always. My mother would be there, as always. As always, we would stay in the taupe hotel, eat the watery room service, and I would wear the used, pin-striped clothes borrowed from my mom's co-worker Abby, clothes that read responsible, ladylike, trustworthy, ecstatically bland. Early in the morning, we'd drive to the courthouse. The sun would blaze the limestone steps. And once inside, I would repeat the facts, because one has to both submit them and recite them aloud to a room full of strangers: I was nine years old when Calvin Boyer molested me and recorded it on a camcorder, nine years old when my parents pressed charges, ten years old when those charges were dismissed; Boyer, now a habitual felony sex offender, continued to abuse young girls, and some girls, girls like Linzie, were offered action, consequences, reverence; Boyer is mentally unwell; he is in and out of jail, prison, and community control; he once lived under the Julia Tuttle Causeway Bridge, and he now resides at Gateway to Grace, a civil commitment treatment program for pedophiles; Boyer has continued to initiate contact, has professed his love, has threatened to *find me anywhere*, has always, and will always, find me—these facts printed on my flimsy sheet of paper, my body, as always, on the left side of the cold, carpeted room with all the other women (sometimes, a single man) and the stupid video looping on the bulky television that hasn't been updated since the invention of television about spousal abuse, domestic violence, the gifts of intuition, while actors on the TV dramatically play us—the *disempowered victims*—cowering and screaming, hands over our ears, ducked in a corner of a staged dark living room, always behind a couch, makeup too blue and streaking, and one by one, we approach the judge, a judge who is bored, a judge who sits unmoving and unmoved, thinking about his leftover meat sauce and four p.m. vodka waiting at home, and we wait for our verdict, for any recognition that might faintly change our lives, the only sound our stomachs, all of our stomachs gurgling, squelching with ache and with hunger like a thousand rusted, closing doors, while, on the right side of the room, our abusers sit stunned, drop-jawed, feigning remorse, feigning surprise, desultory stares of *I don't know where she got this! Get a load of this one!* waiting for the moment it's all over, the papers stamped and handed back, so often *No*, so often *No reasonable person would feel threatened* or *This threat is not explicit, work it out already!* or the alternative: a dull date of time allotted, our names no longer names but serial numbers, the countdown until the next renewal, before the mass of us exit the same courtroom and walk the same halls, which are never divided between perpetrator and victim, they wait until we leave, wait until we're back outside, the sun still striking beautifully those courthouse steps, all twenty-three steps, where the person who wants to kill us might, at last, be free to.

 Calvin hadn't shown up last time. The two times before he had, dressed in the same oversized royal blue suit, his face clean-shaven and older, his whole body clutching for his mother, Mary-Beth, a jerky-tanned tiny blonde with puffy veins up her arms, who walked him down the hall, kissed him between the eyes, and said, *I believe in you, baby.*

Connie came on the juke, and someone booed. Trace reached out and squeezed my hand. Hang in there, Trace said. Everything's about to turn around. We use the letters in court. The podcaster will defuse the Linzie stuff. She'll fade away like every other media mosquito. And you'll come home a new person. We'll find you a new job, and you'll—

Are you my girlfriend or my manager? I asked.

You had your way, now you must pay, Connie sang. I took an accentuated sip of my drink for Connie's chorus, playing a role, a woman lovely with menace. You didn't need to come here, I said. I'm good. I've got my own thing going on here. I'm fine.

Your fingers look like hell, Trace said. She pulled my hand closer to her eyes. I yanked it loose, flicked her in the forehead.

We laughed. I don't know why, but we did. Sometimes it came back to us—laughter, touch, Trace's hand, big enough to wrap my forearm with pressure. She held it down on the table. It filled me with a bright pink static.

Alright, Wilma Dean, she said. You're fine.

When we got home from the bar I thought about the book. Heat radiated from its place beneath the bathroom sink; it hummed from under the towels. Something about Trace brushing her teeth and washing her face and shaking out her hair like a wet dog over the vanity without knowing it was there turned me on. It was something I'd been able to keep from her.

Trace triple-checked the locks on the cabin's door and windows, snapped the blinds closed, pulled a knife from the kitchen drawer. I'd done none of this since arriving on Whidbey and felt a glut of pride. Put another log on the stove, I directed her, and she did.

She made it up the stairs to our bed. I turned off the lamp and kissed her, both of us sitting up at first, but then I rolled on top of her. She tried to grab my hands, tried to flip me back over, but I held her down. I pinned her wrists to the sides of her face, bit her. Really? she asked.

Really.

She tried to reach for her phone. For the soundtrack we'd made on our counselor's suggestion of thunder, rain battering a tin roof, meditative gongs. *I consent to making love*—we were supposed to repeat, one after the other, like vows—*I am safe in this moment of intimacy. I am entering the kingdom of safety.*

I pinned her wrist again. I moved my hand to her cunt.

I don't have anything with me, she said. I didn't think—

Shhhh, we go natural, I said.

I didn't need a silicone cock to be fucked, though I liked that. I once did. Now I wanted to feel her skin and fingers and the warmth of her. I wanted her to keep her rings on. For it to feel sharp and sudden, for her to reach in and let me sit on her whole fist; I wanted her to grab my throat with her other hand and squeeze. I slid my underwear to the side, moving her hand inside of me. She hooked the good spot, and I rocked into it.

You feel safe? she said. Are you in the kingdom of—

I gripped her hair and pulled hard. I kept grinding and she looked at me strange, her black eyes darting quick circles, but she didn't stop. She didn't say anything at all. For once she shut up and fucked me harder, and I opened my legs wider. She gripped my throat until my face prickled with absence of air, absence of everything, and I repeated Linzie's name in my mind as I rode Trace's wrist, pulling it deeper into me until I came all over her saying, *Do you feel that? Do you feel how wet I am for you?* and I repeated Linzie's name and thought of Linzie's face on the book jacket, thought of Linzie's face scrunched crying on TV, as I counted the pulses of my own contracting body, that off-beat heart between my legs, and as I fell over to Trace's side, my legs numb, ears ringing high into the pillow, our stomachs slick, I felt, for that moment, what it was like to be powerful.

Early Wednesday morning, Trace's last on the island before she had to get back to work in New York, we drove to an artisanal coffee shop off a dirt road to taste a specific blend of espresso. Trace was a Yelper, a planner, interested in impractical things like that. The day was already bright, the sun glinting the road into sandpaper; trees bent and swooned from a bay breeze like the world was stirred by the spoon of God. With the car windows down and my feet on the dash, I thought, I could be a real person, like this. Maybe one day. Maybe starting today. That's what Whidbey was for. My body was capable of calm when I let it in, when the radio played loud enough to suck oxygen from the flares of my mind, when I could relax enough to *just be* in the company of this person who was unrelentingly patient, someone who knew what basics I needed—a back rub, a long walk, a new bra or pair of socks—before I knew it myself.

Swarms of cars inched in and out of spots surrounding the coffee joint, and a long line of people stood outside the door. The *true summer* Thelma had warned me about was underway. Sun-hats, stars and stripes, and decked-out vacationers, Obama-bumper-stickered Seattleites here to whale watch or drink organic grapes with Pacific Northwest's techno elite.

I followed Trace in. She wore a tight black t-shirt, arm tattoos blurred blue by sunscreen, low checkered pants she'd had since forever. We held each other by the waists, kissing and groping in that just-fucked morning giddiness we hadn't lived in ages.

I don't want you to go, I said, testing her. I knew Trace would go, she had to go—big prep for an energy drink campaign that would pay our rent—but I also needed her to resist, ready to drop anything for me. Ready to leave her job. Her life. Anything. To love was to pretend.

OK, I won't, she said. She kissed me. Her thumb ring rubbed my cheek. A woman in a woven sun hat stared at us, cocked her mouth in melodramatic revulsion. She your sister? said Trace, squeezing, then smacking my ass.

Patrons crowded the pickup side of the bar. They perched along the window seats in pastel, gauzy indifference. A bucktoothed boy waved a tiny American flag in his mother's face. The place was loud, vaulted ceilings dilating the sounds, and people flinched at the clanging of milk pitchers, the gurgling exhales of steam wands. At the register, Trace ordered for us both. Then she unhooked my arm to pull her wallet out of her back pocket and turned to face me, her back against the glass pastry case. Is that right? she said, yelling a little. Black, iced? Her posture shot up, tense.

Yeah, of course, I said. What else?

What time is it? Trace asked. She rubbed at her nose. The anxious hand wipe. Her neck blotted red. Do you have the ferry schedule? Then she pressed both her hands into my shoulders and turned me around. She walked me to the pickup end of the bar. She pulled my face to her chest and massaged my scalp. A new laundry detergent.

What's up? I said into her shirt. Why'd you just get so weird?

I got overwhelmed, Trace said, by all the options.

Our drinks slid out onto the bar with a shout of *Tracy!* and Trace rolled her eyes, said, Come on, let's take these to the beach.

She took my hand and rushed me out the door. I chewed at my seaweed eco-straw, grainy and bitter. I have to use the bathroom, I said, spinning around and into the building. I hurried to the register, squeezed past the line of new people, whispering *excuse me* and *so sorry*. And there it was, just to the left of the cashier, who was assertively screaming back an order for a macchiato—the pastry case taped with local band flyers, babysitting services, guitar lessons, bunk beds for sale, local taxi cards, and where Trace had stood, I saw what she had been hiding. Her xeroxed face on a sheet of lime green paper:

Elliott Bay Book Co. Presents

Linzie King's *MY TURN: Reading and signing to follow*
1521 10th Ave. Seattle, WA

Friday, July 5, 7:30 PM, Free Admission

I didn't tear the sheet from the board and pocket it, although I imagined what that might feel like. It was in two days, and Trace would be gone.

MARY-BETH

THE POND AT the entrance of Gateway to Grace was a milky cataract blue with a half-spitting fountain in the center. It had been Calvin's job every few weeks to drop the dye packs in the water, buckets of *Sapphire Sun* on clearance from BJ's. Of all his Gateway Community agreements and tasks, Calvin took pride in this job, specifically. When he'd arrived in December, seven months before he died, it had been overgrown with algae, stagnant brown with hot rings of mucus gunk, and it was Calvin who'd suggested the blue. Blue blocked the sun—he'd learned from a brief stint cleaning pools—blue blocked the fish from being seen; it would keep the herons away, curb the algae—plus, he'd added, it'd bring some much-needed elegance to the place. So every third Sunday, Calvin would roll on his rubber gloves and tend to the pond, drop in the packs, stirring the water with a Ping-Pong paddle, all in service of an opaque beauty.

Mary-Beth didn't like to think about the past. When she did, it came in flashes both real and unreal, true memories interrupted by things that hadn't actually happened to her: Hiroshima, Jim Jones's Jonestown, migrating on the great frontier, Mary-Beth's body wrapped in a half-dead, still-warm animal. It would be more legible to have survived such things, more comprehensible to others, because she *had* survived, hadn't she? Against all odds, the conditions of which no one else would ever know. The endless moves—serrated cardboard gnawing at her hands. The debt. Her little brother Alfie's face when his life left him after jumping from that swing—the color of his mouth blue and yellow at once—a stunning, impossible thing (she wondered what Calvin had looked like when that had happened). There was every late-night phone call. There were her teeth that hurt from simply smiling, wind whistling against them like a soldering iron, unveiling the root. Without Calvin, proof of all those survivals no longer existed.

There was no more stain on the road when she arrived at Gateway today. No more caution tape or dead sparklers. It had been over a week. This, another survival.

She sat in her car, just beyond the entrance. It was four p.m., elf hat slumped on the dash beneath her SunPass, her foot heavy on the brake. She stared at that pond. A welcome pond, for those allowed entrance. A showpiece. The bluest blue. Already, without him, the perimeter was foaming. It would go back to shit, and she tried to stop imagining her boy there, fixing it.

Gonna do Cal's room today, she said aloud to herself, releasing her foot from the pedal. The way her Mercury came to life surprised her, and it rolled over the gravel driveway, the sound the slow gurgle of a clogged drain. The Gateway to Grace housing units made a long row—three rows total—cinder-block pale yellow Legos plugged into the ground. Group sessions and meetings were held in two different vinyl doublewides, one of which served as Betty's intake office. Outside the units: shit-for-nothing cars, bicycles hanging from nails, wooden clotheslines affixed like crosses, bubble-rusted washer units, vinyl lawn chairs, lopsided grills, browning banana trees, a few limping, sickly pelicans. In the air: smoke sparkling from constant sugar burn and the always-smell of dead fish. A brick chapel stood with graffiti tags looped on from trespassers, which got painted over in white, then retagged, then painted over again and again in lumpy streaks—the painting, another service task. Mary-Beth could still make out the *BABY BANGERS* and *PEDO SCUM* in bold letters, the red cursive of *FUCK U PERVERT PARK* like taillights breaking through fog.

As Mary-Beth drove past Units 1–4, a few of the residents waved to her. The boys stood in their matching wife-beater tank tops—five dollars for a bag of them at Lucinda's station in Pahokee—low-slung shorts, a tight, pitying look on their faces like smoke held in. Calvin was going to get out of here. Eventually, he would have. He'd earned many of the most difficult to earn certificates at Dade and in his programs since—Hygiene, Excellence in Problem Solving, Work = Ethics—plus three sobriety coins and a GED. Calvin had shown her his math worksheets, long division tricks he'd begun to memorize: *To the left to the left*, he'd move the tip of his pencil to the tune of a Beyoncé song—that was how one successfully moved a decimal. Mary-Beth had feigned interest, her face taffy stretched as if offered the very last key to the cosmos. *Ohhh, that's how*, she'd said, though Mary-Beth knew decimals from North Pole. She knew money.

Unit 5B. Here was Calvin's. A studio unit, a nice one. Mary-Beth parked, got out, stroked the warm, bumpy cinder block of her son's entryway. She wondered when Calvin's hand had last rested on the same place her hand rested now, if she was still picking up cells of him, detritus, sweat or prints or DNA. 5B was more freshly painted, brighter than the rest, Mary-Beth had made sure of it. The other units had been graying with dirt, sand, and pollen spun from tires, paint chipping and peeling like Mary-Beth's drugstore makeup. When Calvin had been approved for Gateway, Mary-Beth asked for the color *Post-It!* by Lefferts Paint Co., and Betty approved of her and Cal spending days with the cans, the brushes, Mary-Beth stabilizing the ladder for her son—*Hold steady, Ma! Don't let go!*—something they could do together under the sweat of midday sky, something that meant they'd be starting over for good, for now.

Once, when Mary-Beth was still a woman worth health and dental insurance and a shred of dignity, she worked at a real Home Depot. Not even a knockoff, but the blocky orange logo and everything. It was her dream to wear that stiff apron with its deep, purposeful pockets. She worked the paint department, and all day long she watched every kind of person stroll up to the wall of swatches, the colors glowing under spotlights like portals to the future. And she saw in the faces of those who plucked lavenders and periwinkles the look of pure hope, a different kind of hope than hers, a hope with vision and promise behind it—a pale yellow kitchen, a sapphire den, the sage of a baby's room.

At the counter, these men or women or families would hand Mary-Beth the swatches, and doubtless they would say something about *the vision*, because people still talked to her back then. They'd hand over the small sample white cans, Mary-Beth plugging the numbers and codes into the Home Depot computer, her bitten fingers typing on thick, old keys, a soft tinkle sound like carbonation. She was so proud of that meticulous typing. She'd trained hard for it in a Broward community class, fifty words a minute with paper taped over the keyboard.

Kids, she'd liked the most. Kids, she's always adored. Children held up by the armpits by Daddy, or egged on by Mommy, kids who'd shyly show Mary-Beth a color, sometimes a gorgeous color and sometimes hideous—Mary-Beth had opinions about them all—and Mary-Beth would then show them the white inside the can before setting it into the paint rattler. She did not explain the ratios of white to yellows, the power of primaries, did not show them the color dropping so quickly into the can they each looked like strings of yarn.

Wave your hand over it, Mary-Beth would say. Perhaps, she thinks, the beginning of her role as *Fairy-Beth*. And the kid would do it, every time—even the older, more cynical children with sunburns and ringed scabs, never too old to believe in transformation, in what might happen, just for a moment. They'd wave their hands. Then Mary-Beth would open the shook-up can to a new color. Lilac, cerulean, chartreuse, gray. She lived for those kids' faces.

When flyers were made about Calvin, right after his second

conviction, right after he'd been added to the sex offender registry at nineteen years old, the paint color thrown on Mary-Beth was called *Aubergine Dream*. A woman had done it. Her child had helped.

Gonna do Cal's room today. Mary-Beth squeezed her key firmly, aiming at the knob of her son's door. Tucked under her other arm like a football, she clutched the box of heavy-duty Heftys.

Mary-Beth opened the unit. She'd prepared herself for the smell of him, but she wasn't prepared for this. His unmade bed on the left side of the room, like he'd just kicked off the sheets. The brass cross above it, still slightly crooked. Calvin. Cal. Calzone, Callywag, Kooky Baby Nugget, his woodsy deodorant, smell of sweat and faded Icy Hot, his always mildewed towels on the floor, the piercing chemical stink of cashed bowls of K2 Spice—the nasty drug she'd know the smell of always—he promised he wasn't smoking it, but she couldn't be mad now, could she? K2 didn't show up on Calvin's drug tests. It also made him paranoid, sometimes mean. She felt disappointed in him for lying and then disappointed in herself for catching him in a lie in this unfair way, a betrayal, because what good was any of it now? All this knowing, for what? Mary-Beth stood in the entrance of her son's dark home.

No detectives had come since the day he died, and still no updates on the case—not even after the funeral protest. On TV, special units often found hints of who'd done it right there in the victim's bedroom, so Mary-Beth had left Calvin's alone. At first, she was angry about the lack of attention—no print dusting or special bulbs. Now she was a little relieved. No way anyone else could or should touch his things, precious things, moving them around, picking up a shirt or belt of Cal's between two pinched fingers, dangling it above their head with judgment. She wouldn't let that happen to him anymore. Not after a whole life of his belongings examined, taken. He'd once saved up years for an MP3 player in Dade, and Mary-Beth always donated to his prison commissary, but all that had been swiped, too.

She started with the picture frames lining his dresser on the right side of the room, then those hanging on the wall. She'd printed and framed and hung them all herself—a *gallery wall*. First slowly, then quicker, she tossed them in her Hefty bag. She'd sort it later. She didn't want to spend too much time looking, longing, all the photos of them—*You like to push on bruises,* Tommy used to say. She tossed and tossed.

You will grow old and live on a mountain; that's what a county fair psychic once said to Calvin. Mary-Beth was there for it, she had heard her say those words. The psychic, Delilah, had held Calvin's palm and mashed her fingers at his skin, stretching the lines. She looked closer and said, *I see a long, happy life.* Calvin had smiled so big, a teenager just out of Duval juvie, the last time he was allowed near a county fair. His genuine smile jutted out his jaw into a boyish underbite. Mary-Beth called it his Blond Boy Smile—*Come on, give me your Blond Boy Smile*—the words all rolled together. Mary-Beth's eyes stung. It was a chlorine sting. She used to have days like that—swimming pools, sun.

You will grow old and live on a mountain. In the years after that psychic reading, Mary-Beth dreamed a life for her and Calvin in Wyoming. Wyoming, with so few people, and therefore so few children—they would be free to live almost anywhere, no 2,500 feet. Perhaps a double-wide on a wide, open plain, crops soft with distance, real weather, sunsets pink as calamine. She wouldn't have to work at a gas station, but it wouldn't be so bad even if she did, that's how nice all the customers would be, what with their fringe jackets and aftershave, the dark denim stiff of jeans. They'd know her by her heart, and they'd understand Calvin's too, because to live in Wyoming meant you were probably flung from somewhere else, somewhere less forgiving. Mary-Beth had never been there, she'd only left Florida once (Valdosta, Georgia, attempt at running away, 1973), but she'd watched *Butch Cassidy* and the Robert Redford kind of movies, and those mountains were something she could trust, something to believe in. Mary-Beth in Wyoming would make her own clothes, she'd buy new teeth, no more baby food or lukewarm drinks, just crocheted blankets, prime rib with bone, leather boots, home-brewed tea. And Calvin in Wyoming. No temptations or parole officers or *danger zones*— no girls seeking revenge. No blow-gasping into car Breathalyzers to stop the blaring, ringing alarm. They'd have their own farm for Calvin to do what he did best, tend to the land, feed chickens and bucklings, build ladders. No Okeechobee winds, no registry deadlines, no bridge rot or dying monitors—even the Pigs would be nice, county deputies who'd come over for dinner, never empty-handed, only looking to serve. Calvin might even have grown a beard there, eyes deepened with crinkles of age, fresh coffee in the morning, fancy stand mixer shining with chrome, cartons and cartons and cartons of smokes, bacon and eggs, a fireplace, yes, Mary-Beth and Calvin in Wyoming. There, in this alternate plane, her son would have lived.

Mary-Beth didn't feel herself falling, but there she was, on the floor of her son's studio, the scarves she'd knotted and hung over his windows letting in a burgundy, mawkish light. AC unit off and Mary-Beth on her knees, his bamboo mat all askew on vinyl, everything gritted with sand. Her hip hurt. Her elf tights were torn in a perfect circle at the knee, her hand and wrist rubbed raw, skin peeled and weeping like a tomato left forgotten on the counter. Mary-Beth crawled toward one of Calvin's New Balance sneakers between the door and the bed, then buried her nose right into it. She wept watery snot and tears, her hand pressing the sneaker to her face until she could breathe nothing but the smell of him, his feet, a smell that would always be his, unchanged since he was a child, since Mary-Beth had squeezed a fat bottle of baby powder at his shoes and it puffed ghostly and she said, *You stink worse than Georgia,* and still he was so bad at changing his socks, at applying any powder himself, she'd gotten used to it, a joke between them, she'd *die of the smell* she once said when she'd taken him to the outlet at Sawgrass to try on some nice chinos for church, when he'd kicked off his shoes everyone else in the dressing room said, *What in God's name?* He'd laughed so hard, and Mary-Beth had been embarrassed, but it was another one of their memories and days together, that pact between them, a shared life of them against the world, on and on and screw the rest, she huffed and held all of him in, what was left of him. Her boy.

She tried to stand up now. She hadn't eaten in who knows how long. Fireworks squealed off in her stomach. Her vision spotted purple dinosaur skin.

She emptied his fridge in the back of the room, the bagel bites, slimy ham in a Ziploc, metallic juice pouches, three green apples, a moldy plum, a melted Slurpee from 7-Eleven, still so red. The fridge lit up the rest of his room in a dreamy paleness that made it look like the past. On the counter, a pack of Newports freshly opened—the wrapper still beside it. Mary-Beth popped the lid. None were missing.

In his bathroom: plastic Adidas shower shoes. She wore the shoes on her fingers like puppets, then dropped them in a new bag. Shampoo, cracked soap on a rope, his clipped hairs—she wiped the porcelain, tossed it all. For years, when Mary-Beth tried to lull herself to sleep at night, she had imagined sealing beautiful boxes, two disembodied hands wrapping each one with bright-colored wrapping paper. She imagined perfect folds made more perfect by a manicured fingernail gliding, the exhale of tape from a dispenser, bright ribbon, glossy Scotch stretching out. She'd kept the many years of Calvin in these boxes of her mind. They were confined in her own history textbooks, Mary-Beth's McGraw Hill, hardbacked and official, the words grammatically correct and proofread by experts, the facts of her son: born July 16, 1977, in Miami, Florida; 3 pounds, eight ounces; slight and sickly. He had felt so much bigger as she'd carried him, so much so she'd often imagined she was carrying twins. When he was born, as they wiped his body and cleared his nostrils, Mary-Beth had felt the distinct pang of a second something, somewhere inside. Beyond all logic, beyond her ultrasounds, she felt two. More. But after the doctor and nurses emptied her body of sac, placenta, blood, shit, the whole flood, nothing else came. Calvin was placed on her chest. No baby hat, no clothes or blanket, only the smell emanating from the top of his head, soft flesh dimpled like hammered clay, hers. He had always been innocent.

Tying each garbage bag and lining them up in her dead son's room, Mary-Beth imagined another one, another *him*, somewhere unharmed—going on and breathing.

Calvin's laptop remained closed on his homework desk near the middle of the room. So many years without one, or with padlocks on Mary-Beth's bedroom door to keep things lawful, but he'd been allowed monitored use here at the program. He'd taken the IBM Mary-Beth had bought him—brand-new, like a real professional—a red nub in the center for a mouse. Mary-Beth lifted the screen now, her reflection a blur not quite in sync with herself. When the computer flashed on and made a noise, Mary-Beth closed it.

She opened his desk drawers and collected his pamphlets, his papers, multiple-choice worksheets offered by Gateway on anger management, impulse control, construction training, etiquette. She collected the books she'd given him as a kid—*The Story of Ferdinand*, *Love You Forever*—Marvel comic books, too, and then at the bottom of his right-hand desk drawer, she saw something else.

Mary-Beth held the book. Linzie looked the same to her as she had as a kid. As she had on those protestors' signs. Pipsqueak of a girl, pushed-in nose, always greasy; at the funeral, Mary-Beth had wrestled one sign from a green-wigged bandit and tried to tear it in half, but it wouldn't give. She stomped on her face instead.

This was the closest she'd been to a copy of the book. She'd sworn to Calvin, crossed her heart (for he'd made her promise)—*Never. And if you see it in the store*, Calvin had said, *you'd better hide it where nobody sees*, and Mary-Beth said she'd do that, of course she would, though she never went to bookstores. So why was it here, in his drawer? For a moment, she wondered if she was in the wrong apartment. Maybe everything, all of this, was a mistake. They'd promised.

Mary-Beth opened the book. The book's spine made a cracking noise. She wanted to feel what Calvin felt, holding it. The heft, the smooth, cool pages. She smelled for him, his hands, his cologne: nothing. She flipped and stopped short. Writing. Calvin's writing. Pencil marks, everywhere. She flipped page after page and covered Linzie King's print with her hand—a promise is a promise—and scanned Calvin's furious notes in the margin, arrows, question marks: *BULLSHIT* and *I AM NOT!* and *LYING CUNTRAG!*

A Polaroid was slipped between the pages, somewhere toward the middle. Mary-Beth's body cooled all the way down as she looked. Her son's flaccid penis, face on, bleached with flash, a background of the room she was standing in. It looked like a sea creature in the deep ocean, but she'd know his hips anywhere. They were hers, too. She closed the book and threw it in the bag.

At the way bottom of the drawer, beneath where the book had been, Mary-Beth pulled out a yellow legal pad, the papers crunchy with folds and scribbles. In her son's writing, she read a list of names:

Jacy Farrow
Wilma Dean Loomis
Judy Barton

A clue. Maybe he had left clues, after all. Maybe he knew what was coming for him. Mary-Beth walked a few paces to his front door and looked out the peephole, then the window. She held the legal pad tight against her chest. *Five times, forward and back.*

Mary-Beth watched the sky. It would pour soon, she knew from the new green of the clouds, the metallic brackish smell near the window, everything darkened and trembling, no more birds. The puddles around her tires dimpled, though the drops were invisible. Like a movie played backward of rain.

Mary-Beth drove south to work, directly from Gateway. The Hefty bags blocked out every window of her Mercury, windshield wipers snoring louder than Syl.

She had been working in North Pole Florida Gas & Save half a decade now, but the past few night shifts, without Calvin, felt ceaseless. The lights too bright, everything too cold, the humming too loud when she stacked the cooler. Stanley pumped the AC to keep whoever was working graveyards alert, and the thermostat couldn't be adjusted—a red plastic devil knob notched in place. Usually, Mary-Beth didn't mind that so much. But since the funeral her feet dulled with an alien tingle, purple under her elf shoes.

Mary-Beth stood at her post behind the register. She was now sore, stiff, from falling in Calvin's room, and she blew gently on her hand. Customers came in and out, pointed to the great wall of smokes. Whenever Mary-Beth pointed back—*Celadon? Pinks? Ultras?*—she remembered her Home Depot days, the swatches. This was as close as she'd get to back there.

She thought about the photograph, the book. Her teeth chattered hard, so she chewed more sugar-free cinnamon gum, washed the flavor with warm Pepsi. Usually, OK, she could take it. The customers. The regulars. The children lit up by their year-round Christmas—it was worth it for them. Worth it for patrons who knew her, those whose lottery numbers she remembered by the birthdays of their kids, their anniversaries, their luckies, those who bought the same smokes from her on behalf of the station's discounts (Seminole land). Mary-Beth was used to sending gas to the pumps, used to spraying the aerosol snow, punching neon numbers, mopping floors, the mindlessness of stocking the cooler. She was used to the deep black pit in her stomach when a patron said, *There's something in the bathroom, miss*, and she was used to sliding over packs of Kools and Marlboros for the younger ones, Nat's and Pall Malls and Bensons for the olds, pink Camel No. 9s for high school girls all with the same shimmering cheekbones, Merits for the businessmen. Fraternity boys, with their sodas and Magnums and Red Bulls and Parliaments, bothered her most. Pimpled brats from Florida Atlantic and FIU, sometimes BCC but never University of Miami (they went out in the Grove), always sounded the bell as if it were a finish line. Sometimes the college boys made jokes about Mary-Beth and her elf outfit. Sometimes she overheard them joking about fucking her as if to prove to their friends they'd do it, they really would, swear to fucking Christ they would, and other times they wanted to fuck her truly, they meant it, she felt it and they told her so, the young men alone, leaning too close, brutal in their breath. Often, in groups, there were jokes about her riding Santa Claus's dick, or *working* someone's dick like the elves *worked* toys in their *work*shop, they'd ask her to keep the hat on, the leggings too, to *ride their reindeer*. Sometimes there were jokes about snow blows and ball freeze, and they told her frankly she was too ugly to fuck, too gnarly to fuck, or too old, too trailer, too grody to fuck—*probably some clap shit*—too yappy or scrawny or toothless to fuck, *Mrs. Claus! Mrs. Claus! Daytona Dumbfuck!* Mary-Beth hated them all, these rodent-faced boys, their lives of leather buckled shoes, school paid for by Daddy or Grandpa or an uncle with *stocks*. These boys had cars. They owned everything. Fake Delaware and Hawai'i IDs that looked like shit, such shit she wanted to snip them in half, but Stanley said, No, take the money, *always, MB, take their fucking money!* And they spat at Mary-Beth so many times she and Petra requested a plastic partition, which had been granted a few months prior, though it was only a partial. She felt this now, as four boys in khakis and polos said, *Suck my dick, elf bitch! HAHAHA!* knocking over the energy drink sleigh on their way out the door, the Monster cans rolling, hissing. And this was ten p.m. on a good night.

Margail stepped out from the stockroom behind the cooler glass, pulled white headphones from her ears. Someone fuck with the goddamn sleigh again? She crouched to pick up the cans, which dribbled as she lifted them.

When Tommy sent the Christmas bells jangling, Mary-Beth thought she was dreaming. Or not dreaming, actually losing her mind. The moment her ex-husband walked in, all time collapsed, and while Tommy had never walked through the doors of the North Pole as long as she'd worked there, he did look the same way he'd looked walking through every door, ever, when they were young and crazed for each other. Tommy hadn't aged much at all—a mustache will do that to a person, Mary-Beth knew. He was thinner, and his hairline was bumped just an inch or two further back on his head, but his gingham shirt was the same. The same strawberry blond, the same splotched skin from lifelong psoriasis, which worsened when he drank or when he ate rich, caloric foods or messed with the wrong fiberglass insulation. His skin wasn't as splotchy tonight—he was probably sober or healthy—and Mary-Beth thought: *Of fucking course.* Of course he'd be better now, he'd look better, while I look like me.

Rather than fussing with herself, Mary-Beth felt ashamed of the gas station and its current condition. The snow blankets were mottled gray. The sleigh on its side—Margail bent over, toweling the ground. Mary-Beth hadn't been fulfilling upkeep tasks since Calvin died, and when she slacked, the others did too. Her favorite task had once been teasing out cotton for the centerpiece tree—jeweler's cotton—not the balls sold in bags, but the fluffy, expensive kind beneath a new pair of earrings, a delicate fibrous bounce. But tonight the frost on the windows had the handprints of toddlers, teenagers, adults who'd fingered *954* and *305* and *PEN15* in the white foam.

Mary-Beth wanted Petra there—a true friend, a witness. But she only had twenty-one-year-old Margail Adams, named after Margate, Florida, hair so bleached it frizzed like a layer of freezer burn. She was an exotic dancer down in Hollywood, known best for her cowgirl outfit and striptease to that sad song—*Johnny's daddy's takin' him fishing*—about the girl who'd survived a mugging and a bad life but still dies after all that *for a baby!*

Tommy walked over to Mary-Beth, hands deep in his jean pockets. Until he began talking, Mary-Beth thought it must have been an accident—he must have stopped here to fill up, or to play a round of slots in the casino, not knowing. Maybe he wouldn't even recognize his ex-wife as he said, *Thirty on pump eight, ma'am*, sliding a bill through the scooped silver slot. But instead, Tommy looked right at her and said: MB, come out from behind there, I need to talk to you—like it was the most ordinary thing in the world. Like a thousand years hadn't passed.

I need to talk to you about Cal, about this situation, he went on.

Margail said, I'll give you two some privacy, though Mary-Beth had not asked for it. Margail would use this excuse to step out for a smoke. She flipped a hoodie over her elf cap to protect it from rain.

Mary-Beth stood from her chair and stepped out from behind the register and partition. It was like a silken straight line had pulled her right back to Tommy, no resistance, no questions asked.

And then it was only the two of them, ex–husband and wife—angels from their realms of glory crying over the static stereo—alone.

BIRDIE

THE STREETS OF Capitol Hill were loud loud, blurred with movement and music, terrific neon exhaust. Manholes chattered under tires. Rainbow flags dangled from storefronts. The weather was warmer in Seattle, true summer at last. I walked into the bookstore.

Linzie's book was propped in pyramids on tables all over the shop, hundreds of her eyes multiplied. Skylights beamed columns of light, and the sounds of the registers, the people, caught me not so much in the ears but behind them, a sour twinge that ran down my neck. In my pockets, my fingers bled. I pressed them tight to the fabric to stanch the bleeding.

Downstairs, a single spotlight directed at a wooden lectern onstage, an old Persian rug beneath it, a microphone, a giant poster of the book. Twenty or thirty people already sat in their seats with Linzie's face in their laps. Some flipped through new copies; others had brought their own, fat with colored Post-its, the spines warped. Just like mine.

I had considered writing a letter and handing it to Linzie in the signing line. In this fantasy, she would have to read it aloud to me right then and there, in front of everybody. She wouldn't get to fold it up and save it for later, wouldn't get to throw it away, or hand it to a friend or assistant to ask, *What's it say? Anything I need to know?* In my fantasy she would read it, word by word, right to my face, her body language hopeful at first—maybe she wouldn't recognize me, maybe she'd think, *Cool new fan*—before her mouth would change, her shoulders hunching *Oh*, as she'd struggle through ragged high-pitched breathing and I'd say, *Go on, Linzie, you can read, can't you? You're a famous writer now!* Then everyone behind me would leave.

But I'd settled on a different plan. One so simple I could rehearse it, and I had. There was only one line to deliver. I'd say it as she signed my book, when she'd ask, *And who's this for?* I wanted to see my pen in her hand. I wanted to see her stop, mid-scribble.

Make it out to Jade Suzuki.

Maybe all I was looking for was fear.

I sat fifth row, right side of the stage. She wouldn't see our faces in a room this dark, her fawning fans, grateful and ripened by her mere proximity. Industrial pipes rattled above, and everyone hushed, checking their watches and phones. The woman next to me smelled like medicine—it radiated—a smell you don't forget once you've been near it, through it, once it's scored its work in you, and I felt angry that I would associate that smell with this room, this night. I thought of my father's freckles. Lollipop sponges propped in a glass. *Just one more day*, he'd said, while other people got to keep on living.

A high-bunned bookseller stepped onto the stage, lanyard dangling from his neck and flashing in the light. The man read excerpts of recent *My Turn* reviews; he called the work *groundbreaking, boldly feminist, a timely exploration of consent and media corruption,* then repeated that it was *a privilege* to host Linzie on their stage. He practically whispered, his mouth so close to the mic it all felt very personal, very late-night radio.

Then Linzie walked toward the stage from somewhere behind us. Behind us—she'd been waiting in the back of the room, and I hadn't noticed—my eyes had been so fixed on the stage, on the man. Linzie took the steps and hugged the man talking. I felt terribly lonely.

Linzie looked like she'd gotten her hair done for the occasion. That dyed black color, *beachy waves* that were too tidy. She wore a dark red lipstick and a floral top that showed off thin, pale arms. On the bottom, black tights with sheen to offer the illusion of leather pants; pump heels with multicolored embroidered cats on them, which bothered me—the book had said nothing about cats. In the book she'd loved only Lucky, her rabbit.

I leaned forward, tucked my hair behind my ears. I was close enough to see her hands trembling, and close enough to see that she was familiar with this feeling; she'd learned and practiced tools to calm herself. A portable AC unit blew behind her, and she kept looking back at it, as if it would nip her behind the knees. I watched her steady her palms on the lectern, her fingers tapping in triplets. She took in deep breaths between sentences, and I felt her count before the exhale. I was breathing in time with her.

—I'm just so grateful, she went on. I never could have imagined what would come of me writing down my thoughts. It would have been enough for a single person to have found comfort in my story, but when I look around tonight, wow.

She brought sips of water to her mouth as her voice shook, a plastic bottle that crinkled and popped at the mic. She shifted her weight from foot to foot, rocking in the precise way I knew. Suddenly I did want her to see me. I wanted to see her face disfigure at the maybe of me, a double take—*Birdie? Jade?* Would she know the difference?

She began reading from chapter 1, and those around me mouthed the words of her opening pages, all of it memorized: *Let me tell you a fairy tale, but told in reverse. Picture a swing set, a school bus, a girl surrounded by porcelain dolls on the floor of her princess bedroom, then pause that frame. Hold me there for a moment, before the story goes on.*

The writing was even more hammy aloud, no nuance—her ideas stale and stilted. *I'm not open for love after what I've endured*, she'd cried on national cable, leaving the show, snot streaking gray down to her chin. *I have walls up. I have the whole Hoover Dam up, it feels like, around my heart.*

I sat straighter. Look at my face, I thought, look at me. Crazy. Calvin's defense had called me crazy. Weak. Precocious. Dishonest. Mentally unstable. Attention-seeking. Untrustworthy. Not consistent. Who cares. Others had called me a statistic. A casualty. A learning lesson. An innocence lost. A victim. Victim B. Survivor 2. Jane Doe. Jade Suzuki.

And here Linzie was, under a spotlight, her real name and real life candied by our gaze, our yeses and snaps and *that's so true*s whispered through a Seattle basement, just so she could be cooed at and comfortable. We held her words—dog-eared, highlighted with importance—and she fed off it. Our reverence. Each sentence she read found more sparkle. Linzie paused and closed her eyes—*I was destined for an extraordinary experience*—and the medicine-smelling woman beside me rested the back of her hand to her forehead, feeling things.

At the end of the reading, Linzie said, *Thank you*, so quietly. I felt knocked from my chair by the force with which everyone rose from their seats, balled tissues clutched in hands, cheeks shining in the dark. They said, *Thank YOU*, right back to her, and she kept her head bowed and took it. She extended one hand, palm out, the other a fist at her heart in a gesture I'd never seen before. Something like *go on, please*, and *no, really, you shouldn't*, at the same time.

I looked right at Linzie as everyone clapped. People took photos of her on their phones, and I wished I'd brought my own with me. I'd have done the same. I longed for her to find me. If she said my name, if she requested I stand for my own applause or join her onstage, I'd shake my head no. I'd lean forward to hide my face between my knees. *No, Linzie, stop.*

Then, after a while, I'd do anything.

A blouse lesbian around fifty stepped up onto the stage to join Linzie. She looked pleased to do this, important with a headset and purple-framed glasses as she plucked the microphone and said,

If you'd like your book signed by Miss King, the line begins in the hallway, near the bathrooms. For expediency, Shelby and I'll be taking your names down for inscriptions. Miss King is taking five and then we'll begin.

Thanks, Diane, Linzie said, loud enough to be picked up by the mic. Blouse lesbian Diane gave Linzie a little pat. Then Linzie said, Thank you again, you guys—see you soon! and walked offstage, waving and slumping and lopsided in her heels.

I found a place in line between two groups of friends, all chatting about what they had seen. One group, I assumed, was a Mommy book club, made up of very pretty moms. The group behind me: Seattle hipsters, maybe college students. The hallway sickened everyone's skin with fluorescents, the echoed voices flushed and brash. I longed for the dark promise of the reading room, now maybe thirty feet ahead, as if we had to earn our place back to her.

She's shorter than I imagined, one of the mommies said. And skinny mini!

Jarringly short, another said.

I feel like she's prettier on TV, said another mommy. Weird chin. But her skin looks better now.

I wanted to defend her. *Leave her alone*, I would say. *So what, it's a chin.*

I gripped the book to my chest. Then I pressed the cover against my nose and lips, a comfort, my own breath steaming it. The moment was coming. The moment, and the girl, just around the corner. *It's me*, I would say. I'd stand, looking down at her, slouched in her seat behind her signing table. *I'm not voiceless after all, huh? I'm alive! An actual person!*

Birdie?

The voice came from behind. And then her face. I didn't understand at first, this person saying my name, chest striped with bones and a gummy smile, arms outstretched for a hug. Birdie! These are my friends, the woman said.

Then: Girls, this is my—you know my cousin, Trace, the one I told you about, this is her girlfriend . . . Oh, I'm so sorry, do you prefer partner? This is Trace's domestic partner, Birdie. They stayed with me a few weeks ago. Remember I told you about them?

Havi, I said, hi. My arms hugged back, and my voice lifted to match hers.

Birdie, these are my sisters Agnes and Koyote, with a *K*. We've known each other since U Dub, Havi said.

You can't cut us, said one of the hipsters behind us. We've been waiting.

We're with her, said Havi, pointing to me. She was holding our spot.

Havi and her two friends scooted next to me in line, annoyed at everyone behind us. The hipsters grumbled and one spat, *COOL!* It always surprised me to witness the casualness with which some people cut lines, without pause, without apology or excuse, they just cut in and kept talking, and people like me would always make room for them.

Birdie, aren't you on Whidbey? How'd you get here? Havi asked.

Ferry, then cab, I said.

So independent, Havi said. Do you come in often? Girl, I could have picked you up!

She smiled and spoke more to the wall than to me, and I suddenly felt sorry for her. No, I don't come in often, I said. This is my first time leaving.

And to her friends, Havi said: Birdie's on Whidbey hiding from her own Calvin. She's doing a digital detox, a spirit cleanse. She's been through so much.

It makes sense why you like this book, one of the girls said gently. It must hit close to home. Is it validating? The girl wore slender feather attachments in her hair—violet, plumed stripes.

We book-clubbed the memoir, the other girl—Koyote—said. That's when Hav told us.

My body shook. Is it cold in here? I asked. My knees ached. I wanted to sit down.

Crazy how pervasive it is, said Agnes. It's, like, one in three women, and that's just those who report—

The women continued explaining sexual assault to me as the line inched forward. Bookstore staff with walkies directed us along, but they seemed suddenly very busy in their headsets. Distracted, uninterested in us, their eyes jotting left and right on the ground, following whatever serious thing they were hearing. The Moms ahead of us stepped to the side to see how much further we had to go. I checked my watch—this was longer than *taking five*.

Havi held two copies of *My Turn* in her hand, and her tote bag looked packed full. I could see the square outlines in the thin, cream fabric. For the rest of our book club, she said. Then she said: Hey, we should totally take a selfie and text it to Trace. She'd be so disoriented.

No, don't, I look like total shit, I said.

Is *disoriented* a bad word to say? Havi asked. Be honest. I'm not great at all the PC terms—

The line did not move forward. I continued to swat away the selfie; Trace couldn't know. It's part of my victim protection plan, I said, covering my face with my forearm. I kept my hands balled, fingers tucked as ever.

LADIES AND GENTLEMEN, one of the walkie guys said. He wore a denim jacket and a lanyard, tight army green pants, dirty All Stars. He projected in a way I found incredibly official. We're sorry for the wait, he said, and sorry to let you down, ladies, but the signing is canceled! I'm so sorry. Please go ahead and browse upstairs.

The whole line groaned in *what*s and *are you kidding*s. Someone said: We've been waiting thirty minutes, and another: We're missing our dinner reservations, you've got to be joking. Another screamed, *Refund!* though the event had been free.

Nobody moved from the line.

Seriously, you can all go home, said Walkie-Talkie. There are books for sale at the signing desk, and upstairs at the register. Thank you and have a good night.

He clapped once, bowed his head, and walked away.

I held the book tighter to my chest. My heart beat into it. How far could she be?

Should we stay? I asked.

Oh my god, mystery solved, said Agnes. She stood with her mouth open, lip gloss lit by her phone as her thumb dragged up up up on her screen. She faced the screen to us but only for a second; I couldn't make out any of the words. Fuuuuuck me, she said. Then she laughed.

Linzie tweeted, Havi said, reading something on her own screen. So, because Calvin . . . book Calvin . . . I guess Calvin, the guy, was found dead.

Oh my god, said the girls.

What? I said.

Dead, said the rest of the line. Phones lighting up. All over the news. More whispering. *That's so crazy.* Dead! Echoed the line. A few more people laughed.

She's asking for privacy.

I mean, this is good, right?

Bye, Felicia!

I would have killed myself, too.

Oh, for, like, sure.

Good riddance, fucking loser.

What's his last name? I want to see.

Look, said Havi, holding up her phone again. Linzie says she'll sign stickers or something for everyone at the reading, bookplates. Bookplates?

Wow, said Koyote. I mean, she really didn't have to do that.

How did he die? I asked. Does it say? I reached for Havi's phone, but she caught me by the wrist. Her hand was damp and bony. Spiritual cleanse, she said, no peeking.

This is probably really triggering for her, one of them said.

After a moment, I realized she was talking about me.

II

LINZIE

ARE YOU READY for this? Yale asked. After calling off the signing, he'd escorted Linzie up the stairs and out of Elliott Bay Books, and now they stood on Tenth Avenue, eight thirty, Linzie shivering in her Victoria's Secret hoodie, her face in the window display behind her.

Yale said: Actually, let's walk. OK? Hello?

OK, Linzie said.

Yale linked arms with her. He smelled expensive. He walked fast. Yale, Linzie's manager—her *handler*, he sometimes joked—giddy like she'd never seen him, and maybe a little affectionate in this moment, too. Up the pace a little? he said, but Linzie's flats were in her suitcase. Her ankles quaked coltishly in new pumps, her calves sore. Yale walked her to the corner of East Pine, near a skate park. Then he walked her one more block, just in case. Finally, he stopped, held his phone in front of her, and shook it like a baby toy.

Tweeted something for you, he said. Wanna know what?

Linzie did not want to be here, outside, in the seventy-degree Seattle cold. Her fans were still waiting back at the bookstore, and she worried they'd never forgive her.

Look at me, Yale said. I want you to look right at me when I tell you this.

Linzie looked at him. He was handsome, mature for thirty. His dark stubble grew higher on the left side of his face than the right—it made his cheeks an almost blue. Cars honked and the wind spun over a seltzer can. The setting sun winked between buildings, pushed them apart.

Actually, no, wait, I want you to guess, Yale said.

All her life, Linzie had hated when somebody told her to *guess*. She guessed stupid things, things like asteroids or celebrity deaths or presidential abductions, every time. Her guesses were never hopeful. She never knew real current events or the punch lines of jokes or where a conversation was going. So she shrugged, here on the street with Yale, sighed at her feet, and said: I don't know, why don't you just tell me.

Calvin's gone—Yale said—out of the picture. Yale smiled a smile Linzie had never seen on him, nose scrunched up like a kid, upper lip bulky, like food or chew were nestled there.

What do you mean by that? she said.

Found dead outside Pedoville, Yale said. Your dad called while you were reading. Heard it on police dispatch and had to reroute some of his fleet yesterday. They found a body. Turns out the body was Calvin's.

My *dad* knows? Linzie said. She felt a lurch. She wanted to take off her shoes.

Now everyone knows, Yale said. Because you just tweeted it.

Yale did not stop smiling his weird smile. His teeth were square and a pale yellow, like each had pierced a perfect kernel of corn. It looked now as though he might . . . cry? Maybe it was the wind. Maybe he was allergic to something. Linzie paid attention to her own face and realized her mouth was tense, molars locked, that phantom-pinched lift of her cheeks—she was smiling back at him, a habit. She let that smile go. *That kind of person*, Yale had said early on, *no one cares if they live or die, would you?*

No, Linzie had said.

Did I do this? Linzie asked now. Like, do you think—

He killed himself, 'cause of you?

Or, you know, the book?

If he did, good, Yale said. You're not responsible for what he did. But I doubt it; narcissists don't kill themselves.

Punkish looking people in patchworked denim brushed past them on the sidewalk. They made Linzie nervous. No one dressed like that in Florida. Linzie clasped and squeezed her hands in the front kangaroo pocket of her hoodie as the sun stretched their shadows into bowling pins. Linzie didn't know Seattle—before this book tour, she'd only ever left Broward County once, and that was for *The Dating Show*. She looked around. She wasn't sure if she liked this place.

Your dad thinks it was a car wreck, Yale said. All the cane loads on his fleet moved down to Belle Glade. Road's still blocked.

Why do you think Calvin's a narcissist?

I know him, Linz, Yale said. Linz, look at me.

Linzie stared at him, tried not to blink. This, a handy trick she'd learned on *The Dating Show*; she could make her eyes well, drop tears after a few seconds of stunned dramatics. *Show me grateful. Show me feeling.* Maybe then Yale would quit talking.

I *know* him, Yale said, maybe better than you do. And you know I'm an emotional guy, but I don't get emotional when it comes to things like this. People die every day. Good people. I almost died, remember—as a *kid*. You think *kids* deserve to die? So what if he died, Linz—he ruined *kids*. He nearly ruined *you*. He shit away his one precious life, so figure it that way. They call this a *comeuppance*. Add that to your word list.

You've never even met him, Linzie said. She sucked her cheek in, bit down the skin. That perfect worm of swelling. Linzie thought of Calvin, of the little slivers she still had of him, somewhere in her mind. She thought about who he was all those years ago—his long and animated fingers, his underbite, a few words she could still hear in his voice, *brave girl*, the way he knew interesting facts about planets, lizards, shells. She could still locate that person. He was a real person, despite all the facts, the transcripts, the lawyers and gavel slams that had followed. Despite the way he had scared her.

Why'd you have to cancel the signing? Linzie asked. Everyone's going to hate me.

No time to waste with something like this, Yale said, typing on his phone. He looked up to the sky; it was beginning to rain. Seattle for you, Yale said. Shake it off.

Linzie, it turns out, could not shake any of it off. In the hours that followed, she could not.

They picked up their bags from the hotel, then headed to the airport for a red-eye to Florida. Yale stared at his cell the whole Uber drive (that smile!) like he'd won something. In the airport security line, without his phone, belt, or shoes, Linzie imagined him as a boy in the hospital, the dying boy he'd constantly reminded her he once was. She tried to picture him scared and hollowed out, dragging around an IV pole in white socks, a room of pretty nurses. It was hard to imagine, though not impossible.

As they sat at their gate, the tweets came. Then news outlets picked up the story, Linzie's face at the center of them all. Yale scanned the articles, made her look at every one—

Child Molester and Subject of Bestseller Found Dead

Dating Show Sweetheart Called Him Out—Then He Died

Convicted Felon Known for Raping TV Queen as a Girl Dies.

Linzie did not understand these headlines, especially that last one. She read it over and over, picturing a little girl dying. The articles were unclear—*The trouble doesn't end for Linzie!* And *Trouble finally ends for reality show star*, so which was it? No one cited a cause of death. Only that the death of Calvin Boyer was confirmed by *several inside sources*, and one of those sources was her.

The airplane took off. Yale sat beside her in the window seat, peaceful on his plane pills, and once he slid his headphones and sleep mask on, Linzie was free. She twirled every strand of hair around her pointer finger, tight enough for the throb, then pulled. She sprinkled the strands on the airplane floor, counting them.

Linzie loved to count. She breathed. She gripped the armrest with her right hand while the other one worked. She wondered if anyone on the plane recognized her, if anyone wanted to hurt her.

Maybe Linzie really was a good-for-nothing low-life scum-dumb-bitch of a person. She yanked more hair, breathed, considered. She'd made a spectacle of Calvin, no longer a life on earth. She had earned *money* in doing that—a few thousand dollars so far—and with the money she'd bought her rabbit, Lucky, a new flip-board for treats. She'd bought organic popcorn from Publix, and a brand-name perfume that looked like an evil apple. Now she knew all of it was at the expense of a life. A whole life that had once belonged to a world. To a family. Calvin had once had friends, probably more friends than Linzie had ever had. She thought of Mr. Boyer, Calvin's dad—he was so nice. He'd remembered their names on the school bus, so attentive. She remembered Mary-Beth, who was not as nice, at least not in the courtroom (*Little cunt!* she'd screamed at Linzie), but she was still a mom. A mom who'd never abandoned her kid like Linzie's mom had, who'd never tied off her bicep and swallowed into a thousand oblivions.

Linzie fell asleep in her seat, scalp raw and alive in the spots she knew how to cover. In the morning, as the sun rose over her familiar ocean, the plane thunked down. She and Yale walked through the Fort Lauderdale airport together and then outside, Linzie only speaking down or inside of her hoodie, embarrassed of her breath.

Get that sweatshirt out of your mouth, Yale said. You look like a baby.

She didn't want to see him. But then there he was, her father, Doug, at the airport pickup median. But instead of angry—for Doug was always angry—he climbed out of their shared Toyota without his cane and pulled with him several pink and purple balloons. Old-school balloons, powdery and oval and darker at the knot, but still—they were beautiful. Linzie and Yale approached him, and Doug said, Come over here, my girl.

Linzie stepped off the curb and walked toward him, toward his outstretched arms in the humid morning air. She didn't know why, but she felt like someone might shoot her dead in this moment, maybe splay her clean in half with a bow and arrow—it was so surreal—Doug's hands holding those balloon ribbons, the pride in his face like a wax double. He hugged her.

Motherfucker's dead, he said into Linzie's hair. You know how good this is for business?

Doug squeezed. Linzie did not say anything, didn't even consider it. Over his shoulder, Linzie watched as two teenage girls snapped photos of her on their cell phones. They snickered, long rhinestoned nails covering their mouths, but not enough to cover *That's her, that's definitely totally her.*

Linzie noticed that feeling in her face. She was doing the smile again.

MARY-BETH

IT'S THE GIRLFRIEND, Tommy said. I think who did it is the girlfriend. Ching Chong's special friend, Tracey. You know what Chong's grown up into? I've been keeping tabs.

Tommy rested his big hands on the cashier's counter of the North Pole, leaning over it as if out of breath, though he seemed calm. Too calm. No ring on his fingers—Mary-Beth checked that first. No paint on his hands, either. Tommy's life had changed since he was married to her; she knew it. He didn't drive a bus anymore, but he still ground a minty toothpick between his front teeth, working it flat.

I don't know about her, Mary-Beth said. She stood next to him, in front of the partition. Great if she's a little faggot now. I don't occupy myself with her whereabouts or whatsabouts anymore. Who cares about her? She's pathological. The courts knew that, and I've known that since before you knew that, Tommy. You're the one who believed her, right? Believed Cal would have done those things. I knew he wouldn't've done those things, but you had all your doubts. That girl's mental, always been fussy.

MB, she's back. She's involved, Tommy said. Doesn't matter what Cal did or didn't do. She and her friend. Maybe she made her friend do this. You've got to listen to me now. I want to make things right. I've got the intel, woman.

There was a twinkling left in Tommy. That's why the fact of him hurt. His skin, something man about it still. Mary-Beth knew even without touching. Mary-Beth's skin had the quality of the tangerines she bought in the bulk netted bags from Winn-Dixie, the last fruits she could never eat fast enough, tiny, deflated footballs.

Cal knew this was coming, Tommy said, don't you think?

Previously, Mary-Beth did not think that. But now she considered the notes from Cal's room, the notes currently stuffed somewhere in those bags in her Mercury. She'd kept the sunshade propped in the windshield for privacy, even though it was night, and her parking spot was behind the station. Those names in his handwriting, the book—what did it all mean? The Polaroid.

I've talked to the guys on the case—Tommy said—*a lot*. All anyone cares about is the King girl, but that's just dazzle camouflage. King's got nothing to do with this—no, this is Chong and the girlfriend. The guys are keeping me updated with forensics and all, whatever they find. Tommy tapped his front jean pocket and Mary-Beth knew—that's where his phone lived. He didn't carry one back when they were married.

Guys on the case—of course they'd be updating Tommy. The father. Man of the house—what house? Mary-Beth hadn't heard from anyone, not once. Hearing Tommy talk so serious, talking *forensics*, made Mary-Beth think of when she used to ride Tommy's face. A mustache ride, they'd called it, in love. Glistening, happy face. She couldn't take this same face seriously.

Our boy's livestock to those assholes, Tom. Our boy's what they grind up for chum.

Police have changed, MB, he said. They're not all un-noble. A human life's a human life.

I was there, at the scene of the crime, Mary-Beth said. Glass all over the road like sprinkles, and they collected it. Every piece. Probably they're matching it to make and models—I think it's a big car, just my two cents, but nobody's asked me. Also, Chong's name is Birdie Chang, which you'd know if you'd paid attention. And she doesn't even live here. You saying she came down here?

Birdie didn't, Tracey did, he said. You've got to listen, woman.

How would you know all this? Mary-Beth asked.

Folks saw her, said Tommy. Near Gateway, at that bar right on Lake O, the Palmyra, you know it? Hours before Cal, you know—they saw Tracey. She's been around's what I'm saying. You don't *not* notice someone who looks the way she does, dressed like a little mister.

All these years, Mary-Beth had rehearsed what she'd say to her ex-husband if given the chance. She'd practiced not one but several speeches before falling asleep, and in the shower on chirping dim mornings as she drove to work—music or no music, radio or not—she could still work through that speech. It went something like, *Thomas Boyer, when we wed in Key Largo, you vowed sickness and in health. When we talked deep about the future, you spoke of wanting a family, and when we found out we were having a boy, you remember what you said? First, you cried. A sniveling, silly cry, reflecting on all the yada yada problems you had with your old man, and with your brothers, you came from a family of boys, yada yada, and this was your chance to fix that past up, you wouldn't beat or blame your boy for anything, REMEMBER! You wouldn't belittle or ask him to be anything other than what he was, you said he was a sign, a gift, your destiny, and for that, do you remember what we did? We named our son after your shitbag daddy due to all that syrupy spiritual thinking. And then you left. It doesn't matter what came between as much as it matters that you left. Your hospital gown had tiny blue flowers on it when you held our son, your whole hand so much bigger than his head. You looked like a man in love before they took him away to that get-better box. Then you said he's so beautiful, sweeter than a Penn Dutch ham, I don't want to sleep ever again that's how much I want to keep looking at him, and what you didn't say is that love of yours had conditions. Or that you would become the same boring-ass daddy you yourself hated, and your son would eventually hate you, too. When the going gets tough, the Boyers get going!*

Mary-Beth had been fine about Tommy's erectile problems, his fungus-spotted feet and toenails like pistachio shells that nicked her calves under the covers—plus, the way his temper went crazy at the worst times. She forgave it all. But the leaving, she couldn't forgive. Not ever.

Now Tommy said, I just wanted you to know that I sometimes visited with Cal, in case he never told you.

Two cars were outside at the pumps, R&B rumbling a bass. Out the door, through the sprayed-on snow, Mary-Beth watched Margail chat up one of the drivers, leaning over to his face through the rolled-down car window. The driver pinched her rubber elf ear, and Margail's body bounced with laughter.

Mary-Beth thought about giving her speech, wondered how she could hurt Tommy most, what she could possibly say back to him—but the speech seemed irrelevant now, dated. She could tell him how she and Cal had laughed at him all those years, when they'd get liquored up enough to bring his name into the conversation cautiously, then hugely. But she said nothing as Tommy went on and on, still not looking at her, going off about signs and signals. Was he nuts? He talked about a pool hall—a what? They'd never gone to a pool hall together. I don't follow anything you're saying, Mary-Beth said. Not following one bit.

On the phone, Tommy said, Cal told me on the phone, days before it happened, about those local folks hanging at the Palmyra—the place where the girlfriend was seen. It's a bar and a pool hall. Lavender and the Vicodin guy, what's his face? Harrison? You know people around there with those Crayola names. Police haven't questioned anyone, so I took it on myself, met up with Harrison, showed him a picture of Tracey from the internet. He knew her right away. He said she probably did it.

Mary-Beth felt the cool, glowing stab of something far sharper than Calvin's body in those bloody frames. The much more painful image: Tommy on the phone. Calvin holding Tommy against his ear, speaking to him. Confiding in him. A *father*. Tommy hearing about, knowing about, Lavender and Harrison and Calvin's daily life. Mary-Beth's legs went tingly—the phone, that was for her and

Calvin. The phone, where so many of their days and memories and jokes had lived, where their *love* had lived. Tommy had been on the other end, too, and Calvin had lied to her about that. She breathed in. She couldn't show that lie on her face, couldn't let any feeling travel up or out of her. She was a woman.

Margail walked back inside, the bell ding-donging. She had a way of breathing with her mouth hung open that killed Mary-Beth. Her bottom lip pink with spit, tongue against her teeth. Mary-Beth wanted to take that shiny lip to a cutting board and go at it with a knife. Tommy kept talking at her, though he paused to look at Margail's tits as she walked past, flipping back her hood, then pulling up her elf corset. That didn't help.

When's the last time you cleaned up in here? Mary-Beth asked her. Margail looked around at no one, as if Mary-Beth meant someone else.

Me? she said, finger at her chest. MB, that's all you. I don't mess with your snow style.

Mary-Beth knew that. She didn't know why she'd asked such a question. She supposed she did it so Tommy might think she'd earned some sort of authority here, that she could ask questions like this of other people, people like dumb bitch Margail.

Harrison can't be trusted, Mary-Beth said. Probably in it for the media. All the attention.

Harrison's telling the truth, Tommy said. We speak the same language.

And what language is that? Mary-Beth said.

She couldn't show him any of it. All the not knowing. She'd never heard of a Harrison or Lavender—she was bluffing. She'd heard of the Palmyra bar, but she'd never been. There was Calvin owning the book, writing those notes, and now this? Tommy the deadbeat. Tommy the traitor. There was nothing Cal didn't know about Mary-Beth except for maybe how Mary-Beth applied makeup, the specific products and brush strokes. Cal even knew about her menstrual cycle. He knew that pads gave her a rash sometimes, but still, he'd stolen extras from the shelter when she'd needed them before her blood stopped.

Tommy kept on talking. Face-to-face like this, Mary-Beth thought of their wedding day again, on the beach—she was twenty years old, once. A tie-dyed purple dress, Mary-Beth had felt pretty for a single day. Their sterling silver rings cupped in a seashell she'd bought from Shell Man on their drive down. Tommy, in his Hawaiian button-down and khakis. He didn't dress up. He never would. In fact, she felt to this day, if he wore a tie or suit, it would be the deepest deception. There was knowing someone and then there was knowing someone. The first kind was knowing what someone tended to do. The second more intimate knowing: what someone would never do.

BIRDIE

HAVI AND HER friends walked me to the Unicorn bar after Linzie's reading. I barely remember the walk. Barely remember the ask, or the yes, or the leaving. I do remember it rained. My hair twisted in cold, wet ropes in our window booth beneath an air vent. Heads were mounted everywhere. Animals, beautiful animals, cheetahs and antelopes and deer emerging from the candy-colored walls like they were charging through to meet me. One doe wore a red ribbon around its lovely dead neck.

The booth pleather snapped beneath our legs. Havi to my left, Agnes and Koyote across—the door ahead of me, always in view. I leaned against the cool window painted in neon zebra stripes, watched people walk by as if through a rib cage.

A waitress with electric blue mascara and little hooped piercings took our order. I pointed to something on the menu. When my drink arrived, it was cloudy peach, practically glowing. *Your Unicorn Jizz*, the blue mascara person said, wearied at this routine, and the girls laughed at the name. They scrolled their phones and eventually said, *Oh, car accident.*

He died in a car accident.

My gut cramped with disappointment. I wanted to press them for more; I needed details to believe it—what kind of accident? Where, and exactly when? Was anyone else hurt? I knew this: every moment of who I was the night Calvin died could matter. If the accident was self-inflicted, or if there was some kind of foul play, I'd be yanked right into this—it would be me, of course, the motive, the vendetta, the scheming embittered *alleged victim* who'd pushed him over the edge, me—and I would need to retrace the evening, provide proof and alibi, nothing off. I needed to be a girl having fun at a bar.

Agnes and Koyote posed for selfies with their drinks clinked. Agnes stuck out her perfect pink tongue as if licking her glass; Koyote tilted her head, parted her lips contemplatively, her eyes cast down at Agnes's chest. They didn't seem embarrassed. The phone kept flashing and flashing as they tried again, *no, come on, one more*, and people looked over quick in that theater stare that said *stop*. I carried this embarrassment alone.

UNICORN JIZZ! said Havi. She pointed to my glass and said, That one's my favorite. Then, close to my ear: I really love that one, I usually get that one. Tonight, I got Cereal Killer. She spelled it out so I would understand.

The girls now pointed their cell cameras at me and Havi, who rested her chin on my shoulder with an unearned, trustful weight. Documenting a verrrrry weird night, Agnes said. I held my drink up to cover my face. They all laughed some more—*Oh my god, stop, you're so pretty!*—and eventually, I relented, smiled. Maybe an alibi would be good. If necessary. Can you not post these? I asked. Just send them to me? More flashes.

A chair skidded across the floor, screeching against the wood. My body winced at it. I imagined a circle of cop cars surrounding the Unicorn bar, blue and red lights whirling through the windows, every patron's face a sudden hologram. Maybe they'd cuff me, an elbow pressing my cheek to the table, all their weight to keep me contained.

Cops had busted into my parents' restaurant once, not to eat (though they did frequent the place to eat; chewy and gruff, Pringles chicken, silverware only) but to barge mean and sweating through the dining room like the place was theirs. I thought they were coming for my father, thought maybe they'd come to drag him back to Chengdu for incorrect or forged paperwork—I was always afraid of that then. I didn't yet understand what cops were supposed to do, or who they were, I was only taught to fear them and to flatter them.

The cops ran to the bathroom of Hei Baby and dragged three children—two boys and a girl—out by their t-shirts and ears. *Ears*—that was my mother's flourish. I didn't remember that, but she'd repeated it always, to prove her allyship: *They dragged out those poor African American kids by the ears.* The children yowled and kicked their grassy sneakers, and I remember the skin of the girl's stomach, the bulbous knot of her outie bellybutton as the t-shirt fabric stretched from the cop's fist, covering her face. The chandeliers were dim, and the cop wore a black wedding band on that fisted hand. The diners spun in their upholstered seats to watch, and one cop came back after the great drag to tell my father the kids had run from foster care and that was why the drama, *sorry.* Those children were my age; I never found out who reported them. I wonder how they'd tell this story now.

Agnes was talking about Seattle summers, how they'd trick anyone into relocating. Don't you want to move here, Birdie? she said. That's how Seattle gets you.

Not really, I said.

So what's Whidbey *actually* about? she said. Hav told us snippets, but that's such a crazy place to go alone.

I'm doing nothing there, I said. Striving for nothingness is the point.

I've read books about that, Agnes said. That's goals.

Is that a trauma response for the thing you went through? Koyote asked. If so, you should investigate low-dose ketamine. It sounds like you might be engaging in avoidant behavior. Koyote slid her lower lip back and forth on the rim of her glass as she watched me, a tic.

I think it's cool, Havi said. She's Eat, Pray, Loving but instead of Italy, Whidbey.

I'm surprised you guys are still on the East Coast, Koyote said. Seattle's always been ahead, an extremely accepting city. I feel accepted here for exactly who I am. She nodded slowly. Her wooden earrings swung.

What do you mean? I asked, after nobody said anything. *Who you are?* Because of your name?

All three women looked at me as if my question were very rude.

Well, I'm queer, said Koyote. Obviously. But in Seattle you can love anyone for the person they are, regardless of parts. Love is love.

I didn't know why this should be obvious to me. There would always be Koyotes—white women in hand-carved earrings who didn't feel valued enough, who made it a point to out themselves to me, to say things like *I'm very queer, OBVIOUSLY*, that love is love is love, why-don't-you-see-me neediness. *In Seattle, you can love anyone, regardless of parts.* Print it on a postcard. The Koyotes repeated the paint-by-number platitudes and fortune-cookie phrases assigned to them by an online shaman, which would, at last, offer to explain who they were, effortlessly. And then it's the platitude they cling to, never a question but the Answer, never the work but the moon finding Neptune or a dragonfly symbolizing hope; with every repetition, further self-confirmation, and with that confirmation, you're the girl who cuts the line, who uses the flash in a crowded room.

Don't tell me you're biphobic, Koyote said. It's 2013.

I didn't answer. More people entered the bar and the girls moved on.

They asked me if I used Korean skin care, which was their way, I knew, of asking if I was Korean. I don't use Korean skin care, I said.

Chinese skin care, then?

Just regular skin care, I said. Bar soap. Basic moisturizer.

They waited. Havi said, I've been really, really into those sheet masks Linzie recommended. It was in *Teen Vogue*, I think.

Sometimes I use a milk cleanser, I said.

This answer pleased them enormously. Koyote nodded her head

and snapped her fingers close to my face, her elbow on the table. Knew there was something milky in there, she said. She drank from her neon drink and bit at the straw until it whitened at the tip.

Botox? Agnes asked. Fillers? Or is that seriously just your face?

None yet, I said. I wasn't against it.

Agnes lifted her eyebrows three times quick, to show me the way her skin wrinkled. Me neither, she said. Look, look at my head. She kept pumping her brows, the skin pleating, a hamburger squeezed. Prove me yours, she said.

My forehead?

Yeah, prove me yours.

I lifted my eyebrows. Left then the right. I was always able to do this, back and forth—Bogart. I said, Speaking of proof, do they know who caused the accident yet? With Linzie's guy? I forgot his name, I said.

Damn, said Koyote, looking at me. It's true. She proved it. No Botox.

What would be waiting on my phone when I eventually had to turn it back on? Would Rich have found me, called me, if he'd done it? Would the police have called, or one of my lawyers? My mother? All of it, darkly closed in that desk drawer.

I have an interesting history with my forehead, said Havi. I could tell she wanted someone to tell her to go on, could tell she'd been quietly rehearsing this history of her forehead so that we all might fall in love with her a little, swept under the spell of girl-on-girl intimacy, the quiet negotiations of friendship. No one spoke.

What did you mean before, about my name, Birdie? said Koyote. Do you not like my name? Or do you think it's not real?

Is it? I asked.

Is yours? she said. We're both animal names. Why's mine different? It's been bothering me . . . I want to know what you meant about my name. Coyotes are my spirit animal. Do you mean to say your name assigned at birth is the only name you should keep? Like that's your most authentic self, or—?

Say more about your forehead, I said to Havi, I'm curious.

Koyote stayed locked on me. Agnes opened her phone and started scrolling.

What are they saying online? I asked. Has Linzie said more?

Oh, you're, like, *really* invested, Agnes said. Remember the episode, did you see the one where Linzie said her life was doomed, that she once dreamed Marilyn Monroe came to her—

OK, Havi said. So, when I was a kid, I had this birthmark in the center of my forehead. People used to say all sorts of racist shit to me about it, like I looked Indian or something—you know how they wear the bindi things, how Gwen Stefani started—anyway, people, or I guess just kids my age, made all these jokes because it was right smack in the center, this purplish brown blob, I'm serious, don't laugh—

As Havi spoke, she met all our eyes for evenly distributed eye contact, about three seconds per person, practiced.

Havi said: So anyway, I hated the birthmark, but my mom . . . Trace's aunt Faye . . . said no way could I remove it until I turned thirteen. That's so Florida, right? Birdie tell them, right? Birdie's from Florida, too.

That's so Florida, I confirmed.

Everyone in Florida got surgery at, like, thirteen. So anyway, there was this restaurant at the mall called Stir Crazy, and you lined up at a long window, and a bunch of Asian hibachi chefs would stir fry your food all theatric and crazy—stir CRAZY. You brought them a bowl of raw food and slid it under the window, then kind of watched them cook your food for you and then the chef serves it back. There were these little circle cutouts in the window, like the size of a CD, can you believe people don't even know what CDs are anymore? That's how big the cutouts were, like CDs. So one day this chef was making my stir crazy bowl, and I used so much extra sauce that day, not just one ladle like you're supposed to but maybe three ladles—teriyaki, peanut, and kung pao. That's what I chose. And I say that because when the chef tossed the wok either some of that sauce or hot grease or a spark from the stove flew out that circle window and burned me in the head.

Did you press charges against the hibachi chef? Agnes said.

No, Havi said. But it was a second-degree burn in the exact spot my birthmark was, so my mom, Trace's aunt Faye, let me get it removed after that. And *no one* at school believed this story about the spark from the wok—I'm still not sure what it was, but I mention the extra sauce because sometimes I think that was actually what happened, like actually it was my fault because I was greedy—but everyone thought I made the whole thing up just to get the stupid birthmark removed. But I can tell this whole story TO THIS DAY with such detail, and how would I do that if I lied? Stir Crazy! I swear, for years I thought of the hibachi spark like it was Hashem, like God knew how much I hated being different and so the spark took it away. It made me serious about my faith for a while, believe it or not. I'm less serious now, though I would say I'm still pretty spiritual. So I've gotten Botox only a few times, and this tiny scar, and that's what came up for me about my forehead while you were talking.

I looked out my narrow strip of window as the girls asked polite follow-up questions. Outside, a world without Calvin, drained of him. The lack of him. And I had wanted it. I'd asked for it, even. I'd dreamed this before, as many times as I'd dreamed of him finding me, or of his bedroom in that UV light—I'd dreamed and yes, wished and wanted him dead. I'd always be guilty of that. But was wanting so bad? Thinking, without doing? Often I imagined waking one morning outside the umbra of him, of what he did, the sun shining on my sheets and skin, my mind finally at rest, muscles relaxed, appetite endless. What would that warmth feel like? Now, for the first time since I was nine years old, I would live a night without him.

Thank you for sharing that, Hav, said Agnes. Thank you for trusting us. I could tell her words were not genuine. That she merely knew the right words to say, but maybe Havi did this a lot—*confessed*—and maybe her friends had all heard the hibachi story before, or the bleaker possibility, maybe they really didn't care.

I gulped from my drink. All sugar and sour, an ache in my cheeks. Now that I was used to it, I wanted another. The wind picked up outside, traffic lights swinging low like a great charm bracelet. Colors all looked different now, without Calvin. Bitingly saturated, magnified like dot candy where raindrops clung to the window glass. Calvin's voice would never be in any room I'd enter again. His name would never be in my inbox; his face would never again turn to see me in a courtroom. And like that, my fear was no longer his arrival. It was what would replace him.

LINZIE

The day I received the call from The Dating Show—*July 22, 2010—I was in an airport. The phone buzzed in my pocket, an unknown number, and by intuition alone, I knew to pick up. Ecstatic, I looked to everyone else sitting at gate 5C to Buffalo, wishing I could tell them the news: my life was about to change, and they were all my fortunate witnesses. I knew I would soon become recognizable, familiar to these small-town people in their pilled sweaters and frizzy hair. Soon, they would adore me. Look up to me. No one would have believed me in that moment, but I had the oracular tingle. I already—*

—But none of that is accurate, Linzie said to Yale. This, the first time they met.

Linzie said, That doesn't even follow what I told the cameras before, which wasn't true either. The producers told me to embellish.

Continuity is the word you're looking for, Yale said, typing fast at his desktop. This airport scene is gold. Airports are everything. Transition, interstitial spaces, movement. Everyone's in love at an airport—this is where you'll get the call. Yale hitched back in his office chair, stared at the ceiling, then closed his eyes. He seesawed a heavy-looking pen between his fingers, thinking. Then he got back to typing.

Yeah, *continuity*, said Linzie, nodding hard, showing Yale she knew what he meant. She knew what he meant! *Continuity* sounds like *continuous*, and she knew that second word, it made sense. In the course of their relationship, Yale would continue pointing out things she didn't know, words and facts like the way adrenal glands and astrology worked, stock markets too, and some French proverbs and competitive sports terminologies. But it wasn't that Linzie didn't know things. She just didn't know them *yet*. She wanted to be as smart as Yale.

Here's the truth. Or multiple truths. There will be many.

The day Linzie received the email from *The Dating Show*—July 22, 2010—she hadn't even known she'd applied. She thought, at first, it was a mistake. Second, a sick joke. They'd used her full name—Linzie Gwendolyn King—with three exclamation marks. They'd also attached a questionnaire and legal forms she was supposed to complete, to secure her *Dating Show* candidacy.

Later, she'd find proof: the email was for real. An attached file contained a copy of the completed application with Linzie's sexiest personal photos already in their possession. Linzie in stringy bathing suits, tan lines a gradation on her ass in the bathroom mirror. She looked good in the photos, enigmatic and blurred, though not entirely like herself. She'd never sent those photos to anyone.

Linzie received the email on her lunch break from working the makeup counter at the mall. This is not actually true, but she'd tell it that way later. She'd actually checked her phone *while working* the makeup counter at the mall—she always snuck glances between customers, and sometimes while working with customers—*so sorry, this is important*—the phone a constant, comforting weight in the front pocket of her black apron.

To her boss at the makeup counter, it was *definitely* lunch break. Linzie sitting at the food court under the skylights, Panda Delight chicken a glossy, syrupy brown in the glittering Styrofoam. The email lighting up her screen.

To the press, local media magazines, and even a national publication or two (!!!), she wasn't eating—how gauche—but at a wedding in Palm Beach, because *The Dating Show* did not, eventually, want her to be a *girl who worked at a makeup counter at the mall*, they'd wanted her to be a *Bridal Beautician*, which was something Linzie had dreamed of becoming, though she wasn't there yet; she was only OK at makeup, actually.

In every version of the story, Linzie used her signature eyedrop look, meaning *a quick flash of widening your eyes and lifting your eyebrows, as if applying an eyedrop* (that's how it would be described in *My Turn*). She'd make her eyes big and soft and dazzled as she told the story, again and then again. And in each telling, no matter who she'd tell it to, she'd use the same term: *totally life-changing*.

And then there was the truth: Linzie was working the makeup counter on a Monday morning. She was on her period, she remembers that—dizzy, crotch throbbing, Midol forgotten again (Linzie was forgetful, though she would never have included that on her application if she'd actually filled one out). Then Bonnie came in, a regular, who liked to get glammed before her retirement community's afternoon bingo. As Linzie pulled Bonnie's shade of concealer from her front pocket, she refreshed her inbox. She had been expecting a different email—a Talbot's discount code—but she read *Dear Linzie Gwendolyn King*. She skimmed it once, fast, then X'd it out.

Continuity doesn't matter here, Yale said from behind his desk. Because we're breaking the new story, the true story. It's only the *last* story that sets the record, and you deserve at least that. Yale stood, hands in his back pockets—or were they tucked into the back of his jeans?—and stretched his body, flat stomach protruding in a child's performance of pregnancy. And even in this pose, chin down with contemplation and tripling with skin, he was secure, he was handsome and wise, he was a fucking pro.

Yale Gutterman, *Story Doctor and Ghost Writer*, was the best of the best. That's how he'd described himself in the Facebook ad Linzie's father had found. *The Dating Show* had contractually blocked Linzie from accepting their partnership book offers, so then there was Audrey, a nasally cold-calling self-proclaimed *literary agent* on the phone—and there was Audrey's request: *Pages. Let's see some sample pages. Then we can try for a deal. The market is ripe for this right now, not the molesting so much but the allegations against the show, the inside scoop. This could be* big money.

Yale was a writer. *The* writer Doug had found. He'd sold *five* self-help books on Amazon, though Linzie hadn't read them. Yale's Wynwood office was white with books framing the wall behind him—Kerouac, Salinger, Hemingway, Wilde. Linzie wanted to pretend this was Yale's office for his writing—*best of the best!*—but actually this was HQ for the start-up where he worked, something about soup or broth for which Yale strategized the marketing; writing was something he did on the . . . side? For "freelance"? Those who greeted her at the front desk of this building thought she was a soup client, she knew that; he'd told her to say it: *Linzie King, here for the Broth Boss.* Perhaps ghost writing meant true secrecy of your profession, your art. Oh god, there was so much she didn't know.

For months Linzie would continue to arrive in heels, appointments at Dry Bar before their meetings so her hair would look full, but the way her coordinated looks tried too hard became all the more stark in Yale's cool presence. She always told the stylists to *mess up* her hair a little more—to *fuss it* into a *just-fucked frizz* over her bald spots—but it always fell back limp, thin, and pretty. *Pretty,* Yale called her, that first time. *Pie-faced simplety-dimplety pretty.*

Linzie sat in her swivel chair, twisting left and right—then stopped. It was annoying, the way she did that, her fidgeting. Many people had told her this, and she should know better. The millions of viewers of *The Dating Show,* in fact, had created all sorts of online message boards to discuss the things she did on TV that they had found *so, so fucking annoying.* The small chip in her tooth—*fix it!* The way her clothes fit, her corny phrases and physical tics, her schlocky makeup job, her compulsive giggle—*fucking CLOYING!* Linzie scratched the fabric on the underside of the chair, itching at the threads.

I'd never even been on a plane before the show, Linzie said. No one would believe that.

We have to write what's true, Yale said. He sat down. He leaned his chair back again. But! he said, you know sometimes truth is relative, because we also have to write what's compelling. And is the truth compelling?

Yes, said Linzie. She believed that her truth was enough.

Of course it isn't, said Yale.

Of course not, she repeated.

The truth is boring. *BOR-ING!* Yale would continue to say this word so much. Sometimes, mid-sentence, as Linzie was describing something that had happened to her, or a recurring dream she'd had, he would interrupt her and shout *BORING!* or *STOP BOR-ING ME!* the latter in a singsong tone she'd hear for years to come, at all hours, every time she thought about her feelings, her parents, the things she missed or hurt for most. *BO-RING!*

The truth, Yale went on, is unwieldy, messy, long, and yes, boring. Think about your days, your mall job, your family, blah blah, boring. Too many people. Too much happens. You wake up, take a shit, wash your hair—Linz, if we're doing this you've got to get used to me. Everybody shits, this shouldn't scandalize you. Truth! We're talking truth. The not-boring truth, for which we pluck and combine and deftly chisel like a statue until it takes shape and has people stopping to take photos, like, of David's dick. Do you even know who David is? I'll text you him.

At first, it astonished Linzie that Yale wasn't gay. He talked about women a lot. He'd made jokes about his ex-girlfriend, Dorkus—that was her name. Linzie had never met a man who allowed himself to bask in flamboyance and words like *deftly*. Men weren't usually like this in Florida. Sometimes Linzie noticed paler streaks of skin on Yale's upper chest and neck and knew he must have spent his weekend in the sun, a lover must have sloppily applied his sunscreen. Sometimes, she'd notice faded black or green stamps on the tanned flesh of his hand, smudged evidence of important nightclubs, elite access. Yale knew things about the world, hard and true things. As a child, he almost died of a rare disease. He named the disease all the time, though Linzie never remembered it. And he was also right: she was boring.

Keep your truth close to your heart, Yale said. He held his hand at his heart. Bitten nails, like her own, under her acrylics. You'll always have that, he said. But this is a *book*. People don't turn pages for girls who work in the shopping mall. Or at a *wedddinngg*—this, in the singsong tone again, his fingers wiggling. This isn't a Hallmark story, you've got actually compelling shit you've been through because of that guy, and that sells. I get no cut until we land this. This is *for you*. Your life is boring, but the bad stuff—that's gold. The bad guy's your hook. But we've gotta help your reader get there.

Linzie said, OK. Why am I flying to Buffalo?

Doesn't your mom live there?

No.

Why not?

I don't know where my mom is, Linzie said. She noodled her legs around each other like a Twizzler, hooking her right foot behind the opposite calf. *She sits so WEIRD! Dating Show* viewers had written on the forums, circulating screenshots.

Your mom's now in Buffalo, Yale said. Where you also do volunteer work. Farming.

Farming?

Are you good at anything else? Any skills? Yale asked.

Pretty good at math.

Yale shook his head—*def no*—then typed at his computer, read aloud: *My amazing mother moved to Buffalo, New York, where I often visit her on her sustainable, organic farm. She is resourceful, an avid canner, and now I am, too.* How's that?

OK, Linzie said. So my mom's not missing?

Not missing, and a junkie no longer, he said.

Buffalo, Linzie repeated.

Overcoming one big trauma makes a hero, Yale said. He put the pen down. But two . . . three . . . any more, then you're a tragedy. Then the problem's probably you.

Dear Birdie,

My counselors at Gateway say I have a death drive. I wonder if you've ever felt this way yourself. I know it's crazy but sometimes I feel like you and me are married. Even with all the things that happened between us and even though it's always me versus you. The truth is we have known each other a long long time, and who else can you say you've known that long? For me basically nobody. I've known you since you were little and you knew me before I was this bad guy. The big bad wolf. I know I became bad after what happened at my house, but how many more times can I apologize for that? I can't change what happened. I only knew what I knew at the time, and I was young. There was a lot I didn't know. I can see that now.

You know how I always sat in front of you in court? I want you to know I always turned around to look at you when you were talking. You barely ever looked back at me. You looked straight ahead like I was a ghost, but I looked at you because I <u>respect</u> you Birdie. Even when I was scared of what would happen, when I would rather plug my ears or die than listen, I wanted to look at you to show you that I care about what you have to say. I wonder how much of what you said was really you talking and how much was stuff your parents and lawyers made you say. Did they write it all for you? I would really love to know if it was you or them.

If what I did was really that bad why did you come to my house after Francine did? Francine told you what would happen. That I liked you both. You really did seem into my animals. I didn't force you to care. Do you remember my snake Pepper? I ask because you mentioned the frogs in the statement but there was the other tank I showed you with Pepper in it, and he ate the frogs. I used to pick those frogs out of the swimming pool filter. They were already dead so I didn't kill them. If they were still alive but almost dead, I would freeze them in a bag because that seemed like a more peaceful way to go, like they would just fall asleep cold. Then they would defrost on the floor, which didn't take much. If you remember my house was very hot because my mom wanted to save on electric. Then I dropped the frogs in for the feeding. I didn't know all that chlorine in their blood would make Pepper sick.

When I explained that all to you, you seemed really interested but then you said in court you didn't want to be there. You made it sound like I kidnapped you or something. Like Francine didn't tell you. Something I find really upsetting is Lindsay said I targeted weak girls, like girls without parents or girls who got bullied. <u>One</u> why would I do that and <u>Two</u> how would I even know about a girls parents? That wasn't the way I saw you at all. I knew you could use a protector or friend because I sensed something like that but that's not the same as weak. You were strong internally and externally. I was scrawny and still am. You seemed to know who you were already, and I wonder who you are now.

It's called <u>pro-contact</u> when guys think it's OK to have done what we've done to children. Like the law is against us but nature is not. These kinds of guys think children have it in them to say yes and consent if they're mature, and that to say they don't know anything or can't experience love takes this maturity away from them. This is not a popular idea I will say. When I hear pro-contact guys talk it's like I've swallowed a cactus and it's stabbing me in the guts. This kind of thinking is dangerous and self-serving. At least that's what I'm taught here at Gateway.

Alright the death drive. That's where I started this. Sometimes I do think I should die for the things I have done. If you think I should die I would do that for you, I really would. I would do anything to make things up to you. When I lived under Julia Tuttle, I don't know if you know this but I got really sick. My ankle got infected under the monitor but no one could get it off and we tried. It blew up into this kind of ball and I didn't know how bad it was until the hospital drained it with a thick needle because my skin actually was rotting. These nightmares took over my body when that all happened. They said it was <u>sepsis</u>. When I woke up the nightmares and real life became the same thing. There were rats under the bridge and they bit. And this one guy had a pet iguana so big he put it on a leash—the rats even scared this iguana. My body got so hot when that infection happened and everything around me got sharp, like teeth. I felt like OK this is definitely what I deserve and this is how I go. I wanted to die so bad it scared me. My only dying wish when I was under the bridge was for you to forgive me.

Back to the topic of Lindsay. I'm sure you know about the book and in it I won't look good. You won't either! Why should I want to die, and why should you when <u>that bitch</u> should die? She was old enough to know what she was doing with me. She wasn't like you or Francine, she went on television with other whores who wanted that kind of attention—boohoo! I don't feel bad! I wouldn't feel bad if someone poured lumpy hot asphalt down her throat. Now everyone will feel bad for her, but why not you? How about me?

I know I'm not supposed to but I write you these things because I hope it can all change if only we understand each other. Maybe with this book situation we could be back on the same page like we used to be.

Sincerely,
Calvin

BIRDIE

I KNOW IT'S sketch, I said, but please, you can't tell Trace I'm here.

Havi said: That is kind of sketch, but whatever, as she opened the door to her Capitol Hill apartment. The ferry service had ended for the night—the girls told me that—and Havi's place was nearby, though it wasn't clean the way it had been when we'd stayed in May. Everything had a film of stickiness to it now, a drugstore lilac sweet perfume, C's of dark hair on the granite countertops. *Haven't changed the sheets since you and Trace, so I guess that works*, Havi said.

We stood in Havi's ground floor kitchen, small and tiled, one fluorescent lodged in the ceiling flickering a sterile white. In the sink, a plate smeared with peanut butter. Havi leaned against the fridge for support and said, Can I let go of my pants? I don't usually get fucked up like this, but when nurses get nights off, I don't know, we get fucked up like this.

Havi unbuttoned and then unzipped her child-sized jeans, releasing a long, theatrical groan. Her cat paced the floor around her feet, rubbing its body against her ankles. Silver gray, with those big green eyes, it meowed and meowed.

Aw, Patricia came out—Havi said. She picked up the cat, a loud, forced kiss at her cheek. Remember she didn't want to come out when Trace was here? I think she hates men, and maybe she's confused by Trace. She's a Russian blue—they're special. Aren't you special, Patricia? Do you hate men, Patricia?

Did you see the cats on Linzie's shoes tonight? I asked.

My Patricia's hungry, Havi said. Pat only comes out when she's hungry. Havi set the cat down and opened a cabinet, pulled out a can of food with a purple label. She hooked her finger into the metal loop, then peeled it open in a burpy tear. She dropped the can on the floor and it clattered in a drumroll before settling. Patricia sniffed it, then bit into the center delicately, her neck jerking as she ate.

I'm not gonna lie to my Tracey for you, Havi said, leaning at the counter. I don't like liars.

It's only a lie by omission, I said, and it's Trace now.

Do you want to talk about what happened to you, Birdie? Havi said. Like, really? I imagine this whole night, Linzie and that guy, must be pretty activating for you. You can talk to me. Nothing fazes me.

What do you already know? I was sincerely curious.

I know my cousin's paying for your little retreat because she loves you, but you still want to lie about where you are, which isn't very nice. And that the bad guy's been writing to you guys. Like, he's a stalker now. You and Trace both? Or just you, or just Trace? I don't get that part fully.

I don't either, I said.

I wanted a glass of water. Or another drink. I walked over to the fridge, opened it. A sodden, dented box of baking powder. A single spear of pickle jarred in neon juice. Wrinkled plums. In the freezer: one carton of cigarettes, a few dark Ziploc bags. There was nothing.

Do you have a liquor cabinet? I asked.

Havi stood against the kitchen wall beneath a Hello Kitty clock. She bent over into a low squat, unzipping the back of her leather booties. She spread her arms out a few times to regain her balance as she worked to remove the shoes, Patricia paying her no attention. She wore thick white socks she'd folded halfway over her foot, and she took those off too, tossing them.

You know, I said. You and Trace don't usually talk much. So if you wouldn't talk to her otherwise, why would you tell her about tonight? Tonight's no different than any other night—

Why's tonight different than all the others? Havi laughed as she said this. Do you get it? Ma Nishtana? She stood, got close to me. Black eyeliner gathered at the pits of her eyes, and I noticed, for the first time, the feathery blonde down on her cheeks. She spun around, gripped the counter, and lifted herself onto it after two hard pumps. Her feet were red and swollen. Pale, fuzzy lint stuck mold-like between her toes.

You don't know that by now, Birdie? Why's tonight different than all others? Why this night we are all reclining? You've been dating a Jew how long?

No, I said. I don't know what you mean.

And I do talk to Tracey, why do you think I know all this personal shit about you? Can you get me a cig? Havi said. There are Asian Jews, you know.

Havi rested her face onto her knee now. A serious expression turned sideways. Her face tugged down, revealing the inner pink moon of her undereye. I wondered if she was the blackout kind of drunk or someone who remembered. I wondered how mean I could be.

What did you think of Linzie? I asked. What do you think really happened to that guy?

—You could even get bat mitzvahed, Havi said. Oh my god, please get adult mitzvahed. I need something to look forward to.

I opened her freezer again. I pulled a pack from the white carton of Parliaments. The plastic wrapping was cold and slick with condensation. I handed it to Havi, who bit into the plastic with her teeth, pulled, then spat.

Do you smell that? she said. Dill.

Dill?

I once ordered like a million bundles of dill by accident. The herb. Because I order online. That's a Seattle thing. I must have typed in the wrong number of bundles, so I put all the extra dill in the freezer next to my cigs. Cigs go in the freezer, do you know that, Birdie? Keeps them fresh. Same with denim. All of a sudden, my cigs started smelling and tasting like dill, and I became kind of obsessed with that. Now I can't go back. Once I light this, you'll smell it, she said. Like smoking chicken soup.

She worked to speak legibly through the drunk drag of syllables. Listening, I wondered what my own sound sounded like.

Havi pulled a baby-blue lighter from the bowl of a nearby candle and clicked it a few times. She took a few pulls, then ashed on the plates in the sink. I love when it's cold from the freezer, she said, wiggling her cigarette.

Hey, come sit next to me. She patted the counter.

I lifted myself up beside her. Havi scooted forward and swung her feet so they dangled off, to match mine. The booze emanated from her pores, and behind that, a perfume laced with vanilla, something dated that made me feel more tender toward her.

Just because Tracey was adopted doesn't mean we're not close, Havi said. We're a tribe. We're the same. Then she said: Birdie, do you think I'm hot? You can tell me.

I think you're a little gone, I said. I stared the cat in the eyes. She meowed.

Would you want to sleep with me? If you weren't with my cousin.

I wouldn't sleep with you, I said.

Are you all the way gay? she said. Or halfsie? Bi? Are you a bi-con?

I did not answer. I cheated on Trace once. We'd talked it over for years in couples' counseling until the memory boringly blunted. It was with a man, and I was ashamed of that. I would always be ashamed of that. Trace still referred to it as the *male situation*, or the time I hit my *cock bottom*.

He was not the frail, effeminate type I sometimes found myself attracted to, movie star wispy, men smaller than me that I could imagine topping, or pegging, or hurting. Nathan was a huge man. A slab of thick, pink bacon, with dark holes around his lip and eyebrows from teenage piercings. When I met him, he was a sports jock at a sports bar placing football bets with a bookie on his phone, a username or passcode he spelled out and repeated with one finger plugged in his ear: NateDawg38.

Nate loved his grandpa and mom. All that was left of Gramps was a pair of eyeglasses Nate sometimes wore, though they gave him a headache. Nate dreamed of a life back in Charlotte coaching high school football, helping kids. He was a Republican fiscally, but socially liberal. As a child, he used to swim with pet ferrets—four of them—in his swimming pool. He was thirty-two and a Pisces. He was afraid of underwater trenches, of the murderous murk so far down—what could it contain? These are all things NateDawg confided in me over the course of three cheap drinks, though I never asked.

Calvin had said I was only gay because of what he did to me. This was the beginning of the letters; Calvin's name in the sender line to an old email address he'd somehow located. I was twenty-two when I received it, and I didn't know how he'd learned about Trace—we'd been dating less than a year. She'd only just found out about Calvin, which changed the way she looked at me. I read Calvin's message and deleted it and then I wanted to feel a man's hands and mouth and cock and have it be my own call. I wanted to ask for it, beg for it, wanted to make a grown man whimper. It was both complicated and mutinously simple.

If you make decisions in reaction to him, my fourth or fifth therapist said—*you're still allowing him control. That is not autonomy.*

I kept the email in my trash even though I could still read it there. I read it again and again before pulling an old crushed-velvet skirt up my hips, the elastic tight. I wore a black top. Clean sneakers. I took the train to Manhattan, then up to Murray Hill, sure of what I would do.

I'd told Trace I was working the theater that night, turned off my phone when I found the perfect place—a bar with corny neons, chicken wing specials posted in the windows, loud TVs. I saw

NateDawg at the bar, sat next to him, told him my name was Louise. I touched his thigh as he talked to me, so that he would feel very interesting.

Nate lived in the financial district. He called it "Fi-Di" in the cab and stroked my hair a few times. He lived in an apartment with three roommates, and one of them played games in the living room with a headset on, waving and winking to me as I entered Nate's room. In the dark I sucked his cock, surprised at how obvious it was. Utilitarian and easy. His boxers were at his knees, I didn't pull them further than that, I didn't want him to move. I heard the roommate scream into his headset. I spit on my own fingers. Nathan lay on the bed, and when my eyes adjusted, I saw how bewildered he looked, almost confused, like a man who'd just seen his favorite childhood toys at a garage sale. I still had my sneakers on but no skirt, and with two hands I held him, half-flaccid, and centered myself on top. I eased him in, bounced lightly until my thighs shook, then rode him while I ran my fingers through the stupid hair on his chest. His skin was damp. He smelled like man. He smelled disgusting, like the sweat-wet rope from gym class. I focused on the smell, and the disgust made me wetter, made moving on him a little easier. He looked up at me with his mouth half open like he was the luckiest son of a bitch that ever lived. I pictured the way I must have looked to him, Louise, pale chest and sharp ribs and dark nipples *exotic*, maybe the first Asian to ever fuck him, or maybe Asians were Nate's *thing*, even his buddies knew that. I told him to come in me, teased the words slow the same way one imagines themselves driving right off a bridge and into the Atlantic, the spurring ache with which we tempt ourselves with our own power—and he did. He came. I barely felt it, only the warm mess after.

I read Calvin's message over and over the next day, blinds drawn, back in the plastered dim blue of my studio apartment. I hadn't eaten in a long time, which was always the case after hearing from Calvin. Soon after, the message expired and disappeared.

Havi put her hand on my shoulder. I want you to know you're not alone, she said, soft and babyish. It may feel like you are, but lots of us have experienced guys like your guy, just look at Linzie, and you're stronger for what you've gone through. Havi lit another cigarette, stumped the previous one into her candle. Everything happens for a reason, she said. She coughed once, hard. You want?

I don't smoke, I said. I'm pretty tired. Can I head to sleep?

Birdie, I want you to know you're like family to me. Tracey is my family, so you're my family. Do you have family? Like, your own family? Like, in the States?

Yes, I said. I'm from Florida, remember?

Are you close?

My mom's still in Florida. My dad died when I was eleven. I'm an only child.

Was your dad murdered? Havi asked.

I said, Why would my dad be murdered?

Oh, I don't know. But I know you've had a lot of tragedy in your life. I can feel it coming off you. And that's why you act like a bitch. That's your thing, right? Being kind of a bitch.

My dad died of stomach cancer, I said.

That's a hard one, I'm sorry, Havi said. At the hospital they say Asians get stomach cancer the worst—the rice diet or something. The stress. Is that a myth, do you think? Birdie, you know I once modeled? I used to go to these open casting calls at the mall. They had these modeling tables with agents. Did you ever see those? And it was one of those agents from a table—he ended up taking my pictures. He's the one who abused me.

I said, The modeling agent abused you?

Yeah.

More than once?

No, just once, Havi said. She said this with a tight smile, the upbeat voice one uses not to cry.

Then that's an assault. Not abuse, I said.

See, Birdie, you're really a bitch.

Why did you ask if I'm bi?

I wanted to know if you'd kiss me, and I feel like you'd tell me the truth. Also, I know you fucked that guy from the sports bar. That wasn't very cool of you, was it? Told you I talk to my cousin.

The overhead light made a low hum. All the smells churned my stomach, the sweet punch of fruit in Havi's diffusers, the cigarette smoke, the dill. I wouldn't kiss you, I said. I would never kiss you.

I still have the photos of me hanging up, Havi said. The modeling photos he took. Did you see the headshot in the bathroom, when you were here last? That was me. And the guy, his name was Randy, he took that picture. I still had the birthmark on my head then, in the pictures. The purple mark I told you about before, with the hibachi chef—

Why would you want that in your bathroom?

A reminder . . . Havi breathed hard. Of what I've endured.

I'm going to bed now, I said. I'll take an early ferry.

I hopped off the counter, opened cabinets to find a glass. The cat was gone, the food can empty. I didn't remember her leaving.

Can I tell you something? Havi said. She laughed, spitting smoke, then coughed. She covered her mouth as she kept laughing, her eyes watering now. Come here, she said, Birdie, Birdie, come over here. I wanna tell you a secret. I'm not gonna kiss you, I just wanna tell you something.

I went to her. She cupped her hands around my ear. Her boozy breath puffed as she spoke, and the hair on my arms perked at the feeling.

I already told Trace you're here, she said, giggling. Like, a looooong time ago. Don't hate me, you fucking bitch!

In the guest room, I sat cross-legged on the sheets. Havi's cell phone warm on my thigh. *Just call her*, Havi had said. *Why would she be mad?*

I knew when I spoke to Trace, something would sever again. There would be a new before and after. To talk about it, to face it, would make it true; Calvin would really be gone, and an appropriate reaction would be required. I'd have to change, grow, flower with maturity and difference. It would finally be time to move on.

I touched Trace's name on the screen. Saved in Havi's phone as *Tracey Cuz*.

She picked up right away.

Hav, how'd it go?

It's me, I said. How'd what go?

She paused, then started to cry.

Breathe, I said. What is it, talk to me.

He's dead, Bird. It finally happened.

I let those words sink through me, lasso me at the throat.

Calvin died, she went on. Maybe you heard.

Car accident, I said, I know. I'm staying at Havi's. I'm sorry I didn't—

Bird, Trace said. I need to—No, that's not it.

I don't remember the rest of what was said. Only that she kept saying *murdered*.

Date of Intake: 12/8/2012
Name: Calvin Thomas Boyer
DOB: 7/16/77
Age: 35
AoA/Sex: females, 6–12. Boyer reports age of attraction only activates in higher range when female is or appears to be prepubescent.
Primary/Secondary Orientation: Minor attracted, exclusive; no secondary reported
Temperament: mild, friendly
IQ: unknown
Registered SO: Y
Last registered: 11/9/13; quarterly SO registration completed on time since '97

Electric Monitor: court ordered GPS EM; Boyer wears Omnilink OM400 in addition to SCRAM
Medications: none current
Prior Offenses: sexual misconduct, sexual obscenity, lewd/lascivious molestation, possession of CSAM, poss of Lolicon, drug poss (misdemeanor), DUI, stat rape, violation of probation, B&E, see Appendix
Programs: B4UOFFEND, anger management, hygiene 3, ladder 2 dignity, urge awareness

Notes: Boyer has applied to Gateway twice (2008, 2012). Denied first due to offenses against minors -12; transferred to Julia Tuttle bridge colony after serving MD sentence; Boyer admitted to G2G in 2012 due to program expansion. At G2G he is attending court ordered Anger Management and has taken initiative to enroll in other elective programs of his own volition. Boyer's AoA consistent with pedophilic disorder; Boyer says he prefers this label over "minor attracted." Boyer has been medicated with both oral NPA and CPA to curb urges and says they helped but made him sleepy, suicidal, and "chubby"—he then stopped. He has reported offending against minors fourteen times but says he is committed to a life of no contact and no offending. Boyer has tried various modes of SOSE to change sexual orientation including exposure to ammonia, smelling salts, and manual self-harm with lighters and safety pins beneath his nail beds while viewing images of children within his AoA brackets. No success noted.

Boyer has admitted to the use and creation of CSAM and exploitation material (see DOJ investigation) and admitted to hiding thumb drives in the tank of his mother's toilet. In intake, Boyer reports feelings of guilt and shame over the use of such materials, which he viewed as "not always real kids, sometimes fakes or drawings." His reasons for not wanting to offend include fear of future incarceration and "God's judgment." Boyer will remain drug tested via SCRAM monitor at G2G. He is uncomfortable wearing monitors due to substantial medical complications incurred with previous Omnilink model while living under Julia Tuttle, resulting in Septic Malleolar Bursitis (med record attached).

Boyer's mother, Mary-Beth, supports his programming and "keeps him on track." Boyer says he has a "complicated relationship" with father, Thomas. Boyer is polite, well mannered, well appearing at intake. His assigned service at intake is to treat the community pond; he will also work the cane. Boyer presents symptoms of potential NPD and accompanying paranoia. He remains fixated on a book which he says is being written about him and has repeated: "soon everyone will know." Boyer is capable of mood and feeling articulation. He displays curiosity and complexity of thought.

Boyer reports a recognition of his AoA at 9 years of age. He reports no longer indulging in any fantasies of minors, as he claims fantasies exacerbate his urges and likelihood to reoffend. He is aware of the possibility of civil commitment via Jimmy Ryce Act if found guilty of pending charges ("I deserve whatever punishments I get"). He eats well with no other health problems reported. He has volunteered to set up and break down chairs for meetings. He has expressed interest in becoming more involved with the G2G church and grounds keeping. Boyer is in possession of an iPhone with limited data; no internet access, as mandated by FDLE DOC/CCS. Curfew 10 PM-8 AM. We believe he is a strong candidate for G2G with high probability of success.

MARY-BETH

MARY-BETH WOKE ON Calvin's birthday with cake on her mind. She'd slept in late after a graveyard shift, and it was two p.m. Syl knocked on the bathroom door and said, *Gotta get moving, sissy. Day's long until it's over.*

Mary-Beth could not resuscitate her son from the dead, but she could pick up a cake—a red velvet half sheet cake with cream cheese frosting from Winn-Dixie. She'd ordered it in advance, two weeks ago, when Calvin was still alive. Spelled his name with the tiny blunt pencil at the grocery store bakery, her hand shaking as she pushed hard, curved the *C*.

The sisters would drive to Winn-Dixie, then Gateway. Syl asked how old Cal would have been and Mary-Beth, in the passenger's seat, said, *Thirty-six today, you ought to know that.* Heat squiggled silver over the road. The crepe-skinned man in a bathing suit sold mango from a cooler on Loxahatchee, an iguana perched on his shoulder. Mary-Beth did not know him personally. Still, she raised her cigarette hand out the window. He always waved back.

Mary-Beth reflected on the day Calvin was born—jaundiced in that box, Calvin's face so serious and scrunched, gnome-like. Tommy and Mary-Beth both pulsed in the light of that room, and they'd gripped each other's hands, a prayer like *God, if we make it through this—*

You remember that day? Mary-Beth asked.

Born good, Syl said. Everyone's born good.

No one's born good or evil, Mary-Beth said. Come on, now, babies don't even got kneecaps, never mind morals.

Syl turned up Katy Perry on the radio. Mary-Beth hated the girl's voice. She decided that Katy Perry's voice would henceforth be an *omen*—that this would not be a good day.

Inside Winn-Dixie, a young, tattooed baker gave Mary-Beth a free balloon with her cake—Mylar, with rainbow, cursive lettering, bobbing like a sky dancer.

Why's it free? Mary-Beth wanted to know. She pushed her ticket across the counter.

Recalled, said the baker. He pointed up. Says *Happy Birthlay*. He handed her the ribbon.

Mary-Beth looked down into the warbly, plastic window on the top of the cake box. There was Calvin's name, spelled just right, bubbly flowers and vines in ornate florescence. Chartreuse—she'd always remember that color, close to *Citrus Burst* or *Yellow Finch*. Mary-Beth wanted to jam her thumb into the center of the cake, it was so beautiful.

Happy with it? asked the baker.

Little frilly for a boy, said Mary-Beth. Don't you think?

Betty had invited Mary-Beth and Syl to Gateway to lead a birthday prayer for Calvin. Betty and Lief and the others all hugged Mary-Beth and Syl when they got out of the car. Syl took the hugs even though she barely knew them, which pissed Mary-Beth right off. Syl could take those hugs with her closed-eyed serenity face now that Calvin was dead. Syl rocked every hug left to right, left to right, before letting go.

Any word yet? Betty asked Mary-Beth outside the trailer. Sweat clung to the soft hairs on Betty's cheeks. Any leads?

None, said Mary-Beth, only what Tommy'd said about those Palmyra folks.

I told you, said Betty, those folks are good, honest people. I asked, and they know nothing about any of it. Nothing at all. All we've got's reporters still sniffing around here.

Mary-Beth knew from TV: the first month of an investigation was important. They were soon approaching that threshold, leaving behind any hope of a hot clue. She didn't want *reporters sniffing around*, didn't want Linzie King's face or name on her prime-time cable, in her tabloids, *anywhere*—though sometimes she was grateful. Sometimes she was glad. It was a secret that sloshed like acid in Mary-Beth's stomach, a shameful truth she suffered alone—without Linzie, she knew, no one would care about her son. And without the coverage Linzie had stirred, for better or for worse, there would be no possibility of interest, or an answer. In a way, Linzie was hope. Driving up to Gateway today, Mary-Beth had noticed new plastic window blinds inside Cal's unit—his scarves were gone, even though Mary-Beth had purposefully left them. The sight of those blinds made her swallow different. Everyone would move on. But Linzie might slow the process.

The group of them walked up the tinny stairs to the double-wide propped on cinder blocks. When Mary-Beth tugged the balloon's ribbon even slightly, it hunched all the way down to meet her, a little too alive. The trailer was where Gateway held court and state mandated support meetings, though she had never been invited in before today. Inside, the lights were bright and loud, inspirational posters taped to the walls. Betty had set up liters of soda on the folding table, and Mary-Beth let the balloon go. Lief turned on a standing fan. The poster corners flapped like moths.

One by one, more men entered. Some Mary-Beth recognized, others she did not. A few looked dressed up in ill-fitted collared shirts and khakis for their mock job interviews. Others, she could tell, came in from fields or maintenance, tangy sweat and chemicals abrading her nose. The men popped folding chairs into a circle. Some tipped baseball caps, said, *Good to see you, Fairy-Beth*, grief still dragging its hooks through their voices.

At four p.m. on the dot, Betty asked everyone to sit down and zip it. She clapped three times. Rolled a large television away and into the corner, turning it around as if it were in trouble. Then she introduced the sisters and invited Mary-Beth to offer her prayer. Mary-Beth stood and wiped at the front of her pants, instinctively. The fifteen or so men, plus Charmaine, sat in silence. Knees open, hunched backs, hands clasped behind sunburned necks. Most of them stared at the floor.

Afternoon, Mary-Beth said. Syl looked up at her with an expression that could almost be mistaken for love.

Some of you know me as Fairy-Beth, and to others, I'm just some crazy lady up here in a butterfly shirt. Just want to tell you I believe in you boys—and you, Charmaine, I don't forget about you—and I'm counting on you all to go out there and do good with your lives in honor of Cal. If you didn't know my Cal, he was the one murdered here earlier this month because of evildoers and the hate in their hearts. Cal, like all you, I know, was a victim of the system. He could never get up from under it once it sucked him in. It's like a fucking cancer. You cut a little bit out, and it grows back all over, leaves all sorts of defects and mysteries for later. Makes you weaker every time.

Anyway, Mary-Beth said. Today would have been Cal's thirty-sixth. This would have been his ninth month here, and he was doing well. Boy, did Cal loooove his cake. Loved birthdays. He was the sweetheart of my world, and you know . . . you know I'm pretty angry about what happened to him if I'm being real with you right now. If I can be real with you, I think I'll stay pretty angry for a long time. So thank you, boys, for seeing him. I know you got no blood relation, but he considered you all his family. Least those of you who've been here some time. And I guess with that, I ask we bow our heads and pray.

The men, plus Charmaine, plus Betty, plus Syl, reached for each other's hands. Mary-Beth crossed her own arms in front of her chest and felt her heart in her thumb. The whole group dipped their heads as Mary-Beth spoke to their Lord and Savior and thanked him for the bounty and the cake of which they were about to receive. Happy birthday, Calvin Thomas. *Amen.*

Betty clapped her hands together, just once this time. The men followed and clapped. Now, before we get to cake, Betty said, let's do a five on this unit, and our vow. Mary-Beth and Sylvia, she said, you're welcome to step out, or as faithful allies, we welcome you to join us.

Mary-Beth sat down next to her sister, right as Syl stood up to go. Mary-Beth yanked her back, and Syl whispered, *Sissy, this ain't any my business.*

The men all took out pieces of paper from their pockets, their backpacks, their nylon briefcase bags. Some carried binders, others unfolded the pages and smoothed them over their thighs. Wobbly Bic pen inserts were passed around, no outer plastic casing, and when Mary-Beth received one she delighted in the familiar bend of it. It had been a while.

This so I don't get stabbed in the eyeball? Syl said. She flopped the ink tube at her eye. Mary-Beth felt unexpectedly giddy to be in the know in these criminal ways, to know more than Syl did about anything. Betty passed them both sheets of paper—worksheets, Mary-Beth could now see—*For if you want to follow along*, Betty whispered.

One of the men stood up, said, *Ma'am.* He wore low cargo shorts and a tank top, rubber shower shoes over white socks. Black facial hair looked Etch-A-Sketched around his chin and jawline. He was twentyish, Mary-Beth thought. Twenty-five, tops.

Afternoon, name's Zephyr, he said to the room. Like the water, he said to Mary-Beth and Syl, and I'm on service today. I'm a MAP. *Hey, Zeph*, everyone said. Zephyr lifted his paper above his head. Anyway, I been doing this work back at bunk and thinking, like, thank God I'm here, right. Miss Mary-Beth, what you said about

Calvin—we all talk about him here like he's not even gone. He was someone I looked to when I first came in, even though he was taken from us just a couple days later. Cal took me out by the pond when I arrived, and we sat at the water, and he told me what it meant to be a VirPed. I ain't never heard a term like that before he opened my eyes to it, that you can rise above what you've done, day by day. Cal felt real bad about what he'd done to his lot, but he disciplined himself. He was sorry to those girls. Ms. Mary-Beth, you should know he was someone we looked to. I sure did.

Mary-Beth reached over and squeezed Syl's hand. It was a surprise, how her own hand could betray her. *I need to go*, Syl whispered. *MB, I am not a part of this.*

Mary-Beth gripped harder.

Betty, you been talking about violent proclivities—Zephyr looked to his paper now. His own inked writing had bled through. Cal may not have had it, but I got that rage, I know. The whole room nodded. But to know it, to say we know it, that's how we trap it, right?

Right, Zeph, Lief said, snapping his fingers. Come on, now, that's exactly right.

So today, I'll lead our vow, Zephyr said. I am not a monster, he began, and everyone joined in. I am a Minor Attracted Person. I am a person deserving of dignity and life. Lord grant me the serenity and strength to accept that, while I cannot change my afflictions, I can choose to be virtuous. I will not inflict harm upon myself. I will not inflict harm upon others. And I will especially not inflict harm upon the children. I am on the pathway to grace, and I will be virtuous, turning away from darkness and into the light.

Charmaine's voice trailed a beat behind the rest as they concluded the vow. *Amen.*

The room was silent as the fan spun, the balloon rising and falling. Something tightened in Mary-Beth as she watched it.

It was as if the balloon's ribbon were pulled and knotted around her organs, her lungs bound like two slabs of steak. A trenchant, black howl wanted to come out of her, but didn't.

She heard a sound like leaking water and looked around for its source. It was the sheet of paper, trembling in her sister's hand.

BIRDIE

I'D LEFT HAVI'S in a rush the morning after the reading; finger-swiped my teeth with her toothpaste, a too-hot jostled cab ride up the I-5 to the water.

The Mukilteo ferry terminal was swarming with people this time. A Saturday. A holiday weekend. Tourists and their children leaned over the dock waiting for the boat, big hats rippling like shrimp chips. Men in neon work vests lowered the boarding ramp. I bought my ticket to Whidbey.

The walk from the terminal, up the ramp, and to the seating area in the back of the boat: one minute and fifty-one seconds.

I stared at my watch. Nobody sat across from me—they all stood on the deck. The seat where Rich had sat was glaringly empty, perfectly draped by the sun, as if he might step right back into his mark, on cue, just to tell me about it. I imagined him describing Calvin's face, his final words. *According to the internet, it was murder,* Trace had said the night before, on the phone.

The man on the boat, I'd said.

When I closed my eyes, I saw him again. Remembered him precisely. Rich's cheeks in the afternoon light, his scar, black hair the color of my own, shining. It all came back. It was an image I wanted to keep, press into a locket, talismanic—*don't move, stay.* In dreams sometimes, I saw my father again, and whenever I remembered he was dead, I'd look for a camera, a phone, something to prove that he had come back for me—but there was never a camera in my pocket, and my father's face would distort as if drawn upside down then turned the right way again. That's how Rich felt.

The engine shifted. The boat moved.

I checked my watch again—two more minutes had passed. I searched the ceiling of the boat for security cameras, checked every corner; maybe there would be footage from the day we'd met. I would ask. I would write letters to the ferry manufacturers if I had to, pleading.

A few people walked out to the observation deck with coffees—gawking, looking. Maybe at me. One man's shirt read America the Great.

I closed my eyes again. Rich had a memorable body, the way it slinked and moved, the way it bent. His nails returned. His dark, dry knuckles, rapping on the Animorphs book. He'd carried a plastic bag . . . of what? He said he did *marina stuff*, but I didn't know what that meant. With each new flash, I worried every recall might smudge him even more, each new Rich summoning someone different. I knew what people said: that every time you remembered a person you were only thinking of the last time you remembered them. You could touch a moment too much, stroke it, darken it like silk.

Calvin had recorded what he did, on a camcorder. He admitted to it; the police had found a chat log in which he confessed about the tapes to another man over the internet—a man whose IP address they were never able to identify. He'd confessed that he'd filmed most of us, those of us who came to his house, then his bedroom. He'd asked the man how much money he could get for the recordings. The man responded: *No money, just admission. Tapes prove you're not a narc.* In the courtroom, Calvin's state-assigned defense said the conversation about the tapes—a conversation had when he was nineteen—was an example of the "inappropriate fantasies of a teenage boy." He wasn't a *man*, but a *teenager*, and teenagers make *fantastic mistakes*.

My lawyer, Mr. Proulx, told us the tapes were essential. Mr. Proulx came to my parents' restaurant to discuss this. My father closed Hei Baby for the meeting, a Monday afternoon, the chairs piled high and tucked into the corners of the dining room as if frightened. Dad prepared a bowl of steamed broccoli and chicken for Mr. Proulx, which he never ate. I found that rude. He wore a big gem on his pinky, and I thought: Untrustworthy.

Finding the tapes is not only important, it's essential, Mr. Proulx said to my parents.

My mother had dressed me up in a burgundy velvet dress, and I sat at the table as they spoke—an adult, an equal. I ate a bowl of dad's egg drop soup, which I'd always loved, but that afternoon, as I stirred, it reminded me of snot. Already I missed Francine, who was instructed not to speak to me by her own lawyer. I pulled a wavy thread from the white tablecloth as Mr. Proulx told my parents I didn't need to be there, didn't need to be a part of the discussion, as if the details of what happened to me were inappropriate for a kid my age.

Looking around at the restaurant, I saw it anew. Grand and a little fake, like Epcot. Nothing totally real. My father played a Chinese restaurant CD he'd found at Virgin Records. Once, when I asked if the music reminded him of his childhood in Chengdu, he answered simply: *No*.

What about what he did to her? my father asked Mr. Proulx. He shook his fist as if ringing a bell, elbow on the table, and he didn't stop shaking it. He went on: *Birdie can say very clearly what he did. Francine can, too.* My father spoke with a Mandarin accent, and it was the first time I remember feeling embarrassed by it; in the presence of this lawyer, I wanted to razor his syllables, flatten his tongue.

If there's evidence of child exploitation—pornography—material, Mr. Proulx said, *that matters more. That's a greater charge, more time he'd go away.*

More than what? my mother asked. *Greater charge than what?*

Than the event itself, Mr. Proulx said. He clasped his hands. *Distribution would legally weigh more than the event itself.*

Something in the lawyer's face, the heaviness there—I already knew we would lose.

She's not just a child, she's a person, my mother said later that night. I listened through my parents' bedroom door. *We have to fight. She has her whole life ahead of her.*

Maybe she'll be lucky, my father said. *Maybe she won't remember any of this.*

They found my tape, in the end. This was years later, on a thumb drive, when they searched Calvin's house for stolen electronics—a different charge. They never found the others.

Arriving soon at Clinton terminal, the ferry speakers said. *If you have a vehicle on board, please return to it.* Mountains slowed out my window. Birds formed an arrow in the sky. The arrow appeared, disappeared, reappeared, as the announcements looped in static.

I checked my watch. It was enough time for our conversation to have happened. For Rich to have happened. *Shorter ride than I thought,* Trace had said; but for a single afternoon, a twenty-two-minute-and-thirteen-second boat ride, Rich had recognized something in me, something more than sadness, more than a missing. He'd found the primal, glistening thing, dark and slick, spindled in my body. Someone had finally seen not what I feared, but what I wanted. Consequence. Consequences *for the event itself.*

I sat very still. Imagined he was watching from a distance, sending me a sign.

We've arrived at Clinton terminal, the speakers garbled. *Welcome to Whidbey.*

Thelma was waiting when I arrived back at the farm.

She looked solemn sitting on the bench near my front door, her golf cart parked nearby. If she'd had a hat, I felt she might have removed it and held it to her chest when my taxi pulled up. Instead, she balanced the handle of a basket on her fingers, lifting it in quick little pulses. As I walked closer, I saw that the basket was full of brown speckled eggs.

Well, hey there, world traveler, Thelma said. I zoomed right over when I saw your cab come in. Thelma's silver hair was sweat-damp, darker around the ears. She did not stand.

Hey, Thelma, I said. Can I help you with something?

Been worried. You got some emergency calls—we took them back at the house. She jutted her thumb over her shoulder, though it pointed at my door.

I'm sorry about that, I said.

We ask you tell us when you're leaving the premises, so we don't get worked up like this, she said. Tried your cell to see if you'd gone off island, but went right to voicemail. Didn't know what to tell your mom. Seemed rather *exasperated* trying to get ahold of you.

I thought of my mother, Wendy, her planner full of pressed flowers and loopy handwriting done up with colorful pens. It'd be in there—*Thelma and Hal's emergency number*—probably with some star stickers around it. Outside the orthodontist's office, Mom wore linens and turquoise bracelets from Sedona, leather sandals, a long, red braid. But the Wendy who clocked out of her shifts in her white Toyota Camry was the truer Wendy to me—a woman in Bugs Bunny scrubs, tie-dye clogs, drawstring around her hips double-knotted and frayed.

I'm sorry about my mom, I said to Thelma. Did she leave a message?

Just told me she needed to reach you, Thelma said, shrugging. Called maybe fifteen times last night, and five times today, a bit *demanding*. And she called *late*. Asked us to run the golf cart back and forth to see if you were in yet. Hal stayed up past his usual bedtime to do it, and in the process flattened one of our new lady ferns and woke up the Turkish girl's dog—kept barking all night, so there's that. You might not have a happy neighbor.

Thelma wiped and rubbed her hands together, as if washing them. Her face mottled pink and white, almost pulsing. I chose to focus on the eggs in her basket. I wished I could will one to break. They were so round.

Looks like you had a fun night out, then, Thelma said.

I went to a literary reading.

This isn't really what we're here for, Thelma said. Not really a messaging service, you understand.

Well, I got ahold of her—my mom, I said. I looked Thelma in the eyes now. I thought about telling her about Rich, about everything I was capable of. I wanted to tell her: *You should be afraid of me.*

So what was the fuss all about? Thelma asked. If you don't mind my asking?

She wanted to let me know my dad died, I said.

I walked right past her and into my cabin, slamming the door.

LINZIE

LINZIE HATED POLICE stations. She hated courthouses and FBI buildings, lockers and security checkpoints, bronzed old men and placards lining the walls—she hated the framed pages of illegible, angry cursive.

She particularly hated *this* police station, Broward County's, which still smelled of Windex and pizza. It hadn't changed much since she was a kid. Today, when she came straight off the red-eye from Seattle, the intake hall was crowded. A woman in a terry cloth tracksuit kicked the vending machine, said: Are you fucking shitting me? Beige seats lined both sides of the hallway, bolted to the ground. A cop jangled by with a Pub Sub in his hand and bit the sweet, dark bread. Linzie listened to clinking knitting needles, ringing phones, heels on tile, the angry woman banging her fist against the glazed face of the machine, begging for her Mountain Dew.

Come on in, Miss King, someone said.

Linzie entered a room and sat down at a wooden table. Two officers sat across. One said, I'm Officer Brodkey; the other said, I'm Officer Rutkin, but Linzie would never remember these names, or which cop was which. They were white men with mundane faces, and the thinner man drank from a small metal cup. One of these cops knew her dad, had called him; after Doug had picked Linzie up from the airport, he'd driven her home, told her to shower, *put on a nice top and lipstick*, then he'd taken her to the station. Linzie kept her hands flat and strange on the table now, as if pleading for a spirit. She was hungry. She wanted to cuddle with Lucky, take a nap.

Miss King, said one of the officers. Can you tell us where you were the other night, Wednesday, July third, extending into the early hours of July fourth?

Um, I did a reading in Davie, Linzie said. Then I did a meet and greet at a bar around there. It was Polish.

Your reading was in Polish?

No, Linzie said. The bar was Polish.

And the approximate times of these two events?

Well, Linzie said, the reading was at seven—I mean, you could check that. I was there. Linzie looked up at the ceiling fan, allowed the black blades to blur and sharpen in and out of focus. The reading went until about eight thirty, she went on, then I drove about twenty minutes to the Polish place. That probably started around nine. I stayed until eleven, I guess, then drove home.

You drove after the bar?

Oh, I don't drink, Linzie said. You can test my blood or anything—I never have.

Can you tell us more about this reading? one of them said.

I read from my book, said Linzie. It's promotional. I read to a crowd. And then they ask me questions, like in a question-and-answer session, and then they buy the book, hopefully. And then I leave.

Mary Higgins Clark over here, one of the officers said.

What kinds of questions they ask you? Your fans? the other one said.

Linzie wasn't sure how honest to be. She wanted these cops to respect her, to understand the work she'd put in. Even though Linzie had not written a word of *My Turn*, no one—other than Yale and Doug—knew that, and absolutely no one asked Linzie about her writing. Not even the *hard* questions she and Yale had practiced, questions about *rendering traumatic memory*. The crowds asked Linzie about her skin care. Her sex life. Would she be open to going on dates now? Had Dimitrius reached out since the woman he ultimately chose dumped him for an American Ninja Warrior? Thanks to Yale, Linzie knew how to inwardly count for pauses, how to only answer the question she wanted to answer, which was the opposite of the training she'd received on *The Dating Show*.

They ask me about literature, Linzie said to the officers. She crossed her arms.

Literature, OK! one of them said. He looked to the other man.

The honest truth: when Linzie signed books, she noticed people wanted to share *their* ideas with her, and wanted Linzie to hold whatever it was *they* had to say. They told stories of lousy cubicle jobs and euthanized pets. Of catastrophic real estate losses and friendships torn apart over pyramid schemes. *It's like we've lived parallel lives*, many said, which confused her. Linzie imagined, with her face on a book, a face not crying as it had on the show, but professional—unscabbed and airbrushed together—she might finally be worthy of dainty, dreary thoughts to share about the world. This hadn't happened yet.

Can you tell us about your relationship with Calvin Boyer? Metal Cup said.

Linzie's tongue—a limp, thin petal. She smiled. She said: I think you already know.

They said: Remind us.

Linzie said: Wouldn't that be in your records? Even the county clerk records are online. There's a ton of articles about me and Calvin. I don't really know what more there is to say.

We know you had sexual relations with Mr. Boyer when you were thirteen. And you keep bringing it up years later, which is strange, if you ask me. Would you say you still resented him? Enough to run him over, after your meet and greet?

Linzie wanted to reach to her scalp, to her lashes or brows; she wanted to yank from anywhere at all. She did not. They were watching.

So Calvin was run over? she said. That's . . . really sad. That makes me feel sadness.

That makes you feel sadness? One of the officers wrote that down.

It did. Linzie didn't like to think about it, Calvin's body crushed by tires. Once, driving, Linzie tried to swerve from a turtle, and it was her swerve—her caution—that crushed it exactly. She'd pulled over to apologize, the turtle's guts pushing through shell like a pressed Godiva chocolate. She still felt sadness for that. She felt it for a lot of things.

How much you make for a meet and greet? one of them asked.

Two hundred dollars, Linzie said. She was proud of that number.

The officer with the cup reached into his pocket, then poked at his phone. He showed the other man, who laughed. The phone clapped onto the table and the officer hit Play. It was a YouTube video of Linzie, a compilation of her crying on *The Dating Show*—a remix to be exact—set to a techno beat. Linzie knew the video well. She turned her face to the wall. The men kept laughing.

Linzie started to cry then. Something about seeing her chin crumple in pain on the video made her mirror it, automatic, a live wire attached to this Linzie of the past, *Linzie from Florida, looking for love*. The cops let her—cry. And that's what she'd remember most from this interview, the wet sleeves of her wheat-colored cardigan, the one she thought looked *responsible*; the techno beat as they cackled, her own sniffles echoing through the room. After a while they said, We're just messing with you girl. Come on, it's not serious. Linzie said, Please don't laugh at me, and the cop said, Come on, stop crying, we're just playing with you. My wife loves your show, asked me for an autograph, she loves you.

We had to bring you in, check all our boxes, Silver Cup said.

I got a daughter your age. Really, I mean nothing by it, the other said.

We know you weren't around when the guy got whacked. That's actually very easy to check out.

Then why am I here? Linzie asked.

Soften up, now, they said, as Linzie stared at them, silent. Her cheeks felt Saran wrapped as the tears dried. Linzie didn't understand why men said these things. Soften up. But also, harden up. Loosen up, tidy up, hurry up, buck up, grow up, perk up. She said, Can I go now?

The younger officer had her sign a Starbucks receipt, for his wife. Then she signed off on a police report, and she was free to go.

An opportunity like this, it's going to grow you up, a producer had said, on a final round phone call. This was a few weeks after the initial *Dating Show* email. Linzie still didn't know who'd sent her application, but it didn't matter; she'd remained an alternate. A maybe. And if she said all the right things, she'd get to go to Los Angeles. *Stay just the way you are*, the producer's voice said. *No diet. No changes. You could be the relatable one.*

Linzie didn't want to stay just the way she was. Though she *swore* and *vowed* she wouldn't, Linzie picked and picked as she waited for the show's decision. She woke to the cratered wounds on her face, blood dotting her pillows, the tiny hairs from her cheeks and brows wedged black under her fingernails as if she'd dug for water. Her lips scabbed over as she plucked and pulled away the waxy skin. She didn't even know when she was doing it most of the time, but it was *like a pacifier*, she'd tried to explain to co-workers, makeup clients. *I want to stop but I also don't, you know?*

Christ on a bike, what's with your face? a different producer had said, after Linzie landed at LAX a month later. Linzie had taken an early morning flight from Fort Lauderdale, the first time she'd *ever* been on a plane, a bit high off that accomplishment. She hadn't needed anything, and the plane hadn't crashed, and she'd seen *mountains* out the window (!!!), turquoise beads of swimming pools, even *snow*. From above, solar panels looked like bars of staples. Life could be, would be, bigger now.

When she landed, a producer in the airport took her phone away, dropped it into a fanny pack.

Because Linzie was still a *maybe*, they pushed her through the rough track. From the airport, the producers drove her directly to an Embassy Suites. Inside, the cold room was stripped of everything but a Bible in the nightstand. No television. Nothing hanging on the walls. Black boards were taped over the windows, and Linzie was given a beeper—a pink plastic toy with a glowing glass window. Her assigned handler, Zoë, taught her how to use it: *423 for emergency, 323 for food, 123 for drink*. Zoë wore a belt of black wires and a big army-looking phone and duct tape in every color. She said, *C'est la vie*.

The medical examiner came in first. He was a doctor called Mr. Green, and he wore a blue doctor's mask over his mouth.

Not *Dr.* Green? Linzie asked.

Mr. Green snapped a band around Linzie's biceps and rubbed alcohol over her skin in hard, cold strokes. Then he pinched her without warning. Linzie looked at a gum bald spot on the carpet—a dark ghoul face in it. Tubes of her blood were dropped into a baggie and zipped shut.

Next, Linzie was instructed to pee. Handler Zoë reached around her body to make sure nothing was taped to her, no urine stored under her clothes. Four of them waited outside the bathroom door as Linzie went, listening to her do it. She tightened and loosened her urethra, trying to aim, left hand trembling and tipped. She peed on her hand. Then she twisted the cap, rinsed the cup in the sink. The cup felt warm, and steam whitened the inside. Her urine was too dark, she knew; Linzie never drank water, only soda. They would judge.

The wet is from the sink, it's not, like, from me, Linzie said, as she handed them the pee cup. She visored a hand over her brows, to hide the scabbing. I just wanted it to be clean, she said.

Mr. Green labeled the top of the cup with a smudgy black pencil. Not with her name, but a number. Then he walked out of the room.

After Mr. Green, several other people entered. They all introduced themselves as producers, and part of her team. They said, *Hi, Linzie, I'm part of your team.* They asked Linzie questions about love, about her dream wedding, the cut of diamond she most admired (*I'm not sure, diamond cut?*), her core values. They touched her, looked at her, asked how others would talk about her if she were invisible. Then Miss Shannon arrived.

I'm Miss Shannon, resident psychotherapist, she said, I'm on your team. Miss Shannon was bird-small with a high kindergarten teacher's voice and a voluptuous mole above her lip.

Have you ever wanted to end your own life, Linzie? Miss Shannon asked, right after shaking Linzie's hand. Have you ever wanted to harm another person? Linzie, have you ever been diagnosed with any personality disorders? How would others describe Linzie King? Do you have any friends, besides your bunny rabbit? Would you say you feel generally happy, most of the time? Miss Shannon had a strange tic of saying *mmmm* and nodding to everything Linzie said, even before she was done saying it. Then she'd move along to her next question. Your scabs, Miss Shannon said, her finger tracing a triangle over her own face. Scabs are hard to cover, sweetie. Scabs are hard for Kyle without using prosthetics, and that could take some time in HMU, time we don't usually have. Can you tell me why you do this to yourself?

Linzie didn't know why she did it to herself. Why it hurt her to even blink. Why she had to bring a fluffy fleece sweater in her suitcase to *The Dating Show* so she could shove her pillow inside of it, rather than ruining *The Dating Show*'s linens by plucking herself bloody and bald. She hoped this wouldn't eliminate her. She wanted to stay in California forever. She had no idea which co-worker had sent the *Dating Show* application, but one of them had watched her, thought of her, believed she was worthy of love, that she could be—loved. So she decided that's what she wanted.

This won't eliminate you, Miss Shannon said. So long as you tell me you're on the right track.

Definitely on the right track, Linzie said. And I'm a makeup artist. I'll work on my face.

You'll need Kyle, Miss Shannon said.

Then she left.

Linzie could not remember how long she was in that room. She never ate or used the beeper. She was rarely alone. She may have slept. When Zoë returned, Linzie noticed she wore a new black shirt, smelled like a new shower. Eventually Zoë led Linzie out of the room, down the glassy elevator, and outside. Linzie's vision flared with disco ball spots. It was daytime now—which day, she did not know—and there was a gold-plated golf cart waiting outside the front doors of the hotel.

More producers patted Linzie on the back and told her to sit in the golf cart. *Congratulations*, they said. They shook her, chaotically and paternally, by the shoulders. All the headsets and wires made the producers look like bugs. One of them handed Linzie thick papers on a clipboard. She looked at the numbers on the bottom. There were over thirty pages.

All of this's for me?

John Hancock's only needed on the last page, the bug said, showing her a dotted line. His sunglasses were stretched wide and mirrored. What day was it? It didn't matter. They'd fill the date out for her later. *These rules—sacrosanct*, another bug said. Linzie knew the cliché about girls not reading contracts, and Doug had taught her better than that. She would be more professional than that. So she sat on the golf cart and read all the rules, all the stipulations—that's the part that surprised people most, later.

She had read every page. And still, she signed.

Linzie wore a red, backless dress the night she met the star of *The Dating Show*, the man she would marry, if she won. Red dress to match red lips. *Red'll be your thing*, said another producer, or maybe he was a director—a developer? A coach? He was a long-bearded guy named Todd, always fork-flicking salads from plastic bowls, creamy dressing at the sides of his mouth. The girls in the big house called him *Poor Todd*, and *Poor Horny Todd*, on account of the way he hugged them too long, pelvis pushing, though they liked him.

Do I *have* to have a special entrance line? Linzie asked. They were in a trailer labeled "Holding" just after two a.m. The contestants had been prompted to find an *entrance line* that said something about who they were, what they wanted. It seemed, to Linzie, that other people always knew what they wanted. It also seemed that other people had something crucial she lacked: taste. The *Dating Show* girls knew what made food classy or cheap or unhealthy. They knew their face shape—heart or oval—and could coordinate shoes to their purses, perceive deep messages and meanings in songs Linzie either hadn't heard before or considered the most weird and boring. The girls knew *symbolism*, and *signs*, and they talked about it all in *real conversations*. The only way Linzie could hold conversation was to simply copy what other people said, their mannerisms, inflections of speech. And Linzie could not speak the way the other contestants spoke. She spoke like Doug, the way he said *all y'all*, her father from Milton, the Panhandle, which was a *different nation* of Florida, he'd reminded her.

Just let the girl come out of the limo, no gag, said Zoë. Zoë always seemed disappointed in Linzie. She sighed a lot. Her left front tooth was brownish smoke-stained, the other one white. Zoë held a clipboard and showed everyone on set their marks with a pointed finger. She spoke often of feminism, and of one day leaving the industry and moving to Spain.

Come out of the limo Linzie did, Linzie from Tamarac, *Bridal Beautician*. Red twinkling dress bought by Doug at Dillard's, tags still on and tucked for return (when Linzie had slipped on the dress the night of filming, one errant tag sliced her in the earlobe). She smoothed the area over her thighs as she stood, then walked toward her future love—Dimitrius "Poseidon" Doukas—Olympic bronze medalist rower and amateur home cook. (This information available in Linzie's pink plastic *Dating Show* binder, which was also full of thought exercises and statistics, plus a brief history on the art of confession: *Since the dawn of time,* one page read, *confession has been necessary and, in fact,* essential, *to human connection. Since cavemen and their hieroglyphic art. Since the beat poets. Since Bob Dylan, and Joni Mitchell, and* The Phil Donahue Show. *We have needed to CONFESS!*) Dimitrius was six feet four, with tanned Greek skin, dashed lines of makeup. He had big eyes with squiggled vessels in the whites. The starkest collar. When Linzie approached him, she said what she was coached by Zoë to say: *Dimitrius, I'm Linzie with a Z . . . so our—maybe our unique names is the reason we are meant to be.*

CUT! said Todd. She flubbed the line. Bring it back!

Bring it back! the crew repeated, and Linzie was told to get back in the limo. The cameras reversed on their elaborate tracks.

The following week, Dimitrius asked, on camera, what Linzie was looking for. They sat on a velvet couch in a very cold room. His arm was around her, lifeless as a mannequin, and she didn't really like his breath—something ham-hocked and minerally, like he'd just sucked on a beach pebble. Linzie's growling stomach kept ruining the take.

I'm looking for love, Linzie said to him, nodding. And maybe that's in you.

Why are you looking for love?

(Because her mother left her when she was thirteen.)

(Because she'd never had a real friend in her whole life, besides her carnival-won bunny.)

(Because Doug. Because her father.)

Well—Linzie tried—who isn't looking for love?

Zoë asked her to give them more. They rolled camera as Linzie was asked for *more more more*. Then Dimitrius left the cold room, and they had another guy—Marco from the crew with Dimitrius's same dark hair—slip on Dimitrius's jacket. Replace him. He sat on the couch looking at Linzie while the camera filmed over his shoulder at her face, working the lines again. Marco the crewman silently mouthed lyrics to the Folgers coffee commercial—*trick of the trade*—but at one point, Linzie swore he mouthed: *Go*.

Linzie and eleven other girls slept in one room in the big house, all of them in bunk beds, cardboard sealed over the windows. She stayed up later than them—the vigil, the watcher—and liked listening to the whining mumbles of their dreams, somebody always chasing them. Often, in the middle of the night, Zoë or Todd or one of the other handlers would come into their room and shake one of the girls awake. They'd lead her—usually Tricia, Michaela, or Betsy, wrapped up in a blanket—past the Control room to the Confessional tent. Hours later, the girl would return sniffling and alone, and Linzie would say, *You alright?* And the girl would say, *I'm fine*, dismissively, and then, always: *I gave it to them*.

The producers taught the girls to have a *spectrum of feelings* for such occasions. In their binders, they were given mood charts with illustrated faces, expressions that looked like the ones Linzie saw in the Emergency airplane pamphlet on the trip to LAX. *Jealousy* was different than *envy*, and that was different than *sorrow*, the producers reminded them, and Linzie was encouraged to meditate on times she'd felt these things to build out her spectrum. *Show me angry*, Zoë would instruct her, pointing to the illustration. *Now show me sad*. For *sad*, Linzie imagined her mother, Irene, performing motherly things:

Irene playing charades in their living room or clapping a plate of pot roast onto a clean dining room table. Five daily ITMs (in the moments) went quicker this way, when Linzie could pinpoint the memory, use it—*Give me somber. Milk it, hammer it in. Can you hold on to that now? Bring me that moment.*

    She got good at it.

    So when the Broward County reporters rushed Linzie as she left the police station, when they moved the cameras in, the foamy microphones offered like bouquets, when they said, *Linzie, tell us, do you have feelings about Calvin Boyer? Are you glad he's dead?* Linzie knew what to do. She perked up and gave it to them.

BIRDIE

I CALLED MY mother from the pumphouse in the middle of the woods. It smelled ancient inside. Dry and dusty, a single standing lamp with a flame-shaped bulb. Old magazines piled in the corner next to an unplugged mini fridge and a stack of firewood. On the desk: *Yellow Pages*, a metal toolbox, a propane lantern filled with dead flies, the navy-blue phone.

Hi, Wendy, I said when she picked up. I rolled my chair closer to the window. Looked out.

He-who-shall-not-be-named—she began.

I felt nothing, hearing her voice. I didn't miss her, did not want to hug her or smell the essential oils she slathered on her skin. I said: Yeah, uh-huh, I know. I said, you need to stop calling Thelma's house. She said you called, like, twenty times last night. They're gonna kick me out of here.

We need to *process* this, my mother said. *You* need to process it. This is a *major life event, Bird*. She sounded distant, tinny.

Am I on speaker? I asked.

No, honey—and then the sounds on the other end rustled, grew closer. I'm meal prepping, sorry, she said. So, how do you feel with all this? What's going on with you, I haven't talked to you. You don't call me. We need to know when you're coming home.

We?

Trace and I. We need to book your tickets. I emailed you some options.

There's no email here, Mom. Remember? Why would I have email?

I wondered what my inbox looked like, wondered who may have reached out in the past twenty-four hours. Press, looking for a statement. Or maybe the podcaster again. Trace had checked my emails, daily, since the letters from Calvin started again. She kept them all in a folder on her desktop called "C." I wondered if she'd still check now that he was dead, if she'd ever break the habit.

Birdie, seriously, how are you? How do you *feel*?

I said, I feel fine, I guess.

Just fine? That's what you feel?

I looked up. In the corner of the ceiling, a drooped strand of spider's web. The sun slipped over it like the glisten of a hook. I said, Yes, Mom, that is all that I feel.

You remember what Dr. Flood said, about ego-resentment, about splitting and ego-sublimation, that way you often—Trace told me what you shared, about your boat experience.

Do not therapize me, Wendy, I said. I'm not dissociating. Do not fucking therapize me.

This is a major life event, Bird. You need to listen to your feelings, to your metronomic organs. Remember, the inner work yields the inner pasture. The healing pasture will—

Once, my mother was angry. She ran yellows and didn't recycle and ate veal Milanese. This was before my father died, before my case's dismissal, before her *higher road*. The vein at her right temple as she spoke to lawyers—I'd never seen it so defined. I'd never again heard her use terms like *this piece of shit* and *that sick fucking bastard*, but she did, back then. She wanted things, back then. Now it was a life applying balls of wax to pointed metal brackets, clip-clapping retainer cases, her voice permanently lilted for bratty kids. Now it was guang chang wu dancing, slow and grunty, in the living room. Gemstones charging on the dashboard of her car, manifestations written on her mirror with organic, coral lipsticks. Everything about her embarrassed me.

What's the difference between me splitting and you meditating on your phone app? I said to her now.

You don't have any friends to talk to, my mother said. I wish you did. Maybe you should call Francine, huh? I know she'd like that. She's probably feeling all the same feelings as you. You two could work through it as a team.

My right arm got hot, lit up from the window. I said: Do the police need to talk to me?

The police? Honey, why would they want to talk to you?

About where I was?

You're there, Bird, my mother said. No one needs to talk to you.

Judge Roberts? Calvin's POs?

Birdie, my mother said. Those people are over now. He-who-shall-not-be-named is gone. You can come home now. You can go to Trace, or home to me. There's no more court. No more reinstations—you can delete those from your calendar. You *should* actually, as a closing ritual. We could plan a trip together, maybe that spa in Arizona, with the rope challenges and the broccoli, huh? We could burn all the paperwork. That could be nice.

We both sat silent for a moment.

I think they're going to want to question me, I said. We should give it time.

Well—said my mother. I'm following the forums, and all the conspiracy theorists are focused on Linzie.

I walked back to my cabin after the call. Sap dripped and glittered on bark. I breathed in the pine needles, clean as laundry. The sky was deepening its blue.

When I turned the corner to my place, the Turkish woman was sitting on the front bench where Thelma had been. Her husky sat statuesque at her feet.

Hi, I said, approaching. I lifted my hand, a half-hearted wave. You need something?

The woman said, with little expression: Thelma told me your dad just died, that I should look after you. What's your name? she asked.

My name is Jade.

That's right, I remember.

Up close, the woman's face was tan with pinkish clouds on her nose, skin recently peeled. She had bushy black eyebrows and a big smile when she shook my hand—crooked, lovely teeth. I think you know I'm Nevra, she said, and this is Amanda. She pointed at the dog, who didn't move.

I've never met a husky named Amanda, I said.

Amanda sees spirits, Nevra said. Bad ones. Sometimes she hears voices. Then she said: Spooky here, to be all alone. You're here alone, Jade?

All my life, the answer to this question had always been, unwaveringly, *no*. The *no* so automatic in my mouth, so trained, it felt illicit to catch it, stop it. I said: Yes, I am alone.

Me too, for now, she said. The quiet makes you a little crazy. Nevra scratched at her beanie, and her tucked hair fell from it. It was bright Kool-Aid red, freshly dyed. She pulled a knotted rope ball from her jacket pocket, threw it for Amanda.

What do you have going on here? I asked.

Nevra described her PhD program, her work with University of Washington, her studies abroad away from her home, in Istanbul. She said her partner would be joining her soon. His flight had been delayed due to the PKK militants blocking the streets.

Do you want to come in? I asked. I have some wine.

She did. Her dog came too. Inside, Amanda the husky finally sniffed me, pawed at my stomach, allowed me to lean over and stare at her as Nevra took off her shoes. I never liked big dogs. They knew too much.

Nevra stood in my living room, looking around. It was messy with towels strewn over the banister to dry, empty bottles of Cab lining the sink, Linzie's book, face-down on my desk. Nevra said,

Nicer than my place, and sat down on the couch. Then: Jade, why are you here?

To be unplugged, I said. Everyone needs unplugging, right?

Very American, she said. America isn't everyone. Only Americans think that. You know, back home I have a wolf. I thought it was a husky in a box. A box left right by my trash can. But that baby grew up and started catching birds in her mouth, and I thought, Oh she's a wolf. You could see it in those instincts. Her name is Sasha the wolf. It's nice to have Amanda be a dog.

Nevra pointed to the picture framed on the mantel. The one I had brought of Natalie Wood. And who's that? she asked.

That's my mother, I said.

She's beautiful, Nevra said. Then she asked, So how did your dad die?

I thought of my father. The way he looked at me like he was trying to remember me, exactly who I was, especially at the very end. In health class that year, we watched snakes shed their skin on the television set. Every part silvered into a snake-shaped wrapper and then the old version was gone.

He was murdered, I said. I just found out last night, it was a total surprise.

Everyone is dying back home, Nevra said. Everybody. Car bombs, abductions, have you seen what's happening? Do you know that everybody's been dying, besides your father?

I shook my head. I didn't feel meanness in what she was saying.

They are, she said. She shrugged, slumped in the corner of the couch. Look around, Jade. Everybody's always dying.

I poured us two mugs of wine, finishing a bottle. The sediment clung like drowned ants to the deep green glass. Nevra and I clinked our mugs together, and I sat on the floor, next to Amanda. Then Amanda jumped up onto the couch, away from me.

So I take it you're leaving now, Nevra said. She used her thumb to rub the dog between the eyes and the dog blinked slow, as if hypnotized. Does your dad have a funeral?

No funeral, I said.

Family to see?

Not really, I said. We'll all do better grieving on our own. I think I'll stay here a while, actually. In the quiet.

Nevra and I finished our mugs, opened a new bottle. We talked about the food she missed from back home, her childhood on the Aegean coastline. Eventually Amanda whined for dinner, and Nevra sat up on the couch, slipped her hat back on to leave.

Be well, Jade, she said at the door, like we would never see each other again. I bolted the lock behind her. Then I moved to the window, watching, until her cabin lights turned on.

What they don't tell you is this: to live without fear is lonesome.

MARY-BETH

THE SISTERS WATCHED TV on Calvin's birthday, following their afternoon at Gateway to Grace. It was one of the tried things they did together. Rather than speak of their lives, it was often easier for Mary-Beth and Syl to predict every plot twist, missile insults at their favorite characters. Bitches and wives of Beverly Hills, hair-sprayed news anchors, soap opera sweethearts with tits to their chins (and yes, *The Dating Show*, up until Linzie's season). Tonight, Mary-Beth and Syl sat on the floral couch, a little drunk on wine coolers and therefore, a rare love between them. On the screen, an infomercial for edible hair wax breaking up a detective show, the model running the stick of goo over her already hairless leg, then licking the goo-stick like a lollipop. Both sisters coughed up smoke they laughed so hard, Syl rolling up her tabloid, batting Mary-Beth in the knee.

The detective show came back on. Soft-core porn music thrummed over a kidnapping reenactment. Heavy, booted footsteps. Shattered glass. A young actress gagged with a pretty scarf.

Hey, hey, what if we hired a private investigator? Mary-Beth asked Syl. Like one of those you see taking the black-and-white photos of husbands with their hands on some slut's titties? They solve murders too, right? Every show's got one.

Syl said, Psssshhh, frankly, Elvira, I don't know about all that.

They were approaching that one-month marker, and both sisters knew it. The case would be dead soon, dead as Cal. Syl checked the online forums, daily. Mary-Beth had called Officer Durham a few times, but she only ever asked boring logistical questions, like *how much did Calvin make last year?* And *did he get preapproved permissions to leave the county in 2012?* He's dead! Mary-Beth wanted to scream. You want to lock up a dead man? It occurred to her, in this juridical way, that not much had changed postmortem.

Seriously, let's find us a good investigator, Mary-Beth said. Investigators don't choose sides. They just want their money. Maybe they can look closer into those Palmyra people, and Chang's friend—the stuff Tommy talked about—I could get their histories and stats. Get your lapdog.

Syl got up and unplugged her laptop from the kitchen table, where it always sat. *Jesus, woman, OK.* Mary-Beth did not own a computer anymore, hadn't for years—too many logistical hoops if Calvin came over to visit. Instead, she used the library's desktop when she needed it, which was only to register Cal as a sex offender four times a year, a deadline for which she'd become solely responsible. She wondered if she'd ever have the nerve or occasion to open Calvin's laptop, which had sat in the back of her bedroom closet ever since she brought it home.

Syl's computer was absolutely uninteresting. No desktop mess, only a background photo of her business logo—River Run Farms—though there was no *river* anywhere near Syl's property in Ocala. The logo featured a badly illustrated horseshoe and a white horse head peeking over it, the horse with a strange toothy smile.

Mary-Beth googled: *how to hire private investigator.* The little hourglass somersaulted, then blinked. Mary-Beth's nostrils burned—Syl had opened her little round tub of polish remover. Syl poked each nubby finger inside the spongy slits, moving them in and out. When's the last time Howie did you like that, huh? Mary-Beth said, and the sisters laughed like sisters.

A website loaded top to bottom: *So you want to hire a private investigator?* A magnifying glass spun, and Mary-Beth thought,

Bingo. The website had a questionnaire with white boxes in which she should type her answers. *Who are you trying to catch!? Why are you trying to catch them!? Is it time for him to face the consequences!? Have police failed you!?* The website said things like *state-of-the-art recording and tracking devices!* They would look up records and do background checks on suspects. They would trail people, deliver photos. And most importantly, they would solve your case in seven days or less, otherwise money back guaranteed. It didn't say how much money, but it did say they solved 99 percent of cases, which Mary-Beth thought was quite a lot, perhaps an exaggeration, but she understood—business was business. She answered all the questions and hit Send.

Mary-Beth and Syl popped the caps off new wine coolers—Wild Cherry, their favorite, Mary-Beth's with a straw. Syl flipped the channels. She fussed with her BlackBerry phone, clucked at her tooth. Mary-Beth tried to remember what Syl looked like as a girl, before she looked mean.

Sorry, Syl said, Genie's in charge while I'm here, and she's screwing the pooch.

How's it screwed? Mary-Beth asked. She killing your horsies?

Horses are fine, Syl said. It's just that she's letting the girls, my riders, my clients, she lets them get away with too much.

What do horse girls got to get away with? Mary-Beth asked.

I've no more patience for these prancy little bitches, Syl said. Grow up in that world, you get prancy unless you work. And I work them. They got fancy gloves now, tall boots with zippers, hunched shoulders like they're eighty fucking years old already. These girls are like cotton candy under a hose, I swear to Christ.

Then why don't you go back? Mary-Beth said, jiggling her sister's leg. You've got no reason to be here. This is the way it's gonna stay. Cal's gone. I'm still going on with things.

The only thing Mary-Beth could think of: maybe Syl was having marital problems with Howie. They never seemed to like each other much, so maybe this was an excuse, a vacation living in her sister's empty bedroom, an out. Maybe Howie was bending over some rodeo star in sparkling chaps, ass exposed and slap happy. Which gender, she did not know.

You're a woman in mourning, Syl said. You don't leave a mother in mourning, all alone in her house.

Mary-Beth wondered what was waiting for her, in that aloneness. She felt something was.

Her phone buzzed alive. Mary-Beth picked it up and there it was, a private investigator on the line. She liked the confidence in his voice as he introduced himself as Detective Shawn Ulrich, former military. Mary-Beth flapped her hand at her sister, telling her to shut up. Mr. Ulrich, said Mary-Beth. Thank you for your service, sir.

Now, how can I help you? the detective said. Mary-Beth allowed herself, for one moment, to imagine Detective Ulrich as a man who might save her. She imagined the two of them meeting at Flanigan's by the beach, iced slushy rum drinks in bright colors, a shared basket of curly fries under a swinging lamp. The two of them would discuss Calvin's case, and in the dark of that bar slash diner slash restaurant, Mr. Ulrich, former military, would see what the big deal was about Mary-Beth, her cunning, her pluck, the woman she was beneath, well, circumstances. She imagined Ulrich in a trench coat with nothing underneath it, then she imagined her own body the same—a detective and detective's wife, bringing bad guys down together. They'd screw in the back of his car whenever they solved a case—Tommy tied up in the passenger's seat forced to watch, or maybe hog-tied in the trunk—and then they'd promptly find a new mystery and start the whole thing over.

Did you read my answers? Mary-Beth asked the man on the phone. Her own tone of voice gave her the creeps. She didn't know when she'd started using it, but she could hear it—something needy in there. Something hopeful.

Detective Ulrich said to even speak to her, before deciding if he'd take her case on, he'd need a deposit of one thousand dollars.

And if you don't take this case, that money comes back when?

It doesn't, he clarified. This is a very selective system.

Mary-Beth had heard all she needed to hear. A crook knows a crook knows a crook. When she hung up on Ulrich, she already had six missed calls blinking on her phone, some text messages, and another call buzzing through. Look how many detectives want in on this, she said to Syl, pushing out her phone like a badge.

I think it's all crock, Syl said. Syl typed hard into the laptop. Google tells me the real deals are a load. That website's a scam.

What kind of load?

More'n replacing those teeth of yours, sissy.

Mary-Beth tossed her cell onto the coffee table. Syl flipped the channels again. ISIS all over the news, a new heat wave coming, another competitive show with muscular, muddy people in bathing suits. One commercial for back-to-school Snow Day coming up at North Pole, which made Mary-Beth squeal—*I'm a star! I'm gonna be a star!* Then there was Linzie.

Hey, pause it, Mary-Beth said. Hey hey, stay here a sec.

Come on, Elvira, you don't need—

Mary-Beth snatched the remote from her sister's hand. What's this prissy princess gotta say?

I'm sorry he died, Linzie said to a Botoxed, permed interviewer, *I really am, but maybe this was his comeuppance.* The background: a staged, dark kitchen. Then the special flashed to older footage, footage Mary-Beth had already seen—Linzie leaving the Broward County police station. *If I'm honest, the whole thing makes me sad, but there's nothing I can do about it now.*

Do you forgive him?

Sure I do.

The permed interviewer: *That is extraordinarily empathetic, Linzie. You must have great capacity for forgiveness in your heart.*

Linzie shrugs. Pushes out her lower lip. *I guess.*

Then it's an ad for an upcoming prime-time special on Linzie, an exclusive for *The Fix*.

Whore, Mary-Beth said.

Gotta tell you something, Midge—Syl seemed all the sudden serious. She lit another smoke, something she only did when she drank, and she held the cig funny, awkwardly propped between two stiff fingers. Her face cleared of feeling, like she'd eaten something bad. She wiped her forehead with the back of her hand, fingertips matte cracked and white from the polish remover. That King girl, Syl said quietly. Too quiet for Syl. Her people came up once. Up to the farm. Her boyfriend assistant person came to ask me about Cal.

Oh, come on now, Mary-Beth said.

Syl nodded. It's true.

And you did what?

I talked.

And what did *you* have to say? Mary-Beth wanted to know. She stood but didn't know why. Then she took one hard breath and sat back down. She grabbed both sides of her face with her hands and pedaled her bare feet into the tile, slap-slapping. Sylvia, tell me now what you did.

MB, cross my heart, I only said the best things. You know I've had doubts about Cal and his intentions, you know I wasn't thrilled with how you've covered for him, how you lie. I don't take back those things. I've been honest about those things. Look at the things those men said at the meeting today, just open your goddamn eyes. But I didn't let on, for that book, any of that. I told my part of the truth, that he came to live at the farm a summer, before the registry. Helped with the horses. Did a good job with them.

You said he did perfect, Mary-Beth said. *Perfect.* Her phone kept buzzing and lighting up with more detectives.

He did, and that was hard work, Syl said. Even learned to braid their tails. Girls taught him that. Did you know that? That my girls taught him that? They're good girls, MB.

Many times, Mary-Beth had imagined digging Linzie's book out of the trash bag in her closet. In this vision, she licked her finger to flip every page, wearing glasses she didn't need or own.

She'd highlight every sentence about her son that was wrong. *Wrong! Incorrect!* She imagined submitting proof—a photo album, discharge papers, a yearbook—she'd run out of highlighter, doing all that, licking the tip of the marker, a strip of hot yellow down her tongue.

Nobody knew her Calvin. Not the way she did.

Why're you telling me this now? Mary-Beth asked. Talking for that book's as good as yapping to Pigs.

You can read where I said what I said—nothing bad, Midge. Family's family. On my word. Nothing more important.

Then why'd you talk?

Syl changed the channel to a cooking show, then looked Mary-Beth in the eyes. She shrugged her shoulders. Haunted feelings, I guess.

LINZIE

LATER, YALE WILL call this Linzie's *instigating incident*.

The producers requested the talk with Linzie in a trailer, not the tent. Trailer talks were more private, no crew present. Zoë and Poor Horny Todd sat in the back, inviting Linzie to sit between them in the horseshoe-cushioned seating area, and only Zoë spoke. Todd nodded along, pushed the button of a recorder.

So, Linz, said Zoë, how would you say this journey for love's been going for you?

It's going good, Linzie said. It's an amazing opportunity.

Is the journey rewarding?

Very rewarding, Linzie said. She stroked her eyebrows with her index fingers. *Calm.*

Do you think you've made your mark? Zoë asked. Not your mark on the floor, but your Linzie-shaped mark, on Big D, in a way that translates to viewers? Zoë leaned in close, her voice soft and coddling, almost like she might kiss her. Do you think you've formed a real connection? Because Dimitrius, he's feeling you (Linzie remembers Zoë leaning back here, crossing a foot over her opposite knee), but I don't think he thinks you're feeling him.

At first Linzie thought, Liar. Zoë was a liar. Everything she'd said—when they would eat, when they could nap, when Linzie could make a bead bracelet—had proven this. But the more Zoë spoke, the more Linzie wondered if Dimitrius really *had* been feeling her. If maybe she was too oblivious or stupid to notice, to reciprocate normal-people cues. So she said—

Really? He's falling for *me*?

Amazingly, you.

And *he* doesn't know if I like *him*?

Zoë pursed her mouth to the side, shook her head. Linzie heard voices squibble in Zoë's headphones on the table. They sounded like the voices in Linzie's head when she fell asleep at night. Angry voices.

Of course I like him, Linzie said. I *love* him. We all do. That's the point.

See, that's what I thought, said Zoë, animated now. That's what I told him when he talked about choosing you. I said, *Linzie? My girl Linz? She's a favorite. She's a match*. But he still didn't believe me about you. Nobody thinks you want this.

Linzie wondered if she should apologize, and, if so, to whom.

You have to show him who you are, Zoë said. She pressed both hands at her heart. Like really, really, deep down—all those demons, we all have them. That's the journey.

I can do that, Linzie said. I'll hold his hand, kiss him, or whatever everybody wants. Linzie was tired. She was sunburned and dizzy and always cold. She wanted to leave the trailer.

What should I do to show him? Linzie asked.

Linz, Zoë said, you know I'm a producer, right? You know my job is to produce. Basically, I make sure everyone's safe and happy. And part of that goes like, when you signed on, when we took you off the alternate list, we did a background check. We dug around to make sure you are who you say you are. Are you Linzie Gwendolyn King?

Linzie nodded. Licked her lips. They burned.

OK, phew, just checking. Zoë laughed. You remember signing those forms of consent?

Sure, Linzie said.

Zoë snapped her gum here; she sat crouched forward, knees open, fingertips like *here is the church, here is the steeple*. We always do our homework, she said. Of course we do. Me and Todd, all your family here in production, we know you were a minor at the time of your incident. But we did figure—it's easy to figure—we know about the situation you had with that creep in Florida and the DOJ. How you did the brave thing, helped lock him up.

Linzie's ears began to ring at that word—*brave*. Then her ears felt hot, plugged with Popsicles, numb and wrong and not hers. The back of her neck tightened in a nauseating pang. Her mom flooded back to her. This was not the way she liked to remember her mom's voice. This was not the pot-roast fantasy, but the real tone of her mother outside the courthouse: *You'll pay for what men do your whole fucking life*. Linzie had tried so hard not to believe her.

Linzie said, Zoë, I'm on a journey for love.

And Zoë: Forget the cameras. Forget Marco and Dan and the whole crew. They're not even there. Forget America. It's just you and me here, talking, OK, woman to woman (Poor Horny Todd nodded at this, too), and, Linz, this is *reallllly* important information for your future husband to know who you are, don't you think? We're giving you the opportunity to explain this on your own terms, don't you want that? A relationship built on honesty, and not lies?

Linzie said, There's other things I could share. I was the best at math in my whole grade growing up. I think it makes me good at color theory, like, with makeup. My mom left me when I was— (she'd already told this story while six of the girls sat around her in the hot tub one night, jet bubbles slipping up Linzie's spine like an ominous finger).

We know, Zoë said. You've already shared that. So have other girls here, about their moms. Big D already knows. It's time to show him what you've really endured.

Would he want . . . that kind of wife?

Are you kidding me? Zoë said. She rested her hand on Linzie's wrist. It was so gentle. Her hand looked bloodless. Any guy worth a damn wants a strong woman, she said. Do you have any idea how strong you are? You're not a little girl, OK. You're a woman. And women protect other women. That's our job. There're women living in caves of shame, Linzie, survivors everywhere. You're gonna turn the flashlight on for them. You're gonna show them the way out. Do you have any idea how strong you are, Linz?

Linzie did not. She had never heard this about herself, and she'd certainly never felt it. Even the DOJ attorneys had never called her *strong*, not even after she'd spoken before the judge, impact statement in her hand, in front of all those strangers. The lawyers had called her *utterly broken* and *ruined*, actually. After the sentencing, in the hall, they'd thanked her for cooperating. Said they'd be *on her team for life*. As a federal witness, she'd be *protected, guarded, invaluable*. Then she never heard from them again.

If Big D doesn't continue this journey with you, Zoë said, do you want to have to wonder if it could have gone different if only you were honest?

I don't think I would wonder that, said Linzie.

It's time you finally break down those walls, Todd said. This was the only time he spoke. I can tell you have big walls up, he said. Men can always tell. You've got to tear them down, brick by brick, unless you want to be stuck behind your own moats and starve to death like Caesar's people.

Fun fact, Zoë said, Julius Caesar invented the modern calendar. He was a genius. We fucking love him here.

But not the Caesar salad, added Todd.

Linzie may not have known what she wanted, ever, but she did know what she didn't want, and there had never been anything she wanted less than this—remembering Calvin, talking about him with Zoë and Todd in this trailer, or with her future husband. She didn't know how to explain the water park, the chats, the other girls, without Dimitrius thinking she was too much baggage, a mess. *Where bugs gather*—Doug used to say to her—*trash*. Calvin existed in a place outside of Linzie, the same way looking at old photos of herself felt weird. The hairdo all wrong, obviously wrong, but where was the memory of having the cut? That's how Calvin felt. Something true she'd experienced but didn't understand, void of detail, of feeling. He'd happened to another girl, another Linzie. She'd made the wrong choices, but she was young. She wanted to forgive herself. It was the last year of her mom.

What that man did was sick, Zoë said, and you no longer have to carry that burden alone.

I don't feel like I carry that, said Linzie, shaking her head.

Beyond your obvious perseverance, Zoë said, imagine how interesting a story like that would be, to share. This many beautiful women—look around you, everyone's beautiful—don't you want to at least be interesting?

Alright, the scene of coercion, with the producers, that is *perfect* for a book, Yale said.

That sounds like a depressing book, said Linzie. I wouldn't want to read that.

This, a Friday. This, almost a year after that talk in the trailer. Before *My Turn*, before Calvin's death, before all the rest that would come, it felt like a special occasion when Yale had left his office to spend a lunch hour with Linzie. He took her to the front patio of News Cafe on Ocean Drive, and fans spun, misting them from above. Sinatra played. Behind Yale's head, tiny legs kicking clouds along the horizon—parasailing season. In Yale's prescription glasses, a siphoned sky.

Thank fuck you did tell them—Yale said—'cause in a way, not the best way but in a way, Calvin made your life. *This* is your purpose. He happened to you for a reason.

Linzie described the pivotal night with Dimitrius, the Big Scene, and Yale ordered her a tomato soup. He scrawled fast in a fancy notebook. He'd already had a few beers, bright gold.

It's all a goddamn CON, Yale said. He removed his glasses, wiped the lenses with a frilly looking cloth he pulled from his pocket. Can you see that now? They CONNED you. They chose your narrative, and you followed like a duckling. This is Manipulation Tactics, 101.

Linzie considered this. She knew not to say things like CON about *The Dating Show*. The producers had told her this, and she'd signed forms promising not to. But here, on Ocean Drive, she didn't need to ask Yale to believe her—he simply did. He believed her. And phone-agent Audrey had liked the sample pages. Now she'd requested a *whole book*.

Here's the real question. Did you *want* to tell him, on camera? Yale asked.

Who would *want* to tell a story like that? Linzie said.

Yale said, I've read the tweets, the comments, the forums. And people know there's more to the story, that there's more to you. They *like* you, Linzie. They're interested.

In me?

In what happened to you.

Linzie pulled the spoon from her mouth, set it down. Her own face warped in the reflection. That's so crazy you'd say this, Yale, because you know, I told Big D the story about Calvin, and he didn't even look surprised or anything, like he already knew. And when they called *cut*, he didn't even talk to me between setups. He just sipped his water and looked anywhere else but at me. And then HMU came and touched up his face, but they didn't touch up mine, with all the makeup running down my cheeks. I felt like, *Wow, here's my biggest fear coming true. I'm bad, I'm baggage,* and then my handler, Zoë—

I know Zoë, Yale said. I've called her a few times for quotes. Not the happiest girl (hahahaha!). Not my biggest fan. How about this, Yale said. How about I'm your handler now. I mean that metaphorically—no one handles you but you. But you've got an advocate now.

Linzie felt suddenly hyper, sharing these feelings with Yale.

With Sinatra on the restaurant speakers, his voice a backing track to her own, the telling now felt legitimate. Zoë came up to me during setup, Linzie went on, and my whole body was shaking, like, convulsing. I thought maybe eating would help. I hadn't even realized I liked salmon, but the show had made it taste so good, and I was so hungry, and Zoë said, *Linzie don't you even think about touching that fucking salmon! It's a continuity issue!* (There was that word again!)

Why was the salmon so good? Yale asked. He stared at Linzie, hard.

Huh? Linzie said. She sipped her Sprite, and the straw sputtered liquid onto her nose.

The salmon, Yale said. You never liked salmon before that particular salmon. Why?

Linzie looked at Yale, the way he was leaning over his notebook, legs crossed, his genuine interest. She just shared all that, and here was Yale, picking up on the details, the *little things*. That must be what made him a writer, she thought. This level of attention, the way he examined her like she was someone worthy of preference, of thought.

It was crispy, Linzie said to him, carefully. Yale wrote that down. She went on, I'd never tasted a salmon like that. With crispy parts.

Go on, he said, sorry for that interruption. He smiled as he spoke. The tape recorder sat on the table between them, and suddenly the small black device was no longer menacing, but a comfort. Linzie leaned in closer to it. She said: Zoë fed me the words. Zoë said, *Can you not say you had sex with that man?* And I said, *Well, what else would I say? That's unfortunately what happened.* And she said, *He raped you, Linzie. He raped you at a water park.* She said I was *groomed, stalked, and assaulted by a serial statutory rapist.*

That's why you used the word *assault* on the show? Yale asked.

That's the word she used. And that's what the lawyers used. But that's not really how it was, Linzie said. Not in a strict sense. Like, I liked Calvin. I wasn't a kid like the others, I just turned thirteen the month before. No one put a gun to my head. I'd been talking to him online.

But you didn't share any of that.

I mean, no, I wouldn't say that now. I know what he's done to girls. Really helpless little girls. There's no way to forgive someone sick like that. I learned about the others in court, and I'm just saying I wasn't the worst of them.

Well, Yale said. He was a lot older than you. Teenage boys are horrendous horndogs, I apologize on behalf of my species (hahahaha!). We can't help it. But he knew more than you. He should have known better. This is something different. Have you ever heard of power dynamics, Linz? Prefrontal cortex?

He wasn't a teen, Linzie said. He was twenty-five.

Yale sipped his beer. We come to everything slow.

I wasn't *young young*, the way you might think of it. I was grown for my age.

That kind of person, Yale said, no one cares if he lives or dies. Would you?

No, Linzie said—and this response, this moment, what would ring through Linzie's whole body outside that bookshop in Seattle, Yale shaking the phone, *He's gone, out of the picture*. Indeed, she cared, the rush of sorrow one of the most potent feelings of her life. *Show me sad.*

Yale scribbled for a long time, then finally said, *Linzie*, like it was someone else's name. Linzie, you've been coerced. By producers you trusted. By every creep on that set.

Marco from the crew actually stood up for me, Linzie said. During the salmon dinner. He threw his headphones into one of those fake plants and told Zoë she'd gone too far. That she was doing it for a pay bump. That they should send me home and pay for my therapy.

And what did you do? Yale asked.

I didn't want to go home. Linzie shrugged.

Yale shook his notebook. This book, Linzie, *our* book, this is where you get to own what's happened to you. You're not the girl crying in a red gown anymore, are you? Look at you. You're having lunch with me, on Ocean Ave. And you get to reclaim who you are.

Linzie liked the sound of that word—*reclaim*. She really wanted a new life, separate from *The Dating Show* or her sad bedroom in the leaky garage of her own sad house. Linzie grew up living in the garage; her dad had transformed it into a bedroom when she was a toddler. The row of high rectangular windows, the industrial smell, the dark—she could leave that all behind now.

Linzie wanted to show her mom, wherever she was, that she was capable of being somebody worth a damn, that she had become *something*, and maybe that something was *author*. Her heart had been broken a thousand times—every time her mom disappeared behind the bathroom door, when her mom disappeared for good, when Dimitrius walked her out, dumping her, the night she told him—and, later, America—who she *really* was. He'd said, *This isn't for me*. And Linzie knew she had become "this." Then he kissed her on the cheek to say goodbye, though they never showed any of that footage. The only evidence: Linzie telling Yale about it now over lunch. Zoë said they had to figure out a better way to exit her, and then they'd recorded Linzie dismissing herself. *I'm not ready for love*, she cried. They promised this would offer her story *more dignity*.

When Linzie was asked to cry for camera, and it was many times in those final few days, she opened her eyes for the sting. Just beyond the sting came water, and she liked that—the high-pitched, disciplined pain. As she cried into the lights, she imagined somewhere out there, in a motel room, in a jail dining hall, or in a bar, her mother would be watching her on television. She hoped Irene would think she looked good—her little girl, grown up. Irene would be so proud of her, maybe even stand on a stool to turn up the volume, say, *Don't we look alike?* to a crowd of people. *Can't you see it in the cheeks?* She would hush anybody around, for her daughter. She would want her to win.

MARY-BETH

MARY-BETH DIDN'T LIKE Odette from the moment she said her name. O-what? O-duck? Croquette? Odette called and called, first at home, her voice spatting nonsense on the voicemail machine—*Mary-Beth Boyer, I'm here to hear your story. I'm here to help you and your son, to bring justice to Calvin. No one will care the way I care, Mary*—then she called North Pole, Petra screwing her eyebrows up high while offering the white plastic phone, *MB, some Yankee pants looking to solve Cal's case.*

Now listen, girly, Mary-Beth said to O-derp on the phone. Petra stared at her, no one else in North Pole, which emboldened Mary-Beth to make the call sound a little more dramatic than it needed to be. She'd do that, if only to see Petra slap the counter, Petra's dark molars showing like the pebbles at the bottom of Cal's old fish tank. Mary-Beth went on: Girleen, you're rushing up the wrong stalk. I know all you detectives are a sham, won't stop blowing up my phone, and I ain't paying, so why don't you go get humped by a dolphin.

Petra huffed and puffed and shoved Mary-Beth on the shoulder with that *you bitch* crinkled-nose expression she loved. Petra, a sister in all the ways Syl had mostly missed—never any judgment. Mary-Beth suddenly wished Syl would walk in and see them laughing like that.

I'm not a detective, Odette said on the phone. I'm a journalist. I'm in podcast media, and people should know what happens to men like Calvin, the treatment of them. You know the police aren't going to prioritize this case. It's been almost a month. They're not going to follow this . . .

Mary-Beth did know—it was as good as over. Last week, she'd tried to find the private detective. Since then, she'd left fourteen messages with Carmen Durham, even showed up to the station once—*Nobody here's on that case, they'll get back to you, miss.* Mary-Beth knew she could drag Cal's corpse into the station, knife stuck in his throat and floured with prints, and every officer would stare dumbly. They'd step over his body, hers too. Oh, she knew this. But she didn't like somebody else, this girl on the phone, knowing it— that to law enforcement, to anyone so-called righteous and good, Cal's life would never matter. It would never have a point. Not now that they couldn't punish him.

Mary-Beth watched two teenage girls in the gas station's convex mirror. Next to the Christmas village train, the teens stuffed bags of chips and white cheddar popcorn beneath their sweatshirts. Mary-Beth jutted her chin: *Petra, nail 'em.* Petra ran over.

You can't trust anyone, said Odette. When media's involved, money, headlines—and with your situation, with Linzie, you've got all that—people will sell you out from under them.

Odette Carlisle, Mary-Beth said into the phone. Who hated you enough to name you that? You don't sound like a redneck, but that sure's a name.

I rather like my name, the girl said. She argued it for a moment, then said: Mary-Beth, I live in New York, but I'm willing to fly to Fort Lauderdale tomorrow just to meet you. Will you meet me if I do that? That's a trip, a not insignificant trip, and I'm willing to do it for you. For Calvin. I swear, I'll book a ticket right now.

Petra yelled at the teen girls, banned them from North Pole. Both the girls laughed with plum faces, tears rising, then ran from the station with the chips anyway. Old Frank walked in, a regular, and Mary-Beth turned around to grab his usual Reds before he even asked.

Odette was still talking. More about looking up flights.

You being paid to bother me? Mary-Beth asked. This *Candid Camera*? I'm working.

I know that, Odette said into the phone. I found the number for your place of employment. I know you're at North Pole, because I called you there.

Oh, Mary-Beth could read her. Odette was *that* kind, the kind who'd always underestimate her, find her poor and therefore stupid. It was in the way O-duck enunciated her words, said her name too much. The wimpy little sighs. Mary-Beth liked to notice the ways people changed their voices according to what they wanted. With Cal and his friends, she noticed the way they pitched up in tone and inflection when they didn't want their title, that forever rotten rind—*threat, criminal, sex offender*—when they needed to be boys again. Syl had her Oprah tone. Mary-Beth herself tried to never change who she was.

Would you be opposed to me coming in to see you tomorrow, Mary?

You could say I'd be opposed.

How about a dinner, free dinner? As many leftovers as you want. I'll compensate.

Let me think about it, said Mary-Beth. Then she locked eyes with Petra, who was back at the register. Nudge of the pupils, twitch of the mouth—NOT! Mary-Beth said. I can pay my own dinner, you dumb little shit. Petra leaned all the way over, gripped her stomach. The pompon on her elf cap skidded across the counter like a fishing bobber.

Ms. Boyer, Odette said. Linzie's book's an abomination, we both know this. And she's directly profiting off the death of your son. You want Linzie King, Miss Priss of *The Dating Show*, to have final word on Calvin, to set the record for how he's remembered?

I don't want to hear about that great Dean Koontz classic, Mary-Beth said.

I think this could get millions of listeners, Odette said, that's the blessing and curse of Linzie. I want to give you a platform to speak your truth, your son's truth. You should have the space to counter the other girls who accused Calvin.

Chang?

Francine Gerber—now Frenchie Levine. I've been in touch.

Your nose is everywhere, huh, Mary-Beth said.

We can figure out who killed your son . . . That's what I truthfully want. The attention will no doubt bring in tips we need, and I want you to have that peace. I want you to drive the car—I'm so sorry, I didn't mean to reference a car. I was attempting to build a metaphor.

Frank exited the station. Petra pulled a clipper from her back pocket and worked at her pinky nail. Behind the counter, she straightened a rack of lotto tickets.

Who'd listen? Mary-Beth asked, quieter now. You've got a squirmy little voice, you're no Osgood.

Take the story back, Odette said. You can't trust anyone. Not even your friends at Gateway. You know Betty the director sent me Calvin's intake forms? His homework assignments? She was thrilled to send anything, asked me for money after she sent it, and that's your son's confidential information. Who knows who else she's sending those forms to. Who knows if she's in on something, maybe an inside source for people who harass the guys, those guys at the Palmyra?

Mary-Beth stood at her counter, receiver pressed warm to her ear. Almost one month, that mutilating deadline, her time up, one more failure of a million. *They'll get back to you, miss.*

If I talk, Mary-Beth said, here's the condition. No Thomas Boyer on your podcast.

Then Odette booked her flight.

BIRDIE

BEFORE CALVIN BIRDIE. After Calvin Birdie.
I made the lists like I was supposed to. I'd done everything I was supposed to. For years I'd followed blinking lights in therapy, and I'd done hypnosis like a person traumatized is supposed to. I repeated back affirmative chants, did tap-tap therapy at my sternum, chugged herbal teas and swallowed supplements like I was supposed to. Down on Mott and Canal Street, a Chinese doctor once gripped my wrist to feel my pulse or heartbeat to diagnose me, and the gripping of my wrist made me reach out and smack the doctor in the arm, which I was not supposed to do, but perhaps it was a response I was supposed to have. I used happy lamps like I was supposed to, installed motion sensors in every apartment I'd lived in, like I was supposed to. I'd leaned back for acupuncture, needles flicked into my hands, forehead, the hardest pinch at the feet and inside the ankles—starry, hot—I wore pressure point stickers on my ears like I was supposed to. I burned mugwort and healing candles, dotted essential oils all over. I'd taken every self-defense class at the Y like I was supposed to.

None of that helped, after Calvin was gone.

None of it brought me back to the present. To the *Walden experience*. To my island of healing. I didn't leave the cottage. Didn't take any calls. I collected the pine needles that had stuck to my shoes and the welcome mat, lined them up on the desk to mark hours, then days.

Every day, it's the first thing I wish for. Him gone, I'd said.
Now, there was nothing left to wish for.

All of us girls met Calvin on the school bus. His dad, Thomas Boyer, drove it. Calvin was a high school dropout and did outdoor work at Dole Grove—pool cleaning, lawn maintenance—and he took the passenger seat next to Mr. Boyer after the last bell's dismissal, up where none of us were allowed to sit.

Every girl called him hot. He was Mr. Boyer's son, and he was hot. There was something scandalous, hilarious, about Mr. Boyer—with his thick mustache and rashy skin, newly *divorced*—having a hot son. Because Mr. Boyer wasn't a person to us then. He was our bus driver. He was the man who'd make jokes every morning about what we were wearing. He knew our routes, our parents. He knew, somehow, who was not speaking to who, or who had asked who out, or who was grounded for what. He loved us, we thought. He worked for us.

Calvin wore blue all the time, and Francine said it was on account of gang affiliation, that he was a Crip, and that we should wear red if we wanted his attention.

I saw it on PBS, Francine said, *about the Crips.* We sat under a sheet fort we'd built in my childhood bedroom. We'd propped the TV radio on a chair in the center of the tent as it played music videos. TLC dancing in a warehouse.

The PBS special explained all about the Crips, and he is definitely one, Francine said. Francine, with her splatter of dark beauty marks and freckles, thick red hair, silk pajamas just like TLC, highest soprano in choir. She was one year older and looked more like my mom's daughter than I did. I was jealous, though I never told her that. I said, *Don't you have to commit murder to be in a gang?* And, *Can you be in a real gang if you're white?*

It was hot in our tent. The ceiling fan billowed the sheet above our heads in a steady pulse. Our breath clung to each other's skin, warm as static.

I think he's committed some things, Francine said. Or did she say that?

At school, rumor had it that Calvin was fresh out of juvie, that he'd had his driver's license taken away, that's why he rode the bus with Mr. Boyer even though Mr. Boyer didn't really like him. Calvin was tall, always covered in skateboard bruises, and his Adam's apple bobbed when he smiled with an underbite. *Underbite*—I learned that word because of Calvin's smile. Because I asked Francine: *What's that called?* and she knew everything about everything, especially Calvin. He smiled a lot.

Francine and I were both in the third grade; she'd been held back a year. Together we learned spelling with Mrs. Gladstone, and I was advanced, embarrassed of this. In Mrs. G's classroom, she'd made paper footprints on the floor laminated with glossy packing tape. We'd have to spell things aloud to move along the prints, to go anywhere, even back to our desk.

One day, Mrs. G pointed to a manatee on a wall calendar. I said, *M-a-n-a-t-e-a.*

I misspelled it so Francine would like me. So she wouldn't feel so alone. I stood in the middle of the room the rest of the period.

Francine Gerber, my first friend. My best friend. Before Calvin Francine dreamed of being a marine biologist, stole her parents' money to adopt a manatee in a mail scam—*this mana-t-e-a is dedicated to us, let's call it Brancine.* Before Calvin Francine, who'd punched Ben Priggs in the nose after he'd made a silverware-down-the-stairs joke about my name; Before Calvin Francine, who wrote notes and poems full of code words and secret languages we'd made up, *Soulmate twins,* we'd said, before him.

Francine got off the bus before I did, somewhere near Monroe Street, following Calvin. It was winter of 1995, I was nine and she was ten, and I didn't want her to leave me there. I said, *You're going with the Crip?* Then I watched her walk off, following Calvin, several stops early. Key chains jangled from her JanSport slung low, which pulled her skirt up in back. She'd worn a red bandana as a headband that day. Mr. Boyer said *goodbye* to them both.

It was After Calvin Francine—who'd suddenly changed her name to Frenchie—who'd told me not to do what she did. Frenchie, who'd begged me not to go over to Calvin's house weeks later, when he'd asked me. The look in her eyes when she pleaded, round haunted owl eyes—*He's bad, Bird*—the two of us back in our fort, twinkle lights bleeding through the sheets.

Pinky swear, she said, *on Brancine's life*, and we hooked our fingers, kissed it official.

But of course I went. I was a kid. He'd asked me. I thought I was supposed to.

And I already told you, I was jealous.

LINZIE

DOUG SAID: CASSEROLE. Every woman can make one of those.

Linzie's father insisted she learn how to cook; he'd been on this ever since *The Dating Show* aired. Now, to prep for Linzie's primetime special on *The Fix*, Yale was coming over for dinner. He'd never seen their place, not in all the time he'd spent researching Linzie's life for the book—she hadn't wanted him to. Now he was coming to *scope it*.

Remember, this's a dead man's meal, Doug said, entering Linzie's room. He limped down from the garage doorway, green plastic bag in his hand. It sagged dark and round, like a battered kneecap. Radicchio, he said, for the rabbit.

What's a radicchio? Linzie asked.

A nice lettuce, that's what. Doug tossed the bag at her on the bed. It nearly missed her. Dinner's gotta be classed up, to match. This one's on the dead man.

Linzie didn't understand this. Why, ever since Calvin had died, her father had begun ordering things, buying everything— telescopes, bright button-down shirts from China, plane parts folded into money clips, antique coins. Doug was a dispatcher, forever on the phone in his plaid recliner, which featured a gloomy outline of his body. Forever sick and on VA benefits, forever tumid with gout. But now he'd bought a new silver cane that snapped open into a collapsible stool. He snapped its jaw open everywhere.

We're not making money off Calvin, Linzie said.

Oh, but finally, my girl, we will, Doug said.

This was why Yale was coming. To see if their home was *primetime ready*. To *restrategize. Rearrange.* To *keep the story alive.*

Linzie googled: *impressive dinner home make*. Casseroles did not appear on the lists she found. The items she scrolled past were daunting: hulking cuts of meat that required thermometers. Chicken cordon bleu and beef Wellington (why so many *layers?*). Crabs and lobsters required in-home murder, something Linzie found impossibly stressful to imagine.

Linzie drove to Publix. She remembered how her mother used to call Food Lion the *Shitty Kitty*, and Winn-Dixie did not seem like the place for a special occasion. Inside, the store smelled like baked bread and fried chicken and cookies. She looked at the fondue recipe on her phone. She would not use cheese from a plastic film or from a spray can. If she was going to do this, she was going to do it for real.

The cheese display looked like a coffin, and Linzie decided she'd buy them all—imagined all the cheese coalescing into one elegant sauce. She chose port-marbled pink cheddar, cratered Swiss, a block of bleu—she knew people liked bleu, even if she didn't. She grabbed a netted bag of Babybel wheels with their shining wrappers.

She hadn't considered dessert. She googled *fondue Dessert make* and picked up strawberries. Near the stems, they were pale yellow, the color of the old blood on her linens and sleeves.

At the register, a woman named Tippi glided the ingredients over the red, blinking laser. Linzie saw her own glossy face crying on the magazine rack next to the Skittles. She tried to psychically counter it, that crying face, by smiling.

This is a lot of cheese, Tippi said.

I'm cooking dinner, Linzie said, proud.

When the total appeared on Tippi's screen, she repeated the number. Took Linzie's cash, smoothed it. And then: Aren't you the girl who killed the guy or something?

At home, Linzie unpacked the groceries. She folded the paper bags into perfect, adult rectangles. Laid the food out on the counter. Yale would arrive by six. She had about an hour.

Linzie double checked her recipe list; she'd forgotten the lemon juice. She googled *what replace lemon juice* and then *what replace lemons*; she read that acids like apples, or apple juice, might replace citrus in an appropriate way. She had Martinelli's in the refrigerator. She was also missing the Italian dressing required to "pack the sauce with extra zing," but she did have packets of ranch powder. Her dad used to mix the powder into mayo and spread it on a burger or onto a baked potato, *Da King's Specialty*, he'd say, chewing.

Linzie knew where the plates were (she microwaved on them daily), but the big pots and pans were mostly new to her. She inspected them carefully, wrapped her hand around each handle, wondering which had been her mother's favorite. She remembered Irene watching Giada on Food Network—pretty smile, dash of this, splash of that. It was true, what they said: cooking made a woman.

She got to work grating the cheese that needed grating, the bleu crumbling against the metal teeth, nicking her thumb. She found a Band-Aid. Inspected her great mound of cheese. *No such thing as too much of a good thing*, Linzie said, trying on her best cooking show voice.

When Linzie had been eliminated from *The Dating Show*, the SUV full of cameras drove her back to the Embassy Suites. The room was still stripped like she'd never left it, but the gum bald spot was gone; it was a different room. Miss Shannon, *resident psychotherapist*, opened the door and pushed in a room service cart.

She looked so weak, pushing it. Metal bells of food rattled as she walked.

Miss Shannon lifted every lid by poking her pointer finger into the hole on top. She lifted them like a scientist would, steady and evenly, elbows pointed. Each revealed a sheet of Saran wrap dotted with condensation so cloudy Linzie could not see the food beneath it, only vague color there, like a wound under one of Doug's bandages. Miss Shannon went on to describe each item on the cart. A brick of chicken. A very nice steak. A hamburger, cooked medium. Spaghetti and meatballs. Linzie watched that mole above her lip as she spoke.

Spaghetti, I guess? Linzie had said. Miss Shannon nodded, pupils like stones.

So you have an appetite?

Linzie shrugged.

Are you having any suicidal thoughts?

Like what?

Are you feeling like you could harm yourself, or others?

What others? Like you?

Like me, yes. She nodded.

Why would I want to harm you? Linzie asked. Linzie ate more. Sauce flecked the bedspread. She asked when she could go home. *I have a very old bunny to take care of.*

You've demonstrated some concerning signs, Miss Shannon said.

Linzie never asked what kinds of signs. Maybe she was afraid to know.

Miss Shannon stood and wheeled the cart out of the room. It rattled the same. Linzie's meals would come and go this way for three more weeks, until production wrapped, Miss Shannon's plates punctuating loose billows of time. This scene, this conversation with Miss Shannon, would never make it into *My Turn*, though Linzie returned to it often. How the door always locked automatically.

Yale knocked. He was early. From the kitchen, she heard Doug answer the door. She smiled, thinking herself occupied with *domestic matters*. She imagined one day wearing an apron upon which she'd elegantly wipe her hands—there would be flour on her face. Linzie straightened her blouse, centered her denim skirt so the zipper matched up with her spine, walked out to greet him.

Yale held a bouquet in his hand. His hair looked wet, though that may have just been gel, and he wore a blue polo, dark denim jeans, the same Rainbow flip-flops as her. No one had come to Linzie's house looking for Linzie since she was a kid—and those were cops—but now here was Yale, his dimples dimpling, holding her favorite flowers. She'd told him this fact early on, that daisies looked like they were smiling.

Absolutely love the place, Yale said. Fuck, this is gonna be perfect. He looked all around, nodding. He was talking to Doug.

Can't miss it, her father said. By this, Doug meant the blue moon color he'd painted the exterior when Linzie was a kid, to match his favorite ice cream. Yale turned to Linzie and spread his arms, waiting for a hug—come on, kid.

Linzie had always dreamed of being hugged like this. She smelled Yale's familiar cologne, which was more like a temperature than a fragrance, really. Like cool mountain springs, dark trees, Alaska. She'd seen Alaska's jagged teeth of floating ice on doctor's office calendars.

Better get these in water before they frown, Yale said, winking at her.

The cellophane whispered in Linzie's hand as she took the daisies to the kitchen. She pulled a tall water glass from the kitchen cabinet, filled it with water, popped the unsheathed daisies in. When she let go, they fell into a split like a ladybug's wings parting. From the living room, the familiar pops and snaps of cans. Linzie heard the men talking about roads and directions, the traffic on US-1 (*Useless 1, am I right?!*). Yale and Doug had spoken *business* on the phone, and they'd met briefly here and there, but they'd never spent a meal together, never something intimate like this. Linzie had read she should *feed a guest upon arrival*, so she arranged the Babybel pucks on a plate, their waxy bisecting flags all facing center. She brought the plate out to the living room. The men did not say thanks.

Back in the kitchen, Linzie turned the stove to high. The metal coils flushed red. She poured the flour in the pot, then handfuls of cheese, then the ranch powder, the Martinelli's apple juice, a bottle of her dad's Heineken. She stirred and stirred, imagining Irene over her shoulder, proud, saying, *Just like that, Linzie girl, you're so grown-up, that's perfect.*

The ball of cheese spun as she stirred. That's what it had become. A ball. The beer and juice hadn't integrated, and instead pooled and boiled around the ball. As the pot continued to heat, Linzie chopped an apple, cut cubes of bread, sliced a chicken cutlet, and arranged them onto three plates. She'd forgotten to buy fondue skewers (how many things could she forget?!), but that's what forks were for. She turned off the stove, watched the neon coil pinken and die. The ball of cheese looked like it had a face now, bubbled eyes, and the eyes were blinking at her.

Linzie brought it all out to the dining room. Yale stood from the couch, handed Linzie the Babybel plate. Might wanna put these in the fridge, he said. The cheese is sweating.

Linzie did not know what this meant, but she said, Oh wow, sure is, and took the plate from him. Then she said: Supper's up, guys!

Linzie sponged off the dining room table, and the three of them sat down. For years, this had been Linzie and Doug's storage spot, the table stacked with bills, magazines, her father's empty pill bottles, crushed cans, copies of the *Sun Sentinel*, fly swatters, crumbling or leaking makeup products, empty boxes of Triscuits, mugs of muddied coffee stinking of vanilla Coffee Mate, the dots of mold floating delicately, like lily pads. Yale would never know this, never know that Linzie had piled all their junk into the food pantry, just for tonight. He simply sat down, rubbed his hands together, and Linzie said, I thought it'd be a nice evening for some fondue.

A stained-glass lamp hung above their heads, the three of them stabbing the bread pieces with their forks and dipping them, one at a time, into the pot at the center of the table. No cheese came out. Nothing stretched or oozed like in the recipe photos on Linzie's phone. She had thought maybe the cheese ball would *settle* or *relax*, the way hair did. Linzie tried it herself; her piece of bread came up wettened by the apple juice and beer, but no cheese loosened. Yale did not comment. He ate a piece of wet bread on his fork and asked her father questions.

Doug tried to dip the bread with his fingers now, no fork, and Linzie hoped and prayed the cheese would give, release, liquefy. Not much of a cook, is she, Doug said.

Yale said: Maybe cast-iron next time, Linz . . . something to retain the heat, disperse it. I believe fondue needs to stay on heat.

Linzie looked around at the dining room, a dingy offshoot of the kitchen. It was so dated, with her father's yellow service medals on the wall. His framed certificates. The wallpaper, bubbled and brown, their jelly air fresheners. Why was this place *perfect* for the TV segment? She stood up with her knife and cut a chunk from the cheese. It reminded her of a great big eyeball—a whale's eyeball—floating in a jar (Linzie's parents once brought her a baby shark in a jar, brought it all the way from Key West. The blue thing watched her always, and at first, Linzie had felt protected by it. Eventually, it started looking at her funny, and bad things started to happen in the night. Linzie buried it in the backyard, dug a weak hole and hit chunks of coral with a metal ladle from the kitchen, white chalky shells everywhere. Her parents never noticed it was gone, but Linzie often wondered how long it would take the glass to break down in the hot earth, shark liquid seeping, a body decomposing, right there next to the sprinkler head).

It's not so hard to just cut it, Linzie said, holding her knife, which darted a Tinker Bell glow across her father's face.

How's work, sir? Yale said.

Thirty-one trucks now, Doug said. Then he went on about load board apps and freight operation.

(Men talking)

Anyway, Yale said, twenty minutes later. With the murder, this is the perfect time to strike. There's podcast movement happening, and I'm thinking we can get more doc work, have cameras follow her, a *Day in the Life* kind of deal. I've reached out to some networks, and like I said, I think there's a second book in here too. I'll get a proposal together for you and Audrey. You know, I wasn't sure about the book, but obviously it gave people something, and after *this*? I mean, we don't even have to worry about legal now. No libel or slander after someone's dead, so we can step away from the public record docs and come from a place of Linzie's raw, visceral emotion—

Visceral emotion, said Doug. He chewed and spoke with a dry piece of bread in his mouth. Visceral emotion and my daughter—Linz, you know what that means? Tell me what that word means. I'll give you three tries. I'll give you three hundred bucks and a new rabbit if you tell me what *visceral* means.

Well, it's related to *viscera,* Linzie said—but Doug cut her off. Started in about the European Union.

Doug King was an asshole, but he was an asshole who had been to war—Linzie reminded herself, watching him wipe beer from his chin. Doug King or *Da King,* as he enjoyed pointing out—*say it fast!*—was disciplined and no-nonsense (*impudent,* Yale would say later) and had a house-rattling laugh, when you earned it. Doug could be sappy over songs. He thought outer space was really something. He liked to explain the way things worked: *This is how to check a carburetor. This is how to load a shotgun. This is how the world functioned when people weren't such pussy morons, when we stamped our tongues with psychedelics, and this is how to drive stick,* and Sasquatch was no doubt real, according to Da King, as were aliens and UFOs, and China had a long plan for our ultimate physical, spiritual, and economic destruction, and salmon—living salmon, muscled and reflective salmon—had some kind of subterranean resilient knowledge after which we should all model ourselves. Doug King was such a fucking asshole, Linzie knew, but she would not leave him. Not even when he humiliated her, which was often. Not as long as the back of his balding head stayed planted in their sunken living room, hand on the remote like a terrified balloon animal. He was consistent. Predictable in his slurry cruelty. Forever he'd whined about the deep dent in his chest, there since he was a boy—one could eat a whole bowl of cereal from the clean, round depth of it, he liked to point out, and Linzie remembered that metaphor was once a bowl of soup, split pea soup one might eat out of the dent in Doug's chest with a wedge of grilled cheese—*that's how big*—but he'd eventually changed it to *cereal*, and the fact of this—the way her father had cared enough to consider this soup/cereal imagery, plus the mysterious decision to change course one day—remained the reason, the twinkling, startling reason Linzie stayed even though her mother had not. She pitied him.

"True crime" is going to be a whole genre, it's gonna boom, Yale said. What we want to do now is distance ourselves from the Linzie on *The Dating Show*. We wrote that book—love, media, resilience—we banked that. Now we swerve into investigative territory. This is the hot spot, right now, before anything's solved. Once it's solved and they find whatever hillbilly hit him, no one'll care. Yale pulled a plastic baggie out of his pocket. He untied the knot of the bag and poured walnuts into his palm. Then he scattered some on his plate like little dehydrated brains. Linzie heard them crunch between his teeth.

Omegas, he said, lifting the bag an inch from the table. Always have 'em. Want?

No thanks, Linzie said. I'm allergic to nuts. Remember?

Yale opened his spiral notebook again and got to jotting. *Ideas, Doug?* He shifted in his seat and crossed his legs, like a girl. Yale in her mother's chair cast a new impression on every single detail of the house, the same way Linzie's perfume, the try-hard dearth of her try-hard soul, became more potent every time she entered his office. The dining room table, which she'd worked so hard on, now looked gross and tacky. Not looked, *was*—a sticky film—each time she lifted her glass of Sprite from its surface it felt like popping off the suckers of her shower mat.

Worst of all, Yale wasn't considering her thoughts the way he had when he interviewed her for the book. She was so excited for that, excited not only because Yale's attention felt good but because she'd wanted her father to witness his questions and her answers, to know someone like Yale Gutterman, *best of the best writer*, could be interested in someone like Linzie. In what she had to say. Yale knew about Calvin. He knew about the crispy salmon. Doug never asked her anything, only the familiar dailies: *what takeout's for supper, what're we watching, where's my mail?* Yale asked about her *feelings* (the spectrum!), always wanted to know, *how did that make you feel?* If her dad listened, he might see her that way too. He might, at long last, know her.

Linzie continued forking and cutting chunks off the cheese, as if eating it like this would make it *on purpose*. Yale ate the apple slices and his omegas. He asked if the apples had been washed, and with what.

Dad, Yale thinks I've survived real trauma, Linzie said, as Doug explained a particular WWE move, one called the Tombstone, a metaphor for Linzie and her audience, See it looks like they're suckin' each other's sausages.

Trauma! Doug said. Then softer, Meant something else in my day. Doug hadn't shaved his stubble for the dinner, and the patchy white made Linzie embarrassed.

Well, trauma is complex, it's not really a binary, Yale explained.

These words like *trauma*, they're just—Doug lassoed his index finger over his head—salad tossed words like words don't mean words anymore.

One day, Yale explained, women are going to feel empowered to be forthcoming about their traumas. Sexual and otherwise. All because of your daughter's life.

But, Doug explained, you think that's a good thing for the world? Rah-rah girl power? How about actual strength? Biting down the bit? Clawing up the bucket like a fucking rat?

Yale explained that yes, it would be a good thing for the world, this empowerment would be a real, progressive, nonviolent action. Honesty is action.

Doug explained that to seek true progression is to seek freedom, and just recently Ron DeSantis signed the No Climate Tax Pledge, and wasn't that a great thing? Did Yale even know about that? Because that's the kind of goddamn progress he's talking about.

And Yale explained the historical connotations of words like *freedom*, the ever-changing ephemeral nature of words, the patriarchal white supremacist constructs of grammar.

Linzie said, Can we please get back to my trauma, please?

And Doug explained how books and liberal arts degrees don't make for true wisdom, ingenuity, and especially not moxie, not gall, because nothing absolutely NOTHING makes up for experience.

And Yale explained his student debt, impending climate change, Mike Dukakis, faulty tax brackets, a summer internship he once held as a high school student at the White House, how he'd shaken hands with veteran John McCain for a photograph still framed in mahogany and hung in his mother's house in Delray, despite his numerous gentle requests for her to take it down, because people change (they have the right to), and moral compasses recalibrate, and just look at Ukraine, just look at Egypt, and don't make him bring up McCarthyism.

The plates shone with grease under the overhead lamp. Linzie said, Yale, I don't want you to think I'm a bad cook. He leaned back and put his hands up like he was pushing something away. A gallant effort, he said, but maybe a fon-don't.

Gallant, Doug said. Linz, three tries for *gallant*. He held up his horrible fingers, elbow on the table. Three tries for three hundred and a bunny.

Yale asked Linzie if she wanted to get ice cream after dinner, just the two of them.

In his Fiat, at a red light, Yale pulled a glass pipe shaped like an elephant from his center console. His fingers wrapped around it like a fine violinist would his instrument—immediate, expert. Linzie wondered what it would be like to do anything that capably.

Want? he asked, smoke held in, an old-man croak.

Is this a test? Linzie asked. To see what I'm like high?

Not everything's a test—he said, breathing out—just offering. Linzie touched the car window. It was so warm, even at night.

Yale lit the pipe again with a Zippo, the flame slithering up his thumb knuckle. Then he circled the bowl, as if stirring a miniature cauldron of soup in one of those miniature-life videos Linzie had seen online. In the videos, real human hands painted dollhouse-sized furniture, chairs and stools the size of thimbles. Sometimes, staring at those videos, Linzie felt the Carrie White inside her bubble to the surface, someone blazing and ugly and dripping with gore, a snapped girl, tiara glistening. The Carrie urge, for Linzie, was the urge to swipe all the tiny furniture from their tiny little rooms and to crush every object into paste. She watched the videos a lot.

Who ARE you, really? The producers had asked Linzie so many times.

Yale smoked as he drove, no music or radio. Need a little quiet, he said, always do after extroverted activities. Alchemizes the introvert, same way this does. He lifted the bowl.

You never told me you did drugs, Linzie said.

Mother medicine, he said. Plant medicine's not drugs.

They pulled into the parking lot of the Cold Stone Creamery off Nob Hill Road. All the strip mall businesses were closed for the night—the Asian market, the barber shop, Doug's favorite liquor store, the place Linzie once took dance lessons as a kid. The slot where Hei Baby used to be—now Plantation Pilates. Linzie thought about Birdie, imagined seeing Hei's ghost face in the dark window.

Yale got out of the car, and she followed. Our secret, Yale said, when they walked into the Cold Stone's. Everyone's got their kink.

Under the white halogens Linzie smelled cake and watched Yale disappear. There was always the moment—after the bottle, the pipe, the flat hand of smoke hovering like ozone—where you could watch someone slip out of themselves, go. When Linzie's mom used to torch rock or tie up or snap her neck back for pills, Linzie counted the seconds after, the same way she'd counted between lightning and thunder to gauge the probability of more. She'd nicknamed Irene *Poppy* once she disappeared, because in Oz, Dorothy and her friends fell asleep in a great big field of those blooming flowers, the witch whispering as they drifted off to their sweet death sleep, a sleep so peaceful sometimes Linzie shamefully felt it—happy for her mother.

The girls in the big house were invariably kinder to Linzie after they drank, the cameras pushing in on them in these moments, especially. The kindness quickly shifted to nonsense which shifted to tears, but there was an ideal spot in between, and Linzie knew it well—the place where others bore witness to the dark currents of their own life, where Linzie was their bright, buoyant preserver. Without her fingers unclasping the girls' necklaces, untying her mother's shoes, Linzie would have no purpose, she knew. It was a departure, a compromise, that would warm her—then leave her suddenly, stunningly, alone.

Her arm extended to guide Yale as they walked around the stanchions. She touched him. And as Yale smiled at the ice cream behind the glass, words stumbling slow as a dreaming person, Wanna split a bucket? Linzie felt plunged by an anchor of love. Like this, she could be with her mother again.

Yale ordered for them—sour candies, Oreos, chocolate base, pecans. The tiny girl in uniform scooped the contents onto a slab of cool metal, mixed it all in a slashing, almost violent, choreography.

I think you should get out of your dad's house, Yale said.

They were parked in the way back of the strip mall lot, facing the street. The car was dark, no other people around. Yale ate the chunky ice cream, spoon on his tongue, tracks of chocolate on the plastic. You're twenty-three, he said. Like, you're a mall worker, I get it, but think of all this, Calvin, as your ticket out. You should have enough savings from the book (*Two-million-dollar deal!* someone on Reddit had said, though in reality, Linzie had only received a few thousand for *My Turn;* Doug handled their shared account).

I can't leave, Linzie said. You don't understand.

Linzie considered taking a big bite of Yale's pecan ice cream, killing herself. She pinched at her eyebrow—relief. In the dark of the car, she couldn't see the sprinkle of hairs dusting her lap, and with Yale disappeared, he wouldn't notice. She pinched and pulled, blinking hard.

I want success for you, his voice said. And there's a failure to launch here.

Dad wants success for me, too, went Linzie. Dad used to want me to be an actor like the Olsens, then a dancer and a singer. He had me practice a vibrato by pushing on my throat with my fingers. He even sent my pictures to talent agencies, or I guess I don't know where. He kept me outside in our yard so I would get tan. I used to hate him for that, *tanning abuse,* my mom called it when he locked the door, but we didn't have any money. That's why the house is so small, why I live in the garage—VA benefits aren't a lot, and I told you my mom worked at Diamond Dolls . . . I really did want to be a star, to help them.

Honestly? Yale said, I think your dad's kind of a creep. Yale laughed with his eyes closed. Like, the application thing. What kind of man does that to their daughter, I mean, *submits* her, for that kind of show? That's kind of a peculiar thing to do. He just told me that factoid tonight. Why'd I hear that from him? I thought you told me things?

Linzie left her eyebrows alone and moved on to a sharper spot, the one at the nape of her neck that never quite healed, skin that wept like the cheese had. She twisted and yanked. She hadn't known. When Linzie watched previous seasons of *The Dating Show* in their sunken living room, Doug had only said: *This is such junk! How could anyone have a brain and watch this junk! Do you have a boiled pea brain?* And Linzie had said: *They want to find love! Is love so bad?* And Doug had said: *Not for these stuffed-for-nothing bimbos.* The photos of Linzie in the application, so many bathing suits. Various ages of herself, her face bloated, or spray-tanned some years more than others. She wasn't sure when or how her dad had gone through her phone to find them. Maybe she'd been asleep. Maybe she'd gone to the bathroom during one of their *SVU* binges, leaving her phone right there on the couch, next to Doug's recliner. Probably she'd just been careless.

Then Yale said: You know, almost dying teaches you a lot of hard lessons. Yale told her about his favorite nurse, an old Chinese lady named Myla—or maybe it was Myra, or Mary—he couldn't remember, but she was definitely Chinese. He began talking about his bone broth business—how the shit hospital broth revealed his life's purpose—as if Linzie had transformed into an investor. She sensed this, what he wanted her to be, and so she became it.

How's your broth different from Swanson? she asked. She leaned her forehead against the window. She pulled more hair.

She remembered the blue-and-white cartons of Swanson's chicken broth of her childhood, Irene heating it in a mug in the microwave, the straw always burning a perfect circle on her tongue.

—pasteurized trash, Yale went on. Real broth is gelatinous—gizzards, feet, if we're talking the authentic stuff. Shit you'd find in the Asian market over there (he pointed over there)—

Linzie wanted to go home. She wanted to ask Doug, *Why did you do that? Why do you do the things you do?* She wanted to hide in her garage that smelled of Lucky's cage and read the cruel things people said about her online: *Who does LK think she is??? AUTHOR?? This is a white bitch from TAMARAC LOL. I think she killed him . . .* The forums hadn't slowed, even a year after the show's premiere. She wanted to get out of the car. She wanted her own ice cream.

When you survive something, Yale said, when you've looked death in the eye, it literally changes your DNA. Mother medicine has provided me that reassurance.

You said I *have* survived, Linzie said.

Yale seesawed his hands, *ehhhh*, then said nothing. He carved his spoon into the ice cream. Who do you think really did it? Who's your guess? Seriously. I think it's his own mom, personally. Mary-Beth. He emptied her out, you know.

I thought you didn't care?

Trust me, I don't, Yale said. It's still fun to play.

I told you I'm allergic to nuts, Linzie said, and you still ordered that ice cream. Do you really pay attention?

Yale said, Shush, peanut oil's in everything.

Then Yale turned his head and looked at her, white spoon handle hanging from his mouth like a tusk. Stupid and familiar, the way he looked at her, eyes tilting down, as if she held something precious in her lap. His head ticked to two o'clock (Doug had taught her to see everything in clock hands; when would she ever see things her own way?), then Yale parted his lips into a smile, biting down on the spoon. Linzie couldn't see much in the dark of the car, but she could see this, his teeth as he pulled the spoon and jabbed it back into the ice cream. She knew what that face meant. That jab. She always knew. And she let him, lean in. Yale tried to use tongue, but she kept her mouth tight and closed. She would break out in a facial rash now. He licked her, chin to the tip of her nose. *You're so annoying, you're driving me crazy*, he said, girlishly, differently. Black foam trembled in the air vents of the car. Yale touched her.

Linzie imagined herself as one of Yale's gelatinous broths. Jell-O hair, face, body, even her clothes. Then she imagined her Jell-O self melting, pooling down to where her ankles were currently crossed on Yale's rubber car mat, seeping out the door and onto the street. Jell-O Linzie slithers to the corner of the parking lot like mercury, like Alex Mack, slides up the lamppost. She solidifies back to herself up there, way up high, looking down. She breathes in swamped humidity, swirling gnats, night matter.

Yale unzipped his pants. He used his fingers to push Linzie's hair back behind her left ear. This language she knew, hard glints of it everywhere if you paid attention. The hands—always the hands—told you when they needed something. Linzie wanted to scratch at her lungs. Her breathing hurt. Her scalp hurt. Her face scorched in the pecan line Yale had licked below her nose. She pulled the hair elastic from her wrist. The elastic was always there—something she snapped against her skin in counts of three when she tried not to yank. She pulled her hair back into a quick, low ponytail. Then her face moved down.

On the lamppost, Linzie studies each bug in the light, the light cold and fluish. Moths collide lazily in the air. They say heat rises, but on Linzie's lamppost there is no heat, only an incredible winter coming on, something she's never felt before. Cars drive past, traffic lights clicking color after color, and Linzie is all the lives inside those cars, lives she'll never, ever know. *Don't be a bitch who cries*, her father had instructed her whole life, but Linzie cried and cried and cried lately, real tears. *Show me sorrow.* She worries the crying will never stop.

I'm gonna—said Yale. He didn't finish what he was saying. His hand came to the back of her head in the way she hated, in the place that hurt. She pressed her head down as far as she could, held it there, so he would stop pushing. She had no gag reflex, always knew how to show her tonsils to the doctor without a Popsicle stick or instruction, she just knew, and Yale now thrust his hips in a way that had her wondering if his dick would leave a bruise.

The light flickered off on the lamppost. The bugs flew away. Day arrived with the scrabbling of birds. Families drove into the parking lot for ice cream, for their Asian groceries, for breakfast. Lamppost Linzie imagined her mother's hand on her shoulder, her mother punching numbers into the strip mall ATM—Linzie's birthday as the key code, 1221, that's how much she loved her—the ATM money not for drugs but for pancakes at the Pancake House, like the morning Linzie's mom ordered a blueberry stack and they shared it, and she let Linzie pour a tiny plastic creamer into her coffee, and she widened her eyes and told Linzie she made the most delicious potion she'd ever tasted. After pancakes she'd driven Linzie to North Pole Florida Gas & Save, and a truck sprayed snow, the sky breathing glitter, heave of the machine over children screaming, Linzie and her mother spinning beneath ten whole minutes of ice, looking up.

Linzie swallowed it all. She felt the life leave Yale's penis in her mouth, a detachable sink hose turned off, his skin suddenly loosened, wrinkled. She sat up, neck aching, face hissing with itch, and leaned back in her seat. Yale lifted a spoon full of half-melted ice cream, airplaned it toward her mouth as if she were a toddler, then said, *Psych!* and took the bite himself.

BIRDIE

THELMA KNOCKED. IT had been a week, maybe more, since Calvin died. Since then, I had left the cabin and walked only once, looking for my slugs, though it seemed they'd burrowed elsewhere for dry season, disappeared. The rain had let up. No more fires were necessary. It may have been grocery drop-off day, but Thelma had no bags or boxes of wine in her arms.

Wilma—*Birdie*, shoot, sorry. Can you hear me? She knocked.

I unbolted the door, lifted the latch, opened it. Thelma's skin was dry, her expression worried. Behind her head, light pierced through the cedars, and near Nevra's cabin, Hal worked with his giant lance, like a gladiator's spear, stabbing a holly bush with poison.

Birdie, Thelma said. Your friend Trace has been calling the house. I left the messages in your mailbox, but she insisted I deliver this one face-to-face, check on you. She says to call her, please. I told her Thelma's not a messaging service, yet here I am.

She wants me to come home, I said. Because of my dad dying and all.

Makes sense, Thelma said. I'm sure there's plenty to attend to. You're paid through Labor Day, so if you want to leave and come back, or skip out early, all that's fine, I just need—

I'm not going home, I said. They've got it handled.

Thelma stood there, working her mouth. She twisted it around in a circle as if there were an itch there, then propped her elbow on the doorframe, thinking. The sun shone through the skin hanging from her arm, a glowing wing.

You sure about that? Thelma asked. Your friend Trace seems worried about you. Said something about you needing *the healing inner paddock*, or pasture, something of that kind.

We're not that close, I said.

Isn't she your emergency contact?

Eventually, Thelma left.

Before Calvin Trace took three weeks to kiss me after we met, and when she did, it was soft and careful. *Can I do that?* she'd asked, after kissing me on the cheek. We sat on a bench in Tompkins Square Park near midnight, 2007, two tallboys of Pabst in brown paper bags. My cheek vibrated where she'd kissed it. Could she do that? She moved to my neck. I said *yes*, then she moved to the space behind my ear. Around us, from trash mounds, rats dove marvelously. My whole body woke to sound.

It was fall. A WGA strike, *The Talent* wrapped, and I was out of work. The next morning, we walked through the Lower East Side drinking coffee before Trace pulled me into a sex shop, her usual carefulness, her timidity, gone. The way she walked through the store and handled the items—different. She picked up a purple cock from a dusty glass display shelf; a tiny spotlight made the dust sparkle. Trace told me to touch the toy, and the silicone felt like skin, like suede, expensive. Trace gripped my hair, leaned into that place near my ear again, and said, *This is what I'm going to use on you.*

We went to Trace's apartment in Williamsburg. Renata was out of town. I lay on Trace's bed, and we left the curtains open, purr of a box fan mounted in the window, dragging the air. I watched the power lines, the club-footed pigeons, the M train rattling above with dark-coated figures inside, arms lifted to the bars.

Trace washed the cock in the bathroom sink. The package—square as a Barbie box—crinkled as she threw it away. I watched her, thought about what she had said in the store, *what I'm going to use on you*. Trace flicked the water off, closed the bathroom door. Then I heard the rasping of Velcro.

She came out of the bathroom with her t-shirt and blues still on. She walked over to me, bulging. Pull it out, she said. I sat up. She took me by the wrist and led me off the bed, to the floor. The wood made sound as my bare knees bit into it. I sat on my heels. As if kneeling on a pew, I undid Trace's buttons, the purple cock springing out into my hand.

Get it wet, Trace said, and I did. I sucked it warm, sucked until it was skin, wrapped my hands around the black nylon straps of her harness and took it down my throat. I wanted it to ream clear through the back of my skull and come out the other side. I wanted to be nothing more than a clean impalement, a pinhole camera obliterated with light.

Trace pulled me up off the floor by the hair. It hurt. I wanted it to hurt more. I wanted to be the first bite of an apple, a surprise in the shape of her teeth. She spun me around, bent me over the bed, yanked my underwear down so fast I didn't even feel it, only felt her opening me up from behind. Trace put her hand on my back—I felt that, too—and pushed me down into the bed, my mouth choked by bedsheets. She fucked hard. When I tried to move a hand down, Trace caught it, pinned it behind my spine. I hoped my shoulder would dislodge like that—every bone released from its socket.

No more touching, she said.

Trace pulled all the way out and let the tip of it wait, made me beg for it. Tell me you want it / yes, I want it / say please, she said, and I said, Please. Say thank you, she said, and I did. We went on this way—*please please thank you please thank you please please please please thank you*—her fist yanking my head so far back I could barely drive out those words, my eyes at the corner of her room, the crack there, the seam.

How had I lived before that moment? I wanted to walk around with that feeling, arms pinned, face pressed into a gilded, pressurized dark. I was wet everywhere, I could feel that too, and that meant my body was capable of it—feeling. A body knew what was right for it, what it could do. *Please. Thank you.* A deep so deep it itched between my ribs, a surge up my throat. I pushed back into it. Trace pulled out and flipped me over, jerked my legs to the edge and let them dangle off the mattress, shaking.

She leaned over, then. Bowed to me. And like the gentlest gesture in the world, opened her mouth. I throbbed down there. I burned. But Trace's mouth made everything softer. My toes dragged across the floor as if magnetized. My fists clenched up by my face. I wanted to crack her jaw so far open I could tongue the fillings out of her molars. Before I came, she took her mouth away, *Look at me when you do that*, she said, and I did. When I came in her mouth, she didn't pull away, or stop, she just circled more slowly with a tenderness that made me want to die.

I needed that void in me to expand, disappearing the body. I'd learned how to leave the body by living in it. Trace didn't know about Before or After Calvin Birdie, not yet, and that was a rare, new power. That, for a moment, was hope.

You are more than what happened to you, Trace said. This, a year after that first day in bed, after the lazy, lovely delirium of those other selves we'd been. Wet sheets. Ice cream out of the carton. *Splendor in the Grass* on the laptop. Joy.

After Calvin Trace: We shared a bathroom, toothpaste, bottles of Advil. We folded each other's laundry. Emergency contacts. Trace called my mother *Mom*.

He doesn't define you, Trace promised.

After Calvin Birdie wondered if that could ever be possible. If she wanted it to be.

Trace never fucked me like that again, not even after I'd asked for it. Not even when I'd tried to re-create the conditions, bought a new toy. I jerked off to the memory of that first time for years, until it didn't work anymore. Then it became a story, some inchoate flashback of the woman I could have been, once, had I not been the girl that I was.

Dear Birdie,

I'd do it for you you know. End it. All this. Your going to be called crazy for the rest of your life and so will I. There's no future for people like us don't you see?? People like us are freak dummies of the system, doesn't matter what side you're on or who did what to who, all that matters is that you were a part of it. Our names forever in those papers. Our faces drawn by that clerk. You and me, we're both on registries now. Doesn't matter if they're different lists. Some people won't ever be more than the list they are on. We're more alike than you think.

Lindsay got out of being a system freak. Lucky her. That's what money does, how it moves. People are SHEEP Birdie and they'll do or think anything that makes them feel like a "good person." I don't think you ever cared about being a good person, you were just you. The same way I was just me, and still am. I KNOW you Birdie. I know how you talk, where you sleep, what you dream about. I know what haunts you. What you really want.

Where is Francine, Birdie? She doesn't answer me. Where are you right now reading this??

You want me to do it, kill Lindsay. Maybe I will. But maybe I should come for you instead. Prove you weren't crazy. Prove I really was this bad guy. Ricin is easy. A gun would be a lot easier. I have plenty of guns—you could even choose. Maybe then Lindsay would learn her lesson, and so would America. A final <u>fuck you</u> from us both. Everyone's attention has been in all the wrong places. It should be on you.

Think about it.

Sincerely,
Calvin

MARY-BETH

MARY-BETH MET ODETTE at a sushi joint in Boca Raton, forty-five minutes away.

She *did not care* about Odette, no expectations, not when she got ready and chose one of her fanciest dresses—an old sky-blue satin number from Sears—not when she hung the dress from her shower rod to steam it smooth, not when she twisted her hair into the pink foam rollers stored under the bathroom sink or when she blow-dried the rollers, her arms lifted in a bow of muscle memory, and not even when she lined her lips with pencil, the nub of dried, sharp maroon. Mary-Beth slid her feet into strappy heels, gummy at the insoles where her skin met flaking pleather. She *did not care*. She'd simply go in with a blank, pliant mind, humoring this girl, ready to receive a pitch.

Mary-Beth found a parking spot behind the pink plaza. She checked herself again in the car's flap-down mirror. She turned her face left and then right, checking for any stray marks or hairs. She wasn't pretty, but she looked pretty, felt pretty, for her. She promised herself she'd wear makeup more often, maybe even soon.

When Mary-Beth opened the restaurant door, she was greeted by a very tall and very handsome Japanese man in a tight black shirt. He said, Welcome, welcome, but Mary-Beth looked right past him and at Odette, who was waving as if they'd been friends a long time. Mary-Beth felt important walking through the center of a restaurant like that, peachy lights sunsetting the walls, toward this waving woman at the bar.

Mary-Beth clutched her purse—also satin, with beaded paisley swirls—under her armpit. Slabs of colorful dead fish lay on ice in front of the girl, and behind all that dead ice, two men in white aprons and hats sliced away, stirred spoons into bowls. Mary-Beth approached the stool Odette had pulled out to the left of her, sat down on it. Odette reached out and slid the strap of Mary-Beth's purse off her shoulder. Purse hook's down here, she said. She moved Mary-Beth's bag under the bar. She said, I can't believe it's you—I feel like I know you already.

Mary-Beth had expected Odette to be prettier, based on her voice. Based on her New York locale and obvious money. Odette had squinty, wet little eyes too small for her face, and dark brown hair pulled into a bun. The hair looked straightened out of its curls, ridged like the roof of a dog's mouth. Florida, Mary-Beth thought, will do that to hair. As Odette spoke, she slipped on glasses with thick black frames that made her eyes appear both larger and smaller at once, which Mary-Beth found troubling. The girl had fine pale skin and wore tight jeans, a stiff black shirt that fanned out around her waist in a half-opened umbrella. She smiled big, and Mary-Beth noticed swollen pink gums. Mary-Beth wished she would stop smiling like that.

Mary-Beth hadn't even taken in the soft music or the menu or the mood of it all as Odette rattled off about sushi quality and her grandparents in Boca West and her relationship to driving. She sipped from a glass of white wine and spoke oddly, like her chin was attached to her neck by a tight cord, her head tilting down, eyes tilted up. She nodded constantly, crazily—a tic. She talked too much—already it was way too much—and Mary-Beth said, Shhhh, slow down, missy, gonna give yourself a hernia.

—it's just that a lot of people can't believe I know how to drive because a lot of New York people, they just can't, they never had any reason to learn, you know? But I had to learn. I wanted the challenge and even the parallel parking—a car is like my *peace place*, when I get—

A woman brought them two glasses full of ice water, then small wooden bowls of thin, white noodles with pale seeds on top. A watery brown sauce drowned it all. Odette slipped her chopsticks out of the long strip of paper and split them like doll legs. She rubbed the sticks together between her palms, and it made a horrible little sound. I think it's an amuse-bouche, Odette said, gesturing at the noodles. Like a palate cleanser, to start. She raised her hand high like a kid in class. When the waitress came back over, Odette said, can you get my friend here some silverware?

Before we go on, Odette said—though she'd been going on all by herself—I want you to know how sorry I am, Mary-Beth. Losing a child isn't the way nature's supposed to go.

Mary-Beth said, Appreciate that.

You must be so disturbed, Odette said.

I don't disturb easy.

Odette asked if she should order for them both. Mary-Beth had barely read the heavy, leather-bound menu, but said, *Sure*. Odette winked. It was like she was the star of her own movie or something, and this quality allowed Mary-Beth to feel more interested in whatever was wrong with Odette, psychologically.

So, you're wondering, why has this Chatty Cathy come all the way down here just to talk, right? Odette was still nodding. It was so irksome.

Mary-Beth said, I'm not really wondering that, because you already explained why.

Odette said, PWL. Sorry, *The Problem with Linzie*. Investors liked that name for the first season.

Noodles kept slipping out from Mary-Beth's fork right before it reached her mouth. She thought other people in the restaurant must be staring at her, though nobody seemed to be. They sat at tall, padded booths with their heads down, phones glowing on tables. Kids and babies sat before perched-up phones, too, like sophisticated little businessmen.

You said the podcast might figure out who did it? Mary-Beth was careful with her voice. She did not want to come across as eager, or desperate, that worst-of-all version of her: hopeful.

Carlisle Files, that's the official name of the show, and yes, I think we have a nine out of ten chance of figuring it out, Odette said, if we work together. The way I picture it now is I'll interview everyone involved. And I mean everyone. I've already got sources you wouldn't believe. I'll talk to forensic experts, locals, Cal's caseworkers from over the years, the guys at Gateway.

Calvin, Mary-Beth said. His name is *Calvin*.

Calvin, my apologies, Odette said. You use Cal, so, apologies. Anyway I'll invite everyone on. I've got people close to this—Betty, as I mentioned. Birdie's mom's already in, and back in New York, I've been meeting with her girlfriend, Trace, and they might not all say things you necessarily want to hear, but—

You got Tracey? Mary-Beth said. What's Tracey know?

She thinks it was your ex-husband, Odette said. But anyway, this is *your* story, Mary-Beth, *your* true crime. You lost the child. The other voices are fodder. You're leading this.

Most of these people hate Calvin. The girls you're after, Francine and Chang, they ruined his life. How's this me or Cal's story if they're involved?

First of all, Odette said, Francine's out. She tried to kill herself last week, and now she's in the looney bin—that's a liability I can't afford. And second, an audience wants to solve something. An audience wants to feel smart, to turn over their own stones. To do that they have to feel like they're getting all the angles. They need someone to root for—that's you—and they need someone to loathe—that's Linzie. Better if it's more than one person, to loathe. But, Mary-Beth, I turn over stones police wouldn't dare to, because they miss a LOT. There is no investigation, you get that, right? Law enforcement doesn't care about your son.

Mary-Beth suddenly felt very bad for the girl. A girl who thought diddling policemen not doing their job was a juicy revelation. A girl who thought she herself could solve this *better than policemen*, like that was a competition. She recognized Odette—her big-girl glasses, her big trip to Florida—and felt pity. No real smarts. Just a webby, gloomy vacancy.

You talk and talk, Mary-Beth said. Has anyone said you talk too much? And don't say much at all? I don't think you know anything about Calvin, or the world.

I know he had a laptop and it's gone now, Odette said. I'm assuming it's with you. And did you know someone got into his unit before you cleared it out? Took notebooks of his? Betty sent me scans of those too.

Mary-Beth did not know this, but she didn't let on—she knew better. She dipped her spoon into the icy glass of water, brought the water to her mouth, then blew on it.

I'm thirsty, she said. Just can't do the ice.

I want you to trust me. Odette straightened herself on the stool. What will it take for you to trust me? Fully?

Mary-Beth slurped the water from the spoon. It was still cold enough to hurt. No offense, she said, but a person like me doesn't trust. That doesn't have to be our end goal.

I'll tell you something about myself. Something I don't tell anybody, Odette said.

Mary-Beth looked around the restaurant, confused, then said, Alright?

My real name, it's Olivia.

What's the big deal about that? Mary-Beth said. That's a better name.

It's a common name, said Odette. You know it's one of the most popular names on BabyNames.com? Literally, number two this year, number three last year, and the year before that.

How'd you pick that new name?

I'm so afraid of being common. It's my worst fear. My older

brother passed the bar like it was nothing, and he works for my dad. He's handsome and dates ethnic models and everyone is so fucking proud of him. He's gonna be on *Shark Tank* soon with wood pellets.

How'd Francine try to off herself? Mary-Beth asked. She miss or something?

Come on my show, and I'll tell you all that, Odette said.

The food arrived on a two-foot-long wooden boat. Slugs of fish on top of rice. Pinks and corals and off-white colors. Heart-shaped rolls dripping with thick, glistening sauce. I'm making you try this, Odette said. She pointed to the saucy roll first. Just try one piece. The fried one.

Mary-Beth stabbed one of the cuts of the roll with her fork. She didn't ask what was in it because she didn't really want to know. Odette took her own bite, covering her mouth with her napkin as she chewed. Mary-Beth chewed, too, slowly. It was somehow mushy and crunchy at once. Sweet. The texture thing she didn't love, but it didn't taste all that bad. She watched Odette watch her swallow it. Some kind of half smile on her face Mary-Beth knew well.

Have you ever had sushi before? Odette asked.

Mary-Beth put down her fork. See, that—that's the thing, Olivia. Mary-Beth bounced her pointer finger in the air. You think I don't know what sushi is. You think you can rope me into saying funny redneck shit you want for your show and that I won't know I'm being made a fool of. You think I don't know I'm eating fish fuck, these little red caviars—ole Mary-Beth must think it's paprika or something because I'm so . . . malnourished and uneducated and I've never had a meal this hoity-toity before. But, girly, you don't know me. You don't. You're never gonna be taken seriously. Not with me, not with any of this you're talking. It's a loser's game, this world, and you're not pretty enough for it. I used to eat the best of the Atlantic right from the line, right on the boat, had my own little grill. You ever catch your own food? You ever skin a rabbit?

Or you just buy their parts at Whole Foods? And let me tell you, I cook my meat; this raw stuff is dirty. Full of worms. Why are the rich always into dirty things?

I don't eat rabbit, Odette said, shaking her head. You're right, I haven't done those things.

I got a clean shot when I was five years old, through one eye out the other, and the recoil on my daddy's 12-gauge hit me harder than a dick, OK? Still, I could goddamn aim, and we ate. Rabbit didn't feel a thing, just went flying across the yard like a fucking football. You know what that life's like? That's a splendid life.

Odette made big L's with both hands and rested them at the sides of her face, over her ears. She said, *Don't cry don't cry don't cry.*

You're a little wimp, Olivia. And you should use that name.

A person can't help if they're born rich just like they can't help if they're born poor, Odette said. I work hard, and I want to do good in this world. It's not about money, it's about being good, being just. I only ever want to do the right thing.

Go knock a cop off the pier if you wanna do good.

Mary-Beth, women, we aren't always taken seriously. Do you feel that? I've talked to your ex, Tommy. I know the way he talks about you. The degrading language. You ever think it's weird he was the witness on the bus and then he turned on Calvin?

Hon—

I want my work to be taken seriously. And you could be serious, too. Because of me. *With me.* Let me ask you this . . . You want to be asked real things? Do you think your son's guilty?

Of what?

The girls, Odette said. Of what he's been accused of.

He's been accused of lots of things.

Molesting them. Recording them.

This is about his murder. What did Ching Chong's mother have to say?

There's a literal recording, Mary-Beth.

There was no audio on it, Mary-Beth said, louder than she'd meant to say it. And no proof that recording was real and not messed with. Christ, you could barely see what was what. And I think what people do behind their doors and the conditions of such is none of my business, not even my son, because I'm not some perv trying to know what gets my kid's rocks off. So I'm gonna stop you—you've never met someone as gentle as Cal. He's gentle and that was the problem. One girl takes advantage and then the next follows—girls will always follow. Hard to get out from under God's ass, excuse me, and Cal tried, but once you've got that scarlet letter of RSO—and you know you've got to renew it all the time, four times a year at the county court, to remind yourself how fucked you are, how lifeless your life will become...I had to post up in the library just to use a computer for that, and once upon a time I had a good job, people said...you know sometimes, Christ, sometimes I'm glad he's gone. Thought finally he was in a good place and would like to think he'd get out of there, but shit—Mary-Beth shook her head.

You really believe this, Odette said. She wasn't nodding anymore. She was looking at Mary-Beth—really, faithfully looking—her chopsticks midair and caked with rice. She had inky globs under her eyes now, moved by Mary-Beth's words. She wasn't 100 percent bad, Mary-Beth knew, only desperate. Mary-Beth had a hunch for these things. She knew desperate.

So she stayed in the restaurant. So she listened, and then said more. And sometime soon, Mary-Beth promised, she'd fetch Calvin's laptop out of the closet. Maybe she'd even turn it on.

The day of Mary-Beth's first visit to county jail, she chose to focus on the weather. The sun. Calvin was allowed sunlight, and that was something. In the parking lot of Dade Correctional, Mary-Beth tilted her head straight up, then closed her eyes, red splashed wings appearing where the palms had been. She slammed her car door shut—she'd had a nice white station wagon back then—and walked toward the entrance of the detention center.

She'd dressed up for her visit. She wanted to look nice for Cal, wanted him to say to the others, *That's Mom, isn't she pretty?* She wore brown lipstick with a shimmer of frost, a camo handkerchief folded into a headband, a clean blouse, her dark blue jeans with the embroidered eagles, prickly, glistening stones that made noise on her car seat. She couldn't control the system, but she could look the way she looked.

The entrance was almost cozy. Could have been the entrance to a doctor's office or a library, with upholstered chairs, framed pastoral landscapes on the walls, a TV going with summer Olympics—slender boys swimming for world records in Atlanta. One boy tore his goggles off and slapped water. He looked no older than Calvin.

Mary-Beth moved toward the arms of the metal detectors.

She dropped her cell phone and keys into a tray. A correctional officer came and took it. Then she walked through, and a bleeping pierced the room as Officer Dwight—according to his tag—asked Mary-Beth if her titties were wired.

I don't work for Pigs, Mary-Beth said.

Not asking if you're wired, Dwight said, but if you're wearing an underwire, under your titties. Officer Dwight had creeper eyes, dark pupils fixed toward the ceiling. Plaque build-up bulged from between his teeth. His hair was gelled and freshly combed.

Mary-Beth was, indeed, wearing a wire under her titties, her good bra from Macy's. The bra was old, but it still worked, even if the wires poked out from the cups.

You're gonna have to remove that, Dwight said, and Mary-Beth saw in his expression that he was not kidding at all. She looked around for any sign of a restroom or changing room. There was nothing. Only that waiting area, the TV, digitized flags stretching across the Olympic pool as those boys kicked and swam, the water so blue.

Mary-Beth unclipped herself, up the shirt, one-handed. Then she wiggled her shoulders and dropped her bra into the scuffed black security tray. Gonna have to confiscate that, Dwight said, without moving the conveyor an inch. He picked up the bra with his gloved fingers, dropped it in the trash. Then he looked to her head and said, Lose the kerchief, too. No camo.

Mary-Beth smacked her lips. Her nipples were tight and showing. She wondered what Calvin would think, if he'd be too embarrassed to hug her. She slid the handkerchief from her head and walked through the detectors again.

You're lucky it's me who's asking, Dwight said. In Japan, they've got robots replacing COs. You don't want a robot grabbing at your titties, trust me.

Don't go thinking I've got it nice and cush here, Calvin said, this setup's just for visitors.

Calvin sat across from Mary-Beth at a picnic table in the courtyard—they would have thirty minutes. Officers lined the perimeter of the space in black uniforms, polyester heavy with blooming stink, Mary-Beth imagined, Pigs sweating like pigs. Around them, other inmates and mothers and surly, skinny wives visored their faces with their hands. She and Calvin did not.

Calvin had bought them lunch from a hot food vending machine. In Mary-Beth's box, a small hamburger, the meat a pock-marked violet. It came with little packets of ketchup and mustard, which she split easily with her teeth. In Calvin's box, breaded chicken fingers that smelled quite good, but when he picked up a finger, she noticed the bloated, pale underside of it—wet from whatever moisture had warmed it—like the slick belly of soap that clung to her tub. He took a bite of the chicken, lips curled away from his teeth. Gets too fucking hot in those machines, he said. When he spoke, steam flickered from his mouth.

Calvin got thirty minutes of outdoor a day, which was thirty minutes more than what some people got. Cal was going to bulk up, his biceps already popping. This was catch-up time, these were the updates. He'd also begun saving for a tattoo poked by a guitar string—gonna get your name, Ma. Or your initials. Or maybe just "Mom." Which do you think?

Name, Mary-Beth said. Front and center. She ran a finger across her neck like a ring of death.

Not worse than Duval? she asked.

Nothing worse than juvie, he said, and she knew he meant it. There was relief, for them both, when Cal was old enough for adult jail, and maybe one day adult prison, which had books and TV and a commissary for Newports. In juvie the boys were trained to kill, and they were trained to never, ever snitch—to snitch was to be killed, and you'd be beaten to Nebraska if you refused to snitch. Mary-Beth would never forget the lazy red expanding in her son's eye, eclipsing white, after a boy named Tidal kicked his face in when Calvin borrowed a CD. Cal was sixteen then.

Miss Lopez says they're overcrowded . . . Think you'll be out sooner than you think.

I don't mind, Ma, he said.

You're gonna miss—you're missing so much, Mary-Beth said. I mean, the Olympics—she made an explosion with her fingers from her skull. These swimmer boys can do it.

We see some of that in here. He chewed.

I'm working on finding us a new place, Mary-Beth said. I drove to four yesterday, but two didn't pass.

By pass, Mary-Beth meant the 2,500 feet. Now that Calvin was a registered sex offender, he couldn't live, sleep, or *reside* within those constraints. Mary-Beth wondered how a person could even measure it—nobody had explained that part to her. Nobody ever explained anything to her, that's how come Mary-Beth was so wise, for all the figuring out she had to do.

Mary-Beth imagined measuring tape wrapping whole building blocks, snaking beneath traffic lights, bending over billboards.

She imagined herself holding the cool metal of the tape measure dispenser. The weight of it. Then Ron Book, scumfuck himself, holding the notched edge of the tape. Around the blocks they'd go, wrapping all of South Florida, tape warping gold, bending at the corners like a tentpole. Then she imagined retracting the tape once Ron made it those 2,500 feet, slick steel tongue zipping back, slicing Ron and anyone else in the way. The tape would snap and twitch like a caterpillar flipped on its back.

Calvin reached across the table to hold her hand. You don't need to find a place for me, Ma. It's safer with me here. Even when they see my papers, they leave me alone. Find a place for you, Ma. Something nice. Maybe the Springs.

She hated watching her son chew that hot food, in the hot sun, in his jumpsuit. Eyes gunky and sad and too old for a boy not yet twenty. She would Shawshank him out of there with a toothpick, a fork, hell, a pencil eraser if she could. But still, as if some other being crawled into her body and made a home there, maybe her younger self or maybe a stranger, the way God sometimes felt, her voice asked: Cal, did you really hurt those girls? There ain't nothing that can't be forgiven, but I want you to live in the clear.

Her son looked at her. He dropped her hand and stopped chewing, and a shaking came over his lip the way it did sometimes when he'd had too much to drink, though she knew he hadn't. He said, Mom? and nothing more, nothing more than that. She leaned over the table and hugged him with all the sorrow in her body, truly sorry for ever asking, before several guards blew their whistles.

But the tone, those words, she'd returned to them. *Safer with me here*. She'd think about the lilt of his voice until the day that he died, torso wrung out like a bloody towel in those pictures on Detective Durham's desk. The crack in his throat—*Mom?*

The question behind it.

BIRDIE

BEFORE CALVIN BIRDIE loved the crunch of fried wonton strips. That simple joy.

Before Calvin Birdie collected cloudy, greasy bags of them. She hid them in the top drawer of her bedside table in her childhood home, and when she finished a bag—her mouth thick with salt and oil—she'd fold it a million times, make cloudy lines on the wax surface. She'd seal every fold between her fingernails until the bags went soft and white.

Before Calvin Birdie loved scary movies. *Poltergeist. Rosemary's Baby. Rebecca.* Most of it too old for her, too over her head. But Animal Planet was too much. The news, forget it.

Before Calvin Birdie liked rumors of aliens. The nauseous thrill of heights. Grocery store sandwiches. The smell of lavender sachets in her sock drawer.

Before Calvin Birdie pushed on fears like Light as a Feather and Ouija board.

Before Calvin Birdie had friends with whom she played Light as a Feather and Ouija board—Francine and Monique.

Before Calvin Birdie made these friends easy and remembered tiny details about them: what flavor Capri-Sun was their favorite and which of their brothers made them cry.

Francine belonged to Birdie, Before Calvin.

Before Calvin Birdie cheated in games, most often Ouija board.

She pushed the plastic triangle so slightly her fingers shook. The triangle slid on its felt pads until the Ouija window blew up letters into names into ghosts.

Before Calvin Birdie enjoyed watching her television. Did she write that already? She did. But she imagined herself into every talk show, Birdie getting a makeover on *Sally Jessy Raphael*, or taking a lie detector from Maury about something life-or-death important. She imagined herself on soaps and in music videos and on the late-night shows especially, her own crossed grown-up legs shimmering with nylons under a spotlight, ladylike heels, the host making sophisticated jokes, and her own mouth laughing.

Then the spotlight deepens, a UV blue.

I didn't know the angle of the tape. *The* tape. Yes, I have wanted to watch it. Yes, other people at the trial watched it. In fact, nearly everyone except me. The tape, likely dusted all over in a box, touched by the gloved hands of a stranger every few years, an evidence room lit dramatic as a morgue—or maybe that's all television. Maybe the tape's now gone, stolen, damaged, spent. But back in my projection booth at the little theater in New York, sometimes I pretended I was screening—rather than *Midnight Cowboy*, or *Persona*—the tape. **Calvin Boyer and Birdie Chang, 1995.** I've imagined the label. Permanent-marker thick. His name first.

I never found out where the camera was hidden. Never knew that angle. Didn't know if it was secured in Calvin's ceiling or air-conditioning vent, or stuffed in a teddy bear, hidden on a shelf, or in plain sight. I have never known if it was a wide angle or something zoomed in, if it would be clear to anyone what I may have looked like. Maybe you could only see my body, the size of it. What would I recognize of that room? What mouthed words would most surprise me?

I've imagined unpacking the evidence tape in my projection booth. My tape. Not his or theirs, not the state's. In my fantasy, the tape transforms to a reel. I take it to the Kelmar bench, secure the spindle, run the frames through my fingers (my skin not picked, but impeccable) and over the light. I fill out the inspection report, no emulsion scratches or perf damage, no clipped edges—everything is there.

I thread my film into the projector. I square up, pull the dowser, leave my booth to sit in the gallery seats of the theater. Then I'm all alone, no popcorn or M&M's, no audience. Let's say row seven. Let's say my arms are crossed over my chest, sneakers kicked up casual as the leader begins over the curtain, and then the curtain opens: Calvin showing me all the neon fish in one tank, the tree frogs in the other. Would I see them up close? Did I? I still see frogs, the undersides of their bellies against his tank, the spread toes in brilliant, pale color. Calvin had a plastic bag puffed huge with jumping crickets. Then he opened the bag and it deflated like a lung. He pulled one cricket out and dropped it in the tank for the frogs—*You wanna see the way this goes?*—and that's where the memory fades, like it's supposed to.

He had glow-in-the-dark stars sticky-tacked to his ceiling, and they shone in the UV light of the tanks. No other lights on. I have remembered those stars. I have wondered if they showed up on the tape, or if the camera had been aimed lower. The memory of it is dark dark, outside the UV blue. His teeth glowed. I wondered if mine were glowing also. I felt embarrassed and thrilled at the possibility. I tried to close my mouth, but that only made me smile more. We both laughed at this. I am shocked when children in movies and shows and even real-life children claim to not remember their childhood. To me the little girl on the tape, nine years of understanding, she was all there. The same hands, only smaller, healthier. A sense of humor, a favorite breakfast. The problem isn't repressed memory, for some of us. Like, Before Calvin Birdie liked little frogs and any animals associated with the rainforest, because to grow up in Florida in the '90s meant everything was about saving the rainforest, and we ate at a new restaurant called the Rainforest Cafe for special occasions, and waiting for our table I'd participate in trivia for kids and I knew so many answers to obscure questions and my father would say, *Look at that education! She knew all about the blue morpho butterfly!* Before Calvin Birdie knew butterflies were technically Lepidoptera, because the colors of their wings were made up of tiny scales forming a larger image. She won a gift card at the Rainforest Cafe for that fact. Her last meal there was the bow-tie pasta with cream sauce. After Calvin Birdie never ate there again.

I thought Calvin's frogs might be saving the rainforest, and I remember thinking what a great deed that was, to be harboring vulnerable rainforest animals. I thought Calvin must have been kind and gentle, selected by men in official khakis and mesh hats to be a nature conservationist. All those UV-heated tanks. Before Calvin Birdie sat on the bed, looking up at those stars. She doesn't know how she got there, to the bed, she doesn't remember that part. There are gaps, is the thing. The particular Birdie thing. There are flashes and then there are the gaps, the splices. The flashes persist for seventeen years, clear as morning, clear as the taste of sencha tea, clear as cold currents in a warm ocean, the rush of that on your kicking legs. The gaps are everything else.

Before Calvin Birdie sat on the bed. She didn't lie on the bed, she never did lie on his bed, but she sat on the edge of it, legs hanging off. With one foot on the ground, Birdie has thought, she could have run, but her feet did not meet the ground. Birdie has slept ever since with one foot on the ground. Birdie sleeps on her stomach every night—she hates to look up at a ceiling—one leg dangling off so the foot can touch down to the ground. Doctors have told her this is bad for her back, bad for her nerves, bad for her knees. Therapist #9 Nancy has told her it's so she can run, should something startle her in the night, which Birdie interpreted as someone coming for her in the night, because there will never not be a night of Birdie's life in which she doesn't believe someone is coming for her, someone is coming for her always, in the car with a highlighted map, penned star over whatever room, or cabin, she's in.

Birdie sat on the bed. Of course, she has wished she hadn't. It's something she has wished she could see on the tape, always, evidence of why she sat on the edge of the bed, and her face when she sat there. Likely, nothing on the face. Trying not to smile. Her eye whites, maybe glowing. Adoration in those eyes for the reptiles. The cricket.

Calvin sat on the edge of the bed next to Birdie. Birdie wishes she could stand here, take the stairs back up to the projection booth, stop the reel, flick the switch of the motor. She has wished for this moment more than any other—here—why she has wanted to see the tape at all. Birdie has wanted to hold this threshold, this interstitial cue, this moment where Before Calvin and After Calvin Birdie splits. One foot on the ground, and she could have moved, but she didn't. Calvin talked about the frogs before he called her pretty. Birdie remembers that. Frog facts and where they had come from. His mom. His mom and dad got in a fight so violent his mother tried to leave out of a doggy door, but it only fit her head. Then Mr. Boyer said he would step on it—her head—with a steel-toed boot. To make up for this, his mother bought Calvin frogs from PetSmart. Or so Calvin said. At nine years old, Birdie believed this. She felt sorry for him and, also, hurt that nice Mr. Boyer could do such a thing. She felt she could trust no one ever again.

Birdie still sees Calvin's face in the UV lights calling her pretty. His blond hair floppy like River Phoenix, darker in those lights. The lint on his shirt shone scientifically. Calvin said, *Birdie you are so pretty for your age, and so smart, do you know that?* And she did know that. Often people assume girls like Birdie don't know their worth, have never known their worth, but Before Calvin Birdie did know her worth; it's After Calvin Birdie who's had more trouble, After Calvin Birdie who resents this cheap predictability.

When Calvin kissed Birdie under the stars, Birdie pretended she was dreaming. Birdie has never wanted to see this part of the tape. Birdie remembers the way Calvin smiled green teeth as he leaned in to kiss her and she remembers his smile between the kisses and for her that memory is enough. Teeth are bone, she remembers. They clacked hers, hard. It is one of the flashes, and it is enough.

Birdie remembers the wet of his green teeth and how much she didn't like the sound their mouths made, mushy, like banana chewing, amplified in her ears in a way she will always hear because that sound is a flash that comes whenever she kisses anybody, everybody ever, even Trace, and she likes music and white noise when she kisses, because of this. When Calvin touched Birdie, she remembered wondering if that's what sex was, someone touching the paler parts beneath her clothes, because she didn't yet know what sex was, and when Calvin showed himself to Birdie she did not like the way it twitched the same way the crickets had sprung in the bag, and she thought it was like Calvin had another pet here, in this thing he was showing her. Birdie, kicked back in the theater, wonders how much of her face was shown on the tape, what angle was used. She remembers looking up. Up. The stars. Did the face in the tape match the face of the girl in the courtroom wearing a tiny blazer bought from Burdine's? It didn't fit well. Pads in the shoulders, thin blue stripes—the first of that lifelong uniform. They called her *mentally unsound.*

Calvin wrapped his hands around Birdie's hands, told her it was OK, he would help, and After Calvin Birdie hates this sensation still. In the year after Calvin when Birdie took the steps she was supposed to take, Birdie's parents hired a drum teacher to help Birdie learn the drums, even though they loathed the drums, even though Birdie's dad was sick, so sure were they that drums would be the instrument to help her, the banging and the thrashing and the loud loud noise. But one day the drum teacher, Miss Paige, came up behind Birdie to wrap her hands around Birdie's hands, which were wrapped around the drumsticks, and Miss Paige made Birdie drum triplets on the snare pad this way, Birdie's hands limp inside of Miss Paige's hands, Miss Paige saying, *I'm not going to do this for you*, and Birdie yanked her arms away and never wanted to play the drums again (she didn't, not once).

She has wondered about that tape, how long it all took—the

exact length lives in the gaps—though Birdie has bet not long at all, because in her mind it went on endlessly, endless as a body falling—Kim Novak in *Vertigo*, *King Kong* in '33—but Birdie knows in the same way one has a false sense of size and scale and grandeur when returning to an old house, she must have the same problem with time, the time in that room a nub of grass yanked from the ground, something pure and slick still under it.

    Did Calvin say anything else after how pretty she was? Did he tell Birdie not to tell? These, the gaps. She knew she wasn't supposed to tell. But she knew to tell, knew there was something dangerous in the telling, something daring, for this was the same age Before Calvin Birdie had done things to test her parents with how far she could push them; she had done things just to piss them off, just to see if she'd be grounded—she and Francine had shaved patches of hair from their calves with Hei's razor, and they'd squiggled *Secret Code* on the side of Birdie's house with permanent markers, and Birdie told Gertrude in youth group that she was *stupid*, which was an extremely bad word then, and she'd pretended to forget the words to "Build Me Up Buttercup" when she was supposed to sing at Hei Baby one Saturday—it wasn't even a special occasion, Birdie just *felt* like not doing it—and like this she knew to tell, without knowing if she'd be punished for it, without knowing how bad she had been, and so she did tell her parents one week after, which is not how she remembers it, she has always remembered it as the next day, but according to Linzie King's *Very Brave Memoir* and her Very Exciting Chapter on Jade Suzuki, the court records show Birdie told her parents one week after, and Birdie does remember them at the restaurant closing early for the night, it was a busy night, and her father's hands flipped the paper sign on the door with the little movable clock to say Closed, and she remembers her father apologizing to every table and spooning every meal into take-out containers, his face tired, almost purple as he scooped, the same purple he'd turned right before he died. Birdie remembers him making some calls on the restaurant phone at the front desk to tell people there was an Emergency and Birdie did not, until much later, understand the emergency was her.

Birdie hid under the front desk of the restaurant. She wanted to stay there, always. She still does. Her father, slacks ironed with the perfect crease, the smell of vacuumed carpet. Her father, he could whistle with a blade of grass. All this, somewhere here, Birdie's father on the phone, one hand punching numbers and the other hand resting on her head—so, so warm there, always petting her head—is where After Calvin Birdie comes in.

Did the frog eat the cricket? She wanted the tape to see it, to know. It jumped and jumped against the tank wall, thrashing. She lost track of the frogs. They were so still, throats pumping, boring her. Birdie never did see it happen.

III

YOU WANT TO know who did it.

You'll know. You'll find out even if the women in the story do not. Even if the women of this story are owed their answers. More than you, they are owed this. But they will never find their answers. They will never find their peace after the war. Women are rarely in receipt of what they are owed.

You want to know who did it, but that was never the question.

Or, it was never the right one.

⁓

"WHAT IS THE question?" Judge Roberts asked. 1997 in the Broward County Courthouse, one of the small hearings before the medium hearings before the big hearing. Birdie's in her padded blazer from Burdine's, the one she hates, and she has tried to raise her hand. She's been told she shouldn't raise her hand in court—*Remember, this isn't school*, instructed her father, *there are different rules, you can't talk to Francine the way you usually would*—but Birdie raised her hand anyway, an impulse.

What Birdie wanted to ask the judge was: "Are they allowed to lie?"

They is the front left portion of the courtroom. Calvin and his sleezed-out pin-striped attorney, plus a security guard. Years from now, this attorney will be found naked and waterlogged in his own swimming pool up in Jacksonville, his eyes open, morphine in his system. But right now, he's calling Birdie *mentally unsound* and *untrustworthy*. He has spat the word *immigrant* about Birdie's father, and the Chang family holds *anti-American beliefs*. He has said Birdie is not a *credible witness*—for one, she is nine. Also, when questioned, she could not remember the date of the alleged incident. First, it was end of May. Then April. Chang has pointed directly to Calvin Thomas Boyer as alleged perpetrator in a lineup, but Boyer also resembles River Phoenix, a photo of whom Birdie has in the front slip of her binder at school. Classmates have confirmed this.

Birdie raises her hand.

"What is the question?" Judge Roberts asks. Notably, the judge does not look at her.

Birdie does not, will not, remember this part of the day, the raised hand, the irritated judge, the *outburst*. There are many things she will forget; it's true she can't always nail down the date, or what she wore that day, or how Calvin asked her over; she's tried to draw the layout of the Boyers' house, though the doors in her mind keep changing—

None of this makes her *untrustworthy* regarding the thing she remembers.

Sixteen years later, Birdie is twenty-seven years old. Calvin's parole officer is on the phone: "So what's your question?" and Birdie *feels* it, *intuits* that impatient judge, pulse beating in her neck. The parole officer sounds tired. Sounds like he's been nibbled by these conversations all day. He sounds like a sitcom version of a tired mother of seven, Pall Mall in hand, a Midwestern accent.

This, after Birdie's forwarded him Calvin's emails. The latest ones.

It's late summer 2012, and Calvin's just been released from prison again. He'll be transferred to Gateway soon. *The Dating*

Show has aired; Birdie is already tired; in less than a year, she'll be on Whidbey. *So what's your question?*

"My question is," Birdie says (she's practiced her lower register for calls like this. She has a voice—this voice—that started long ago, in front of Judge Roberts, though she'll never pin down the origin), "aren't these emails violating my order of protection?"

"You want to go to court over emails?" the officer says. "Give me a break."

Birdie is sitting on the small couch in the living room in the Brooklyn apartment she shares with Trace. Trace is at work. Birdie does not like to make these calls with her girlfriend around. It's not that the calls disgust or devastate Trace, quite the opposite. First, Trace is contemplative, quiet—this lasts a day. Then, she's amped, inspired, manic with investigative purpose. She pulls more espresso from their fancy chrome machine, even brushes her teeth harder, faster, whenever things change in Birdie's case. The bristles flare.

"He's not supposed to contact me," Birdie says into the phone. Her hand is sweating like a cliché. She resents this. "It says *no contact*. And this is contact, is it not?"

"He's slick with IPs. You'll have a hard time proving it's him."

Birdie is correct in everything she is saying. She is almost always correct, for she's had to spend her life studying the ins and outs of law, the clauses and loopholes and nuanced restrictions, calendar calls and Arthur hearings, inmate number locators. But the probation officer will say what the system is designed to say, the default phrasing, because the officer does not have the time, does not have the money, the resources, the energy, to make a fuss over some pervert's love letters. He has a caseload of over sixty convicts. He's babysitting rapists and stranglers for less than 40K a year, and his son needs a new bicycle to get to school. And the thing is, he believes Birdie, knows the emails are from Calvin, knows Calvin is a pedo scumbag. But the officer moves to his script, says what he's been trained to say, which is: "There's no explicit threat here. So there's nothing for me to do."

How does Birdie explain to this man, then, this stranger on the phone in Florida who does not know her, who doubtless knows nobody like her (who has met Calvin, what, maybe a month ago? Along with how many other clients?), that every time she is reminded of Calvin, there *is* explicit threat? That his mere presence is threatening to her. His booking shots online. His name in her inbox. Now: reminders of him on prime-time TV. The words in his email like *love*.

"Call if there's ever an explicit threat," he repeats.

Two months later, Birdie makes the decision. Working ceaseless shifts at the theater for the holiday season, the idea comes to her while a little drunk on the reel. (You may have gleaned by now that Birdie has a drinking problem, exacerbated by Trace's drinking problem, a flask or bottle always on her or nearby even when not mentioned in scene—that's how present it is. The real healing for Birdie will in fact only begin once she gets sober, after this story ends.) It was a Hitchcock marathon, at the theater. *Vertigo* was playing. Birdie's hands were dry and cold on the sprockets. *You shouldn't have been that sentimental!* Jimmy Stewart said through the port glass.

It's good, sometimes, to be another person.

Birdie has always known how to be other people (Wilma Dean, Jacy, etc.). Has always known the way other people talk. *Of course* she knew how Calvin talked—he had been writing to her, chatting with her, speaking to her, for as long as she can remember; his voice even came in dreams—she could never unknow him, or that. His syntax. The facts of his life. And because Calvin was slick with IPs, Birdie was too. *A stalker makes a stalker*, she'd told therapist #7. *You're not safe unless you know exactly where they are, what they're thinking.*

Birdie had received emails from Calvin. So why not write some herself.

The system wants an *explicit threat*. Only then can it punish, as designed. It wasn't a lie, then, not really, for Birdie to show them what was true.

They wanted a threat. So she would become it.

THE NIGHT CALVIN died, Trace Levenson landed not in New York as Birdie believed, but at Palm Beach International on a nonstop from Seattle. The flight was turbulent and longer than expected, and they'd had to circle above the Atlantic in holding patterns before touching down. Somewhere over the Midwest, the plane had shuddered in a way that lulled Trace to sleep, her head plunging back and forth until her own restlessness woke her. Now, in Palm Beach, her neck flinched with pain.

The airplane speakers played *Welcome to Miami* as they taxied. Pressure of the final descent had expanded in Trace's ears like a sponge, and her mouth was tacky. She'd downed several gin and tonics—she always did—but maybe she should have accepted the water, too. An empty cup remained crushed in the seat pocket in front of her; napkin tucked inside the pebbled surface. Trace turned on her phone: 10:33 p.m. The flight to Palm Beach was only about an hour more than the flight to JFK. Trace knew this—she had checked—even though Birdie would never.

Earlier that day, still on Whidbey, Trace had noticed a flyer for an upcoming reading by Linzie at Elliott Bay Books. Birdie would find out about the reading, of course she would, Birdie had a way of knowing everything, despite being *off the grid*, or *unplugged*— that was just her way (also: she'd gone back into the coffee shop to *use the bathroom* but returned with her hands dry). On the way to Sea-Tac, Trace texted her cousin Havi a link to the *My Turn* event. Birdie will prob be there, she wrote. Pls for me, can u request off? Make sure she's ok? and Havi agreed, sent back a heart, accepting the challenge.

Here in Palm Beach the captain's voice, metallic and brute, recited a weather report—*mostly cloudy*—taxiing and baggage claim instructions. Trace looked out into the wispy dark air, the thinnest moon, palms smashing their fronds together in the blue runway lights.

Trace would sober up. Pick up her rental car. She would drive down to Wendy's house in Delray and they'd figure it out together, a team. They'd decide what to do about Birdie. Her mounting paranoia and delusions, her fugue states, plus the Linzie of it all. Trace hated lying to Birdie, and Wendy did, too, but that's simply what you did when you loved someone fully, and when that love was cast by worrying—you omitted some things. You wrapped gauze around every corner of the world for a person you loved.

Off the jetway, Trace walked past the airport Miami subs, preserved alligator heads on their spinning mobiles, the rotten sweet of sunscreen emanating everywhere. As a kid, posing for pictures, Trace had held up so many baby alligators on the Everglades tours, thick rubber bands around their snouts, like lobster claws. They were so alive.

Trace brushed her teeth in the airport bathroom. Her skin looked khaki in the light, the bags under her eyes defined as two scimitars. She spat in the sink, twisted her body until her spine elicited a few satisfying cracks. Then she swam her hands under the faucet to trigger the automated soap; the smell—cheap and cherry. Days and months and even years later, once this night became what it would always, henceforth, be—the night Calvin died—Trace would remember this scent. She'd smile at it, fondly.

Outside, on the curb, Trace waited for the shuttle. Early July, just after a storm. Heat so thick you could slurp it with a straw. Heat that fogged and dripped down your glasses. Weather was its own animal down here. It slackened your posture. Unpleated your clothes.

Wendy texted: Can't wait to see you hunny. Going to sleep. Key under Kuan Yin's head ☺ Help urself to anything and c u in morning!! Yeah!!

The shuttle pulled up, brakes squealing, then lowered and beeped to the curb. Trace carried on her duffel bag then kept it in her lap, arms draped over the hump. She had grown up here, in Palm Beach County, and that was precisely why she was afraid of it. It was one of the easy, transparent ways she and Birdie had first connected; Florida people always seemed to find each other. Florida was gothic and fecund, and it would have its teeth in Trace, always. Sometimes—she was embarrassed to admit—she missed it, wanted to move back. She missed her hands twisting at the paper necks of cold bottles in the strip mall parking lots, those easy warm nights of her youth. There was never anywhere to go, really, so anywhere was good enough, each day its own simple, surprising marvel. It was the opposite of New York.

Still, Trace was a racially ambiguous, gender-ambiguous adopted Jewish butch in Palm Beach. Sweat dripped from her binder in warm, tickling beads. She was sometimes *sir'd* and sometimes *ma'am'd*, and in airports, especially, attendants often groped her in the security line having selected the wrong pink or blue figure from the blinking machines. Trace never wore a packer while traveling for this reason, did not need any extra excuse for an officer to reach between her legs, to spot her silicone junk on the X-ray, bright as a bone. Her dick remained warmly, tidily tucked in the zippered pocket of her duffel. If and when a security officer checked the bag, they'd reach the squish of it with a gloved hand, raise an eyebrow, and quickly close it. It used to embarrass Trace when that happened. Now she lived for it.

Trace wondered if the rental car attendant would be OK. At this hour, in this area code, she had to wonder. It was often a gamble whether it would be the color of her skin or her butchness that would offend someone most. She was tall, and she knew that provided some safety. Florida was full of brown people—Cubans, Mexicans, Colombians—and this also, sometimes, helped. But Florida was also full of hoarded guns and serrated grasses and petrified people.

The attendant, it turned out, was fine. In the fridge-bright Enterprise building, a woman with airbrushed acrylic nails took Trace's New York license. Her bangs were blow-dried with volume and sat atop a canvas visor. There was no one else in the room, only a TV mounted in the corner playing a commercial for diet pills, cartoon bodies bloating and shrinking.

"Thank you, Tracey," the attendant said. She said Trace's name with a hard, satisfied smile, pointing to her own name tag, which read *Traci*. Trace offered a fist bump and Traci-with-an-*i* took it. Then Visor Traci slid the keys for the maroon Ford Edge SUV across the counter, reciting this thing and that about paperwork and insurance.

"An SUV?" Trace said.

"All we got right now," Traci said. "We'll honor your reservation price, no upcharge."

Trace pulled a pen from a chain to sign the form as she heard *Linzie*. She had a way of hearing that name anywhere, despite volume or any present action or conversation, a rift in her consciousness, a rousing. She held the pen still. On TV, Linzie King strolled gloomily around a lake in a tangerine dress. Black-and-white closed captions ticked across the bottom of the screen as a voiceover told the story of Linzie's strength. Breaking: new tell-all book alleges manipulation and cruel treatment from *The Dating Show*. Breaking: Linzie King, survivor of a pedophile, shares all in bestseller. No one was hated more than a pedophile; Trace knew that—everyone knew that—what could be easier?

King says she felt forced by producers to tell her story, the host said, *and that the show's team used the facts of her assault for ratings. The network recently reported a sixteen percent decline in viewers and ad revenue. Producers of* The Dating Show *have yet to offer a statement in response to King's claims*. Linzie appeared back on the screen, in a chair now, in a dim room with studio lights. Thick makeup, dark hair straightened and tucked behind one ear. A box of tissues sat on the table in front of her. *My book is my truth*, she said. *They can't take that away from me.*

Do you feel you were more abused by these producers than the man who harmed you? The interviewer's face looked like something smelled bad.

I think I've been harmed by lots of people, Linzie said. *I think those people . . . they pilfered my joy. That's why the book's called* My Turn. *It's finally my turn, you know, to speak up about the harms done to women. To make it right. I hope people will read my side of the story.*

Trace wanted another drink. Her neck flushed red—she could feel it when that happened, hives like an island chain—and her jaw clenched down, then seesawed its satisfying ache. Trace didn't hate Linzie. She didn't know her, not really, the persona airtight, redundantly rehearsed. Trace only hated what she'd caused, what she'd continue to cause. Birdie had survived so many humiliations, but *Victim Jade Suzuki* was something else.

Trace signed the paper. Pocketed the keys. She took her time, tying and retying her sneaker, foot propped on one of the chairs, to watch the full segment.

Linzie. The reason Calvin had started again, the reason he'd become obsessed. A stack of folded papers bound by a hair elastic lay soft and crushed at the bottom of Trace's duffel. Calvin had been writing again, for months. The emails were strange and sprawling, with little narrative cohesion, no clear cause and effect from line to line. Bad enough when Birdie hadn't heard from him in years. Now he was back, and he was everywhere—on the internet, on the news, *Meet your next favorite book!* Linzie ripping the wound right open to reveal the bedrock of it all. Without permission. Without consent.

Earlier that day, as Trace headed to the morning ferry to leave Whidbey, Birdie told Trace about a *man who might fix things*. A man with *no connections* to her, only a location, a permission, a yes. *That's the plot to* Strangers on a Train, Trace had said, *and the ferry ride's too short for all that*, but Birdie had sworn it. Believed it. The boat man was real, and *he'd be the one to fix things*! Nothing Trace had ever done had fixed things, had helped her end the sadness cycle—not in all their six years together, not in every therapy session, every baseball bat beside the bed, the investments in alarm systems, the endless processing talks and tepid sex and *kingdoms of safety*—but, sure, here was a serious man, likely an imaginary one, who'd finally take care of it.

Linzie cried on the screen. She moved her finger under a tissue and made a tiny ghost of it, then went for a tear. She was good at crying. Trace had watched this woman cry more than she'd ever seen her own self cry. It's what Linzie did—wide-eyed and blinking, her mouth opening and closing softly like a fish thrown in a cooler. There were so many reasons Trace loved Birdie. Birdie was analytical, wry, darkly funny, usually fair. She could find the charming defect in anything, unflappable as a sentry when she wanted to be. Birdie's biggest fear was that she was ruined in some way, damaged goods, because of the way her brain functioned, and malfunctioned, since Calvin. In the darkest gulches of Trace's psyche, the part too painful to look at most days, she believed this was true. She would never say that, of course, but Birdie *was* a little . . . ruined. The kind of ruin that might be irreversible, self-abandoning, Trace feared. Every so often, there would be a glimpse of a different Birdie, someone lustrous, sharp. When Birdie would sleep, peace on her face, a dark tadpole of drool on her pillow, she was there. Or when she would sing to herself in the car, or watch a perfect film, when she would kiss Trace gently, or move her hand over her eyes as she looked at something strange or beautiful in the distance—Trace would see it, fleeting and thin as a drumskin, the woman Birdie would have, should have, been.

Instead, their lives, their *enmeshed life*, was orchestrated by fear.

By Calvin. Birdie lashed out easily. Disappeared into her trances. She wanted her whole life in the cubbyhole of the theater projection booth, in the dark. *Heavy doors*, she'd said, when she started training at the theater, *and all alone. That's why I like it.* No kids, no friends, no greater ambitions than that. Trace had wanted to fill Birdie with a stranger's sperm almost as soon as she met her. She wanted to watch Birdie grow, to make a thousand versions of her fanged teeth, her slanted hazel eyes, her wit. Children of tiny calamities, who would never know true horror. But Birdie said no children, not ever, and no leaving the city, and very little television—their lives had become less and less and less. Trace wondered, often, how much bigger their life would have been without Calvin. Without Linzie reviving him like a ghoulish parade balloon, finally catching its air.

Linzie wiped her tears on the television. Traci, from across the Enterprise room, said, "You seen this? The girl from that show, you watch that show? Hate to say I love that show. Now I kind of feel bad."

Sometimes, embarrassingly, Trace even prayed for Birdie to be a full, healed person. Whoever she was as a kid, before she was touched. Any permutation of that untouched girl. She wished she had known her, grown that girl up. Instead, there were counselors, Birdie's face inside thick black goggles emitting their tiny beams of light for *peripheral eye stimulation* and *emotional transformation therapy*. Birdie was seeing something else inside of those goggles, Trace knew, visions Trace would never, could never, reach. The anticipative look of Birdie in those goggles—the way she'd leaned forward with some hope, at last, in her body—nauseated Trace.

The segment moved on. Trace walked outside, took the thick worm of heat into her lungs. She found the SUV and started it. Wendy's house would have no booze, she knew. Wendy didn't drink or eat leftovers because of some Buddhist law in her handbook. But Trace could use a drink. She *deserved* another drink. She was fifteen minutes away from Gateway to Grace, and she tempted herself with the vision of her SUV taking his exit—it would feel like something, really *something*, to fork off the Turnpike onto Loxahatchee, toward Belle Glade. She'd like to see where Calvin lived. Where the person who'd ruined their lives was free to walk and farm and dribble a basketball. Free to laugh. Maybe she'd drive by, just this once. If she saw him, maybe she'd take the emails out of her bag, get through to him in a human-to-human, earnest way. She'd be calm. Maybe that's all it would take, yes—real, unfettered, late night communication.

Trace drove. She'd get one drink, somewhere. Just one! It would all be a part of her healing. Then, who knows. Florida people always seemed to find each other.

LET'S GET THIS out of the way: Rich is real.

But Rich never went to Florida. While he is not a figment of Birdie Chang's imagination, of course Rich never went to Florida. *Rich the Creeper* is what people on Whidbey called him in high school. Does Rich the Creeper make Rich a murderer, though? Despite Birdie's fiercest hope that he could be, despite her colorism or judgments, despite him seeming capable of what she is not? Maybe it was his brashness. Maybe it was the scar. Birdie thinks about the scar, mentally zooms in on it, when she most wants to believe.

Rich Amani has, in fact, remained on Whidbey all summer. Rich has, in fact, resided with his mother only a few miles away from Birdie on her compound, though neither one of them knows this. Rich is, *in fact*, the adopted son of Lisa-Ellen Parks, sister of pathologically lying Hal, and yes, that's right, this makes Rich the nephew of blustering well-intentioned boomers Thelma and Hal. When Birdie finally leaves Whidbey on September 3, right after Labor Day, Rich will be the one to clean her cabin—that's one of his side gigs. Birdie and Rich will not cross paths. He will not recognize her scent or any left-behind earrings or clues. He will simply smoke some weed, show up in his mom's blue Honda CR-V, and clean the place. He will think of Birdie only a few more times in his life—always on the ferry—before she's zapped from his consciousness; he will never see the news of Calvin or make a connection between the Chinese girl who liked Animorphs and the man rolled into putty on a street somewhere; he'll never know about the airport memoir. Rich has other things to think about. For example, in high school, driving home from a party his junior year, he made a blind turn colliding with an empty horse trailer on Route 20, and while Rich survived the accident, his best friend, Chase, did not. Rich will never forget the tickle of airbag powder down his throat, the way he shook his friend, how he thought, irrationally, he could shake life back into his body. He likes to imagine killing someone *with purpose* might be more fulfilling, might soothe some wicked spire within him, because he misses his friend still. That's why he indulges in murder plots. Plays bloody video games. That's why he fucks with people. *Rich the Creeper*, they called him after that.

Rich does not work with boats. Rich mows lawns. Rich has two priors on his record, so he takes on small, local jobs. Rich mowed the Kaufmans' lawn the day Calvin died, mowed the trap field in Langley the next morning. Worst part of his day? Getting fucked up by nettle.

Here's the question that's obsessed Birdie: did Calvin know? If she finds Rich—and she will continue to try to find him for years—*that* is the question she most wants to ask. She's read all about vigilante kills. She knows Marianne Bachmeier regretted one thing about shooting her daughter's rapist in court: he never turned around to see her with the gun. Marianne shot him in the back. Birdie wants there to be a version in which Calvin felt what was coming for him, and why. And from who. Did he even see the car? Could he hear it? Was the moment long enough for that knowing to sink in?

This question pricks at Birdie not only in the months after

Calvin's death, but her whole life. The knowing before death. The sudden inescapability of one's own truth, one's real worth, defined and certain as a rune. It must be the most terrible thing in the world, Birdie thinks, to be able to lie no longer, to have no further refuge. Her father had spent months in that vista of remembrance before he died—she needed Calvin to have had just one flash of it. Just one second. What she wanted most: everything Calvin had ever done funneling in all at once, her face, Francine's face, Linzie's, all their faces, clear and smiling and interminable.

***

YOU KNOW CALVIN'S mom. It's only fair you know Birdie's. This will matter.

Wendy Chang has been a member (and monthly sponsor) of The Healing Privilege for six years. She'd found THP online before starting her own local chapter, a group that began with nine damaged, peckish women who met in Delray over coffee and pitchers of blackberry Crystal Light, sometimes cocktails after the meetings, depending on how the meetings went. The Healing Privilege welcomed *all victims of sexual abuse*, and because the South Florida chapter started small, the director expanded this to *family and friends of all victims of sexual abuse*. Wendy was qualified in both ways (who isn't), though she only ever shared about the latter.

Wendy Chang loves support groups. She feels appropriately supported by them. Less obscure, more legible and known, in her dynamic complications of pain. Wendy is a widow and an empty nester and has a daughter (a *biracial* daughter) who has suffered tremendously. Wendy has also long harbored the fear that Birdie might be a socio- or psychopath—she doesn't completely understand the difference, despite vigorous internet research—what with Birdie's homicidal fantasies, her desire to watch and relive the recording of her own abuse. Wendy's nightmares about Birdie as a total crazy person, dreams that began when Birdie was a kid, fill Wendy with a trembling, shame-inducing terror. She has needed support for that.

Wendy's always made friends easily, but people in Florida often have their agendas—discounts or trades for their children's orthodontic care, or connections to the Rx pads in the office Wendy shares with many other doctors. In her past life, when Wendy still ran Hei Baby with her husband, Hei, she'd learned to recognize—and then to expect—the delinquent smiles and greased twenty-dollar bills of the people who wanted a good table on Friday and Saturday nights. They wanted their tables *Reserved*, extra platters of Wendy and Hei's Favorites, on the house. They were kind to Hei, but they were kinder to Wendy. In her qipao dress, her red hair up in sticks, her half-Chinese daughter and their musical renditions, Wendy was a validating figure, beside which a person might feel empathetic of other cultures, worldly, a little interesting.

Wendy found most of her support groups on her Facebook page. The pages often had privacy settings requiring a person to tell their story in a direct message to the admin, and *OH!* how Wendy loved writing her stories for that. She loved to *earn it*. Admins were *blown away* by everything she had to share; sometimes there was so much to say she'd had to cut down her story to meet Facebook's word limitations, but trauma was trauma, and Wendy knew this language, the key words, the phrases that would grant her that palatial digital freedom.

She'd joined a group for widows first. Then mothers with troubled children. Mothers with troubled *adult* children. (Were their children truly nuts? Mentally ill? Planning something violent and avoidable?) She'd joined a group for Everglades environmentalists, a group for women with irritable bowel diseases (Wendy long suspected stress-induced colitis), groups for people exploring their DNA and cultural backgrounds through new mail-ordered spit tests (most recently, Wendy's hunch had been correct; she was not only Irish and English but Cherokee, too). She'd joined a group for mothers with intuition, a group for people in interracial marriages (it took her some time to admit Hei was dead—nervous, here, that she would no longer be permitted), groups for people without religion but a keen interest in spirituality and animal magnetism, and groups for Ayurvedic dieting; groups for moms against guns in schools, moms against Rick Scott, Cancer Sucks, Ally Moms of Queer Children, Fleetwood Mac Forever, and of course the groups for Asian and Pacific Islander communities, with whom Wendy was always bluntly honest right away: she was not Asian and would never center or position herself as such, but remained an admirer, fan, and loyal affiliate to Eastern ways of being and thinking. She had a daughter to prove it. And a dead husband in whose honor she still bore a last name, a name nailed in brass letters across her mailbox, a name that allowed her to experience a fraction of racism herself.

The Healing Privilege, however, glowed luridly, differently, more tempting on Wendy's home screen. On the page, women of all ages shared stories about the hands that had touched them. Their memories of smells—there were so many smells women could no longer tolerate!—colognes, the fabric inside of cars, garages, petroleum, grease, sometimes foods like steak or burnt chicken, more often than not, a certain stench of booze; these smells triggered flashbacks that left the women twisting on their beds like a poltergeist had been sucked through their pores. There were women with deep regrets and women who graced their child selves with shrines, photos of their own kid faces smiling, too aware or unaware of what would happen next, what savior would or would not come. Some women were triggered randomly, and the randomness was what most disturbed them; driving, they might black out from a song on the radio. Or by a deer skittering past into the nearby woods. They might find themselves suddenly splayed out on the bathtub floor, water from the shower head bouncing off their skin, the women suddenly terrified of their own nipples, their own knees.

Comments multiplied by the hour thanking each person for sharing: *I have felt exactly this way too.*

Wendy was one of a small number of women who had been through the court system (via Birdie). Most others never reported what happened to them, never had the cold, firm swabs between their legs and in their mouths, no pick beneath the nails to collect DNA, dirt. Most of them were, in fact, abused by their own family members, or close friends of family, and they had not wanted peripheral parties to blame themselves, did not want things to get messy at Thanksgiving dinner, years later. *You cannot change the past, only the future!* these women often said.

Wendy sometimes felt as if she were betraying her daughter by sharing her story with the group. Trace had initially felt that way, too, once Wendy brought her in. Birdie was the one who had been touched. Birdie who had been recorded. Birdie had to live with the fact of that, always, the worst day of her life reduced to a thumb drive or hard drive, passed around maybe, traded or sold. Wendy knew that some victims had court-ordered blanket judgments; all persons found with CSAM would be arrested, then they'd owe the victim a fat sum. But Birdie didn't have that recompense, would never have that. She didn't want to continue pursuing such a thing. There was so little—including healing—that she wanted to pursue.

Oh, there was one more Facebook group. There, she wasn't Wendy at all. Wendy's pseudonym in "the Calvinists": Barbara Haines. Wendy had a whole backstory for Barbara: Barbara had retired from the police force but still had access to *very classified information*, thanks to the favors those in the police force still owed her for saving their lives. Barbara—with all her temerity and brains—would be the one to crack Calvin's murder, this *one final job.*

The rumor: the Facebook group about Calvin was started by someone in his own family. Once Linzie shared her story on cable, the Calvinists grew and grew; people wanted to know who Linzie was, and how the rape had happened, and what Linzie looked like at the age it had happened, and was she mature-looking, or only kind of? Did she have breasts yet, or only sort of? Wendy always found Linzie a bit tragic. Little Linzie, Jane Doe 3, after Birdie and Francine, *molested at a water park*—so matter-of-factly dictated in court records, and Wendy knew that was simply the way it went. The victim did this. The victim reported that. Showed signs of this or that. Thevictimworeitemsof thevictimallegedly thevictimclaimsdigitalorvaginaloranalpenetration thevictimiscredible thevictimisuneducated, etc.

On *The Dating Show*, Wendy was proud to see Linzie elaborate, at last, in her own words. She set a scene for the viewers, told them how it felt, how it continued to feel, long after her assault. She showed *emotions* and *vulnerability* the way Birdie never did. She described the way Calvin found her in the water park, *their secret*, how he'd had a gaze like he was in love with her—that's what she said. *Love!* If only Wendy had been Linzie's mom. She would have taught her the difference.

Wendy knew Linzie's mother was some sort of crackhead, her dad a walleyed, battle-wounded slimeball. They lived in a shit neighborhood known for flooding and meth, and Wendy wished Linzie would pack up and move in with her. When Birdie left Florida, Wendy actually contemplated reaching out, inviting her over for dinner. And when Linzie's tell-all book was announced, Wendy preordered twenty copies from Amazon.

The Calvinists—first a local, then national Facebook group— posted fanatically and often. Before he died, rumors about why he was the way he was: bad parenting, early trauma, broken brain / *he seemed like a nice boy / seemed super off to me / he once cleaned my pool*—*got the pH all wrong / gang affiliation / pedophile / pedophiles can't help who they're attracted to / omg a parent's worse nightmare / I would kill myself / I would kill my son*, etc. After he died: prime suspects, Google Maps screenshots, links to Reddit theories, blurry photos of the intersection of road where his body was found.

Of course, the Calvinists immediately cracked the time and place of Calvin's funeral, requesting a robust attendance.

Wendy pulled the Dole Grove yearbooks from her shelf in the living room. This was not part of Wendy's *healing privilege*. Not part of her constituent steps. Every page that featured the girls was easy to find—the spine had softened and split. Wendy rested the book on her lap on the floor. She raised her phone over the images of Linzie—Linzie in swim club, Linzie in choir, Linzie's yearbook photos in black and white, low-res and speckled, half smiling.

Barbara for the win!!!! The group thanked her. *Barbara you're a fuckin G!!!!!!*

With The Healing Privilege, Wendy had learned square breathing. She had practiced forgiveness through evening nightly mantras; you can't change the world you live in, only your reactions to it. She learned about rules of relativity; accepted dharma as truth; she wore oily tinctures on her wrist that left seedy trails of rose petals. *Let go*, she'd repeat, as she huffed her oils. *Inner pasture*. And she would let go—eventually.

This is what she promised herself as she pulled the black nylon mask over her head. It looked made for a burglar, but she'd actually bought it at the cheap sex shop in a nearby mall. She pulled on her green wig (she'd bought thirty or so green wigs for other Calvinists, on sale at Party City), and she sent the yearbook photos of Linzie to Kinko's, and then she'd mounted those photos on posterboard, then to XL paint stir sticks.

At the Eternal Light Memorial Gardens cemetery, the Calvinists gathered around their cars and Wendy distributed the signs from her trunk. She handed out extra copies of *My Turn*, extra wigs. Wendy introduced herself as Barbara in a low voice; the name sybaritic and strong, and she felt that way—like *Barbara*—in the clingy heat of her mask, eyelashes flattened. She was Barbara. All-knowing PI and former CIA Barbara—who was to say she wasn't?

And so they marched. And so they chanted. The casket was

lowered down. Good. Goodbye, Calvin. Some of the Calvinists already stood around his grave, undercover. They raised their fists in unison, and the way their voices rose and joined together made Wendy feel like she was young again, softly high on good stamps at a concert, blood rushing in her ears, cool rain on her cheeks. She screamed.

When Mary-Beth looked at them, there was no mistaking the hot red of her eyes, eyes brimful with agony. She hadn't changed much, not in all the years Wendy had not *known*, but *seen* her—Mary-Beth's Tropicana bronzed skin, frame like a screen door, bowlegged walk of a Halloween skeleton. The look in her eyes—that was pain. And that's all Wendy wanted, really. That's why she'd be able to let this all go—the Barbara persona, this secret group, their planned protests—eventually. She'd deny it to members of The Healing Privilege later. Maybe she'd deny this part to Trace, too. But there was no other goal, nothing else in the world Wendy Chang wanted. She only wanted to see a mother in pain.

ON PRINCIPLE, MARY-BETH had never gone near the Palmyra Pool Hall on Lake Okeechobee (*Lake O*, as most called it) the closest bar to Gateway to Grace, five miles from the compound. But tonight—just over a month since Calvin died—she would make an exception. The Palmyra was a spot for locals, Mary-Beth knew, and Mary-Beth also knew locals believed they'd been bankrupted by the residents of Gateway, their children and economies doomed by mere proximity, their food nearly all toxic, their hospitals and police force closed down. But Tommy had said *those local folks hanging at the Palmyra*. Odette had known about them, too. Those locals wanted people like Calvin dead.

Mary-Beth would go undercover, figure this out on her own.

Earlier that evening, 8:00 on the dot, Mary-Beth had curled onto her couch—both bare legs kicked to the side like a mermaid—

and tuned in to watch *The Fix*. Syl smashed a handful of popcorn kernels into her mouth. *You tell the elves at Santa's workshop you're a movie star?* Syl asked, as Mary-Beth's own face flashed across the screen: *My son would never hurt anyone.*

Mary-Beth never imagined a person like her could be on television. On a show that didn't feature paternity tests, smashed chairs, or police cuffs. Not even a natural disaster news special, one where the anchor always found some poor soul too hard up to get out of harm's way, flood sucking out their double-wide in the background. Mary-Beth had been on TV only once—more her legs than anything, blown out by headlights as the Pigs dragged Calvin away from a gas station in an episode of *Cops*—so she couldn't believe it when Odette called her to appear on *The Fix*, which would now not only spotlight Linzie, but the unsolved murder. *More eyes, more leads, more press*, she'd said. Odette had set it all up.

On TV, someone labeled an *expert* wore a tight black dress and a string of pearls. She spoke with big words, her hands moving rapidly. *This case is complicated*, she said. *No one is impervious to this kind of trauma. Child sex abuse touches almost every household, and the more you learn about Calvin Boyer and the extraordinary spectacle surrounding this murder, the more complicated and complex the story becomes.*

The TV lady asked the Expert why people might care.

People want to know why horrible things happen. I think it makes us feel safe, or maybe better about ourselves, if those people aren't us.

But what if it *is* you? Mary-Beth wondered. And then the special cut to Mary-Beth again. A voiceover explained that she was the mother, *against all odds, still loyal to her son*. Mary-Beth didn't look like Mary-Beth, exactly, more like a puppet of herself. She was told the studio lights would *balance out all that makeup*, and she had imagined they would—the hot bulbs had made her squint, sweat—but on screen the makeup looked orange and cakey, the bumps and ingrown hairs on her face and neck swollen as mosquito bites.

Her frosted lipstick looked less brown, the way it had in the mirror, and more silver.

You don't believe your son abused children? the TV lady asked Mary-Beth.

Abuse? My son would never hurt anyone, Mary-Beth said. She looked at the woman, not the camera. All the men in the studio had told her to do that.

Oh, I know he did, Tommy said then. Tommy's face, his mustache, a navy-blue button-down, appeared on the screen. Sitting in the same seat as Mary-Beth, he said: *There was something wrong with my son since he was a little boy, something . . . not right. Do I think he should have died? No, course not. But do I think he's guilty?* Tears filled his eyes, and he looked down at his lap, apologized—*Just a minute.*

Without a doubt, he said, *guilty. He couldn't be stopped. Something sadistic to him.*

Mary-Beth stepped out of her Mercury at the Palmyra, and fierce wind from the great lake slapped the car door shut. It was ten p.m. A Wednesday in August. She wasn't in her elf clothes tonight but denim shorts, a Daytona baseball cap that had been Cal's, ponytail looped and pulled through the snapback. Adjusting the snaps tighter to fit her head, Mary-Beth had felt guilty.

She walked the dock that led to the entrance of the bar. Over thirty thousand gators in Lake O, it was estimated, and Mary-Beth could see many of those eyes now, red lasers in the floodlights, looking at her. She hated this body of gray-green swarming water, which curved as far as the eyes could see. She hated the warning signs around it for miles—*Could pickle a toe in it,* she'd often heard, *that's how toxic.* But this is where her son had lived.

Nobody looked twice at Mary-Beth when she entered the bar. It was dark inside and sparsely crowded, one TV mounted between rows of glowing bottles. There were two pool tables, a dart board with no one playing. Mary-Beth sat on a stool at the bar. She perused the menu with a fake, fixed interest, index finger sliding down.

"Can I get you something, hon?" the bartender asked. The woman looked older than Mary-Beth but similar, like she could have been a long-lost aunt or cousin. She had better teeth, silver blonde hair, skin tags like a necklace.

"Vodka soda, no ice," Mary-Beth said.

Ten or so people mingled around the pool tables. On TV now: *Fight Night*, two greased men whacking and flipping each other within a banded square. Mary-Beth prayed the bar hadn't been playing *The Fix* tonight—or this would all be moot.

"Looking for my old pal Harrison?" Mary-Beth said to the bartender. Harrison—the name she'd remembered from Tommy's story. The one who'd *been around*, who'd seen the girlfriend the night Calvin died. The woman slid over the vodka. She said, "Middle of a game," pointing her chin at the pool table.

Here's what Mary-Beth Boyer doesn't know: all these people at the Palmyra Pool Hall, every last one of them, including the bartender, know who she is. They know *exactly* who she is, including who her son was. Erline, in fact? The woman next to Harrison in a sparkling pink cap, chalking up her cue? She's the sister of Charmaine, the only woman enrolled at Gateway to Grace, not enrolled because she's a *child molester* but because Charmaine is Black and an opioid addict and because she once peed near a gutter in Liberty City when no establishment, not even in Liberty City, would let her use their restroom. The police arrested Charmaine for public indecency. Lewd and lascivious behavior. So she'd had to join the registry; her face, name, and address now appearing on websites like Watchdogs, where every predator is color-coded and number-ranked by their degree of respective danger. Charmaine is still code orange.

Mary-Beth does not know that Erline lives in the shuttered windowless projects near Belle Glade and the radioactive lake and the 2,500 acres of toxic-pesticide-pumped estuaries, just to be closer to her sister. Mary-Beth doesn't know that Erline commutes over an hour to work Brahman cows during the day, processing them for slaughter, for meat cuts she will never be able to afford, all to support Charmaine in her pervert park, the pedophile village full of horny bound-for-hell assholes, the court-mandated sex offender classes; all of this for a slim hope of a shorter registry, a partially expunged record, Charmaine's face disappearing from those websites.

"You're real good," Erline says now, to Mary-Beth.

Mary-Beth leans over the felt table, sinks a stripe. She *was* good at pool. Mary-Beth and her three new friends—Harrison, Erline, and some other guy in a cowboy hat—have been chatting about Afghanistan soldiers, hurricane season, Karen Carpenter (playing from the speakers). Then Harrison goes, "Where you visiting from again?"

"Wyoming," says Mary-Beth. "Down here to see family, considering a move."

"Wyoming," Harrison says. "Whereabouts?" (over Mary-Beth's shoulder, a wink from Harrison to Erline. Juniper, the bartender, wipes a glass clean, shakes her head at all of them—*Leave that poor lady alone*).

"Altha, Wyoming," Mary-Beth says. Mary-Beth doesn't know any Wyoming towns, so she chooses a Florida town.

"What's your business?" Erline asks, leaning over the table. Erline, with a short, strong stature, scoots her body over the fabric and closer to the ball, lifting one foot from the ground.

"Fishing business," Mary-Beth says. "Snook."

"Snook in Wyoming, huh?"

"I mean I might start here," she says.

"Wouldn't start *here* here, if that's what you mean," says Harrison. "Rick Scott's shot the lake. All algae. They're rerouting that poison crud to the fields. You want that in your fish sticks? It's a wonder we don't all got three eyes by now."

"What else should I know about?" Mary-Beth asks. "If I'm

looking to relocate?" She taps the tip of her cue three times quick, then chalks up, peels over.

"Hell on the asthma," Harrison says, "all the cane burns—"

"Lotta churches, lotta crackheads," Erline says. "You got kids?"

"Just one," Mary-Beth says.

"Not the best place to raise kids."

"Heard there's a community control village nearby. Like, civil commitment, or whatever you call it. That true?" Mary-Beth says. Mary-Beth moves back to her warm drink as the balls clack, tries to sip calmly, lock her knees, steady her breath. She came this far; she'll give nothing away.

Erline limps around the table. She bends her right leg more than the left when she walks. Then she aims and shoots. The woven pocket quivers as the balls sink.

"The pervs? They're in the yellows," Harrison says. "The three blocks of yellow units with Community Corrections parked out front. Yellows are your pedos, rainbow houses where the Blacks live, right, Erline? You know the color of the people by the color of the houses."

"Oh, shut up, you bitch," Erline says, laughing.

(Later, once Mary-Beth leaves the Palmyra, Harrison will apologize to Erline over these comments. He knows where Erline's sister lives, knows Charmaine's not a pedo, even if all the others are. *Had to play the role*, he'll say, shrugging. Erline will understand. She'll say, *I got you, I played back too.*)

"Only white pedos work the cane now," Erline says to Mary-Beth. "Used to be jobs for us. Now *they* have those jobs. The yellows—some of those units are nice. Paved driveways. New paint. I hear they got hot tub Jacuzzis inside—that's how they get their girlies. Like a friggin country club. You know what we get? Shit, you don't want to know."

"Hot tubs," Mary-Beth says. "That's something."

Mary-Beth considers her angle, her next move. Tommy had said Harrison recognized Trace, so Mary-Beth had found and saved a photo of Trace on her cell phone. She could show the picture, get right to it. *Have you seen this girl-fella?* Or she could keep talking, ease her way there.

"Well, what're they like?" Mary-Beth asks. "The pedos? Can't all be guilty now, come on."

"They're wrong in the soul," Harrison says.

Something sadistic to him—Tommy's voice, wringing Mary-Beth.

"Clearly raised without God," Erline says.

"Molested by their folks or something," said the man in the cowboy hat, chiming in. "That's what I've heard. Molesters were always molested."

Mary-Beth smacked her pool stick against the edge of the table. It vibrated into her hand. Everyone stopped in place, looked at her.

"Can you really tell something like that?" Mary-Beth asks. "I mean, you can't tell what's wrong with a soul."

"Some more than others, you can," Erline says. "That kind—you want them near your kid?"

"I'd have 'em meet my .22 if they came near my kid," Mary-Beth says.

All four of them laugh at this. They clink glasses. Erline covers her eyes with a forearm, then slaps the green. "Wyoming woman, you better come around more often," Harrison says.

This will be the part that breaks Mary-Beth most: she *does* want to come around more often. This Palmyra lounge—in another life, another realm, it could have been a place for someone like her. The stools could have been *her* stools, the people *her* people. She imagines a life in which this crowd, her *friends*, lift her body over the table to get a perfect shot of the cue ball, as if she were a crowd-surfing rock star. These friends would defend her honor, remember her birthday, buy her rounds when money got tight. They'd smack the back-ass pocket of her pants, and know her enough to tease her, nickname her, say *what kind of stuff are you up to again* if she acted out of character for a single evening. They'd even let her bring up stories of her late son. They'd let her mourn him. The sadness of it all roiled inside Mary-Beth. Disgusting—how alone her life had made her.

"Read somewhere one of them became roadkill," Mary-Beth says. "One of the pedos, last month, around Fourth of July. Flattened. You know what happened there?"

"Now, that's something," Harrison says. He looks to Erline and the other man. "Any you hear about this?"

"That *is* something." Erline shrugs. "Must've cleaned up quick."

"You hear of this, Jupe?" Cowboy Hat shouts to the bartender. "Pedo-down, under a chassis?"

From across the room, the bartender shakes her head.

"Funny," Harrison says. "Not a lot going here, but none of us heard anything like that."

By two a.m., at close, Mary-Beth said goodbye and left the Palmyra. Her headlights, sickly yellow tunnels on the muck and sod, smeared the road ahead of her. That road: black like tar, like rot, like sucked-on onyx, *like hell* around here; everyone said it, and it was true. Out here, you couldn't tell what was roadkill, what was palm husk. You couldn't tell sinkhole from tarp. Mary-Beth drove and thought of Calvin, drove and thought of Calvin—How many nights she had driven, thinking of him? The broken yellow lane dividers flitted at her like bullets, then elongated. That's kind of what being Cal's mom was like.

Mary-Beth arrived home. Quietly click-closed the front door, Burbank Blue. In her bedroom, Syl slept hard. A snoring lump in the soft light of *Happy Days*.

Mary-Beth knew exactly where Cal's laptop was in the bedroom closet. She pulled it out, held it to her rib cage. Then she walked out the back door, her flashlight weaving through the lawn and then the tallgrass, for gators. At the lake's shore, she tucked her right hand and flung the laptop like a Frisbee—though it didn't fly like one. It plunked into the water, which dipped and distorted the moon, then settled.

Mom?

She broke her promise. Or maybe she kept it.

—

LIKE IT OR not, Linzie matters to this story. Her suffering matters, and it belongs to her.

Linzie did not kill Calvin—only internet trolls will suggest she did—though she does, eventually, break.

The break (or is this the true *instigating incident?* Linzie has had many) begins here. August. Linzie a *different kind of survivor* now. Linzie with TV specials, real ones, exclusive interviews, her *living nightmare* in the tabloids. "Linzie 3.0," Yale calls her lovingly.

Yale is not a therapist. Not a life coach or nutritionist. Barely even an *author*. Hardly qualified for anything, if we're being honest. We know—though Linzie does not yet know—that he is simply a user, insecure and often bored. He has a person like Linzie who depends on him, listens to him, eats it up when he tells her about planetary placements and bleached coral reefs, who thinks his filtered iPhone photos of street trash are *really cool*—and no one in Yale's life has ever regarded him with this esteem before, no one has ever dreamed of calling him *brilliant*.

Here, in Yale's Wynwood apartment on the fourteenth floor, he sips from his green juice with a metal straw. Linzie, from the steeped ginger and lemon water Yale has been preparing for her—her *grown-up drink*, he's been calling it—which Linzie hates drinking. The grown-up drink is sour and hard to swallow and leaves her with deep furrows of canker sores, which makes her lisp even more than her new Invisalign retainers do. This apartment is now their *headquarters*, where they meet for what Yale calls *immersive sessions*.

Linzie's scrolling a Word document on Yale's laptop, a *Teen*

Vogue interview, Linzie's mouth a swollen hyphen. "It doesn't sound like me," she says. "Nothing about me's in here."

"Can you take those out when you're talking?"—Yale, handing her a wad of paper towels, into which she ejects the retainers. The plastic trays glow with spit bubbles. *Sorry.*

"I just sound like—"

"Don't be facile. You sound like whatever I make you sound like," he reminds her. Sweet Yale! At home, in her garage-bedroom, Linzie reads the published interviews aloud to herself, Lucky's warm fur on her stomach, and she works to swallow the words, to make the answers hold severe, poignant meanings within her. Yale has given Linzie a vibrating rock to rest on her solar plexus at night; the instructions—listen to the voice recordings Yale sends, long, slow monologues. On the recordings, Yale walks her through relaxation methods. TV etiquette. Skin care tips. Vocabulary quizzes and speech methods—*no fricatives!* Her own story told back to her in his soft, academic voice. Earbuds ache her ears, and the egg vibrates on her chest instructing her on when to breathe, and for how long. She listens. Practices. Yale teaching her about who she was and who she *could* be, arcing the thematics of her journey, correcting her life.

Linzie and Doug's fridge is now stocked with Yale's broths. Yale has taught her about gluten, about legumes and trans fats and FODMAPs, *no more microwaves!* She now knows the benefits of garlic and zinc. Yale takes her to Miami's farmer's markets, off the grid and *authentic*, has her squeeze the produce, pinch, and identify all the herbs. *Remember, you worked on a sustainable farm in Buffalo*, Yale said on one recording. *You're a woman of nourishment, not junk. Processed food makes a processed woman.* Buzz Buzz went the egg. She breathed.

Was this a marriage? Sometimes it felt like that to Linzie. She'd never spent more time with anyone, besides her father. She'd never been more known. Yale never asked her for a blow job again (*happens when I smoke sometimes—cannabis plus Mercury retrograde—and there was mutuality*), but he tested her on adaptogens. He asks her about the pros and cons of honey versus agave, and what ingredients cause inflammation. Doug needed *anti-inflammatories*, Linzie learned, *no uric acid*, for his degenerative arthritis, his tinnitus, his gout. Linzie was good at adding up calories. It took two threads of the online commenters calling Doug *fugly*, photos of him pulled from old newspaper clippings, for him to join Linzie's diet plan.

Linzie went to Publix every few days, more and more familiar with it, memorizing the aisles. She tried tofu. She skipped the eggs in pastel Styrofoam. She wanted to say, *See, Dad, Yale is teaching me things. See, Dad, he's good for me.* At home, she cleaned dishes with hot water, yellow gloves; she breathed with the egg; counted backward when she wanted to pick or yank her hair out, and this helped—her face was healing, her scalp too. Then she'd go to bed early, jelly eye masks slugging down her cheeks, aromatherapy diffuser chugging bergamot and rose—*salvific!*—and calmly check the online forums to read what a waste of human life she was.

r/ Linzie King LIES and EVIDENCE
r/ Most annoying shit about Linzie King
r/ Linzie Kings white trash biatchhhhhh

Occasionally, a commenter would stick up for Linzie. They would say something like get a life you fucking losers, or does it make you feel good to bully this poor woman all day she's clearly super fucked up or what happened to standing by survivors??? JFC.

And then, without exception, just below those comments:

HI LINZIE!!! WE KNOW IT'S YOU!!!

IN ONE IMMERSIVE session, Yale asked Linzie to lie on his linen couch. Yale leaned back in his gray recliner—*an Eames!* he'd taught Linzie, *you don't call it a recliner*—a bulbous lamp on, *My Turn* in his lap. It was a Friday night, just after *The Fix* special, and Linzie settled her head into his pillow.

"We'll pick up from the other day," Yale says.

Linzie hates rereads of *My Turn*. Rereads mean she's done or said something wrong in an interview, something inaccurate with Yale's stories in the pages. She can't read it herself, so Yale reads it to her. Alone, reading about her own life, especially *this* version of it, the words swim on the page, like endless credits crawling at the end of a movie.

Yale, though. He *loves* to read the book. Right now, they're somewhere near Calvin and Jade Suzuki (née Birdie Chang), high school—*Picture Jade here. Picture her eyes, two salt-dusted almonds, her childish knock-kneed posture*—and Yale reads his own words, smirking and laughing at parts, underlining with his pen. Linzie drifts, thinking of Birdie. Imagines Birdie driving her away in a fancy car without a top on it, Birdie's black hair flashing in the wind. Yale reads about Calvin's aunt Syl and her twin daughters on their farm near Ocala. "They hate the fucker," Yale says, breaking from the page. "Aunt said all the right things, but I can tell, you can always tell, Linz, when there's true hate behind the eyes. That guy's family fucking hates him."

Then Yale gets closer to the day, to the water park, and Linzie thinks, *No.* She thinks, *Stop.* Sometimes words are as bad as the real thing. Sometimes they're worse. Yale hadn't asked much when he'd written this part of the book; he'd used the legal records, free and accessible online, and he'd referenced court transcripts and footage of what Linzie had already shared on *The Dating Show*. The rest—a warm winter day, crowds gathering outside the concession stands, the sun-blasted pastels of the plastic slides—this is all Yale's imagination, his embellishments and googles, and Linzie is grateful for that.

"This is the clincher," Yale says, "this part matters. You've got to access this in order to *feel*. Stay with me, now."

"I lived it," Linzie says. "I stayed."

Yale goes on, briefly, about method acting. *That's how you've got to think of yourself—like a renowned, disciplined actor: DiCaprio, Day-Lewis, De Niro.* He goes on this tangent often.

Yale's bare feet contract and flex on the Eames ottoman. Spectacular, girlish arches—his feet had a way of moving on their own.

"You've overcome a lot, Linz," he says. "But it's got to read. It's not yet reading."

"I want it to read?"

"You want people—we need people to know you have depth. To feel it, that kind of haunting. Deific haunting. You want it to emanate. Have you ever heard of the word *lacuna*? Do you want to be a little parrot? Or a lion? An African wild dog?"

Linzie says: "I want to be better at conversations."

"Close your eyes," says Yale. "Cover yourself in a blanket of light."

Linzie imagines, best she can, a blanket of light. She imagines the blue flickering lamps of the tanning bed—that warmth. Then, the sun beaming off glossy hoods of cars, the moon flashing off grooved edges of ocean, so piercing she'd have to squint at it. She thinks of her mother. How, in bed, with her head against Irene's chest, she could once hear the gurgles of Irene's stomach. Irene's voice as she shooed Doug out of the room—an echoed, muffled alien. Linzie loved sleeping right there, like that, heartbeat so loud. Her mother loved the beach.

"You are Linzie Gwendolyn King," Yale says. "You are strong. You have persisted, despite your pain. You live side by side with it. You are a woman in pain. Repeat it. Embody that. No, literally, repeat it."

"I am Linzie," says Linzie. "I am a woman in pain."

"And in that pain, you will heal. You will radiate healing."

"I will heal," Linzie said. "I radiate healing."

Linzie drapes an arm over her eyes. Then she pulls the pillow to her face because the lamp is bleeding too much light. It hurts.

"Think of Calvin," Yale says. "Think of that fucking prick. Hear his voice. Think of how he went on touching more kids. Who knows how many. Channel this for them."

Linzie smells the chlorine of the water park. She sees Calvin's face again. He'd had such a beautiful face—he had never looked like a monster. More like a movie star. He gazed at her so devotedly. His wet, pink cheek on the plastic tube as he floated her down the Lazy River; the hair on her thighs blonde in the sun, more and more furry as they dried, she was embarrassed. But Calvin stroked her legs. Then he asked if he could hold her hand, under the water. She thought that was the most romantic thing she'd ever heard. The wind chilled her body above the surface, but her hand in his, beneath all that blue, stayed warm. The dividing line felt real as a bracelet.

"Harness it," Yale says. "Ball the pain up into a prism of light. Do you feel it?"

Linzie does feel it—somehow, she does. Like witchcraft. Like a lit cigarette, twisted into her chest. She hears the echo in the water park bathroom. Swish of the lock. Calvin's fingers and then her least favorite sound—her cold, soaked bikini bottom meeting tile floor. She remembers the gape of the shower faucet. Her teeth clenching and then chattering, goose-bumped skin, she wanted a towel. She'd been asking for that—a dry towel. That's how they'd gotten there. Calvin's hand on top of her hand, both their hands against that grimy wall. Her tooth had hit that wall. He'd kissed her everywhere.

You are a woman in pain.

Linzie wants to go up, up out of this room. Out of Yale's apartment, out of the bathroom of Tsunamis. She wants sky, air, wants to hover above the traffic on A1A, her body a droplet, a glassy pendant dripping from a power line. This is where she goes.

Calvin's face, it disappears before it turns into the other face. There are too many faces in the dark of Linzie's life, too many dark faces, it doesn't seem fair to see them when she doesn't want to. Doug's face looks different when it comes. When it sneaks in like this. It's not that she hasn't *remembered*; it's that she's good at it—the not remembering. And nobody has ever been close enough to hold her memories, to care for them. Doug wasn't hollow at the cheeks, no gray stubble then. He was muscular and meaner and healthier, then. Always an *old dad*, compared to the kids at school. A round face, even in the dark, pocked like a golf ball, like a spat-out moon, white and shining with sweat, *old dad*. He never stopped. *I love you, dad*. Calvin had pinched but not the way Doug had hurt. *It didn't happen*, Doug said, though Linzie knew that it did, it always did, even when he told her it had all been a dream. How many times had he come for her, in the dark? In the garage he'd built his daughter? How many dreams of the same stark vision? She didn't know. She'd never ask. She only wanted to turn the light on in her room, to change the silhouette and the story, to say, *Dad, it's OK, you can stop now, you can stop hurting me now*.

"Stop hurting me now," Linzie says, and Yale comes to her. Crouches beside her, rubs her arm, her cheek—*come back*. She lurches into him, her face at his steady shoulder, and lets out a cry. "We can stop," he says, "this is progress," as his hand moves over her back in long strokes, then two hard pats. He pulls away. Smiles. And she feels the warmth of his neck and his quick-quick pulse when she grabs on to kiss him. But Yale does not let her—kiss him. He leans away. *No, no*. He says, "In this state, come on—I would never, ever do that to you."

~

TWO HOURS BEFORE Calvin died, Trace drove from the Palm Beach airport to the Palmyra Pool Hall on Lake Okeechobee in her rental car. The neon outside was half shot, so it read more like *Pam*. Hair of the dog, something to take the edge off before Trace's week with Wendy and The Healing Privilege, a week where Trace would work on being centered, sober, good.

Trace Levenson quite enjoyed keeping herself in a guessing game, as if every event directly before her could remain an abstract shadow, dark and capricious. But deep down she usually/always knew what would happen next, what decisions she would soon make. Trace was predictable like that, and the fun was convincing herself *otherwise*, of any other way things might go.

Trace paced the dock, cracked her neck, and entered the Palmyra.

It was not New York inside the bar. It was dingy, half empty, and smelled of catfish. Trace took stock of the crowd, around twenty people, Black, brown, and white. Trace wondered if she would pass if she kept her voice deep—or she could pitch it up higher, the unfavorable alternative. When people couldn't register what she was—sir or ma'am—it was easier to give them an answer, an exact integer. It was the not knowing that made people unpredictable, angry.

Trace ordered a double at the bar, on the rocks. The highest shelf was Jameson, and it would do. Across the bar, two pool tables, and nearer to her, a dart board, red wings hanging limply from its center. The darts reminded Trace of a YouTube she'd once watched of bullfighting in Spain, red banderillas stabbed into spine and the red, red blood of the animal. Trace imagined the matador shambling off, oozing through his clothes and reaching for help before the bull finished him. As a child, when Trace had first heard of bullfighting, she'd prayed for that. Then she learned that it *did* happen—sometimes the bull killed the matador—but when it did, the rules changed; another member of the cuadrilla killed the bull anyway.

A woman in a cap walked over to pluck the darts from the board. She wore polka-dotted nylons under a black leg brace which hinged at the knee. She introduced herself, then said, "What's got you here, Mr. Missy?" Erline had glossy skin and dark lip liner, a stripe of bleached hair under her hat, which she took on and off, adjusting.

Trace said, "Oh, um, just passing through," already knowing this would not work, that this was a canned line out of a canned movie, and nobody *passed through* this area—it was a road to nowhere. Erline started tossing darts, fast. She was excellent.

"That right?" Erline said.

"Here for the holiday," Trace tried next. "Independence Day."

"Independence for who?"

Trace lifted her glass to that but Erline did not meet her toast. Between dart rounds, Erline picked up what looked like Coca-Cola with a halo of clear liquid weighing it down.

"How about you," Trace asked. "You live around here?"

"From Clewiston," Erline said. "Not much around, so Lake O folks, we come here."

A few more people entered the bar (this, a much busier night than when Mary-Beth would enter, one month later. After what happened to Calvin, after the Belle Glade force got involved, folks wanted to lay low). Trace said, "I know there was a reading tonight, down in Davie. For that Linzie King book, about a guy who lives down here."

"A what now?" Erline asked.

Trace explained a *reading*.

Erline listened. "I don't know where you come from where that's a thing people would do," Erline said. Then: "Be honest, you come to play piñata at Gateway?"

Trace shrugged. She told herself she did not yet know what she'd come for.

"I don't play piñata," Erline said. "But it's not far from here. You get a few rounds for those ugly fellas at the bar, they'll drive you over and show you some fun."

(Erline, by the way, has a code she texts Charmaine whenever the guys head over with their eBay-purchased Taser guns, their JerryRigs, their bats: GATOR GOLF, is the code. Charmaine knows when to stay at bunk, safe and out of it.)

"You know any of them personally?" Trace asks. "The Gateway pedos?"

"Just the real pieces of shit," Erline says. "The real motherfucking spooky ones."

And here's how the whole sequence starts: Billiard balls crack through low, twanging music. Two men walk over to Trace and

Erline. One, with army tags around his neck. The other, bright white eyelashes. "She's alright," says Erline, gesturing to Trace. Then: "This is Harrison. This is Jeb."

Trace has passed some sort of test, though she doesn't know how. She's *alright*.

"Boys," Erline says. "You know anything about a book coming out about this place?"

Trace considers speaking, opening her mouth. Maybe she should stay quiet. Maybe she should simply nod, blend in, humor them. She chugs her drink. Licks the numb of her lips. Why not, though. She's here, in this bar. In Florida. She doesn't have to be good, yet.

"It's a book about Calvin Boyer," Trace says. "Any of you know him?"

"Mmmmmm," goes Erline. Harrison makes a grunt.

"That one."

"Mr. Hollywood. Our little pony boy."

"Biggest piece of shit of 'em all," says Erline, and she means it. "You can feel it on that one, like a tingle. You ever feel something like that? Like you can just feel the ghosts of the raped around a certain kind of man?"

"I know what you mean," Trace says. She does. She has felt this, often.

—Then, well, you can guess what comes next. Trace pulls the bulk of printed emails from her back pocket. She'd taken them out of her duffel, out of the car. She knew—before she'd even turned the key to the ignition in the Enterprise airport parking lot—of course she knew she'd end up here, exactly *here*, the papers folded into a square, then opened, then fanned out and flattened under her hand on the table of sweating drinks, less than five minutes from Gateway.

Harrison lifts one. It's half wet now, the ink weeping. This one is about wanting to pin Birdie to a board, like a butterfly. "See," Harrison says, "it's the pony boys you gotta watch for."

Jeb picks up a letter. He reads a few lines aloud—lines describing various means of knife torture—then chuckles, motions for more people to join them.

(Birdie wrote both letters, though nobody, including Trace, knows this.)

"This guy lives better than we do. And we didn't do nothing wrong," Erline says. "Pony boy's old lady's gone to seed. But she buys everything for those guys."

"The dad comes around sometimes—" A stranger, chiming in.

"Honestly," Harrison says, shaking his head. "Whole family's a goddamn work of art."

—

DON'T FORGET ABOUT the girls. Everyone forgets about the girls—that's always been the problem, and that is *the* problem here, before Calvin dies. Genie and Nicola Packman, Syl and Howie's only kids, twenty (and a quarter!) years old. Genie, three and a half minutes older than Nicola, the two of them real twins, *twin twins*, not the dopey fraternal type.

Here are the ways in which Genie and Nicola differ. The differences are important, to the girls. Knowing them, and not just what happened to them, is important, too.

- Genie thinks her name, Genie Beatrice Packman, is a nice one. Nicola thinks her name, Nicola Lesley, is a bad one. Genie's is better. Nicola believes Nicola Lesley is kind of lazy—not different enough to be intriguing, or ordinary enough to be cool—certainly not a Jane.
- Both girls are vegetarians, but Nicola misses the taste of meat. Genie, never.
- Genie's eyeglass prescription is .25 more farsighted in the left eye. Nicola has an additional stigmatism. Still, they switch glasses sometimes. Both girls lost the same teeth around the same time. Early braces. Same four cavities, even.

- Once, Genie broke her nose in the swimming pool, racing from one wall to the other. *TIME ME!* she'd said to Howie, as he stood jostling chicken parts at the grill. Next thing: blood. It dripped from Genie's face like something clawed and alive as she slapped her hands on the rough lip of the pool, leaving dark, hot prints there. She lifted herself out and ate a burger bun—all the fixings, no meat, tissues smashed to her face with her head rocked back, chewing.
- Nicola has a freckle on the blue of her iris. The freckle is often remarked upon. People say *cool*, or *that's so pretty*. People love both girls' eyes. Spooked eyes, like shattered glass. Nicola often has dreams in which the freckle disappears.
- Nicola has scarring all over her forearms. On average: one-inch-long, cross-hatched in random directions, raised and a *little impressive*, she thinks. Genie's scars are inside her thighs.

Here are the ways in which Genie and Nicola are the same:
- Both girls used the same scissors to cut themselves when the scars were made. The scissors, small sewing scissors with a black handle, remained in their shared nightstand, between their beds, on top of their Saddle Club and Baby-Sitters Club and Boxcar Children books. The girls always wiped clean the blades after taking their turns, returning the instrument, sparkling, for the other. They never once spoke about this system, even years later. It just was.
- Both girls are bisexual. At least they think so. They have kissed boys, and they have kissed girls, and yes, they have even kissed each other, but that was only in the presence of boys, and only before their mutual torrential understanding of the patriarchy and the male gaze—the boys had joined in, and the girls had made the boys kiss each other before they split off, it was only fair, one for each of them, Genie

on the floor with Robbie and Nicola getting felt up in the bed by Max. It wasn't even that weird—the kissing each other part—according to the girls; it felt a lot less intimate, actually, than the scissors thing, or the way the girls picked at pimples and blackheads on each other's shoulders and backs, or even the way it felt to look at each other sometimes, across the dinner table, or at a school dance, the profundity of seeing a self who is not quite yourself but still *you*, always a bit devastating, and also: wow. In the movie theater, darkness blunting the mirage of this real-life mirror, it was still there, the thrill: same profile, almost the same noses (the fracture, the pool), pale freckled skin, blondish brownish reddish hair that hung, regardless of cut, very cultishly, like the women in that Woodstock '69 documentary both girls love. Both girls—strange-looking, eerily pretty (sort of); they don't look like Syl, and look even less like Howie; the girls lanky and tall with scaly knees and elbows, freckles that color their lips darker after the sun. Speaking of lips, both girls wipe at them often, a nervous tick, a burning dryness. It leaves a bright pink ring like mildew around a drain.

- People say both girls ride horses the same, but this is subjective, false. Genie always had a better leg, more strength. Nicola, a better eye and better intuition. Genie loves riding more. Nicola, technically better.
- Both girls fast for most of the day and then eat whatever for dinner. They don't see this as anorexic, unhealthy, or even restrictive. They are simply never that hungry.
- The day Calvin died, both girls woke to the same sound, and they were both on their periods. They would discuss this later. Extensively.
- Both girls like the smell of sandalwood. They wear the same sandalwood perfume.
- Both girls dance eccentrically. Many people have remarked on this. It is not that they have no sense of rhythm; it's that

they can't follow a beat, mentally. It almost looks like a put-on, a joke. But they are dancing in earnest.
- Both girls think Syl and Howie should get a divorce. Like, for real. Like, yesterday. They wouldn't even be sad about it. They both know Howie looks at gay porn on the internet—he never learned how to clear his search history or cache. They are not convinced their father is a homosexual, only that he is confused. Syl, they believe, wants to sleep with Safety Dad from school. Safety Dad meaning Paul Dwyer, who wore the bright orange safety patrol vest for four whole years outside the girls' high school to get a tuition cut for his sons. Both girls imagine Paul Dwyer as their stepfather. They picture him as a decent dad, affable, harboring inner demons about his own life. Paul wears a single diamond stud in his left ear, which doesn't, rationally, fit. It is the reason, both girls know, that their mother wants to fuck him.
- Both girls masturbate the same way. Left-handedly (both girls are right-handed), two fingers. They fantasize similarly—medieval hay bales, spells cast, clattering armor—both girls have talked about it. They don't see any harm, or strangeness, in talking about self-pleasure.
- Both girls have met men off the internet at Universal Resort in Orlando. CityWalk—that is where young girls often meet men off the internet in central Florida. Arranging it is easy.
- One guy, his name was Drew, was eighteen but looked older. He came for Nicola; she was the one who had been chatting with him using an avatar, though he ended up kissing both girls. Over dinner at the Hard Rock Cafe on the CityWalk strip, he asked both girls, *What's something you don't know about each other?* The girls said, *Nothing.* He then asked if they were telepathic. They said, *Sort of.* He then corrected himself and said, *I think I meant telekinetic.* He'd once heard from his mother that twins were capable of all kinds of supernatural stuff, and also both girls looked quite a bit like Carrie

White before all the pig's blood. The twins said they were not telekinetic, not that they knew of, and Drew wadded up the paper sleeve of his straw and rolled it into a little ball. He put it on the center of the table at the Hard Rock. Drew said, *See if you can move this, you go first.* He pointed to Nicola. She stared at the paper ball, and it didn't move. Then he said, *Now you go,* at Genie. She stared and stared, surprised at how much she actually tried to make it move with her eyes, like his challenge made her suddenly care, and that care made it suddenly possible. She moved closer and squinted her eyes at the ball. Then she breathed out her nose just enough that the ball darted toward him. *I knew it,* he said, and smacked his forehead like it was some kind of disappointment, a reaction that confused both girls, later. In Drew's hotel room, both girls took turns blowing him in the dark; his dick smelled of Play-Doh. They left the room not traumatized, no contrition, and more like, *That was all pretty weird.*

BOTH GIRLS WOKE to egg songs the day Calvin died. The hens were busy laying—the new Rhode Island reds Syl had bought for twenty dollars each—with their rusty, shining plumes, distant eyes that never quite caught Nicola's, not in the way she wanted. Hens were imbeciles, she often thought, but they were kind, and their kindness was enough. She'd watched her parents ax off their heads, sometimes they'd use the Stanley knife, the fat birds thrashing headless for minutes after, all those eyes in a single bucket. Days or weeks or months later, their pale breasts were plated for dinner, each portion the shape of a bisected, grill-marked heart.

Chickens were stupid, maybe, but Nicola would not, could not, forget the purr they emitted when happy, or the sweet expectant stance they took knowing they might be picked up in her arms, or the head-up-skyward joy when offered watermelon or worms; then her father hanging them upside down by a clothesline. The killing cones, the strings of blood into the white white bucket and then the blood going frothy as stout. Nicola could not shake the scalding water and then the torch, chicken parts soaking in salt to soften their muscles after death. The onset of rigor, lactic acid—Howie explained—happened to all animals, including human animals, when they croaked. Growing up, Howie made both girls inspect roadkill. The stiff legs of armadillos, raccoons, and cats—iridescent bugs clustering. They pulled over on the sides of country roads so he could teach them, so they could look.

The stiffness stayed with Nicola. It seemed, to her, the very proof of the shock of death, eyes petrified by whatever they saw in the after.

Nicola did not understand why the herd had to be culled. Sometimes the chickens had to die, but the roosters did not. The meat birds had to die, but the egg birds did not. All the birds, murdered, the horses, not. The horses were groomed and smeared with liniment and massaged by a woman named Sally who came by to rub her firm hands all over their flanks, pushing and kneading and saying *hmmmm*. The horses were grazed and clucked at and fed peppermints and carrots and pies. When a horse had to be put down, it was cried over endlessly. Nicola watched a euthanasia once, and once was enough. Bright pink liquid, like bubble gum cough syrup, in a syringe fit for a giant. *You don't think of an animal that large dying while standing up*—this, something Nicola has repeated.

Her college therapist, Dr. Xu, who always says, *Call me Vivian*, had been trying to get to the root cause of Nicola's problems. The self-harm. The dysmorphia. The depression.

Animals always seemed to be a part of it.

It's a whole scene, Nicola said. *Then you hack off their tail to remember them.*

And? says Dr. Xu.

And the hens are hung by a clothesline, Nicola says.

TYPICALLY, THE GIRLS asked each other about everything. They asked about dreams and favorites and would you rathers and *would you kill me if I kissed Brenden from biochem*, and *what if I got him to seriously love me and then we switched places not only so we could test his love, allegiance, attention to detail, and perceptiveness, but so you could see what it's like to kiss him too?* The girls asked, *Did you use my toothbrush or razor* and *did you not say hi to so-and-so on purpose just so he would think I'm a bitch* and *do you think Paul McCartney really died* and *is the soup at school just repurposed sauce?* The girls asked, and they did not lie, never to each other—that was their mutual understanding, a blood pact.

But of all the questions in all those years, they never talked or asked about Cousin Calvin. They never talked about the summer he'd lived at the farm when both girls were ten, and he was twenty-six. Why Calvin was too afraid to sleep alone, or why he always slept in Genie's bed. Nicola knew both Genie and Calvin were awake, because she would hear Calvin talking to Genie, high-pitched whispering like a girl-ghost. That question, the most obvious, was too much. Some questions were like that for the girls: so big they held the pressure of the ocean. So big, to speak them would pop a leak in their mutual submarine, both girls together in their pitch-black unencumbered depths of knowing. To let it in would be to offer themselves to implosion.

This was the scene: every girl in their college dorm gathered in the Rec room wearing pajamas and fuzzy slippers for their weekly viewing of *The Dating Show*. Some brought blankets. Some played with each other's hair. Jo-Jo poured red wine from an expensive thermos. Everyone placed weekly bets on the show, and the losers would have to do embarrassing, hilarious things.

Linzie King, at twenty-one years old, had looked familiar since the very first episode, but she also looked like most other girls on the show, young and spray-tanned with too much makeup, too much cleavage. She was different, though: her teeth were not white and straight, and she was not even a little punched in to the language of the show. Linzie spoke slowly with strange arrangements of words (*it was a real rad time we had had doing that, let give and let God*), an unfamiliar diction, a clenched, constipated, ice-cream-biting smile. The girls knew Linzie was from Florida, but most contestants were from Florida (in fact, they'd made a drinking game of it, a shot for every Florida—then they'd had to get specific with cities). Linzie was four years older than the girls but acted kind of like a baby.

It wasn't until the episode where Linzie told the Greek guy about being assaulted that the twins remembered her. Almost ten years ago—she was *the girl*. The *little liar bitch*, Aunt Mary-Beth said, that wanted a payout, that wanted their whole family to look bad—Calvin was older, wrong place wrong time. *Precocious* was the word some of the grown-ups had settled on.

Later, in their dorm room, Genie didn't make a big deal out of it. She said, her voice steady, as if she'd practiced saying it for a thousand years, as if it were the most ordinary thing in the world, like saying which way to the nearest gas station, or, my ear just popped on this plane: *We should talk*. That was Genie's voice after she came out of the shower and sat on her bed. She kicked her shower sandals off and onto the floor. Blue Adidas, the rubber tearing. Her shoulders were splotched with hives both girls got from heat (showers, long days in the barn, embarrassment). Genie was Genie when she said, "What Calvin did to Linzie he did to me."

Nicola nodded like, *of course*. Eventually she said, "Yeah, I know."

Genie nodded back. They synchronized their nodding.

Then that was the end of it for a while.

NICOLA DID A lot of googling to understand her sister in this new, confirmed way. She googled *adult victims of child sex abuse*, and she learned all about acronyms like CSA and CSAM, and she learned that this kind of abuse often happens within the family; *unexceptional*, was the word that she read, which was a very upsetting word to read in regard to what had happened.

She learned about pedophiles and tried to understand why they did what they did. It seemed people called everyone pedophiles these days; creepy cashiers and sucky politicians and celebrities who had younger girlfriends—the term had become a catchall. She learned that VirPeds were pedophiles committed to virtuous celibacy, and that all the VirPed communities online had been shut down. Nicola wanted to know if Calvin was a pedophile or just a super psycho creep, a murderous sicko, a horny, repulsive person who preyed on the young. Was there a line?

Then she looked up the death sentence and wondered what it would take to get Calvin fried in one of those antiquated chairs or on a lethal injection table. Florida, it turns out, was the right place for that. She knew it wasn't cool to want those things, to want to play God, but she wanted those things very badly; she understood, at last, why a person would opt in on witnessing that kind of death through an observation window, why a person would want to pull the lever or push the button (despite the twins' new evolved politics); Nicola looked up evidence of heaven or hell or reincarnation—the Buddhists had thoughts. She wanted to know it all.

Then she spent time contemplating the years of lies their mother and Howie had told them about Calvin and his crimes and who he really was. When Calvin wasn't locked up, he was in *treatment centers*, which Syl had told them were treatment centers for drugs and depression, and now Nicola wondered if Calvin was ever on drugs or ever depressed even a little, or at all. The family didn't talk about Cousin Calvin much, and they didn't talk about Aunt Mary-Beth, not unless it was some kind of worst-case-scenario-joke. Aunt Mary-Beth didn't have a degree or much of a future. Their mom had offered her financial help for dental work, but Mary-Beth had flatly and pridefully refused. (Syl talked about that refusal for years, even still—*Who rebuffs generosity?*) Mary-Beth had moved around a lot to support Calvin, *chased out of town*, according to Syl, but their mother was often dramatic and exaggerated about things. When Uncle Tom left the first time, around the time Calvin came to stay at the farm, Syl and Howie had said it was because Aunt Mary-Beth had *totally let herself fall off* and *a man is still a man.* The girls knew their mother thought Aunt Mary-Beth batted for her own team—they overheard Syl say that, whispering the word *queer* and then *batting for her own team* to Howie—which both girls thought was hilarious in the second grade. Later, they didn't care if Aunt Mary-Beth was a lesbian or bi or a carpet-muncher or a free-lover; in fact, that might be the one really cool thing about her, despite everything else.

Now that the secret was out, now that the leak dripped in, Nicola and Genie would do something about it. It was like Genie's confession activated something in Nicola—a memory, visible again—a fingerprint finally pressed to ink and then there it is on white paper, in detail. People needed to understand that bad people came in all packages, even their handsome psychotic cousin, who was now confirmed Blue Ribbon Scum of the Fucking Earth. People needed to know who—what—their cousin was. They would tell their friends to stop making fun of *Linzie-Dimsy*, to stop doing her voice and making her weird eyes because it wasn't very feminist or cool of them to tease a survivor just because she was maybe a little slow. Linzie had suffered, and suffering should be respected. They'd defend her on forums, make sure she was believed. Linzie King, the sort-of-pretty dumbass trash scab from Florida, deserved at least that.

The egg song—the shriek of hens—is what Nicola remembered of that morning, July 3, the last morning of Cousin Calvin's life. That, and the wraiths of black smoke curling upward in the distance, neighbors burning their trash. Syl and Howie's Fourth of July party went on for days. It was legendary. Both girls hoped the smell wouldn't last.

As kids, Nicola always slept on the right side of the bedroom, facing the doorway. Genie always slept on the left. Both sides had their own windows with similar views: oak trees, a scorch of sky that discolored the carpet in an angry rectangle, a cell tower that blinked red. At night, both girls took turns with their views of the moon, clouds sliding over it in their deep blue ways.

Calvin showed up in the doorway as soon as he started staying with them that summer. That's how Nicola remembers it now, at least—that there was no real time before it started happening, that Calvin appeared with his summer duffel and then it simply *was*. The hall was dark. Calvin never turned on any lights. He just opened the door, soft and soundless, his facial features and floppy hair sharpening as Nicola's eyes adjusted, Cal's eyes glinting wet as teeth. Some nights, Nicola could see better than others (in science class, Mr. Trott asked everyone to track the moon using a paper towel roll as a homemade periscope; Nicola paid attention to tides, light). Calvin wore baggy plaid pajama pants, socks, ribbed white tank tops he called *beaters*. He was scared, he told the girls, of all the new noises in the dark, so far out there in the country. That's how Nicola remembers it; Calvin was frightened. He wanted to sleep with them the way girls longed to sleep with their parents, or with each other. Calvin always went left, where Genie slept. Nicola did not question this. Genie was, had always been, the Brave Girl. Genie, at ten years old, did not flinch at the rearing, bucking horses and ponies. When she was thrown, she allowed the wind to funnel back into her lungs and then climbed back on, jerking the reins. Genie did not cover her eyes in movies or television shows, was not afraid of Candy Man or Bloody Mary. Nicola was terrified of all that.

Genie's nose healed a bit crookedly, after it was set. It became different than Nicola's, a betrayal in that bump, that spur of misplaced bone, a new degree of difference. With each difference, something they could never gain back. Nicola, so *stupid*—she would call herself in therapy—for never questioning Calvin's fear, Genie's courage. It made sense, when he went to the left side, the other side, never Nicola's side. Not even when she proved herself awake. Not even when she coughed, or flipped over.

Not even when Nicola wanted him to turn around, choose her.

DON'T DO IT for you, do it for the other girls. The ones who come later. They WILL come later. Do it for the girls who don't have a voice like yours; for the girls who don't have a voice at all. Do it for your younger self. Do it for your future self. Do it for all the selves you could have been, all the ones you might still be. The selves you've lost. And if you don't speak up? Oh, you want that fucker to win? Do you want him to get away with it? Do you not believe in accountability? Do you not seek justice? Are you too self-absorbed to remember the others?

If you let go, you let him win. If you live in fear, you let him win. You're not weak, you're strong. You're resilient. You are setting an example, so long as you open your mouth and talk. Spill. Write that story and write it right. You've got to say what he did, exactly what he did. Details. Sensory details. Make them believe you. Where did he touch you and how did that make you feel? What were your dreams after? What have you lost, besides yourself? Did you find him attractive? Of course you didn't—you were a child. You were never a girl like that. Did you eat after? Did you sleep that night? Do you have trouble sleeping now? Do you have trouble with intimacy, with sex? How about friendships? Do you have a good relationship with your family? Do you trust anyone fully? Do you have trouble digesting food? Do you wet the bed? Do you struggle with constipation, incontinence, hypochondria, chronic fatigue, anxiety, bad periods, or PMDD? Well, if I'm talking to you, if any of this is ringing a bell, I've got a solution for that. UP NOW is a supplement made from all organic and sustainable ingredients harvested from rare plants in East Asia and South America, and let me tell you, because it's changed my life already, this stuff will take you from cower to power. An all-encompassing supplement that, well, perks up every system if you know what I mean. Live your life again—you deserve it. Don't stay in bed, use UP NOW instead. Thank you to our UP NOW sponsors; you can read more about them on CarlisleFiles.com, and use code getmeupnow for 50 percent off your first subscription. Stay tuned, listeners, this is *Carlisle Files*, episode two, "Linzanity!"—when beauty's only skin deep.

ANOTHER INSTIGATING INCIDENT. This one, Linzie's:

The bathroom at Tsunamis water park was dimly lit. A square room, with squared off benches in the center of it. On one side, showerheads hung like drooping, deadly sunflowers. White cheap curtains slid across cheap plastic rods. Calvin walked past them, his hand out, as if high fiving the wind.

"Why are you afraid of the big slide?" Calvin had asked, in the Lazy River. This she remembers clearly. Linzie had separated from all the other kids on the school trip, just like Calvin had instructed her to do. Calvin's hair came down in fangs, parted in the middle.

Linzie was afraid. She really, really was. She explained this. How she didn't like the abrupt drop of the Plummet, the slide steep and hooked as a dentist's pick. Linzie had gone on smaller slides, though she didn't like those either. The metal stairs to the top rattled weakly under her, and the plastic-echoed screaming almost made her faint as she waited for the green light.

The bolts and seams of plastic bit at her butt and shoulder blades. Her back—red and scraped when she emerged. Calvin laughed and said, *Let me see*, etching a finger along her skin in the shape of a wing. She shivered, when he did that. He called her *brave*. A word Linzie had always, and would always, hate.

Linzie and Calvin looked in the bathroom mirror together. Or maybe it was a locker room, a shower room. It was an empty and dark room somewhere near the back of the park. Linzie was looking for a towel, and Calvin stood behind her, his chin on her shoulder, and she liked that. He wanted to look. The mirror was nothing but bent, dimpled metal, and they were merely twisted figures with the suggestion of skin. At some point, he'd locked the door. Linzie remembers that—the swishing sound. Calvin put his hand on her head. He pulled her hair back in a ponytail, cinching two fingers like a napkin holder around the chlorine mess. It stayed like that.

"Am I burnt?" he asked. He spun her around to face him, took her hand in his, then pressed her fingers to his chest. His skin felt so warm, and she wanted to jerk her hand back—but he pressed and pressed. Glitter polish, painted for Linzie's birthday party last month, made little floating islands on her nail beds. Her fingertips left whitish yellow ghosts on his skin. She said, "Yeah, you might be, a little."

Then he touched Linzie's chest the same way. And he checked her shoulders, too. Linzie shivered again. Her feet rubbed in her flip-flops. A blister would inflate between her toes, she already felt it. "You don't look thirteen," he said.

Linzie thought he'd meant she looked older, that that was a good thing. It would take years for her to understand.

He pulled her by the hand into one of the shower stalls, behind a curtain. The faucet kept looking at her in that black, angry yawn. She remembers the kiss. Her eyes adjusting to the twilit blue. Cold, she was so cold, but the kiss was warm.

Calvin looked at her with lazy eyes, half-drawn, the way Irene looked when she'd go to her place in the poppies, the place that made her pupils possessed. That's how Calvin looked at her for what felt like a very long time. No words, just that looking, before he kissed her again. Linzie had never been kissed on the mouth before. She held her hands at her sides and tipped her head so far back it made her dizzy. With his thumb at her chin, Calvin opened her mouth wider. It wasn't hard, she thought, to kiss. To be kissed.

There was no window in the bathroom that she could see, but a faint light coming from somewhere. Where? Her skin pinpricked all over, reptilian. She felt her teeth chatter, felt her nipples tighten.

Pinched, tiny nipples—embarrassing—that's what she was thinking about, how she hated the way her nipples looked when they were cold like this, wet after the pool, like the wrinkled pits of fruit in her father's napkins. Calvin turned her around again. She remembers that. His hand on her hand, but this time, against the tiles of that wall. The tile: warm. Laid sloppily. A creamy, gluey pudge between each tile. Her cheeks: cold. Her mouth without the kissing, her hair against her back: cold. Then, the sound of her bathing suit moving to her knees. The scrape of Calvin's nails. The rolling wet nylon pinching hair on her legs as it came down—it made her eyes water.

He called her *brave* some more as he touched. She felt his hands, and then his penis, behind her. She did not know what was what, what was where, only the familiar artichoke feeling in her ribs and throat, a soft needled choking. The pain snapped at her. Her body went brittle. She wanted that window. Her mouth hit tile. Chip in her tooth that would never go away. He told her, *Relax*. Linzie had been told this before. Then down her leg: the hottest hot she'd ever felt. She thought she was being burned, it was so hot, before she saw and then smelled her own urine on her flip-flops.

Later that day, Linzie would walk back onto the bus to leave the class field trip. She would sit, row seven. Out the window she'd search the longleaf pines, the hurricane-bald glades, the bus's engine grumbling beneath her thighs. Her tongue at the new ridge in her tooth—grainy, unsettling. She turned her body away from anyone who came near her. She would do this for the rest of her life.

At home, she blocked him online. He had a stare she could feel, and now—even in her room—she felt it everywhere.

And a few months later, before the DOJ trial, Calvin would find Linzie near the entrance of her school. He'd grab her arm as she walked up the front steps, push a wad of ripped notebook paper into the center of her palm. As she walked inside the door, she opened it, pulse speeding. Scalp raw. In the scrawl of his writing, it said, *talk to me. your breaking my heart.*

THE NIGHT CALVIN died, Sylvia Packman flipped the London broil in her special potion: soy sauce, garlic powder, Worcestershire, salt. It was four p.m., and a few people had already arrived with their tents and campers for the Packmans' annual *get more blasted than fireworks* weekend. Syl watched her neighbors out the window, cigarettes lit, plastic cups of moonshine, kegs rolling. She punched her fork all over the meat.

Genie and Nicola had made the potato salad themselves this year. It looked terrible—watery and too pink, the wrong cabbage, the waxiest baby carrots—but they had been proud. Syl took the mixing bowl of pink potatoes out of the fridge, set it on the counter.

That's when the girls walked in from outside.

"Mom," Nicola said. "Genie's got something she's been wanting to tell you."

Syl had noticed her daughters' eating habits first. When the girls were ten, Genie stopped eating breakfast before school, and then Nicola stopped, too. Both girls gave up meat, even the meat processed at home, meat which came from the animals they knew had roaming, spoiled little lives, animals which, they knew, were never to be considered *pets*. Syl never knew if both girls shared the same thoughts—wavelengths, telepathy—or if one was always copying the other, and it didn't matter who was copying who; they matched in such close succession, like two brains interacting as a single network. Were musicians doing this when they improvised together? Syl wondered. Were men in sports, men at war?

Growing up, Syl had never felt like that with Mary-Beth. There was never anyone more foreign to her than her own sister. Syl wanted things. She wanted a farm, a husband, children, and a Volvo, that was the order of want; eventually, she'd gotten all of those things. Syl knew what she wanted a horse to do under saddle, and she mostly got that too (*there are no problem horses, only problem riders*—she taught every student this). Mary-Beth, on the other hand? Her whole life just happened at her.

Mary-Beth. Big hearted big sister MB. Her wants were blunted out by her drinking, and then, eventually, by her son, which seemed convenient, actually. With Cal, Mary-Beth did not have to think about her own wants ever again, and thus could never fall short of them. It all frisked by when she drank, alternative versions of her life; Mary-Beth would blow smoke hard out her nose, stub her Misty three stern times, then say: *Fate comes at you like a bitch* or *Guess God had other plans.*

Syl loved having a plan. When Mary-Beth and Syl's brother, Alfie, died, Syl stepped easily into the role of planner. She and Mary-Beth were only eleven and thirteen, respectively, but Syl used her father's .22 bolt action Remington to start taking out squirrels and rabbits for dinner, and she was a great shot. She skinned them quick and easy. She was never squeamish like Mary-Beth, who missed her shots purposefully, Syl knew—could never kill anything, a little pathetic. To Syl, life was life, and everyone died, and all that mattered was grace at the table, a little bit of gratitude.

So it pissed her off, quite frankly, when the twins stopped eating their meat. Syl tried every tactic to talk them out of it. She tried the cycle of life—animals eating other animals—then, they were protecting animals from greater ills, bald spots from pecking order, hormone induced obesity. Then, *Only wimps think that, do you want to be a wimp?* The girls chose wimpiness. The girls shrunk thinner. Breeches bagged dramatically over their boots, frowning at the knees.

Calvin ate whatever Syl prepared for him and stayed thin regardless. Boy bodies would always be like that, Syl knew. Boys, who didn't deserve this blessing. Calvin loved sugary cereals and French toast and when Syl made bacon, he'd lift the limp purple strips off his plate, open his mouth, and swallow. Grease always shone on his chin. Syl thought, What a guy.

Syl knew her nephew was a fuckup but didn't know how bad of one he was. Mary-Beth had said: *Drugs, but not the serious kind.*

Mary-Beth had said: *Boys will be boys*. So Calvin would spend the summer on the farm learning discipline—fastidious, detail-oriented, Syl-directed discipline—and Syl and Howie wouldn't have to pay a cent for the help.

To Syl's surprise and dismay, Calvin did well on the farm. He listened intently and nodded along as she showed him how to pull, push, lift, and sift the horses' shavings with a pitchfork, to check for density beneath. *Peed-on shavings are heavier*, Syl explained, and he took the pitchfork in his own hands and immediately understood the poetry of mucking, blond flakes thrashing at the wall. At first it angered Syl, how easy he'd made it all look; he moved a wheelbarrow with perfect balance, scraped the chicken's coop so thoroughly it lightened the wood. But then: *Thank you, Auntie Syl*—that's what changed it.

Syl was responsible for his maturation, his rural knowledge, Calvin's great big turnaround. She would be the person to teach him properly—not Mary-Beth.

Calvin was good with the girls. Not very smart, at least Syl didn't think so—quite a *simpleton*, she'd joked to Howie—but he was fine enough to help them with their second-grade work. Calvin sounded out words. He drew shapes for them, showed them numbers with his thin thumb pressed onto a ruler; together, they practiced subtraction. Howie liked having Cal around, too. He had always wanted a boy, and late at night he'd offer Calvin tastes of artisanal rye, and then he'd lecture Calvin about canned hunting and tractor-trailer scams, plus the existential threat of corn oils.

Syl was happy, if she's honest with herself.

But the death haunt in their eyes, their plates full—Syl missed the way the girls looked before their pupils turned to UFOs, unblinking across the table, a pact. Arms and calves shrinking, Genie thrown from her mare more and more. Later, the cutting. The bracelets that covered Nicola's ruddy marks—still, it was obvious. Embarrassing, to Syl. Their weakness. All their laundered clothes stained with blood, which dried in streaks of brown, orange, yellow.

Calvin's arm around Genie when he helped with those math problems, the longer words.

Syl knew. A mother always knows, at least in retrospect. And this: he was the only person who could tell the girls apart.

"Mom!" Nicola says. The three of them standing in the kitchen, the fork in Syl's hand.

"Mom, pay attention! Genie has something to tell you."

IT'S LABOR DAY. It's back-to-school Snow Day. A North Pole, Florida, tradition since the Gas & Save (*plus casino!*) opened in 1978, to mark the end of summer.

Mary-Beth has done her job. She has hung the snowflakes from the North Pole ceiling; fishing line weighted by small crystal beads. She has sprayed the windows of the station, a white fur of aerosol. There is cotton packed beneath her fingernails, tiny threads showing up in her soda bottles, on her tongue, in her lashes. She has snapped out each and every branch of North Pole's artificial tree, fluffed the aluminum body, and sprayed the needles with pine scent.

Several years ago, her boss, Stanley, had surprised her with a package. It was a box, gift wrapped in candy cane paper. Stanley brought it to the register at the end of her shift, and when Mary-Beth tore off the ribbon and shimmied up the lid, the two of them stood there staring into the box as if the contents held the answers to the universe. The wig, the red hat and red dress with white trim, polyester prickly and shining perfect.

"Really, Stan?"—Mary-Beth slapped both hands over her mouth.

Snow Day, the one day a year Mary-Beth would be Mrs. Claus. The one day each year, every year, of her own.

This Snow Day, by early afternoon, the new Santa showed up a little drunk. Mary-Beth could tell; it was the sway of him, plus the messiness to new Santa's mouth when he said: *Looookie the snow mobile*. Santa's job was to sit on his Santa sleigh—the one Mary-Beth and Petra had dutifully shined and wheeled out into the parking lot—then children would squeeze and cry at his knee, tell him what they wanted.

"Ivan," the Santa said, shaking Mary-Beth's hand. They stood in the parking lot, near Joe's snow truck. "You my Mrs.?"

"Reporting for duty, sir," Mary-Beth said. Mary-Beth did not like Ivan. She found the smell of him grating and fruity, like he'd been popping that zebra gum. The way he smelled smelled disrespectful, but he was a man. And she was his wife, for today.

Mary-Beth explained how this had all gone in years prior. The line along the tape. Petra and Stanley at the tripod counting down from three for the picture—about thirty seconds to a minute per kid. "I'm assuming you know all the Santa things to say?"

Ivan slid his thumb around his phone screen. He said, "Sorry, I do greyhounds. Keeping up with the tracks."

Mary-Beth walked Ivan to the sleigh, the one that typically displayed Monster drinks. The sleigh was heavy and wooden, only three wheels working of four, so the dead one spun and scratched the asphalt when Mary-Beth pushed it. "Here's the monitor that says if you were naughty or nice," Mary-Beth said, pointing to a painted square. Mary-Beth moved her hand in an open circle, as if she were one of the ladies on QVC selling an expensive can opener.

Ivan took a photo of the sleigh with his phone. "You got any chips for me, my Mrs.?"

Inside the station, Mary-Beth grabbed Santa his bag of Lay's. Margail stood, dressed as her usual elf, at the counter. She snapped gum. Today, glitter on her cheeks, and she'd recently started wearing a single, silver tooth. She smiled at Mary-Beth, "Nice look."

"Jealous?" Mary-Beth asked, curtseying in her Mrs. Claus dress.

"Hell, nah," Margail said. "I like my AC. I don't like being around no kids. They give me the creeps." She flipped through a magazine at the counter, lifting a flap to smell the perfume inside. Then she rubbed her whole wrist over the flap like she was working a stain.

"Make sure you're on today," Mary-Beth said. "Once Chuck E. Cheese took off his head outside a birthday party to have a smoke, and my boy, Calvin, he was messed up about it forever. Hated all mice after that. Fed them to reptiles and savored the act. Didn't even want me to smoke—for years he would cry if I did, like I was in cahoots with that mouse. Then he grew up, and what do you know—started smoking himself. That kind of thing can leave a real impression."

"Sucks," Margail said.

Sixty-two days—from the day of his death to Snow Day. That's how long it had taken Mary-Beth to think about Calvin, and to talk about him, in the past tense.

Outside, Mary-Beth watched the cars line up on the curb. The children came running. Some were snapped into strollers. Others, in canvas wagons. Two toddlers with leashes attached to their waists. Ivan the drunk sat down in his sleigh, pleather belt loose and glossy. Mary-Beth joined him there. Her post. Her husband. His dark brown hair poked out from under the wig, his face all sweaty. Mary-Beth noticed the sweat kept changing—fat droplets, then tinier, then dripping.

Joe the Snowman's snow truck was a Peterbilt 379, red cabin with all the machinery in back on the cargo bed. An unnervingly dark slit opened in the side of the cargo, like a giant coin slot. Mary-Beth often dreamed she had a coin slot just like it in the middle of her chest, between her ribs, near her heart—a dark, faithless slit—that's what Joe the Snowman's truck was like.

The children lined up. Little paisley dresses. Little socks with ankle eyelets. Teenagers came, too. Boys, who slapped skin with each other, cigarettes balanced behind their ears—girls, with their gnawed-on short-shorts, belly rings swinging. Most of them had come every year of their life, and they would forever and ever, so they swore. A gaggle of women with no kids lined up. They wore matching green wigs and reindeer masks. Florida was full of all kinds of people.

Joe the Snowman held his hose. The machinery grunted and wailed.

Every year, the best part, it's this: the earsplitting shrieks. Fingers forking whistles, then fists in the air. Joe the Snowman: *Are you ready?* as if dinging the Vatican's bell. He waits until the crowd grows loud enough. Until the speakers blast "Jingle Bell Rock." Then the hose turns on. Then Mary-Beth takes her mental picture. Then the sun drips down everyone's throats as they all look up.

SYL THREW A suitcase onto the quilted comforter of the bed. The leather case was soft, stained, and looked helpless there, hanging open like that. Syl threw in her blue jeans. Her nonbarn shirt that smelled of cedar and perfume. Toiletries. A paperback. Mary Janes and a skirt, who knows why. She didn't think—couldn't think—about what she was packing. She only knew she needed to be gone.

In her pants: Mr. Freddy. That's the name of Syl's gun, a lead-heavy SIG Sauer that clips sweetly in her holster. She didn't know what she'd be getting into, but better safe, always. Syl could take a quail out from over fifty meters away; she could blow any flying disk, any snipe.

She flipped her hair up into a baseball cap. Considered a drink, but no. A queasiness ran from her legs to her eyeballs. People still decked the yard with their USA plates, their plastic cups, twenty, thirty people now, throwing shreds of food into the coop. Barbecue leftovers, including wing bones, which the hens pecked at innocently. It was eight p.m.

This world was full of sick fucks. Out her bedroom window,

friends and neighbors tossed beanbags for cornhole, their back legs swinging. Surely, one of them would try to mount one of the horses soon, bareback with no helmet—that's what this crowd did when they drank. Tonight, Syl would have to let that go.

The silver zipper smiled at her from the center of the bed.

She went downstairs. Threw the bag into her trunk. Pink-duct-taped luggage tag that wouldn't budge. Syl opened the gate and walked into her yard. Out back, Howie wore his apron at the grill, *The Grillfather* one. His cheeks were sunburned and shiny. Genie and Nicola were playing beer pong now, drunk off their asses, laughing away. They fixed each other's makeup, licking a finger here, a finger there, swiping. They wore denim shorts and matching white knee socks. White, *to ward off summer ticks*, they said. The girls came home from college with all sorts of ideas about how to be safer, how to be smarter, more progressive, or communist, anarchic. They made it a point, to proclaim their newness. Syl hated it all.

Syl kissed Howie on the cheek, said: "Gotta go see Elvira."

"Cal into something?" Howie said. Howie aimed his flashlight, and the burger patties cried pink on the grill slats. He would overdo them again.

"Yes," Syl said, and then: "I'll be back by tomorrow for the fireworks. And don't worry the girls." Syl thought about telling Howie more. Thought about breaking through into something real, something true, startling him. *Did you know*, she would ask, *what I now know?* But then Adler came over and asked Howie about fencing, and Howie moved into his patter of mechanics, wood, paint, the How Things Worked Best of it; it was what he always did, more so with a fifth Coors Light in his hand.

From thirty feet away, Syl watched Genie slap a mosquito onto her arm, a dark, smudgy streak. Nicola tossed a Ping-Pong ball, and it missed the cup on the other side, bounced flatly across the grass. They were gloriously grown, her girls. Orange in the light of the tiki torches she'd bought for the party, cell phones bulging out their back pockets. They were limber, unbothered, and Syl was jealous;

when you were young, drinking could still be charming. Life could still be possible. She could die, sometimes, at how tall and lovely they were.

Roughly four hours from Ocala to Palm Beach County—that's a long time to think, in the dark. Syl smoked out the car window, which she didn't like to do anymore, night sounds coming in wild. The nicotine gave her the chills, and the chills made her guts rumble.

Syl tried to pretend this were any other night. That she was just driving to Seminole Feed or the Outback. She made her way to the Turnpike, the tipped green exit signs glowering. She turned up the radio; a *scorcher out there, possible intermittent storms*, this Fourth of July weekend. An overflowing Lake Okeechobee; poisoned estuaries; an earthquake in Indonesia.

They were so matter-of-fact, the twins. Syl and her girls, hours earlier, in the kitchen. Smell of smoke outside. The bird clock watching over the sink, long hand on cardinal.

"Mom, Genie's got something important to say!"

And Genie, "We've been talking to our counselors at school. We're both a part of this group. It's not our burden to keep secrets anymore. Trauma spills over unless you disarm it, like a bomb. We're breaking the pattern, this *intergenerational pattern*, so here comes the truth—"

The girls held Solo cups. This confession: egged on by the moonshine. Syl put the fork down because one of the girls said, "Mom, put the fork down." The girls kept talking, and Syl's London broil suddenly looked very gray. The holes she had made all over with her fork—so black and pronounced. Syl wanted something new to do with her hands. The girls said, *Are you listening? Mom, listen!* They took turns explaining about their emotional growth, gesticulating with their hands the way they always did—fingers elegant, nails too long, it drove Syl crazy—you couldn't tend a barn with nails like that.

Calvin, she heard, and as soon as she heard his name Syl knew the rest. How was that? How had she known and not known? They described it all. The nights in their room, right upstairs from Syl and Howie. Genie's blue nightgown the first time it had happened, the moon low and swollen out Nicola's window. Syl remembered that nightgown. "Scalloped neckline?"

"Cotton?"—*yes*. "Pretty?"—*yes*.

"Nicola had a matching one, in purple?"—*yes*.

This was something they could all agree on, something they could all remember in detail, so Syl dwelled on the nightgown a few minutes—where it had come from, and where it had gone. Howie opened the door and said—"Where's the apple cake?"— and Syl gave him a look like, *Please, Howie, get in here, please*, but the girls said, "Dad, can you get out? This is private." Syl did not know why her impulse was to slap both girls. She should have felt shame about that, she knew; none of it was their fault. It was a truth, like many others, to be investigated later.

It had happened right above them, and she had slept through it—that's the part Syl couldn't get over, hearing the story. No motherly intuition had woken her up. No interruption of her dreams. And oh, at that age, how she'd wanted the girls to grow up. She'd wanted more than anything for the girls to toughen, for the flesh of their palms to harden; she'd wanted them to awaken to the responsibilities and hard work and hard truths of the world. Since the day they were born, she was uncomfortable with all the *soft*. It was the *soft* that rose in her throat, the translucent baby bodies, the doughy heads, too much soft for Syl to bear, so fragile it made her sick to even think about. Anything could harm them. A food allergy, a slipped hand or twist of ankle when she carried them over the concrete front steps, a too-hot bath, any other person. She wanted the tooth fairy and Easter Bunny blown, immediately. She wanted the girls to see the chickens die, wanted them to watch the taper of blood, the kill cones made from water jugs they'd drunk out of the night before, the hens' stunned feet clawing at the sky. Syl wasn't proud of all that; it was just the way it was. She could help them in this way, grow them up, batten them against the dreck of the world. Mucking stalls at sunrise. Buckets of blinking chicken heads when she culled the flock. No gloves on new reins. They would develop their husks, their calluses, and in this way they would not suffer. That's what she'd gone for, tried for anyway, as a mom.

This, too, was the difference between Mary-Beth and Syl. They both knew it.

Mary-Beth loved children, and Syl did not.

⁓

"HAVE YOU BEEN good for Santa?" Mary-Beth asked. It had been an hour of snow, the parking lot pristine white, the sled mound growing. Mary-Beth held a young girl's hand. It was pudgy and purple from some kind of snack. Mary-Beth smiled her long, closed-mouthed smile, which crinkled her nose. It was the smile she hoped wasn't scary.

The camera was acting up again. Petra took a few test shots on the tripod, then showed Stanley, who gestured that the frame looked right. All day, Stanley would push the digital shot, wired to his insta-printer, which sat on a fold-out table next to the tripod. Ten dollars per picture in a *North Pole, Florida, Winter Wonderland* paper frame.

"I think I've been good," the girl said. The girl was four or five. Behind her, her mother, in zippered gym spandex. She tapped away on a cell phone, looking upset about something.

Mary-Beth crouched down, at eye level with the girl. "Key is you've got to *stay* good till Christmas." Mary-Beth said this part loud, hoping to win over the mother. She said, "What's something you want this year, more than anything?"

The girl whispered into Mary-Beth's ear: *Powers. I want powers.*

"Bet you already got some," Mary-Beth said. She had not smoked, not once, when playing Mrs. Claus. She didn't want Misty on her breath. Mary-Beth stood and turned to lead the girl to Santa when the mother pulled the child's arm. Hard.

Like this—saying *Ow!*—the child let go of Mary-Beth's hand.

The mother looked at Mary-Beth. Then back to her phone. She had eyes like a Disney ride robot, one of those animatronics meant to be people. She whispered to another mother behind her, someone who may have been a friend, or maybe not. Some of the green wig reindeer women came up and joined them beside the line.

The next children stepped up to the sleigh. Brother and sister—maybe ten for the girl and thirteen for the boy. The girl had crookedly cut bangs and wore shorts with daisy patches on them. "Sup Mrs. Claus," the boy said. He had dark red lips, vampiric, and introduced himself as *Ross*. The girl was *Amy*. They stood on either side of Mary-Beth, and Petra took their picture.

As Mary-Beth smiled for the next photos, hands on her hips, she saw the spandex robot-eyed woman speaking to Stanley. Mary-Beth will not understand what's happening, not yet, though she will know something is wrong by the way Stanley holds the printing cable in his hand, as if asking, *What do you want me to do with this? This cable or that one?* Three of the green-wigged women approached Stanley as well. As the robot woman spoke, she looked right at Mary-Beth. Then she pointed. Petra said, "Say Snow Day!" And the children did, and the camera went off, and Petra cackled. "You did greeeeaattt! Mwa! Beautiful!" She blew them all a kiss.

"MB—Mrs. Claus—hold up a minute," Stanley shouted, his hand out as if stopping traffic, and this is when Mary-Beth understood.

The children stayed on Ivan the Santa's lap—Amy on the left, Ross on the right. Ivan, who'd definitely snuck more booze since arriving, spoke to them about what they've been up to in school. What did they want to be one day. The boy said something about Dan Marino, he wanted to be like Dan, he wanted to place football bets one day, and as he spoke, Santa put a gloved hand on the young girl's knee. Mary-Beth watched Santa move his hand up with every other word, closer to the young girl's shorts, as he spoke to the boy about football. The girl stared off in the distance. She looked at nothing. Santa shifted in his seat, pressing the girl's leg to his leg. His hand was far up now, moving on the inside of her thigh.

"Mrs. Claus, a minute?"—Here's Stanley.

"Say goodbye to Santa now, kids!" And here's Mary-Beth, "Santa's got to prepare some special treats for you!" Mary-Beth presses the girl's back, pushing her, but Santa keeps her clasped there. Amy's back is hot and bony, and she breathes sadly and slow. The boy keeps talking to Santa about football. Mary-Beth does not see any parents assigned to them.

"Kids!" Stanley shouts, facing the long line behind them. "Mrs. Claus is going for a quick cocoa!" He pulls Mary-Beth away from the sleigh, by the hand.

"MB, shit," Stanley says. The sky, so blue behind him. "I'm sorry. These women—the book and all, the news—I'm sorry. You know it's a money thing, not a moral thing." Stanley looks down at his shoes. He nods.

Mary-Beth knows that nod. She says, "Understood."

"It's business," he says.

"Understand," Mary-Beth says. "Business is business."

Mary-Beth tears off her hat and wig, shakes out her hair. Immediately, with all the crumpled polyester in her hand, the whole afternoon becomes a memory. She waves to the children, says *Merry Christmas!* as she walks back into the station. The children cry for her. They scream, *No! Mrs. Claus, come back!* and Mary-Beth says, *Don't be naughty, stay good for Santa, now!* But then Joe blasts more snow into the air, and with that, everybody turns away, and there's no one left to hear her.

SYL ARRIVES AT Gateway to Grace around midnight. She's never been here before, and tomorrow, with her sister smoking in the passenger seat, she'll have to pretend it's the first time.

Syl turns down the radio, veers left. She slows the car.

Cars line the dirt road, right before the turn-off to the entrance. Fords and pickups and a rusted ATV; all the vehicles empty. Perhaps there are guards at a place like this, secret booby traps—Syl wonders. She pulls her car behind the others. Her car dips to the right. In the bed of the pickup in front of her, a swivel office chair. Syl flicks the headlights off, steps out.

How long had the girls planned the talk with Syl? Who were these doctors and counselors at college (were counselors doctors? Were those the same as a shrink?), and who were these friends in these collegiate support groups, supporting her children? How utterly *humiliating*, for these strangers to know before Syl knew; Syl and Howie, some redneck negligent parents.

Syl walks the gravel road, the one that will lead her to the rest of her life, and the one that leads to her past (sometimes, these roads are the same). She inhales the rot of Lake O, the char of crops. The moon above her, barely a sliver. There is no entrance sign to Gateway to Grace, only markers she'd looked up on Google Earth earlier that night: two one-lane bridgeways, three portalets, the bridged entranceways hidden in gaps between trees.

Then she sees it, Calvin's welcome pond, next to a small gate. She'll remember this pond. Sheen like the lining of a show blazer.

Syl bends over and steps through the bars of the gate. Horse people can find a way through any fence or gate—electric or not—and this fence is not humming with current. It is just a gate. Mosquitos circle Syl's ears, and she slaps her cheeks without pause. She hears a countdown—*ten, nine, eight*—in the distance ahead of her, somewhere beyond the housing units. Fireworks let off a sour sound. Flames jump, caper the air the color of honey. The honey drips down the sky in arcs. Balletic, gentle hoverings.

There are three rows of housing units. "The yellows" Mary-Beth has described. Syl sees Calvin's row, the southernmost row of the complex, the one with gray square roofs on Google Maps, straight ahead. Gravel chomps under her paddock boots. Dogs bark from somewhere, as if broadcast from the sky. This row of blocky, miserable homes: some windows dark, others lit from within. The blinds, the drapes, all drawn. Syl notes shadows of spiny plants. Shadows of men—some fixed in their chairs, some moving. There are duct-taped AC units and windows strobing. An outdoor dryer machine judders hard, tossing a sneaker.

Then it's the freshest paint. 5B.

Syl will always remember how unsurprised Calvin looked when he answered the door. He did not smile, though he had smile lines now—two deep indents that plunged down his face. He looked older, in the doorway; just like Mary-Beth in the tense, tanned forehead, the watery eyes. Syl had not seen Calvin in many years and wondered—in that expanse within a second—if her nephew even recognized her. With a wave of his hand, he motioned her in.

Syl enters Calvin's studio apartment. There are no overhead lights on, just jewel-colored scarves thrown over lamps (Syl knows a Mary-Beth flourish), the same scarves nailed over the windows. The only other light is Calvin's laptop, which sits open on his desk, the glowing square reflected in picture frames hung across the wall. This apartment smells bad—like banana peels, cologne, acerbic potpourri, body odor. Syl breathes through her mouth. She says, "Calvin."

"What's up, Auntie Syl?" he says. More a statement than a question. He hikes up his jeans, which hang low, on the bones of his hips. He's wearing a black tank top, a *beater*, not tucked into his pants but pulled over them, bumpy at the beltline. There's something more cowboy about him now, Syl thinks, as he half walks, half limps over to the laptop on his desk, closing it slow with his pointer finger.

Syl says, "Calvin, we have something to talk about." Syl's back aches near her tailbone. Her knees hurt—she's forgotten to wear her brace again. Her eyelids feel pressed by sharp stones, and she has to pee. But she hangs tough, fakes it. That's what Syl does.

Calvin packs the Newports from the counter against his palm. This pack, what Mary-Beth will find later. "Not supposed to be here," he says. "This is considered after hours." Syl notices a blanched, shiny scar on his chin—it's new.

"What'd you do to your chin, Cal?"

Calvin holds the Newports but does not open them. He stands there, staring at her. This is his place, and in it Syl feels suddenly, grossly, defenseless. Then she remembers Mr. Freddy.

"Is it Moms?" Cal says. "Mom need me?"

"It's not your mom." Syl regrets saying it, right away. It was the only power she had.

Calvin is barefoot, and Syl cannot see the lump of his ankle monitor under the sag of his jeans, but she knows it is there. She is banking on it, feels oddly protected by it. One year, for Christmas, Mary-Beth had shown Syl the faux ankle brace she'd bought Calvin—black, neoprene, Velcro-strapped, fancy—designed specifically for people like him. It covered the monitor with stretchy fabric. There was no better vision, for Mary-Beth, than Calvin in shorts, legs free in a wide-open public, where he would be seen as injured rather than bad.

"So what can I do for you, Auntie Syl?" Calvin asks. He leans back on the counter, still holding those cigarettes. The outline of his ribs appears and disappears as he breathes.

What Syl wants is to take the hair on Calvin's head—that damp, full head of hair—and bite onto it, wrench it out with her teeth. She wants whole clumps of scalp and skull. She wants to blast a full round of Mr. Freddy into Calvin's eye sockets. For decades, Syl has practiced loading 9mm bullet rounds into magazines while watching TV. Back of the round, back of the magazine—she works quick, her thumb red-hot at the tight spring. It is good for the Sig, good for the bullets, and it is absolutely good for Syl.

She says, "I have something I need to discuss with you, young man." She says this in a very measured way. She breathes in through her nose, gets used to the smells.

"OK?"

Syl imagines saying it all here. Laying it bare. Her words coming out sheer and decisive, like the maw of scissors across wrapping paper. She speaks of the girls. Of the women they've become—bold, honest women, unruined. She speaks of Mary-Beth, the reverberating *nothing* he'd made of her life. A woman who'd been homeless on his behalf, friendless, toothless, unemployed, sallowed out. He would have been better off dead in his preemie incubator; Syl could have pulled the plug or smothered him with a sweater; she wishes she had.

Instead, Cal says, "Whatever it is, you can't hurt me. My life's already my life."

He blinks at her, fast. Syl hates that she can still see the child there, when he blinks. Good-for-nothing boy, pitchfork in hand, the Vans sneakers he wore back then—once, this man was her nephew. Syl focuses on the objects in his room, to snap out of it.

Or back into it.

"I need to know what kind of person," Syl says.

"What kind of person. What kind of person, what kind of person, what kind of—"

Nothing is coming out anymore. Not words, anyway. More like little gasps, gasps that stanch the syllables. Sounds leaking through her clenched teeth. She clenches her jaw so hard her molars might blow. The sound coming out of her—it's high-pitched as a whistle.

"Never seen you cry," Calvin says calmly. "Want a tissue?"

Syl bends, hands at her knees. Her bad knee, which locks in place now—convenient! She might puke on the floor. She might piss her pants. She says, "Cal. What kind of person are you?" *Person* comes out high, girlish, somebody else's voice.

Calvin doesn't move. He stands in the same position, but he is no longer looking at Syl, no longer speaking to her. He is barely paying attention to her, actually; it's like the room is suddenly a Magic Eye test, and if he adjusts his eyes to the wall, to the front doorknob, it might become something new, and she might disappear. Cal wants to go back to the business of his laptop, wants his aunt to leave, his sun-weathered bitch of an aunt, the repulsive look on her face—he knows why she's here. He knows she knows.

Syl's teeth clench so hard her nose trembles. She breathes harder, faster—so fast she sees colors now, blotting the scene. The whistling sob-sound from her body goes off again, this time unfurling into something like a roar. It is a sound she hasn't heard from her throat since giving birth to the twins, the sound that came when her skin split, the too-bright lights in her face as Genie's bald head destroyed her, the keenest pain of her life. Calvin takes one step backward, hand to the counter. The sound! She wasn't some languid, faded woman after all. She wasn't gullible or dense, wasn't a stocking stacked with Campbell's cans in the shape of a person—she was furious and she was alive.

Syl scared him. She saw it in his face, saw it in his dirty bare foot stepping back, away from her. That's all she needed to do to feel what she needed to feel, and that's why she left his unit still screaming, hands raking through her hair. She didn't care that Calvin followed her; didn't care to know why—*Auntie Syl?* She ran past all the windows and all the units, past the pines, the satellite dishes, the leaning fishing rods and propped trailers, a Ford pickup on its way home. This place, this woeful swampy place, would never be her life. Behind her, in a driveway, men setting off fireworks. And behind that, only a few moments later, her nephew entering the woods—chased into the woods, actually—pyrotechnics blitzing over the sweep of the furrowed earth.

WHAT SYL WILL never know:
They took Harrison's F-150 pickup from the Palmyra bar after the fourth or fifth round. Erline in the passenger seat texting Charmaine GATOR GOLF, Trace and Jeb in the back; "R.O.C.K. in the U.S.A." on the radio, Harrison turning up the knob.

On the drive to Gateway, Trace repeated some of her new friend's favorite lines from Calvin's emails: *I couldn't handle living with putting out some kind of light in you*, and *people hold all kinds of mercy for other sick people so why not me!* The four new friends sang these words to Mellencamp's tune. *Why not me! Why not me!*

What Syl will never see:
Trace and Co. pulling the Ford just outside row one of the yellows. They've got clubs and paper-wrapped fireworks rolling in the bed of the truck, the wrappers cheerful, a little wet from a brief rain. *Is that him?* Then: *Is it you?*

The funny part, the part Trace will repeat back to herself as proof of fate: they hadn't come for Calvin, specifically. They'd come for anyone who might be outside, setting off those fireworks—*anyone* would do—and who knows, maybe Trace would then have time to find Calvin if they weren't chased out by the cops. That many vodkas deep, they'd settle for *anyone* upon whom to strap a cherry bomb, anyone could be made a glowing man.

But he was waiting outside his unit, right there.

"Is it you?" It was like he'd been waiting for Trace, summoned. Trace with her club, with the emails folded in her pocket. Trace swinging the club through moths in the air, yellow motion light blinking sporadically, *You remember her? She was nine. She was only nine.*

It's only the four of them, surrounding Calvin. Everyone else is one row down, lighting fuses, running from their spinning flames.

"I don't remember her," Calvin says to Trace. He pauses. Then he smiles.

It's the underbit smile Trace has only seen in mug shots.

Trace gets in one good swing, a *crack* in the rib cage with that Calloway driving iron, before Calvin runs.

SYL GOT INTO her car. It chimed at her, the dome light on, a sobering bright. She unclipped Mr. Freddy and moved him to the gun case beneath her seat. Her swallows felt hot, branded from all the screaming; it made her want to smoke. She pulled a filter into her mouth.

Syl turned the key, all her key chains—bottle openers, rabbits' feet, flashlights, a miniature barn—rattling. The car came to life. The dome light turned off. She reversed, the swivel chair still in the pickup ahead, and pulled onto the gravel road.

Syl thought of Calvin, his room. She hadn't seen regret on his face, no reckoning. But she did see his life in that apartment, a space that was lived-in, food on the counter, pictures on the wall. In one of the picture frames, she had also seen a family. Her family. She and Howie and the girls and Calvin, from the summer he stayed. From the summer he had worked. Everyone in the photo wore blue jeans. They stood outside, near the oak tree, the girls smiling in the center—braces gleaming. Syl did not remember ever posing for it.

It's drugs, Mary-Beth had said. *And these precocious girls.* Syl had known about the other girls—that's what she'll never admit to anyone, not as long as she lives.

She'd thought her own girls would be different.

Syl's whole family, Syl's whole world, every person she'd ever loved, blighted by Calvin. None of it could be returned to her. Syl drove forward, then swung a U-turn. With the car window open, she heard more booming. She drove toward Muck Drive, the black gravel of Loxahatchee. Syl turned up the radio—Dusty Springfield. She thought about calling in, requesting a song. She'd request something whimsical and sad, something about tomorrow being a new day.

That's when he comes to her.

Calvin. About fifty feet ahead of Syl, barefoot, in the center of the road. In her headlights, it looks like he's on the moon, having just arrived, looking for a souvenir to bring home. He spins around and around, breathing hard. Then he puts his hands on his knees, then his waist, his leg buckling; he's hurt. There's movement in the trees behind him, a darkly dressed figure emerging, the flash of a club or bat, and then the figure turns back to the woods, disappears.

All humans were animals, Syl knew, but that was no excuse. The back of Calvin's head glowed like a dime. She knew she could watch this happen—watch these club-wielding people beat her nephew the way they often did at Gateway—they might bind him with rope, shove a chrome barrel into his held open mouth—Or!

Syl pushes her foot down into the accelerator.

Turn around, she says to herself, cheery, friendly. She wants him to look at her, to look into her headlights—and then he does. Calvin looks. Like she'd willed it. Blissful, to see his face like that. Mouth open. Then, when she nears, the face twists. His forearms move up to frame his skull, and his eyes squint with something unmistakable. Terror. The trees quake with movement again.

Syl doesn't hit him as fast as she wants to; she doesn't want to damage her car. But this is OK, because she also wants him to feel it. Wants him on the ground, twitching in slow motion, wondering—then knowing—why. Syl wants the pathetic slide-show of his life flashing vividly, every veil of comfort removed (she does *not* want him to think of her girls; she'd prefer to scrub any detail of them); the sound of it—the first thump—she'll remember that. Treasure it. Bottle it up for when she needs it most; she'll dream the sound while taking a bath, for years. She'll dream it when she goes to sleep an old woman, next to Howie. And on her deathbed, both girls holding both her hands. The car tosses his body further than she expects. She thinks she hears a sound from him, under her—something like *No!*—but maybe she's mistaken. She decides to believe herself.

Syl stops the car about ten feet ahead of his body, backs up. She knows the pressure and discharge of bones cracking. Syl can butcher a chicken in one minute flat. She knows every joint and socket, the proper yank, the neck's triumphant release. Knows how to kill painlessly. Not for food, but for the sick or injured, she would do that for them. The special ones. The move is like a hug, the hen's warm body to a torso, their eyes under the pit. Then you jerk, a perfect cervical dislocation. It's humane. Simple. Nature's course. Sometimes, it's the right thing to do.

She moves the car forward again. She aims the tires just so. Chest, neck, head. In the taillights, in Syl's mirror, Calvin purses his mouth erratically as if waiting for a thermometer. She swivels the steering wheel in her hands and backs up. While over him, she swivels again, feels the tires *twist*, her SUV lifting.

Oh, everybody suffers—Syl knows. Forward one more time, this one quick. The world was cruel. But cruelty could be sutured, made smooth again, slick as a tongue; this was greater than herself. She could save others with the push and release of the pedal under her foot. She couldn't change the past, but she can ensure a better future. Simple. Some animals weren't so simple; hens who'd fed them eggs for years, the sweet cry of them when they laid—agony or pleasure, who knew—they called that an egg song. Then they died.

Syl drove away now, fast. She kept going. She turned off her headlights. She did not see a lump in her rearview mirror. She did not see any people or their clubs. She saw nothing, in fact, at all. Syl smoked down to the filter. Out the window it went. An upbeat song came on. Something by Billy Joel.

Syl would find a motel. They were everywhere, around here. Wellington Horse Show—FEI summer circuit—horse people with weird hours, impossible weekends. This place was good for blending in. Tomorrow, tomorrow. She'd clean or patch the car (a *deer* would be the reason; always *a damn deer*). She'd tend whatever needed tending to. She'd scrub herself in the motel shower, that cheap soap, soap she'd take home and add to the endless stack of soaps she'd accumulated all these tedious seasons, a chubby rainbow of them forming a whole new bar. Sylvia Packman was economical like that. She was practical. She was good. Her sister in her arms the next day, smelling that cheap soap on her neck, *Why are you wetter than a tramp?*

Syl would give Mary-Beth her life back.

―

MARY-BETH STOOD AT her register. Margail's elf clothes were baggy on Mary-Beth's body, the bust puckering, the waistline loose. The clothes felt damp with Margail's sweat, pungent with artificial rose, a different brand of smokes, a body odor that was not bad but not Mary-Beth's own.

Mary-Beth was allowed to keep the Mrs. Claus patent-leather shoes on; they had not fit Margail. Mary-Beth leaned down, tightened the strap. Out the frosted window, cackling joy. Laughter churning under Joe's hose. The Christmas carols played inside and outside the station, slightly off time and out of sync.

Margail looked better in the Mrs. Claus outfit than Mary-Beth had expected her to. Somehow, it all fit her. They had shared the single bathroom stall when they'd switched. Margail stripped with no hesitation, pierced nipples on newly fake breasts, fresh scars, rusty tape all over.

Mary-Beth pulled off her round glasses. *Need an unzip?* Margail had asked, but Mary-Beth would reach around, do it herself.

In the mirror, Margail applied the Mrs. Claus red lips, and Mary-Beth wiped her own face with a brown paper towel. It was rough, and she was sweating. She blotted at her skin as if it could remove the whole situation. Margail said, *See ya, MB*, and stepped out of the bathroom. Mary-Beth opened the metal trash can with the toe of her shoe. She held the wad of paper in her hand. Inside the can, peering right up at her, was the book.

Now, at the register, Mary-Beth flipped through its pages. There was no one else in the store. In the pages, she saw her son's name, *Calvin Boyer*. Something about it on this kind of paper—*book paper*—was so different than the way his name looked on legal documents. Something about it made Mary-Beth think of hope. Like he could have done something, been somebody, if only she'd done something different.

The aluminum tree—it glowed. The lights twinkled on their timer. Mary-Beth stepped to the side of the partition and took in all the work she'd accomplished, all this work for beauty. She took such care in her life, and for what? What for? Years it took, perfecting the snipped-out snowflake. Years collecting the trains, the miniature, snow-tipped cities. For snow, Mary-Beth used jeweler's cotton, never the cheap stuff—the cheap stuff looked fake, and all she wanted was for those little ones to believe.

Mary-Beth picked up the book again. Looked at the girl. She really, really looked, trying to pierce her soul somehow. To voodoo her alive. She imagined Linzie's face coming to life with breezy movement, Linzie's mouth mouthing something snarky. Or maybe telling her what she wanted, needed, to know.

Once, Mary-Beth had had a life. And what a life it was. That was before her time became shaped by Calvin's: his curfew hours, his sentences, his prison visiting days. Nights she can barely remember. She'd wake on the tile floor, Skyy bottle between her bare legs, decades of phones gripped in her hand, waiting for Calvin.

There was time before her son, and an after. This after was different.

Mary-Beth pulled a Misty from the cup of her corset—Margail's too-big corset—and bit the foamy filter.

She read a little from Linzie's book. It wasn't all that bad. A few lines made her laugh.

Sometimes, it was like a phantom could take over Mary-Beth's body if she willed it to. If she talked to herself about herself, *Mary-Beth did this* and then *Mary-Beth would do that*, she could momentarily step outside the spiraled seashell of her past, her future—both felt equally fixed.

Mary-Beth's arm reached out to the Bic display at the register. Cutesy zip of the American flag with her thumb—it snapped a single blue spark as the flame took. She breathed in nicotine and tar, harbored by her Misty.

The kids laughed outside. They screamed like it was their last scream on earth. Mary-Beth thought of Ivan and his hand there, limply and then firmly, on those daisy shorts. On the girl. *Amy* was her name. Mary-Beth snapped the metal teeth of the Bic again, this time at the corner of the book. She watched Linzie's face curl, smile, then disappear.

Mary-Beth tossed the book. It was easy. It thwacked at the foot of the tree, and the tree—with all its white foam and white lights—whooshed. That's what happened first. Her beautiful tree—silver to gold. It was gold, now. Then the flames spread to the rest of the blankets of white. Mary-Beth inhaled the Misty, breathed out. A moat of fire, smoke layering like a fancy dessert, intrepidly black but also: the most orange orange. *Tucson Peach* orange. Mary-Beth saw the fossil of the place—this place she had loved, and there were so few places for a love like that—before it was gone. Black crept up the white, eating it, an upside-down dripping. The snack bags crinkled into metallic curls of origami. The song still played from her speakers—"Holy Night"—Mary-Beth's favorite.

The shelves collapsed from their centers. The blaze beamed in stratas of color, like Saturn, like when Mary-Beth learned about those dumb planets as a kid. Mary-Beth imagined smoke rising from her bones days later. Her sister sent to *identify body*. The elf costume would still, somehow, be intact, laid out on the ground like the first day of school. Like ruby-slippered legs beneath a house—but where was the woman?

It had snowed only a few times in Mary-Beth's real life. Real Florida flakes—nature made. She thought, sometimes, she'd dreamed it. But there was the paper, and the records. The accumulation up north, when Mary-Beth was a girl. She'd held out her small hand. That midair shimmer was enough for her, the air alive.

Sirens blazed in the distance. Red on red on red, she imagined, when they would come. But she would be gone at last, arrived at the place she had for so long imagined, the place she'd revered, place of ease and ablutions, maybe, of mercy and laughter and whipped cream sundaes. A creek in her ears, real lavender—her whole life, her girlhood, returned to her.

There, beyond the flames, beyond the walls, on the other side of this interstice, Mary-Beth Boyer wondered if she would see him again. What would he have to say? She imagined her son's face, right there. Right at her counter. Calvin, beautiful boy, all up in smoke. Her own face in the dark of his computer screen. Then the dark face of the lake. The sinking sound of what she couldn't see.

Mom?

Mary-Beth leaves out the back door, ducking low, elf hat palmed against her mouth. She jumps into her Mercury in the employee lot, jerks the gear shift into reverse, *drive*. A firetruck speeds around the corner, and one last time, she pulls out of North Pole, Florida, cranking her window.

Mary-Beth will drive now. Who knows how far, or for how long, but trust that she won't stop. She's got a carton of Mistys. A warm two-liter of soda. Wyoming on her mind.

The last thing she heard was the children.

"WHAT IF WE fake my own death or something?" Linzie suggested.

This was Linzie's favorite idea, her favorite pitch; she'd tried it a few times. She and Doug sat in their living room, in their respective spots. A hot October evening, and Doug was plodding on again about his *master plan*, how they would bring Linzie back into the spotlight.

"I could drown or something," Linzie said. "That's dramatic. The news would love that. And then I could, you know, disappear. If it's unsolved, the coverage could last, and I could—"

Doug told her she was dumber than a sack of gerbils. Stupider than a sack of shit. He threw the remote at the couch—aiming at her—and it bounced from the cushion, thudded on the carpet.

Doug searched for every mention of Linzie on the internet, every hour. Between his freight calls, he'd had the time. But those mentions were drying up, the interview invitations were over. There was a new season of *The Dating Show* with a new *code of ethics*. Odette's podcast had been canceled after the great North Pole fire, Mary-Beth Boyer still on the lam. *My Turn* was on the discount rack at every store. Even Yale had moved on to write a new tell-all exposé book about factory farming.

Linzie was not dumber than a sack of gerbils or stupider than a sack of shit, and she wanted to prove that to Doug. Wanted to prove herself a grown woman, someone who could fold napkins, someone with a knuckle in the soil of a house plant and she'd know, immediately and instinctually, that it needed more water. More sun. She didn't need press or media anymore, didn't want it. All she wanted was a do-over. A new hair color and name, maybe a condo in Naples—just her and Lucky.

"What are we watching tonight?" she asked Doug. His favorite, he said. He softened at the gory ones, the loud ones, women chased through cornfields or beheaded by their own garage doors.

Linzie picked up the remote from the floor and handed it back to Doug. "Cue it up," she said. She fluffed the pillow behind his back—doughy and spit-yellow, without a pillowcase. "Popcorn and smoothies?" Doug nodded.

"I'm tough on you because I love you"—that's what he said. What he always says.

In the kitchen, Linzie grabbed a washcloth to wipe the blender, still damp and resting upside down from morning. She took out the frozen bag of spinach from the freezer, the chilly stalks of celery from the fridge. She cut up a banana and an apple, added a splash of pineapple juice. She took out the bag of black cherries—Doug's favorite. She plucked the stems, dropped the glossy black globes in, whole. Then, from Yale's special wellness market, the one he'd introduced her to, Linzie pulled out three logs of cassava and a bag of bitter almonds. She chopped the cassava logs into white disks, a handful of roots. Antioxidants. Anti-inflammatories. She pressed High and watched the stems and roots and nuts flutter in a tympanic VROOM.

Linzie looked around the kitchen. It was her kitchen now. She had cleaned the stove coils so many times. She'd scrubbed the pans with baking soda. Replaced the lights. She'd come so far since summer, since the fondue. The lid on the Dutch oven balanced lopsided on top of the pot. The lid grinned at her with an underbite. It looked like Calvin. She walked over and fixed it.

The popcorn was popped, the smoothie was done, and she poured it into Doug's favorite glass. The tall beer glass, curved like a bell. "Here you go, Daddy," she said, as she walked back to the living room, handing it over. She dimmed the living room lights. She took Lucky out of his pen, brought him to the couch for cuddles. Doug wore his Bubba Raceway t-shirt, the logo long faded. Her father sipped the green smoothie. He did not say *thanks*.

Doug clicked up the volume. Linzie sat on the couch, to the right of his recliner, where she always sat. His hand fondled the remote, and he chose the movie with the clown. Doug smacked his teeth and said, *Bitter*. Linzie hated the way he smacked his teeth and gums. Always, when she opened shampoo bottles in the shower, she heard it.

The clown laughed. Rain poured into the clown gutter. Everybody fell for it. Linzie had seen this movie a thousand times, so she watched headlights trail outside their living room window. They glowed through the blinds in a spellbinding way. "Daddy, you good?" Linzie started, as Doug made horrible, purplish sounds. Lucky's ears twitched softly between her fingers; she was so relaxed. *Daddy?*

Spittle came up from Doug's mouth, and he wiped at it. A crowd of veins on his face popped his skin like a fishnet. His finger pushed the clicker button and kept pushing, like he couldn't release it, the volume up and up and up.

Linzie fed Lucky grassy pellets from her hand. She remembered the way her father's hand, which opened and closed now, as if grabbing at an invisible star, had pressed against her mouth all those years. The rings on his fingers clacked against her teeth, nicking her lip, leaving sores there. AC vents in cars, AC vents on the school bus—the bars of those vents always reminded her of fingers over her mouth. Of the way she couldn't breathe under fingers. He had never said sorry. All those nights, not once.

Cyanogenic glycosides are found naturally, everywhere. At the farmer's market, in the produce aisle, in your own backyard. She had read all about it, in Yale's texts. She had learned so much about food, farming, health. Plus, Linzie had always been good at math. The body made cyanide. It was easy.

Sometimes, long ago, she'd found Doug crying to himself in his chair. Did he cry the mornings after he'd come into Linzie's room, the mornings after Irene spent all night working Diamond Dolls? All those days had mushed together. How bad was it, how shameful, that Linzie had continued looking forward to Doug coming into her room? Not because of what he would do to her, but because, to Linzie, there was always the chance that he might change course, act differently, not do it. He could, at last, say the fatherly things Linzie had dreamed of. Monsters weren't real. The dark was nothing but the dark. The sound she'd heard that scared her most—the sound of Doug walking to her room—was simply a leak, a branch, a pipe. Someone else.

Doug's body slumped in his recliner. The upholstered chair that had become molded to him, shaped like him. When Doug wasn't in it, Linzie could still see him there, see his thighs, his ankles glaucous with gout, two dying man-o'-wars. She'd get rid of this chair now, she thought, drag it down the driveway, to the street. She wouldn't have to see him in places he no longer was. She would never again say *sorry*, either.

She pulled the wooden lever of the recliner. Doug jolted all the way back, *supine*—another word she had learned! Thanks, Yale!—and looked at his daughter, but it was difficult to say if he was really looking, if his eyes were still his eyes or if they were simply screens upon which she could project whatever it was she wanted. When he'd cried all those mornings, when little girl Linzie found him crying in his chair like that, she'd imagined it was for her. But when she'd approached him, he'd smudge the tears away with the back of his hand, smack her hard, then tell her to fuck off and go busy herself and be somebody.

She pushed the chair's lever in the other direction. Doug folded forward, his gurgling more high-pitched now, a little squeal breaking through bubbles, the movie still blaring. Green vomit dripped off the clicker and onto the carpet, and Linzie walked barefoot to take in all the angles. Lucky hopped a circle, following her.

Through the carpet, Linzie felt sharp pinches at her feet—the foundation of the house, years of crumbs and dirt and rabbit shit, whatever DNA was left of her mother. She touched the skin on the back of Doug's neck—still warm—and as his body seized and then slackened, she imagined how the news would cover her, this time.

LINZIE KING FREE AT LAST.

Would she be a hero? Oh, probably not.

She was beginning to get it now.

GENIE DROVE TO the Lockwood Women's Correctional Institution in Gainesville, Florida. Nicola directed the forty-three-minute drive, GPS lighting up her lap. Both girls wore skinny jeans and sweaters—black and blue stripes for Genie, festive houndstooth for Nicola. It was December, a cool, sunny day, Christmas music on every other station—in and out, static then smooth—Genie turning up "Drummer Boy," Nicola saying, "This is the worst one, are you kidding?"

They parked. Looked at each other in that twin-knowing way as they both flipped the mirror visors down, checked their makeup. Thumbnails—with matching polish—between both girls' teeth.

At the security checkpoint, the officer asked what kinds of bras the girls were wearing. They were both wearing cotton bras, Nicola said. Genie cupped both breasts with her hands, without thinking. Their belongings were collected and placed into a locker. The girls walked through the machine, spread their arms and legs for extra pats. It all felt very official, to do this. Two college girls, for the first time, visiting a woman in jail.

How would they remember it? Genie decided she would remember the songs on the radio that day. Nicola: the way Genie's hair looked. Down and loose and blonder than usual.

The girls stood in the waiting chamber while others went through security. They watched a woman unclip her fanny pack, lay it gently down. Then a skinny man in steel-toed boots. Two teenagers in Miami Heat jerseys. They all stepped forward and raised their arms into crosses, the wands chirping their roving circumscriptions. Each person looked at the ceiling. Then, after an OK from the guard, they all moved into the waiting.

Genie and Nicola sat down at a table in a large common room, which looked, to them, like a school cafeteria. It smelled stale and dank and like meat loaf. The walls were cinder blocks, and each wall featured a dreamy mural painted of nature: waterfalls, swinging vines, bumblebees, the sun. Officers guided inmates in their oversized khakis into the room, some with handcuffs, some without. Lunch trays and cuffs clanged all around them—they'd remember this. Both girls looked for her.

Genie spotted her first. She grabbed Nicola's hand. Then they held hands under the table, sweating. They stood up. Dropped hands.

"Hi there," Linzie said, smiling. Linzie, cuffed and bound in loose chains. The chains wrapped her waist and looped onto both wrists. Her feet were chained the same. It all looked very heavy to the girls, and Linzie looked very small.

"Hello," the twins say, in unison. They bob their heads in greeting. No hugs, no handshakes. Rules are rules. Three women sit down at the table.

"Happy birthday," Nicola says.

"Thanks"—Linzie smiles so big her lips shake. This happens still, a stress response. She says, "It's really nice you came."

"Capricorn?" the girls ask.

"Cusp. But I don't really know what that means. The women here believe in that stuff."

The girls explain that they are Virgos. Twenty-one. They are *Virgos to a tee.*

Linzie relaxes her smile. Relaxes into herself. Both girls will later discuss—and then share with friends at a holiday mixer—the poses and facial expressions that did or did not look like the Linzie they knew from television, her eyes without makeup, freckles that made her somebody new. Linzie's teeth were different now, straighter. Her skin, much smoother. She looked so young. She looked healthy. Her hair was growing back a warm brown the color of bread; below the temples, it was still black.

"You guys look like him," Linzie says. "I'm sorry, that's so bad to say. But Calvin. The face, the eyes." She traces her pointer finger down the slope of her nose, her chains clanking. "Kind of spooky."

"Oh," Nicola says.

"Unfortunately strong genes in our family," Genie says.

"It's like he's alive," Linzie says.

"I can assure you, he's not," Genie says.

Linzie shrugs. She says, "Sorry about your whole family, I guess."

The girls: "We've been writing because . . . we want to support you—" Genie takes over, she's best at speaking. "Outside, people support you. There's money pooling for you to get a better attorney before trial. Even Dimitrius wore a Linzie shirt on *Ellen* the other day."

"That guy's an asshole," Linzie says.

"Oh!" Genie says. "Yeah, totally. You could tell."

"People want what's best for you," says Nicola. "What you deserve. Maybe you should write another book."

Linzie stares. "I get a lot of letters from people," she says. "It's nice."

"Rumor is you're going with insanity?"

"Histrionic personality disorder," says Genie. "We looked it up. That could help."

"Some people say you could get out in a decade," Nicola says.

"Maybe," goes Linzie. "But it's fine if not. I'm learning to crochet. I can take classes and earn my GED once I'm transferred. I mean, I killed my daddy." (Linzie says this part laughing, a moment that chills both girls, a moment they'll recap later, with the friends: *Insanity isn't that far-fetched.*) Linzie lifts her hands to focus on a split end. She peels it back like a hangnail.

"So you're not . . . miserable?" Nicola asks.

"Look at the waterfalls," Linzie says, gesturing at the murals. Both girls hate the sound of her chains. "And I have friends. The only bad part's I miss my bunny. Someone from the mall took him. Maybe you guys could visit him, bring him treats. Tell Lucky if I get out of here, we're going on a vacation."

"Well, *when* you get out"—Genie says, though she was not planning this part, and Nicola will playfully slap her in the arm once they return to their vehicle, *You're so bad*—"When you get out, you can come up north. With your rabbit. We don't know what we're doing after college but maybe Tally or Jacksonville. You could come live with us?"

Linzie imagines a life with these girls. These twins who look like Calvin. She imagines a life of their inside jokes and hair braiding and secrets. She already has that in here, but better.

"I'll try," Linzie says. "I really will try."

"Good."

Both girls promise to keep in touch. Both girls describe their farm in Ocala, the house they grew up in. The horses and sweet hens out back. The way peace comes in nature—that was *scientifically proven*. Outside the girls' bedroom window was a blinking cell tower, no other tall buildings. Syl could cook for Linzie one day—world's best mac 'n' cheese, world's best mom. There was so much for her to look forward to . . .

"Well, it was nice to meet you," the girls say, standing from the table. "We hope the holidays are nice in here."

Then Linzie is escorted out, back to her cell.

In Lockwood, Linzie's let outside twice a week, into a dry courtyard with concrete and bleached grass. The women in their khakis stare up at the sky like reptiles. Earthworms bake onto the sidewalk in wiry, indistinguishable shapes. Linzie doesn't know where they come from, how the worms get in, but she likes that they do, likes making a game of deciphering meanings in their shapes. It's like a sonogram, the way she can squint and see a foot, a face, a heart. These two hours a week are all she needs, most often: the clouds, the air, the blue behind the twist of barbed wire, which sparkles in a lovely way, if you look at it right.

She'd seen that same sky in the twins' eyes. The bluest blue. Their creepy, long faces.

Linzie does imagine getting out one day. She allows herself to fear it, indulge in it, as she's falling asleep. Her cellmates would cry at the news of her leaving, and she'd put real clothes back on—maybe they'd be tight by then, maybe baggy—and driving away, she'd get a Slurpee from 7-Eleven. She'd drink something that cold, all sugar delight, and maybe she'd make her way to Ocala, to Marion County. She'd knock on the twins' door. No bag. No belongings. And the twins would dress her, feed her a *famous mac 'n' cheese*, listen to her. They'd teach her how to ride a horse, something Linzie has always wanted to do, sit way up high on a breathing, clenching animal. Maybe that's who she'd be, who she could be, when this was all over.

But there was nowhere, no future, yet. No way up or out while she was inside. One day—maybe soon, maybe upon transfer—she'd find a window. One day, a steel-webbed glass. That's all Linzie needed, really, to leave whatever place her body was in—and that was a power, actually; that was hers. Tonight she imagines living in the warm, bright bedroom the twins described. Under soft sheets, like a normal girl, Linzie will look out at that cell tower, at the light there—however borrowed—blinking steady against the dark. And she will go to it.

MAYBE BIRDIE CHANG is the forgotten one, now. This, too, happens.

This happens to Birdie whenever she tells her stories; we know this. It happens whenever Birdie tells her truth.

Thelma knocks. It's end of summer, Labor Day. And the end of Birdie's (Trace's) payment plan, so Birdie finally has to go.

"Need help with anything?" Thelma says. "We can take it on the cart."

"I'm good," says Birdie. She's completed her exit checklist. She hands it over.

Thelma says, "My nephew's gonna help clean out the stove, so don't touch the ash; we save it."

"Got it," says Birdie. She's hanging her owl helmet on the wall, one final time. She's drinking from her water bottle, barely paying attention.

Behind Thelma in the doorway, Hal zooms a couple with two children to one of the cabins. On the golf cart, wind turning his shirt to a marshmallow, his calf pumps and pumps.

"Can I use your phone once more?" Birdie asks. "Then I'll be out of your hair."

It's hot in the pumphouse today. Out the window, a sun shower, misting in the light. Birdie only knows a few phone numbers by heart, her fingers able to trace the paths of those numbers like a Rubik's Cube. She has looked up this number a lot—*a stalker makes a stalker*—and hopes that it works.

Hello, Francine's voice says. She still sounds like herself.

Birdie begins to talk before understanding it is a voicemail.

It would have been nice, for Birdie and Francine to speak here, at the end of the story. It would have been a nice way to wrap Birdie's summer on the island, her suitcase and boxes packed and piled at the door of her cabin, her *one final call*. She'd come here to leave herself, to escape something, hadn't she? She'd come here to forget. But here's the thing about Whidbey, its promise—*safety*. Until this moment on the phone, until leaving, she'd never actually arrived.

Hello? It's Bird.

You want to know what Birdie and Francine will say. They will say it all, soon.

The taxi arrives at the compound by two p.m., and Birdie loads her suitcase, gets in. On the radio: a bus accident in Kenya, a Syrian war. Tomorrow the news will cover a gas station fire in Florida.

Today, Birdie rolls her window down.

Their taxi bloats and stretches in convex mirrors nailed to the trees. Crops whip by in long, lavender brushstrokes, and Birdie imagines a microphone above her, the boom held by a gaffer, whose only job is to lift, lift. Birdie turns on her phone. She wonders if, once she gets home, the clothes in her bag will still smell like this place, like some other person. She promises to remember the red-veined alders outside the cab, the trembling quake of aspen, the simple danger of stinging nettle. She'll remember the pine, like statuary, spears standing endlessly up, angry against this midday blue. One day, she knows, all of this will shrink in her mind, like almost everything else.

Birdie will be a new person tomorrow, maybe even today, once she gets on that boat. Once she gets to Florida. And she will, go to Florida. She will find Francine (*You're still you*, Francine will say when she sees her, and Birdie will know there's a *you* there, still). This will be the next stop before Birdie returns to New York. It will take a month to pack her things from the apartment she shares with Trace, and after Birdie signs a new lease on the south side of Brooklyn (Trace will move back in with Renata), the weather will begin to chill, early Halloween decorations festooning their block in Greenpoint one final time. Birdie will be standing outside the moving truck the day the breaking news about Linzie is released. The truck's silver dimpled ramp rolled out, Birdie's arms holding a shoe box of toiletries—that's when she'll tell Trace about writing the letters. Maybe she hadn't gotten Rich to do it. But she'd gotten Trace.

It's never too late, to be a new person.

Birdie gets out of the taxi at the Clinton terminal dock. She lifts her bags, and her shadow stretches in many layers. There, before her, is the familiar horizon. There, that loamy breeze, cooler with every step closer to the water. Drone of an engine in her ears, the egrets dipping, always hungry. She snaps the handle of her suitcase up.

Then, there was her boat pulling in.

Content Warning

A Note from the Author

Whidbey is a novel largely about suffering, the commodification of pain, and the refusal to see it and to name it in others. What it means to look away from these violences, and at what cost. It is also a novel about who we believe. Thus, it was important for me to render scenes of abuse, including sexual violence against children, without looking away. I have done my best to write these scenes with utmost care, and in steadfast solidarity with any person impacted by CSA. As Sarah Schulman once wrote, "There is art about what could be, what should be, but there is also art about what is."

Acknowledgments

During my time on Tscha-kole-chy (what is now called Whidbey Island) researching this book, I learned that sword fern, an antidote to stinging nettle, grows naturally beside it. Spores on the underside of the fern are said to neutralize the acidity of the nettle, cool the wound.

I considered using this fact in the book. I considered Birdie having a nettle experience in the woods; she would find that the healing thing is as abundant and near as the thing that hurts. The metaphor, of course, was too on the nose. I'm not sure Birdie ever gets there in this story, though I'd like to think eventually she would.

Acknowledgments, though, are allowed to be on the nose—at least for this reader. Corny, earnest, much too much. So I bring in the nettle fact because I've learned other plants are also like this—the neighboring antidote right there where you need it. This book hurt tremendously to write. The animals within deprived me years of proper sleep. And though I do not appear as any of these characters, the throbbing center—the barbs and questions that shape these women—lives in me.

As does the sword fern. I have desperately needed my shade providers. Those who remind me always of the calming after, the nearby relief, the ways in which the natural world—and some people in it—will hold you and mend you if you trust them with the task. Hannah Beresford, my sword of swords, has taught me this most. My first reader, greatest friend, romance of my life, my bear in the woods. H, I love you entirely too much and somehow more with every hour. You, the red road, the glowing path, to the rest of everything.

Jin Auh, you told me I was not a memoirist trying to write a novel but a novelist who wrote a memoir. It was exactly what I needed to hear to keep trying. Again and then again. No words capacious enough to express my gratitude for your wisdom, fierce support, friendship, your hawk-eyed readership. Style, in all ways. Thank you to the Wylie Agency. Thank you, Abram Scharf, Elizabeth Pratt, and Maggie Aschmeyer.

Jessica Williams, editor of *Whidbey*, you've been rolling up your sleeves for the real work since day one. Thank you for your tremendous mind, your innumerable talents, your taste for the darkest dark, and every last phone call. Peter Kispert, for your keen readership and bolstering kindness. You two are the opposites of Yale.

I cherish every person, every fact check and deleted comma and gesture of belief from those at Mariner who've made this book possible, including Eliza Rosenberry, Kelsey Manning, Ana Deboo, Kimberly Kiefer, Hope Ellis, Stephanie Vallejo, Jennifer Hart, Caroline Zancan, Peter Hubbard, and Liate Stehlik. To those who gave a face to *Whidbey* with the cover and interiors of my wildest dreams, thank you: Ploy Siripant, Jackie Alvarado, and Katy Leigh Holley. Shirley Cai, what a train ride. Every photograph with you is an adventure and a marvel.

Great thanks to the writing groups who have kept me accountable, humble, always learning, always surprised. Justine Champine and Molly Tolsky—the hours typing away on our quiet screens, the tacos and challahs—your friendship means everything to me.

And BAWS. Chelsea Bieker, Genevieve Hudson, Allie Rowbottom, and Cyrus Simonoff. You've illuminated the possibilities of all things narrative, human, bloody, and Bachelor-oriented—my adoration and awe are endless. You're each as legendary as you are kind, and that's saying a lot. Stalwarts in the worst days, thank you for showing me love.

Acknowledgments

To earliest readers, buoys, most trusted companions, me ka mahalo nui: Kristen Arnett, Adam Dalva, Lauren Groff, Sydney James, Megan Kamalei Kakimoto, Jana Krumholtz, Kayla Kumari Upadhyaya, Danielle Lazarin, Carmen Maria Machado, Ariél Martinez, Dantiel Wynn Moniz, Leah Schnelbach, Ursula Villarreal-Moura, and Esmé Weijun Wang. Benjamin Schaefer—always, more bite. Chanel Miller, I wouldn't be the person who could begin to write this book if not for you. Lauren Hilger, there's nothing you miss, no syllable untouched by your wizardry. I'm a bolder writer, friend, and observer because of you and our nights on Alice's Bed. John Bean, I can live both in my art and in my life because you showed me the metaphors and with them, the laughter; no more sails in the water. Ian Carlos Mormeneo, I know you'll never read my books, but maybe you'll read this page. Since we were kids, you were down for any drive in service of any story; nothing has changed. Thank you for being the best friend I could ever ask for, and also for telling me when it's time to turn the car around. Lidia Yuknavitch, a decade ago, you asked me where my rage lives. This novel, I hope, at long last, answers.

To all friends and contributors of *No Tokens*, you're my favorite writers in the world.

Kyle Lucia Wu: *potentate, sybaritic*—I finally got them in. So much of this book was written in soundless correspondence with you, and always, every draft, to dazzle you. Thank you for walking through the shadows of wreck with me, for showing me the truth and valor on the other side. Is it time to have more fun yet? I think it is. Meet me at the club. Bring Dan.

Thank you MacDowell, for the support of a lifetime. Backup typewriters, chicken coop tours, whole walls on which to build stories; what haven't you done for me? Thank you, College of Charleston, for a Dean's Discretionary Fund in service of this project (and to CofC fam: Malinda, Tony, Jonathan, Gary, Myra, Robert, and every brilliant student).

Acknowledgments | 371

Hedgebrook, this book is for you and because of you. Your stewardship, hospitality, and banana slugs have changed what I knew to be possible. To those I met at these residencies, you not only shared your art, you showed me the kind of artist I want to be. To the Midnight Society. To Vagalanche. *Keep your secrets, trees*, said Eirinie. We keep them.

With profound thanks to my ʻohana and kūpuna near and far, in ancestry, in hakuhia, in ola and makani, including my mother, Sherrie Lokelani, mahalo nō for sharpening my sword—my Joan of Arc, friend of every pua. Cynthia and Paul, thank you for the many, many fortresses of safety. Jeanne Kam. Jon and Ruth. Erin and Pete. Randie. Mary-Beth Lindenmuth (for the moxie of this very different Mary-Beth). Blake, Tiffany, Shawn, Tricia, Marjorie, Pedro, Seth, Mike, and Sorawit—every drive, every boat, every soup, every star. Sarah Kamakawiwoʻole, each grain of sand a whole universe, as is my love for you. A hui hou, bitch.

I could not have written this book without consulting the scholarly work and experiences of experts and medical professionals. Some have spoken to me on the record, some off. I am indebted to them all, and especially to the work of Amelia Evans, Dr. Elizabeth Letourneau, Dr. Elena Lopez, Luke Malone, and Dr. Allyn Walker, for your advocacy in the prevention of child sex abuse. Dr. Alan van Giessen, you made chemistry so much fun—thank you for the perfect recipe. Finally, I'd humbly like to thank and acknowledge those who've complexly explored CSA and dynamics of consent in their literature, art, and journalism, including Kathleen Alcott, Dorothy Allison, Rachel Aviv, Russell Banks, Alexander Chee, Susan Choi, Melissa Febos, Jaquira Díaz, Mary Gaitskill, Kyle Dillon Hertz, Adam Johnson, Heather Lewis, Ruth Madievsky, Alex Marzano-Lesnevich, Kate Elizabeth Russell, Sarah Schulman, Mona Simpson, Andrea Skinner, Lisa Taddeo, Brandon Taylor, Joy Williams, and Alisson Wood. This is not an exhaustive list, but I offer this particular work, in part, because you were all daring enough to offer yours.

Acknowledgments

Thank you to my friends on and from Tscha-kole-chy, who have shown me how to love such an extraordinary and storied place. This abundance would not be possible if not for the stewardship of the Coastal Salish, including the Lower Skagit, Swinomish, Suquamish, and Snohomish people, among others. "Whidbey" will always belong to the people who ancestrally belong to the land, in perpetuity. I'm humbled to have spent time there as a visitor, learning. 'Ea. Thank you. With deepest respect.

Cathy Bruemmer, Amber Flame, Lisa Siders Kenney, Kimberly A. C. Wilson, Jen Will-Thapa, Nancy Nordhoff, Britt Conn, Mirja Heide, Aaron Parks, and Holden Sandal, I am so grateful. Tamara Knapp of the Anderson Farm, thank you for sharing your dahlias and your cows, year after year. Alex Almaguer-Matthews, for the Lone Star magic. Ash and Angel, so many pages of this book were written while staring out your windows.

Thank you, Projectionist Extraordinaire Lillian Hardester of Nitehawk Cinema Prospect Park, for showing me the wonders of the reel. Thank you, Holly at Elliott Bay Books.

And those at Stewart's gas station, who helped me bring Mary-Beth Boyer to life.

And my family at Philly Typewriter. For overnighting ribbon when the ink ran out.

Suzanne Hoover, to whom this book is dedicated. Before you taught me how to write, you took me to the movies. In all our afternoons together, you've also taught me how to live. I will tend to our plants, our stories, forever. Promise.

Finally, for every person and every child harmed not only by individuals, but by the very systems purported to protect them; for the Genie Wileys of the world, and to those misnamed, renamed, revised—you are remembered, you are loved. I write, always, with an open meadow of hope for a more equitable and gentle future, one full of sword fern and jewelweed, and one in which our suffering is no longer commodified; for you, for me, for us.

About the Author

T Kira Māhealani Madden is a diasporic Kanaka ʻŌiwi (Native Hawaiian) writer and the author of the acclaimed memoir *Long Live the Tribe of Fatherless Girls*, which was named a *New York Times* Editors' Choice, as well as a finalist for the National Book Critics Circle John Leonard Prize and the Lambda Literary Award. She is the founding editor of *No Tokens*, a journal of literature and art, and has received fellowships from the New York Foundation for the Arts, Hedgebrook, Tin House, MacDowell, and Yaddo. Winner of the 2021 Judith A. Markowitz Award, she is an assistant professor of creative writing and Indigenous literatures at Hamilton College and served as the distinguished writer in residence at the University of Hawaiʻi at Mānoa.

RAISING READERS
Books Build Bright Futures

Dear Reader,

We'd love your attention for one more page to tell you about the crisis in children's reading, and what we can all do.

Studies have shown that reading for fun is the **single biggest predictor of a child's future life chances** – more than family circumstance, parents' educational background or income. It improves academic results, mental health, wealth, communication skills, ambition and happiness.[1]

The number of children reading for fun is in rapid decline. Young people have a lot of competition for their time. In 2024, 1 in 10 children and young people in the UK aged 5 to 18 did not own a single book at home.[2]

Hachette works extensively with schools, libraries and literacy charities, but here are some ways we can all raise more readers:

- Reading to children for just 10 minutes a day makes a difference
- Don't give up if children aren't regular readers – there will be books for them!
- Visit bookshops and libraries to get recommendations
- Encourage them to listen to audiobooks
- Support school libraries
- Give books as gifts

There's a lot more information about how to encourage children to read on our website: **www.RaisingReaders.co.uk**

Thank you for reading.

hachette UK

---

[1] OECD, '21st-Century Readers: Developing Literacy Skills in a Digital World', 2021, https://www.oecd.org/en/publications/21st-century-readers_a83d84cb-en.html

[2] National Literacy Trust, 'Book Ownership in 2024', November 2024, https://literacytrust.org.uk/research-services/research-reports/book-ownership-in-2024